RED LETTER DAYS

RED LETTER DAYS

SARAH-JANE STRATFORD

THORNDIKE PRESS
A part of Gale, a Cengage Company

Copyright © 2020 by Sarah-Jane Stratford.
Readers Guide copyright © 2020 by Sarah-Jane Stratford.
Thorndike Press, a part of Gale, a Cengage Company.

LIBRARY OF CONGRESS CIP DATA ON FILE.
CATALOGUING IN PUBLICATION FOR THIS BOOK
IS AVAILABLE FROM THE LIBRARY OF CONGRESS

ISBN-13: 978-1-4328-7992-1 (hardcover alk. paper)

Published in 2020 by arrangement with Berkley, an imprint of Penguin
Publishing Group, a division of Penguin Random House, LLC.

Printed in Mexico
Print Number: 01   Print Year: 2020

We are what we always were in Salem, but now the little crazy children are jangling the keys of the kingdom, and common vengeance writes the law!

— Arthur Miller, *The Crucible*

I cannot and will not cut my conscience to fit this year's fashions.

— Lillian Hellman

I believe in Liberty for all men: the space to stretch their arms and their souls, the right to breathe and the right to vote, the freedom to choose their friends, enjoy the sunshine, and ride on the railroads, uncursed by color; thinking, dreaming, working as they will in a kingdom of beauty and love.

— W. E. B. Du Bois

Prologue

Washington, DC, 1956

"Don't make jokes."

It was the first and last thing the lawyer instructed. No one was allowed to laugh at the proceedings. Especially a woman.

As she looked up at the panel of men seated at the high table, glaring down at her, she thought she'd never felt less amused. She couldn't even comfort herself that the accused women in Salem had faced worse. She didn't want to go to prison.

It was like a television play. A script she'd tried to write and then discarded as too absurd. But this was all too real.

The gavel banged, the room fell silent, and the interrogator locked eyes with her.

"Phoebe Berneice Adler. Are you now, or have you ever been, a member of the Communist Party?"

It didn't matter that they already knew the answer was no. That wasn't the point. It

7

never was. The hearing was just for show. Pure theater. And she had to play her part.

She clenched her hands together to keep from wiping them on her skirt. She took a deep breath, and leaned toward the microphone.

CHAPTER ONE

Greenwich Village, New York City
Spring 1955

THE GANGSTER CORNERS MOLLY IN
THE ALLEY.

GANGSTER

Give it up, sister, you're
through.

MOLLY

You ain't got me yet.

MOLLY SCRAMBLES UP THE FIRE
ESCAPE. SHE'S FAST, BUT HE'S
GAINING.

SHE TAKES OFF A SHOE AND FLINGS
IT AT HIM, HITTING HIM IN THE

FACE. IT ONLY BUYS HER A FEW
SECONDS. HER OTHER SHOE FALLS
OFF AND HE CATCHES IT, TAKING
NOTE OF THE POINTY HEEL.

HE SMILES AS HE CLIMBS STEADILY,
ABOUT TO REACH HER AS SHE'S
WRIGGLING INTO AN OPEN WINDOW.

Phoebe slammed the typewriter carriage back and pulled out the page. She read the scene several times, trying to view it through Hank's eyes. He was a discerning story editor with a heavy hand. Phoebe grudgingly conceded that his edits improved her scripts, but she always strove to have fewer edits each time, and she was gaining on him as readily as this murderer was gaining on his victim. She needed Hank to see her as his best writer. He was going places. Phoebe wanted to go there too.

She added the page to the pile and took several deep breaths. She always needed a break before writing the final scenes. The final murder, the final arrest, the final quip. Goodness and decency prevailing. A sameness she had to make different every time she wrote it. Television — or, at least, the fourth-rate detective show she wrote for — followed a rigid formula. There were better shows, though, with opportunities for real invention, and Phoebe was clawing her way to a spot on one of them. It didn't matter how many ridiculous murders she had to write to get there.

She leaned back, giving herself over to ambient sounds. The grunt of the wooden chair's spine. The faint hum of Anne's radio in the apartment across the hall. A news program. Phoebe thought she could hear the announcer saying something about Communists and the Soviets. She couldn't remember the last time a news broadcast didn't talk about the "Communist threat" and the "Red Scare" and the efforts of the House Un-American Activities Committee and J. Edgar Hoover's FBI to keep America safe from Red Russia and the Reds that were assumed to be crawling all over the country, especially in Hollywood and unions and wherever Negroes were organizing. The House committee was in the news so often, it was referred to by one and all as HUAC. Phoebe wondered how Anne could concentrate with such accompaniment, but Anne said the best artists kept up with current events.

"How the heck is it current?" Phoebe demanded once, when Anne was listening, enthralled, to Senator McCarthy's yowls.

11

"Those HUAC hearings started in 1947, for crying out loud!"

"And now it's in the Senate, too, isn't it?" Anne answered. Though McCarthy himself actually had gone away, censured and disgraced after the Army-McCarthy hearings. People still used the term "McCarthyism," but only because it was a useful shorthand, with more zip than "HUACism."

Phoebe stacked up her newspapers, all folded open to local crime reports, and put up another pot of coffee. She lit a cigarette and sat on the makeshift window seat, wrapping her stockinged toes around the jamb and letting her skirt flutter outside the open window in what she hoped looked very devil-may-care without being too saucy. It was warm, and many windows up and down Perry Street were open. Phoebe took long, luxurious drags on her cigarette, reveling in all the street sounds. Other typewriters, of course, clacking away, and music everywhere, some single instruments, some groups, rehearsing or creating or teaching. Next door was the Disorderly Theatre Company, a clutch of young men in a living room, shouting scenes from a political play that even the bohemians of Greenwich Village would say was laying it on a touch thick. But there was always the chance it would blossom into something that would make the world sit up and take notice. That happened.

Shop doors were open, and Phoebe watched the steady flow of commerce in and out of the butcher's, grocer's, and fishmonger's. If she leaned out a touch farther, she could see the regulars draped over the outside tables of the Coffee Nook, where the proprietors Floyd and Leo made cappuccinos more addictive than cocaine. It was a sign of being a true Village artist if one was allowed to give a reading or play music any night at the Nook, especially a Thursday. Floyd and Leo presided over the lineup with a severity that would have been the envy of Stalin.

The bread seller came down the street on his bicycle, accosted on all sides by housewives vying for the freshest loaves. The artists tussled for the best day-old bread. Phoebe was tempted to run down for a loaf, but was too comfortable in the sunshine. It was like being in an Italian film. Those first early scenes where everyone is poor but happy, scraping along and dreaming big. Anything could happen over the next hour and a half.

"Hey, Adler!" Jimmy shouted up at her. Phoebe sighed. In a film, the neighbor from across the road might or might not turn out to be her true love — the very idea of which Phoebe found snort-worthy — but he would at least be charming. He would keep the audience guessing. Though Jimmy wasn't without his usefulness. Phoebe had written three different scripts in which a scrawny, moonfaced buffoon of a young man turned out to be a criminal mastermind.

Not that she really minded Jimmy. As she said to Anne, "He's charmless, but harmless." "That's as may be," Anne replied. "But I wish he'd try to close his mouth when he's around me. Not even a bloodhound drools that much." There was no use in pointing out that all men drooled around Anne. Jimmy's insistence on being friends with Phoebe was mostly based on her friendship with Anne. Phoebe's comparative writing success and general cheerfulness might be other reasons, but they were a distant second.

"Do a fellow a favor, huh, and lend me a gasper?" he begged from under Phoebe's window, where he was weeding Mrs. Pocatelli's front garden.

"She'll rip your head off if you smoke among the squashes," Phoebe told him. "Then she'll use your torso as a planter." Mrs. Pocatelli, Phoebe and Anne's tiny, wizened landlady and the general terror of Perry Street, would make a terrific fictional criminal, but Phoebe had yet to write a script about a crime orchestrated by Mrs. Pocatelli that wouldn't run afoul of the network censors.

"I'll take my chances," Jimmy said, and Phoebe obliged him, tying the end of a ball of yarn around one of her Lucky Strikes and unwinding the ball until the cigarette landed in his hand. He freed it and she wound the yarn back up to her knitting basket.

"You'd better not need a match," she warned. He grinned and produced a lighter from his pocket. She saw him cast a furtive, fearful glance into Mrs. Pocatelli's window before lighting up. "I'll leave you to it," Phoebe said. "I don't mind the sight of blood, but I don't have time to be dragged into a murder trial."

"You working on a paying job up there?" Jimmy asked, his voice carefully casual.

Phoebe sighed. Jimmy wasn't the only Perry Street denizen who made it hard to escape back to work with grace. He was a writer too, and good at what he did, but here he was scrabbling in the dirt for two hours, to earn one dollar and a few lesser cabbages and beets. Not that Phoebe didn't struggle herself. Most of the month she lived on potatoes and eggs. But Phoebe was undeniably on a different level from the other strivers on the street. She had written for radio, and now a television show aired scripts with her name emblazoned on the credits. It didn't matter that it was a lesser show on a lesser network. Phoebe Adler was that strange and glorious thing: A Working Writer. Some men dismissed her success as mere luck, as she'd started writing during the war when they were off serving (she spent her days building fighter planes but was the first to insist it wasn't at all the same). She knew they thought she should be living a different sort of life now, allowing them her opportunities. But they also knew why she needed to work so hard, so grudges were never held long.

"Yeah, another shabby whodunit," Phoebe admitted with a shrug. "As if anyone couldn't guess who did it within two minutes. But another couple of these and maybe I can pay some high flier to build a bubble so Mona can go outside." A fantasy. Her sister hadn't been allowed beyond the controlled atmosphere of the sanitarium in years. "Though, really, it'll take getting on a good comedy or *Playhouse 90* for that. Still, I don't mind slogging away on the silly stuff

16

to keep Mona well looked after."

"No, of course," Jimmy muttered, ducking his head. "How is Mona?"

"Good as she can be," Phoebe said. She liked his embarrassment, but every time a variation on this conversation took place, she was seized with the furious desire to secure that comedy or television play. Something, anything, to give her more than the two hundred dollars she earned for a monthly *At Your Service* script that paid her rent and the basics while also helping with the sanitarium costs. It must be possible. A woman was one of the two writers on *I Love Lucy*, the biggest hit on TV. She must be making a fortune. Hank could be made head writer on a show like that and bring in Phoebe as his "gal writer." Soon, she hoped, for Mona's sake. In the meantime, everyone always had to help each other out where they could. One never knew who someone might be tomorrow.

"Listen, Jimmy, Hank says he'll look at some stuff, he knows a radio fellow who needs a good jingle writer. Wanna give me something to take in?"

Jimmy gazed at her with awe. His mouth was open and Phoebe swore she could see drool.

"You're a real peach, Adler, you know that?"

"Eh, we all have to do for each other as we can, right?" she said, waving away the compliment as she ground out her cigarette.

"I mean it," he insisted. "You're a real good egg."

"We'll see if you're still saying that when I demand ten percent off you," she said with a laugh. "Want another cig?"

"Better not," he said with another glance at Mrs. Pocatelli's window. "Say, I don't suppose you want a drink later? You and Anne, maybe?" he added carelessly.

She was tempted to ask how much fertilizer he'd have to spread to afford the sort of drinks he had in mind, but felt sorry enough for him to smile and decline.

"Deadline, you know how it is. Drop your stuff off Sunday night if you can, okay?"

"Sure," he said, but still looked crushed. Phoebe wondered why men always seemed to think they could get a certain girl, even though she obviously didn't like him. Too many damn movies, probably.

She rolled a fresh sheet of paper into the typewriter and stared at it. The next scene would be back with the detectives who were the stars of *At Your Service.* Now the audience would learn the detectives had woven an intricate plot whereby they could capture both the woman delivering papers to her crime lord boyfriend and the rival gang leader preparing to kill her with her own shoe. The detectives had hoped to keep the woman alive for the sake of her testimony, but another dead gangster's moll was nothing to cry over, and the censors preferred it when a bad girl was killed if there wasn't time for her to reform before the commercials ran.

Phoebe picked up her knitting and knit several rows of a cardigan, thinking about the final few minutes of the script. The music and chatter outside, even the screeches of Mrs. Pocatelli, who must have seen Jimmy putting out his cigarette, faded as the sharp heel of the moll's shoe flew toward her neck before the scene cut abruptly to the detectives' dingy offices.

The phone rang, jolting Phoebe back to her bright apartment, where everything was painted green and pink and nothing went more than three days without polish. She took a breath, composing herself. It was important to answer the phone at just the right moment, with just the right tone. It might be someone offering work, and so you mustn't sound desperate, or too available. Serene, composed, unruffled, that was the only way a lady writer was allowed to come across. It was not unlike what women on the dating market went through, or so Phoebe was given to understand.

She picked up just as the phone stopped ringing. "Well, of course you would do that," she grumbled, slamming it back down again, taking little pleasure in the tinny *bing* that echoed off the walls.

"You should get an answering service," Anne called through the door. Phoebe flung open the door to admit her paint-spattered friend. "I was about to knock," Anne said. "Got a cigarette?"

"What am I, the corner store?" Phoebe asked, handing Anne the last of a pack. "Here, finish these and buy the next ones, all right?"

"Sure thing." Anne grinned, producing a match from the depths of her coveralls and striking it on the bottom of her work boot. Phoebe shook her head, smiling. Even with no makeup, her red-gold curls bound under a bandanna, and oversized denim coveralls hiding her Marilyn Monroe figure, Anne was a head-turner.

"It's ten years since we stopped building fighter jets," Phoebe said. "And here you still look like the world's prettiest model for Rosie the Riveter."

"Now I'm covered in acrylic paint, not grease," Anne pointed out, poking Phoebe's shoulder. "Going all right?" she asked, jerking her head at the typewriter.

"Fresh piping-hot justice will soon be served," Phoebe said.

"That's how we know it's fiction," said Anne. "Sure would be something if just once the criminals got away clean."

"Fantasist," Phoebe chided her. "Go on, get back to the masterpiece."

"Peggy Guggenheim will open a new gallery just for me," Anne promised. She and Phoebe pointed at each other, an old gesture that meant this was a promise that would be kept, and shut their doors.

Ten years. Phoebe didn't miss building planes, and she certainly didn't miss the war — but she missed the easy camaraderie of the women working on the assembly line. The day Phoebe's first sketch aired on the radio, Anne and Dolores Goldstein had rounded up the whole crew to listen. Anne decreed the fifteen-dollar check from CBS "a glorious thing." "Not so glorious that I won't hightail it straight to the bank to let them worship it," Phoebe rejoined. Anne kept her old Brownie camera in her locker and insisted on taking a photo of the check. Though Phoebe protested against making a relic of her first pay for writing, the photo lived in her keepsake box, and she couldn't imagine it ever being anywhere else.

Dolores Goldstein, their forewoman, claimed she was going to be the manager of a factory within seven years. Instead she'd married within one and had three children. Possibly more, but she'd stopped answering letters over a year ago. Most of the women at the airfield were married now. Only Phoebe and Anne had pursued their dreams all the way to Greenwich Village. "I bet they envy us," Anne liked to say. Phoebe hoped not. If there was one thing all those women deserved, it was happiness.

The phone rang again. Phoebe took a long, deep breath and answered in her most mellifluous tone, "Adler residence."

She heard a crackling, a vague buzz, almost like the hum in a meadow's air on a hot summer afternoon, but nowhere near as soothing.

"Hello?" Phoebe asked, trying not to sound uneasy. "Is anybody there?"

If they were, they didn't say. After a few moments, Phoebe hung up.

It was the third time in ten days. It was getting to the point where she had to stop pretending it was nothing. But she couldn't. Not yet. She just couldn't.

■ ■ ■ ■

Monday morning, Phoebe got up early so she could enjoy her breakfast before she went to her meeting with Hank. She soft boiled an egg and thought how nice bacon or sausage would be, but such things were treats, only allowed one morning a month, after a check cleared. She switched on the radio, listened for half a minute to a news report about Communists in the National Association for the Advancement of Colored People, then clicked through the stations, hunting for a new comedy she could send a submission to. The only female voice she heard was that of Hedda Hopper, the vitriolic Hollywood gossip columnist whose nose for scandal earned her a radio program along with her much-slavered-over nationally syndicated newspaper column. "Everyone in Hollywood knows," she purred in her affected mid-Atlantic accent, "there are Reds under the bed!"

"Attention, housewives!" Phoebe intoned in her deepest boom. "The newest-model Electrolux will suck up those Reds with just one swipe!" *Ah, I oughta be an announcer.* She shook her head, wondering if kids were actually frightened of Communists, if the specter of them under the bed had replaced the bogeyman. She flipped away from Hedda Hopper before the woman could reel off a list of Closeted Homosexual Actors of the Week whose careers she would promptly ruin, and settled on Jimmy Witherspoon singing "Ain't Nobody's Business" as she finished her coffee and went to put on her makeup.

Hank's tiny office was on the top floor of the Linwood Theatre, which housed the studios where *At Your Service* and several other shows on the Adelphi Network were filmed. The Linwood was on Sixth Avenue, just within sight of the heart of television: Rockefeller Center. "Greatness adjacent," Hank labeled the Linwood. Phoebe rather liked the sleek structure, made of all the glass and steel that was her shiny dream of Manhattan. Staff entered through a side door and went straight upstairs, so as not to interfere with the soundstages on the ground floor. Only the head writers on Adelphi shows had permanent offices on-site, but Phoebe knew that on better television shows, on the big three networks, there were staff writers who came in every day and had assigned desks. Phoebe was sure there could be nothing greater in life than walking through an office door with your name on it. Hanging up your coat and hat, and settling yourself at your very own desk. From there she would have no world left to conquer.

She took the bus to Midtown. The subway was faster, but it was more fun to watch the people in the streets, and the progression of the buildings as they grew taller and grander the farther uptown they went.

Phoebe liked to imagine the stories her fellow passengers told themselves about her as they traveled. A career girl, through and through. Plenty of women wore suits to go out in New York, and plenty were sentenced to glasses, but Phoebe knew her attaché case and air of purposefulness set her apart. One or two men flicked her an approving look she knew well — the one that said she wasn't pretty enough to marry, so good for her, making something of herself. Then they turned away and forgot her. She didn't care. It was much easier, not being noticed. It meant she could study people openly, wondering who in the crowd was the kleptomaniac, the con man, the workplace scofflaw, the would-be romantic — who would start romancing his secretary after his wife had their third child.

She nodded as she turned ideas over in her head, smiling, not caring if anyone watched and thought she was off her rocker. Let them watch. Let them remember that smile for the day she won an Emmy Award.

Outside, a messenger ran in front of a taxi, and there was the usual jazz trio of brakes, horns, and howls. The bus passengers with the best views rated the show, bringing to bear all their knowledge and expertise. Then came the inevitable: "Awful shame for a lady to have to hear language like that."

You fellows are lucky you weren't with me at the airfield. If a shipment was late coming in, we ladies used language that would have shamed sailors.

Her stop was next, and she took a deep breath, readying herself for the excitement to come. The bus had fallen silent again, the men's eyes back on their newspapers, Phoebe's eyes on the most story-worthy men. She almost didn't notice the tingling in her neck, her own realization that she, too, was being scrutinized. Probably by someone who regretted calling her a lady, if she was the sort who ogled men. She glanced behind her, but only saw hats peeping over newspapers.

She alighted in front of Rockefeller Center so she might give it a salute, remind it she existed and was heading its way, before strolling down to the Adelphi offices. It might have been the lingering effects of her character studies, or all those mysterious phone calls, or simply that all the women in her scripts endured it, but she felt sure someone was following her. She whirled around into another sea of hats, and a massive man in a pinstriped suit plowed right into her.

"What's the big idea, sister, you trying to break my neck or something?" he shouted at her.

"What neck? I only see chins," Phoebe muttered. More passersby stormed around her, offering their opinions on people who stood right in the middle of Sixth Avenue and where they ought to stand instead.

Been reading too many crime stories, Phoebe decided. *Oh well, they say heightened sensitivity is the mark of a true artist.* She put her nose in the air and marched to the side door of the Linwood Theatre, congratulating herself on not being a glamour-puss. Those women had to live with being stared at and followed all the time. *No wonder some of them end up emptyheaded. That sort of thing can drive a gal to distraction.*

Half an hour early, Phoebe indulged in her usual twenty-minute coffee in what was optimistically called the staff canteen. She settled at her favorite table with the morning copy of *Variety.*

"Phoebe! Good morning!"

Geraldine, the actress who played the secretary to the detectives on *At Your Service,* hovered by the chair opposite Phoebe. "Do you mind if I join you?"

Phoebe didn't. She liked Geraldine, who made good use of her own glamour-puss status to play the game of Being Seen. She would do better in a chic little bistro in the shadow of Rockefeller Center, or Sardi's if she was aiming for Broadway, but you never knew who was preparing for meetings with whom, and reminding everyone present that she was a model of wit and vivacity was all to the good. Phoebe was glad to help, not least because she might work in a few good jokes. Together, they could help each other into the big time.

"I simply adore your latest script!" Geraldine gushed in her well-trained voice. "It's such fun to rehearse."

"Gosh, thanks," Phoebe answered in the boom she'd honed on the streets of the Lower East Side. "Writing for you is a dream, there's nothing you can't make even better."

"They taught me well at the Actors Studio,

but truly, I never know what you're going to throw at me, and I know the boys feel the same."

Phoebe doubted "the boys" felt any such thing, but Geraldine was awfully convincing. Her personal gratitude, at least, was no act. Phoebe was the only writer who gave her lines beyond "Let me get you some more coffee."

"Well, I like to keep things interesting," Phoebe said. "I'm working on what might be a real doozy for next time."

"What fun! Can you spill a bean or two?"

Phoebe glanced at her silver watch, her only good piece of jewelry and the only grand present her parents had ever been able to give her ("So you'll never miss a shift at the airfield," her father had said).

"I'd better get up to Hank. He panics if I'm not five minutes early."

They bestowed their prettiest air-kisses near each other's cheeks, and Phoebe headed for the elevator.

Hank's door was ajar, but Phoebe knocked anyway.

"I don't know why I don't just set our meetings five minutes earlier," Hank greeted her. He was a reedy, sandy-haired man with huge tortoiseshell glasses who always pumped Phoebe's hand like he was hoping to produce water.

"It'd likely ruin Miss Ebbs's appointment book," Phoebe said, wringing out her sore fingers behind her back. Miss Ebbs was the lone, and long-suffering, secretary shared among head writers.

"Who?" Hank asked. "Oh, of course. All right, always ready for one of yours, let's have a look at it. The gal isn't *too* tough now, is she?"

"Just tough enough," Phoebe said, smiling. Hank never seemed to realize they had this exact exchange every time.

Hank flipped through her pages. "People like soft ladies," he muttered, shaking his head.

Phoebe knew what he meant, but never understood it. She supposed she presented as rather "soft" herself — a shortish, plumpish woman with a big bust and hips, though her big bust and hips had nothing like the effect of Anne's. *Hurrah for girdles,* she thought, ignoring her frivolous desire for regular deep breathing.

"They may like soft ladies, but everyone loves a bad girl," she pointed out.

"Long as she gets hers in the end," Hank rejoined.

"Painful spot to get it," Phoebe said, "plus the censors would die of apoplexy."

Hank ignored this. "All I mean is, I think some folks get squirrelly about a gal writing hard-boiled gals."

"Lucky for us no one ever reads credits, huh?" said Phoebe.

Hank sighed. "I'll get your check sent out today," he said, and Phoebe knew she'd won. He settled down to business. "Whatever you're cooking right now, back-burner it — I want you to do one about a star ballet dancer who gets iced. Try to include a lot of background dancers, all right?"

"Lots of leg, I get it. Why me?"

"All girls like ballet, right? You know the lingo."

Phoebe didn't have the heart to remind him she'd grown up about as far from the sort of New York girls who like ballet as Genghis Khan had from Bonnie Prince Charlie. One trip to the library would give her enough lingo to seem like an expert.

"That's super, Hank, thanks so much. Oh, and I brought my neighbor's stuff for that fella who wants someone cheap and quick." She handed him Jimmy's samples. Anne couldn't understand why Phoebe didn't ask Hank to help *her* get more work elsewhere, but it wasn't the done thing. Hank considered Phoebe his discovery. He knew she'd done other work and needed more — and

31

he knew she needed that work for Mona, more than for herself, but he didn't want to share her. Phoebe nominally had an agent, a man much more focused on his film-writing clients and who would be hard-pressed to remember Phoebe's name. He was only for show. Phoebe had always gotten work on her own and saw no reason to change that as she forged her path upward.

Hank dropped the script on a pile and grinned indulgently at Phoebe. "Say, want to come down and watch your latest magnum opus start rehearsal?"

"Are you kidding?" she cried, bounding to the door. "They won't mind?"

"So long as you don't bawl if you hear a line altered, no, they won't mind. Won't even notice, most likely."

Hank chose a quiet corner of the empty auditorium for them to sit and watch the rehearsal. Phoebe held her breath, expecting to be transported by the magic of watching actors bring her own words to life, trying them out in different intonations before finding the delivery that would be filmed before the audience on Friday as it was aired on television sets throughout the country. Instead, she was disappointed to find the director more focused on blocking and lighting. No one tried to make any of it come alive. She kept a pleased look on her face for Hank's sake, wondering how long she could wait till she could make an excuse to go home. Then Geraldine spoke her line: "Well of course the letter's in code, the woman is saying you're handsome." And everyone, even the actor playing the maligned detective, chuckled.

"She's good, isn't she?" Phoebe whispered.

"*You* give her good stuff and she knows what to do with it," Hank said.

Off Phoebe went into a fantasy of a show written by her and starring Geraldine. It became a bigger and bigger hit, so that when she vaguely heard someone ask if Phoebe Adler was there, it was no surprise. Until Hank said, "What the hell does Kelvin want you for?"

Kelvin was the producer, and Phoebe had never laid eyes on him. Now, apparently, he knew where she was and had sent Miss Ebbs to bring her to his office. Phoebe's heart swelled. Producers only met with the best writers, meetings that usually resulted in the offer of more work. No wonder Hank was miffed. Phoebe might slip through his fingers after all.

"I'd better come with you," he said, taking her elbow.

"It's all right, I won't trip," she said, attempting to free herself. His hand tightened, and she followed his stunned gaze to see what must be Mr. Kelvin, standing by the stage manager's table at the back of the auditorium. A short, barrel-chested man clasping and unclasping his fingers, he wagged a playful finger at Hank.

"Hank, you know you're supposed to be upstairs."

"Sure, Mr. K, I know. You gonna take me to the woodshed?" Hank asked.

Mr. Kelvin threw back his head and laughed, reminding Phoebe of a Macy's Santa.

"You writers with the mouths on you, it's too much." He grinned at Hank, who grinned back but still clutched Phoebe proprietarily. "Now then." Mr. Kelvin turned his bright eyes to Phoebe. "You're Phoebe Adler?" he asked encouragingly.

"I am," she said, presenting her hand to shake. "Pleased to meet you, sir."

"You're fired, dear."

Chapter Two

London, Spring 1955

"Avast, ye hardy!" Rhoda cried, leaping onto the armchair and waving her cardboard sword over her head. "The battle will begin at midnight, in the middle of dawn! We will kill all the prisoners, and then we'll tie them up and make them dance for us!"

Hannah hid her laugh in a cigarette. She couldn't imagine anything more delightful than the stream of consciousness that flowed from the imagination of a five-year-old. Especially her own child. Hannah swooped Rhoda up and directed her toward a low wooden stool.

"I know you're the pirate king, darling, but please don't ruin the armchair, we've just had it restuffed."

"Bah, humbug!" Rhoda answered. " 'Tis a pirate ship, matey!"

"Sail out for open sea," Hannah suggested. "I hear there's treasure to be found on a distant isle."

Rhoda promptly sat on the stool and began to chart the course. Though she gave occasional instructions to her crew, she was mostly silent, her eyes tight on the blue-green wallpaper, her hands steering an imaginary wheel. Hannah followed Rhoda's gaze, wishing she could climb inside her daughter's imagination as the wallpaper turned into a sea. She hoped it would be a long, long time before Rhoda stopped believing in the wild worlds she could conjure, just by insisting they were real.

Hannah sighed and turned back to the script she was reading. Not much of a world conjured here. Another detective thriller. It made perfect sense for writers to submit variations on what was popular, but television was opening up huge vistas for drama, provided it passed muster with the censors, and she wanted her scrappy little production company to make its mark.

Her company. Incredible. She had a pile of scripts, each one addressed to Hannah Wolfson, Executive Producer, Sapphire Films. She didn't like the reason she and Paul had left New York for London, but it had changed her world. It all still made her giggle like a schoolgirl.

"What's funny, Mama?" Rhoda demanded, steering quickly to shore so that she might share the joke.

"Oh, nothing really, darling. Only I love my work."

"You make stories!" Rhoda cried triumphantly.

"Not the way you do," Hannah conceded. "But I read stories, and when one is good, I give the writer money and then hire people to act it and others to film it. And I make an arrangement with a network, who puts it on television, and then people watch it."

"Exactly, you make stories," Rhoda insisted. "And you tell everyone what to do, just like at home!"

"I beg your pardon?" Paul asked, joining them.

Hannah smiled at her handsome husband, still so boyish despite gray-speckled hair and deepening lines around his eyes. They'd met at a press conference the day the Allies crossed the Rhine, and spent the next four hours discussing how Roosevelt could expand upon New Deal policies once the war was over. She knew she would marry him three weeks later, the day Roosevelt died. Paul came over, bearing four dozen long-stemmed roses, then put his head in her lap and sobbed for their beloved dead president until she worried he might give himself an aneurysm. They'd wiped each other's eyes, drank a bottle of Gordon's gin, and got engaged on VE Day.

"Just explaining my work, darling," Hannah told Paul.

"Ah!" Paul laughed. Hannah knew he viewed her venture into television as a step down. They'd been journalists on rival newspapers when they met, and he saw no profession as more noble. "Mama's just having a sojourn," he said to Rhoda. "And lucky for her I can pay for it."

Hannah gave him a playful swat. Paul's grandfather had been a banker — a distant relation of the Rothschilds, though he'd changed the family name to Rutherford — who liked to give money to inventors and anyone who put their inventions to good use, assuming these would lead to shares in stock. He'd invested in the development of dental floss, zippers, and hearing aids, and managed things so well, the family came to possess the sort of wealth that Hannah, born and raised in a Lower East Side tenement, could still barely comprehend. The Rutherford fortune moved her to the foreign territory of Central Park West, where Paul invited her to choose their home from several apartments his family owned.

Two years later, HUAC, citing the Soviet

threat, held their first hearings into Communist activity in Hollywood. People throughout the industry were subpoenaed, suspected of Communist loyalty or sympathy, or any sort of "subversive activity." They were forced to come to Washington to answer the committee's questions about that activity. There was outrage, of course, and a group of ten screenwriters and directors pushed back. They not only refused to answer questions, they denounced HUAC for asking them. It went against everything America stood for, they said. Hannah and other liberal journalists applauded, and Hannah wrote an impassioned defense of the rights of Americans to hold unpopular political views. But then the "Hollywood Ten" were cited for contempt of Congress. They were tried and imprisoned. It seemed impossible, but it happened. When the other leftist journalists Hannah knew stopped expressing outrage — in fact, stopped discussing it altogether — that was when she became truly afraid. She soon saw that anyone known for being outspoken was likely to land on the chopping block. Rhoda was on the way, and Hannah had no intention of being chopped. Rutherford money helped her and Paul decamp to London and buy a flat in Chelsea, then financed the setup of Sapphire Films after Hannah's short stints on a few productions proved she had a knack for the quickly growing world of television.

"Daddy helped give me a start, but my company is making its own money now," she assured Rhoda, ignoring Paul's snort. Sapphire Films wasn't quite breaking even. "And you're right. I have to keep on top of what everyone's doing, keep track of several dozen things at once, make sure it's all going well and everyone's happy." Being an executive producer was not unlike being a wife and mother; it was surprising that most people thought a woman couldn't manage it.

Then again, no one had expected Hannah to become a successful reporter either. Low expectations could be useful, she found. They left a lot of space for you to work your way up long before anyone noticed.

"And have you found your 'something big' yet?" Paul asked.

"Not in this pile," Hannah said. She consigned the script to the "rejected" stack and reached for another.

"Well, even my busy bee must break for lunch," he said, adding: "Shoes."

Hannah was in her stocking feet — she did her best thinking when she wasn't wearing shoes. Paul didn't insist on his parents' starchy formality, but as Hannah joked to her friend Shirley, he put his foot down on bare feet during meals. Hannah slipped on her shoes and sat at the table, marveling at the glory of her beautiful family gathered for Sunday lunch. Paul, Rhoda, eighteen-month-old Julie. Also Gemma, whom Hannah called the nanny extraordinaire. Hannah had been advised she could pay Gemma half the wages of "a trained English girl," since she was a Jamaican émigré. Instead, Hannah paid her above the going rate. Hannah had never thought of herself as someone who would "keep help," but she'd never thought of herself as becoming a mother either.

"All mothers need help," Gemma had said unprompted, a week into her new job. "Not enough can get it."

"I suppose I'd do better if I weren't working," Hannah replied, surprised enough to be candid.

Gemma eyed her shrewdly. "You're the sort who has to work or lose your mind. It's no good for children, mamas without minds."

Hannah was very pleased to have a strong mind.

After lunch, Julie went down for a nap,

41

and Gemma took Rhoda into the square's garden to terrorize the neighbor children. Hannah, needing a change from the thrillers in the living room, went into the master bedroom, where comedy scripts were piled on her bedside table and melodramas were on the vanity under her hairbrushes. She chose a comedy — everyone wanted a hit comedy — tossed her shoes into a corner, and returned to the sofa.

"Do you really have to do this reading all the time?" Paul asked. "Even on Sundays? That Scotch guy who works for you, can't he do it?"

" 'Scottish,' darling, not 'Scotch' — that's offensive," Hannah corrected, in the gentle lilt that had first captivated him. "Sidney reads too, of course, but I'm the one who's going to find the show that puts me on the map. And anyway, you know perfectly well that a lot of these submissions are entrusted directly to me."

Paul frowned worriedly and looked as if he were about to scold her. To her relief, he just asked if the script was any good.

"It would be all right for a film," she said, scowling at the pages. "I'd sure love it if more writers understood television's not about shrinking a picture. It's a whole new medium."

"I'm sure you'll be the one to tell them, dear," Paul said, laughing.

Hannah laughed too. She reached for Paul's hand, wrapping both of hers around it and drawing it to her lips. He had perfect rounded fingernails, neatly pared always; so unlike her own nails, which were invariably chipped at the corners and uneven. During their brief courtship, one of her favorite things to do was marvel at their intertwined hands. Urban sophisticate that he was, his fingers were nonetheless brown and strong, while hers were small and white and dainty. She loved that he didn't care if she eschewed nail polish — sometimes she wondered if he even noticed — and that her fingertips were always dimly ink stained. She loved that he loved to hold hands.

He kissed her forehead. "Say, darling, since you're reading anyway, I don't suppose you can look at my story?" Paul was a long-form journalist, often spending months on a piece that became a cover story for the *New Yorker* or *Atlantic Monthly*. He had made a minor name for himself during the war, writing in-depth pieces on slices of ordinary American life in wartime. His story about the messenger boy who received the wire that his own father had died was made into a film — a would-be weepie that had nowhere to go after the first act and only ran a week, but a film nevertheless. After Paul and Hannah married and she started editing his stories before his editors did, his work became even more popular.

She looked at the pile of scripts she hoped to get through, and into his expectant brown eyes. It was her work, not his — or not yet, as he said — that had spooked them into upending their lives. She hadn't named her company Rutherford Films as he'd hoped ("so at least people will know we're related, darling"), but chose "Sapphire" — a cool blue stone that was remarkably hard and resilient. She smiled at Paul. She loved helping him. He wanted a Pulitzer Prize, and she wanted that for him.

"It would make a lovely change," she agreed. "Speaking of lovely change, let's get Julie and join Rhoda and Gemma in the square. You can play with Rhoda and I'll read your story. It's not too cold. Heck, it's even downright sunny."

"Are we sure it's still London?" Paul asked.

Hannah laughed and went to gather the sleeping Julie, who hardly stirred as she was laid in her pram.

Paul had put on a tie and carried his story in a slim folder. He cast his eyes over Hannah, still dressed in a cardigan and a pair of his old tweed trousers.

"Don't you think you should change, dear? These people, you know."

"That's exactly how they talk about us," Hannah said with a laugh. She knew Paul meant a skirt, and a skirt meant a girdle. Hannah's stomach and hips were still spongy from her last pregnancy, and she hadn't yet decided if she cared. She presented herself smartly for business, but she was determined to be comfortable on a Sunday. "Anyway, it's just the square."

She saw the flicker across his face and changed her mind.

"Well, now that I think of it, why scandalize people if we don't have to?"

Her gray-checked hiking skirt would do for a cool afternoon. It was a touch too short for the trends, but Paul's smile was all she cared about.

The garden was full of neighboring families who thought it a good idea to brave the nippy air, bringing hoops and hobbyhorses and whatever else might encourage children to run mad outdoors, sparing the furniture another day. Hannah saw Rhoda was at the helm of a platoon poised to attack rival pirates.

"I don't think pirates use horses much,"

Paul observed, watching their daughter gallop around on her red-and-white hobbyhorse.

"Failure of imagination on their parts, if you ask me," Hannah said. She could work anywhere, and she read Paul's story — survivors of the Blitz in the East End remembering their neighbors as new houses were finally built — and listened to the children go wild with equal delight. The sun wasn't warm but it was pleasant, and the birdsong, combined with the shouts of the children and murmurs among the adults, was relaxing. This was the world everyone had fought so hard to preserve during the war, and here it was, carrying on. Hannah glanced around at every father on every bench. Each, perhaps, thinking how lucky he was. She hoped they were happy. They deserved it.

She turned over a page, her mind now wandering to her own week ahead. There was casting to approve for an original play. Set designs to go over for the next episode of the police drama. Option meetings, accounts, script revisions, and time found for all the problems in different quarters that popped up more regularly than crabgrass. It wasn't much different from working for a newspaper, really, and in its way, each day provided the same little zing of shocked delight she'd felt the first time she held her children in her arms.

But the story, the television series that would bear her name as executive producer and be a hit, that still felt like a rainbow she was chasing. They would fight about it tomorrow, she and Sidney — or rather, have a free exchange of thoughts — and this was always something to look forward to. Sidney was a clever, shrewd man, an excellent associate producer in the office and program producer on a set. Every day Hannah walked into the upstairs suite on Cadogan Square that was home to Sapphire Films, she thought how grateful she was, for Sidney, for Sapphire, for Paul, for the new life she'd been able to seize and the endless possibilities it offered. Liberal journalists she'd worked with in America had been summarily fired, and here she was, happy and thriving. She knew just how lucky she was.

She knew, too, that it was foolhardy to compromise that luck. But she couldn't help herself.

CHAPTER THREE

Phoebe swayed, all her insides blown out of her, leaving her perfect-posture exterior. It was a joke, it had to be. Or Mr. Kelvin must mean to say he was taking her off *At Your Service* and hiring her for a better show. She was one of Hank's handpicked writers. She could not be fired.

She looked to Hank for sense. His face was puce. She could see him struggling to speak without the sort of language that would get him fired as well. Except that she *couldn't* be fired, so he might as well comment on this rotten joke with all the tools at his disposal.

"Mr. Kelvin, you're kidding me," he sputtered.

You tell 'em, Hank!

"Phoebe's my writer. You swore I had total freedom over my writers."

Mr. Kelvin's avuncular face snapped closed. "And *you* swore you wouldn't hire any Reds."

He wasn't loud, yet the word shot around the vast room, a pinball hitting every target with a piercing ring before it slipped between the levers and disappeared.

Reds. Reds were Communists, supposedly in league with the Soviets. Anyone called Red in entertainment was put on the blacklist — that list of people not allowed to work in the industry because they might be a "pinko traitor," irrespective of truth or proof. It was the end of a career, the end of everything. And this man was suggesting she was one of those.

She shook her head wildly, a dog trying to rid its ears of fleas.

"I don't understand," she said in a squeaky voice that sounded nothing like her own. "I don't understand."

She seized Hank's arm, certain he was the one sane person in the room. The doubt in his eyes made her recoil.

"Phoebe," he began, and she could feel his mind working, wanting to ask the question carefully. "This is . . . just a misunderstanding. Isn't it?"

"Of course it is! I'm not even political. I'd forget to vote if people didn't remind me when it's Election Day."

"Listen, girlie," Mr. Kelvin interjected.

"You don't look like much of a rabble-rouser to me, and I believe Hank wouldn't have hired you if you were, but he obviously has a soft spot for you and didn't do all he could to make sure you were okay. He'll do better from now on, won't he?"

His eyes twinkled as he gazed at Hank, but his intent was perfectly clear, and Hank paled. Mr. Kelvin turned back to Phoebe, and his tone was almost kind.

"I've got men to answer to and the show's got the sponsors. Rules are rules. We can't have any named Reds working here."

Each sentence crashed over Phoebe like Dorothy's house on the Wicked Witch of the East. She knew how this went — as apolitical as she was, the stories were hard to miss. A few distant acquaintances had ended up on the blacklist. But it was something that happened to other people, something that, until this moment, seemed as remote from her as Easter Island.

A named Red. *My name! On a list! That's just not possible. How . . . who?* Her stomach lurched. There were any number of ways a person got blacklisted, she knew that well enough. They might have supported the freedom fighters in the Spanish Civil War, they might have signed a petition supporting European refugees, they might have

50

expressed any sort of left-leaning opinion. Even people who touted the virtues of the New Deal were suspect. But most people on the blacklist got there because someone gave up their name. The idea that someone who knew her — a colleague, maybe even a friend — had spoken her name, out loud, to someone who added it to a list made the bile rise in her throat. *It doesn't make sense, though! I'm no Communist, everyone knows that. Heck, old Dolores Goldstein actually was one, registered and everything . . .*

The train of thought shuddered to a stop. The other big reason people got on the blacklist was because they were in a union. All of the Hollywood Ten screenwriters weren't just suspected Communists. They had also been active in the Screen Writers Guild, which the studio heads loathed more than a poor box office return. Phoebe wasn't a member — she was still too lowly even for Writers Guild membership — but during the war, at the airfield, she'd helped organize a union to fight for equal pay. It had infuriated the bosses, and memories could be long. Maybe someone somewhere *did* read the show's credits. Though anyone could lose any job if they were fingered as a subversive.

Of course, it doesn't have to be the bosses.

It could be Dolores Goldstein. It could be any one of them.

Phoebe gripped the edge of the little table. She knew it made her look weak, but she'd look worse if she fainted, or asked to sit down, or threw up. None of that could happen. She wouldn't — couldn't — lose control right now.

Hank's touch on her arm jolted her back into the moment. It was a kind touch, solicitous. She felt herself exhale. Hank would still fight for her.

"Sure, of course, we can't have the wrong sort of people on staff," Hank said. She knew he was just trying to mollify the producer, beginning with a hedge. A smart move that did nothing to abate her chills. "I've worked with Phoebe a long time, she's always been a good kid. Maybe there's something we can do to sort this out?" But he wasn't saying this was madness. He wasn't saying it was wrong.

Mr. Kelvin turned jovial again and waved a piece of paper at Hank.

"I thought you might say that. I was sent this to offer her to sign." (Phoebe noted automatically the man was talking about her, not to her.)

He laid the paper on the table and Phoebe read the heading. A loyalty oath.

"More and more are signing them these days," Mr. Kelvin said conversationally. He might have been talking about a new style of hat. "High school kids, if they want to graduate. Workers. Probably it'll be everyone, soon."

Phoebe glanced at Hank again. She didn't know if she was looking for his approval or for him to say if he'd signed such an oath. His face was carefully blank.

She gripped the pen. She could not lose her livelihood, she could not be blacklisted from the industry. She could not have her name destroyed. If there was only herself to consider, that might be one thing, but there was Mona.

Mona. She read ten newspapers a day, and a story just a few weeks ago about loyalty oaths had sent her into a lather. "That's something Stalin would make people sign, isn't it, and then throw them in the gulag anyway because their handwriting wasn't nice enough." Which was easy for Mona to say, because she wasn't out in the world, and the hospital staff liked her and could shrug off "subversive talk" as the ramblings of someone ill and unlikely to live much longer, things they'd said about Mona for the last fifteen years.

She'll understand. She won't want to risk

being booted to a state institution. Anyway, I am a loyal American, so what difference does it make?

Phoebe didn't bother to read the paper. She gripped the pen tightly, forcing her hand to stay still. Then she looked into Mr. Kelvin's eyes.

"And this will clear my name?" she asked. "I'll have my job?"

Mr. Kelvin threw back his head and laughed again. Phoebe felt like she was the hero in a bad horror movie, confronting an evil villain.

"Don't you read the papers, sweetheart? I'd have thought anyone who knew they were in danger of being blacklisted would know this score. We can't have you back till the boys at HUAC or the FBI or wherever say you're clean. Worst case, you go for one of those Congressional hearings, but you'd be a good girl, right, play smarter than those Ten boys and keep yourself out of prison."

The pen fell out of her hand. She gazed back down at the oath. She should sign it. A drowning person grabs what they're handed. But it was saying they had a right to force her to do this, to effectively admit she was guilty of something she wasn't. She didn't give a fig about politics, she'd always said so. But this was different. This was her name.

"Phoebe." Hank's voice was low, both a question and an urging, though it was impossible that he was suggesting she go through with this. She looked at him, seeing her own trapped expression reflected in his eyes. Whosever side he was on, she couldn't guess, and he couldn't say.

She turned back to Mr. Kelvin. "I think I'd better get some advice first."

He smiled broadly. "Well, well. I must say, I thought if we'd ever get a Red, it'd be a man. Please leave the building. I'm assuming I don't need to have you escorted out." That was meant to be kind. A favor, a final shred of dignity he was allowing her. She knew she was supposed to be grateful.

"I can walk just fine on my own, thanks," she said, but with nothing like her usual swagger. It was hard to talk after being sucker punched in the gut.

"I'll see you out," Hank said. Probably this was also meant to be kind.

"I'm fine, thank you," she said stiffly. She had to move fast, before she lost control and started to cry. She turned and saw that the actors and crew had all edged as close as they dared to the proceedings, attracted by a drama in real life.

She locked eyes with a pale, openmouthed Geraldine. Phoebe knew it would be dangerous to acknowledge their friendship, dangerous and unfair. But she wanted to assure Geraldine what no one else there, except hopefully Hank, knew. That she didn't deserve what was happening to her.

Phoebe stepped forward, and the little group took several giant steps back.

"Oh, for Pete's sake," Phoebe boomed. "I don't have the plague."

"But you are a dirty Red," Geraldine said. "The sooner you're gone, the better."

Phoebe knew now that she was wrong. What she'd thought was a sucker punch was nothing compared to this. She bit her lip and turned away from all those eyes, then walked as quickly as she could without looking as if she was running. She didn't feel herself breathe again until she was out on Sixth Avenue.

She stormed down four blocks, but could still hear it. *Dirty Red.* What an extraordinary way to slap a person across the face without raising a hand. Geraldine would remember this feeling of power forever, would use it in her acting till her last job. Phoebe understood. It was known they were friends. Geraldine had a lot to lose. She had to make a stand, make her own position clear. Now she would be admired instead of suspected. Whereas Phoebe would just be dirty.

It was apt. She had never felt so dirty, like all her skin needed to be scraped off before she could feel human again. "Red" was accurate too. The color of humiliation. The scarlet letter.

She ought to get on a bus. Sit down, stop moving. Get home. The sooner she got home, the sooner she could put her head on Anne's shoulder and cry.

But she couldn't stop walking. She couldn't stop the same thoughts from turning over and over in her mind. Her name had been dipped in compost. She might not get to work as a writer anymore. It was the only thing she'd ever wanted, ever since she was nine and her teacher, the harassed and irritable Miss Wittkins, a woman who never seemed to know any of her students' names, shook Phoebe's essay "I Watched Them Paint a WPA Mural" in her face and snapped, "You're brighter than the others. You better keep making an effort." Phoebe had. Now she wondered if praising Roosevelt's Works Progress Administration had been the first tick on a list.

When she reached Bryant Park, she wandered down one of its paths toward the big, beautiful library, which might have books that could help her, tell her how to fight back. She was nearly at the door when logic reminded her that top blacklistees like Dalton Trumbo and Ring Lardner Jr. had retained excellent lawyers, and that didn't prevent them from being brought before Congress, asked about their politics, and tossed into prison when they refused to answer. Even the American Civil Liberties Union chose not to defend accused Reds.

But maybe there's something. Maybe I can be like a gal in some story — the nobody who finds the key no one expected and blows it all wide open.

She was at the card catalog, making a list of likely books, when she remembered that the FBI scrutinized people's library records. And what arcane point of law did she expect to find, anyway? The First Amendment was right there for anyone to see, and it had thus far saved no one.

Phoebe plopped into a wooden chair, pulled out her handkerchief, and wiped the sweat from her neck. *Wonderful, now I'm going to stain my good blouse.* A flicker at the end of the card catalog caught her eye. A man's hat. He was watching her.

Bile rose to her mouth, and she pressed her handkerchief to her lips. She jumped up and ran for the stairs, even though she knew it made her look more suspicious. She couldn't stop running now, not until she was underground, on a subway, heading back to the sanctuary of Perry Street. She glanced around the lightly populated subway car. Mostly women. Were any of them watching her? Women were no less dangerous than men and could be far more so — Hedda Hopper might as well be a ranking member of HUAC, having fingered at least half the Hollywood denizens who ended up blacklisted.

Mrs. Pocatelli was nosing about her garden. The tenants often wondered what had become of Mr. Pocatelli. Phoebe had been disappointed to learn she wasn't the first to assume he was feeding the beets, carrots, and cabbages.

"You!" Mrs. Pocatelli shouted. Phoebe shrank from the bony finger pointing at her. "You promised me sfogliatelle from Veniero's!"

The buttering up of a lifetime ago. "I'll get them later, Mrs. Pocatelli," Phoebe assured her. The landlady looked skeptical — Phoebe could feel her scowl all the way up the stairs and even as she turned down the corridor toward her door.

She heard Thelonious Monk's "Straight, No Chaser," in Anne's apartment and pounded on the door.

"Holy cannoli, what the hell happened to you?" Anne said on seeing Phoebe's face.

Phoebe opened her mouth and a giant sob came out. She dropped her bag and sank to the floor, howling.

"Come on, let's get to your place," Anne said. Her furniture was covered with tarps while she worked on a complicated painting. She grabbed a bottle of bourbon, heaved Phoebe from the floor, and soon settled them on Phoebe's love seat. Anne poured bourbon to the brim of two amber cut glass Victorian tumblers — a lucky secondhand shop find — and Phoebe downed hers in one gulp.

"I've been blacklisted," she said. It was like speaking a foreign language, the word weird and twisty on her lips.

Anne whistled low and topped up Phoebe's glass. She flipped through albums, put on *Call Me Madam* at top volume, and sat close to Phoebe.

"If there's a listening device in here, it doesn't stand a chance of hearing us over Ethel Merman," she insisted.

A listening device! Phoebe wrapped her arms around herself and glanced around the cozy apartment she loved so much. Pale green walls, pink and yellow curtains, the art deco love seat Anne had helped her re-cover. Her desk and typewriter. Had some-one been listening to her when she thought she was safe in her home?

"Stay calm," Anne instructed, reading her face. "They want you to break."

Phoebe finished another tumbler of bour-bon and strode to her Roseville cookie jar, the last thing her mother ever bought. It was filled with change, mostly nickels and dimes. No more than ten dollars altogether.

"I've got this and about seventy-eight bucks in the bank," she told Anne. "What do I do? You know the score. No one's sup-posed to hire a blacklisted writer, Constitu-tion or no Constitution. I'm no big shot like Dalton Trumbo. I can't afford to disappear, become nobody."

The phrase caught in her throat, and she added gin to the last of the bourbon.

"You can get some crummy job to tide you over," Anne advised. "Then you'll sell a script under a fake name, people do that."

"Not easily, they don't. And even crummy jobs can check names. No one wants to hire an accused Red. How am I supposed to cover me and Mona?"

For the first time, Anne looked doubtful. "I don't know," she whispered. She frowned in contemplation. "Why you, though? Unless . . . the airfield?" she ventured.

"It's the only time I remember being radical. They might get you on it too."

Anne nodded. No doubt nearly everyone on Perry Street was the sort of person who might end up on a list before long, if they weren't already.

The phone rang. Phoebe recoiled. "It's being tapped. I know it. It's been ringing with no one there. That friend of Floyd and Leo's said that was a giveaway."

"Geez, the FBI must be feeling flush — they're pouring more money into you than the network is," Anne said. She snatched up the phone.

"It's Hank," she told Phoebe, wrinkling her nose and holding the receiver out between two fingers, like it was a rotting carcass.

Phoebe was tempted to ask, "Hank who?" but took the phone.

"Well, hi there, Hank, what's new?" she asked brightly.

"Phoebe, honey, let's have lunch Saturday, all right? You pick a place, drop me a line."

The phrasing was too perfect, designed so that anyone listening wouldn't know the meeting spot. Phoebe shivered. Hank had done this before. She hung up and looked at Anne.

"Maybe I should suggest Hell's waiting room," she said.

"Isn't that a bar on the Bowery?"

Phoebe managed a hollow laugh. She lit a cigarette.

"What the hell am I going to do?"

Anne opened her mouth, closed it, opened it again, and then just wrapped her hand around Phoebe's and held it tight.

The next day, Phoebe posted a note to Hank telling him to meet her at Desiree's, the nicest restaurant in Greenwich Village. Might as well get a decent meal out of him.

Then she went to visit Mona. The Brookside Sanitarium was nowhere near a brook, but it was a fine facility and had given the Adler family a very good rate in exchange for the honor of subjecting Mona to countless tests. The doctors had never seen someone with virtually no natural immunity, and certainly no one who lived to adulthood. Phoebe had long given up real hope of a miracle cure, but the doctors' desire to understand Mona's body meant Brookside took good care of her, and that was enough. Phoebe hurried through the ritual of scrubbing her hands and face with surgical soap and putting on a white coat before she passed through to the patients' quarters.

"Baby sister!" Mona squealed when Phoebe walked into the dayroom. She wheeled herself across the room at breakneck speed, careening around a cribbage game and coming to a neat stop before Phoebe.

"Glad I caught you before you went ice skating," Phoebe said.

"Don't be ridiculous," Mona scolded. "Tuesday is horseback riding. Don't you remember anything?"

Phoebe hugged her, glad to feel no more bones than usual. Underneath the scent of hospital disinfectant and carbolic soap, she smelled the Shalimar she had sneaked to Mona on her birthday. Rules or no rules, if Mona wanted, as she put it, "a proper, grown-up perfume," she was damn well going to have it.

Phoebe wheeled her sister into a quiet corner and sat down next to her.

"How come you don't have a rug over your legs? You're going to get cold," Phoebe scolded, knowing she sounded fussy.

"Don't be fussy," Mona scolded right back. "I'm fine. You're the one who's not. Don't contradict me," she said as Phoebe started to protest. "I know your face, you can't hide anything."

64

That was going to be a problem.

Phoebe hesitated, realizing she wasn't sure what was safe to say. Anyone could be listening, waiting for her to say something they decided mattered.

"I think I'm in a little trouble," she whispered.

Mona lit up. "Are you pregnant?" She answered her own question. "No, you couldn't be, that would involve actually going on a date. With a man and everything."

"It's not that I don't want to date," Phoebe said reflexively. *Good lord, we're not going to have* this *conversation, are we?*

"Well, I do, and I need to live vicariously, so live it up a bit, will you?" Mona stopped smiling. "You don't have to be so careful all the time, you know. You don't have to always worry about hurting your career."

"That happened anyway." Phoebe leaned closer and whispered the whole story, taking strength from the red rage that spread over Mona's face. For the first time in years, she looked almost healthy.

"This is how they treat people who helped win the war? What a joke."

"I'm not the only one," Phoebe conceded, thinking that a lot of the blacklisted men had been in combat.

"No, but you're the only one who's my sister."

They fell quiet for several minutes. Then they looked at each other and burst out laughing.

"When the hell were the Adler girls ever quiet together?" Mona cried. "Daddy would think we'd died or something."

"Good thing he's not alive to learn about this," Phoebe said.

" 'Horatio Adler,' " Mona mused. "He must have made that name up."

The Adler parents were always angry and tired, and worried about Mona. They rarely spoke, so Phoebe and Mona became avid talkers, filling the silence with sound. The girls decided their parents had an interfaith relationship and were thus shunned from their families. Horatio never acknowledged being Jewish, but their mother, born Mary Smith, once divulged she was a Quaker. To the girls, that meant the man with the big hat on the oatmeal box, who seemed an unlikely relative. They treasured the idea anyway, as they knew of no other extended family. "You're American!" Horatio would shout when they asked about religion. "That's the only religion you need." Phoebe pressed him, trying to make him understand the tribalism of New York City public schools, the particularities of expectation that insisted she align herself with a group so as to accept her label and know her place.

"Tell them you're a New Yorker," Horatio insisted. "That's more than enough for anyone." Mary, preoccupied with keeping the house sterile for Mona, batted away such trivial concerns with flicks of a dust rag.

Phoebe's playground explanation that hers was a family without religion could have relegated her to a childhood peppered with regular beatings. What saved her was her ability to make people laugh and, later, her telling of strange and scary stories. Nothing original at first, just variations on things learned by sneaking into movies she wasn't supposed to see and devouring library books she wasn't supposed to read, but none of the kids knew enough to know she was paraphrasing. Plus, she had the distinction of a sister with a mysterious illness, who went to hospitals rather than school. Such things were respected. The newspaper seller's daughter was too strange to merit friendship, but she was, mostly, left in peace.

"They've been tapping my phone," Phoebe murmured to Mona. "And I'm pretty sure I've been followed."

"She-eesh," Mona breathed. "I could sure

do with a cigarette."

"How the heck do you get cigarettes?" Phoebe demanded.

Mona chuckled. "A few of us sneak down the fire stairs a couple times a week. Tubercular Ben gets them, he won't say how, the worm."

"Don't tell me you can get down the fire stairs on your own," Phoebe said, glancing at the wheelchair that had been Mona's only transport for ten years.

"Oh, where there's a wheel, there's a way," Mona said airily. Phoebe groaned. "Now listen, Phoebe, you need to make a plan."

"I know."

"Because they might drag you in for a hearing."

"Only if they're scraping the barrel, surely?"

Mona ignored this. "So you'd better leave the country."

"What!"

"You got that beautiful passport and you've never bothered to use it!"

"Well, for one thing —"

"Don't make me an excuse," Mona warned, laying her finger on the tip of Phoebe's nose. "They're not going to boot me out now."

Phoebe glanced at a barrel-armed nurse

wheeling a patient into the room. The Adlers had sold everything to buy Mona ten years in Brookside, which was the longest she was supposed to live. That was fifteen years ago. Cancer claimed Mama within six months of Pearl Harbor. And their father — stout, ferocious Horatio Adler — tripped and fell in front of a streetcar six months after that. Phoebe, who had dropped out of school and lied about her age so she could build airplanes, felt like she'd walked through a doorway from her childhood and fell flat on her face into the mud that was a sudden adulthood at seventeen. Every penny she earned for the rest of the war plumped up the family fund that supported Mona in Brookside. Her money now kept Mona in a private room.

"I can share a room," Mona said. "It's probably better if someone's on hand to see me start to check out — stop it!" She pinched Phoebe hard to quell a protest. "Be realistic. If you can't send money, we'll manage. The real danger is if you have a hearing and refuse to testify, which you *would,* because it's disgusting our government is even asking such questions, and then you'd go to prison. Brookside might balk at having a jailed Red's sister underfoot."

"I think only famous people have hearings," Phoebe said.

"You think wrong, you need to read more," Mona scolded.

"What I need is to be here, I need to see you."

"Put everything in hock, borrow from everyone, and get on a boat. You ought to see the world. One of us should, and it seems increasingly likely it won't be me."

"It's running away." Phoebe shook her head, disgusted.

"No, dummy, it's living your life. It's telling the FBI and HUAC that they're wrong, a waste of taxpayer money, and you're going to take care of yourself until someone finally puts the kibosh on them."

"Take care of myself," Phoebe said in a flat voice. "Like there's nobody else for me to take care of."

Mona batted this away in an exact imitation of their mother with her dust rag. "Just be ready, all right? Have some cash, pack a bag. Know the times ships sail. And don't tell anyone."

Mona's eyes glittered and she couldn't stop grinning. Phoebe suspected that if Mona had been healthy, she would have distinguished herself during the war as a spy, and brushed off all honors afterward to live as an adventuress. Despite everything, Phoebe felt her lips twitch. It was nice that someone could enjoy all this.

"Wish I could take a plane." Phoebe sighed. "Maybe I wouldn't mind running away if I could fly."

"Too expensive," Mona agreed. "I'd offer you a kidney to sell, but it's not worth much."

Phoebe sighed again and looked out the window. She could just see the tip of the Chrysler Building.

"I don't want to go anywhere. This is home. I'm a New Yorker. I don't ever want to be anything else."

"No one would ever take you for anything else, not with your accent. Now get out of here, you've got work to do," Mona ordered, allowing nothing more than the usual hug and kiss goodbye. When Phoebe reached the door, Mona yelled, "And bring me some dirty magazines next time!"

The phone was ringing as she walked in the door.

"Phoebe Adler," she answered.

"Hello, this is Hank, from *At Your Service . . .*" came Hank's voice, sounding tinny.

"Hank, I know who you are!" she shouted, but he was still talking.

". . . is Phoebe available?"

"What the — ?"

But Phoebe's mouth snapped closed as she heard Anne's voice, telling Hank to wait a moment. Her heart pounded harder and harder as she listened, and then it came, her own voice: "Well, hi there, Hank, what's new?"

She slammed down the phone on Hank's response suggesting lunch. The whispered rumors had said this could happen — that a bugged phone meant sometimes you'd hear a recording of one of your own conversations. A glitch, presumably. Or not. The FBI might not care if you knew they were listening. They wanted to unnerve you, to scare you into capitulation, into confessing anything they suggested, into naming names. Phoebe backed away from the phone, wiping her hands. She grabbed her bag and ran out to find the nearest travel agent and get the departure schedule of every ship soon leaving New York, bound for somewhere that might give her safe harbor.

CHAPTER FOUR

"You certainly can pick them," Sidney marveled, stroking the script Hannah had insisted he drop everything else to read. " 'Tis a cracker."

"It'll be a good one-off drama," Hannah agreed. It was a play about a black GI attacked by other GIs for dating a white girl in Liverpool, and the city's protest against the American attempt to implement race laws. "But it's still not a series. And no one will air it in America."

"Ach, 'whit's fur ye'll no go by ye,' as they say," Sidney said in his broadest Scots. He grinned, bouncing on his toes as he did when a script showed promise.

"Translation, please," Hannah asked.

" 'What's meant to happen will happen,' " Sidney said. "Our audience will love this, it'll let them congratulate themselves on being superior to the Yanks."

"They're not wrong," Hannah said. "My

friend Shirley and her husband are Negroes. They were Red-hunted out of America for being activists, but she says that here they are treated with decency wherever they go, skin notwithstanding. Not that they've been everywhere," Hannah conceded.

"Isn't it Shirley whose husband is Will LeGrand?" Sidney asked. "The famous civil-rights activist, sociologist, author, all-round genius? He's someone the literary crowd would give a place of honor even if he had three heads."

"As they should," Hannah said with feeling. "He's one of our most brilliant minds and spent his whole life fighting for Negroes to be equal. He deserves scads of adulation, though it should be in his own country."

"Yanks," Sidney said, shaking his head. "Chasing blacks, chasing Reds, they're *craicte* enough to be committed to Bedlam."

Hannah grinned. There was some Scottish that needed no translation, though she wouldn't dare try to pronounce it.

"Never mind," she said briskly. "Let's get to work. I'll get the option secured this afternoon and we'll need a terrific actor. And director. And a top cameraman."

"We cannae afford all that," Sidney protested. "A corner must be cut."

Hannah gave him a baleful look. "You

have to spend money to make money. Good quality pays for itself."

Sidney stumped off to make the calls, and Hannah chuckled. She'd grown up enduring taunts about Jews being tightfisted — even though her family could barely make rent. *Those people should try getting a penny out of a Scot.*

She looked out her window down at the leafy Cadogan Square. Her childhood bedroom window on Orchard Street had looked onto an airshaft. She'd known she would go far, but even her vivid imagination had never conjured anything like this. Her own company, and a man as her second-in-command. She and Sidney had met when they both talked their way into minor production roles on a television movie and discovered they had as much acumen as the entirety of the seasoned crew and a shared passion for work labeled "controversial." He thought they should start slow, but Hannah was far too restless for caution, and had been told too many times in her life to moderate her reach. Once she understood the basics of television production, she knew she could do it, and Sapphire Films was born the next day.

It was only when they produced their third television film — and got it aired on CBS

— that Hannah asked Sidney what he thought of the blacklist. She knew he was a fervent socialist who was keen to hire the best writers, provided they came at a bargain rate. But potentially ruffling the feathers of an American television network might be a bridge too far.

"How can a country like America have a blacklist?" Sidney demanded when Hannah brought it up. "How is it not aping something your man Stalin would do?"

"How to explain the inexplicable?" Hannah said. "You're quite right. The studio heads in Hollywood have always been a strange breed. They want to be seen as innovators, but are terrified of criticism. So when some politicians and religious conservatives yowled about films being filthy, in came the Production Code. Really, they want to be seen as patriots, good Americans. Important. Well, so when HUAC starts huffing and puffing about 'Commie propaganda' in movies, the studio heads could have said they'd make the pictures they wanted and let audiences decide, but being them, they all agreed to wipe Hollywood clean of anything even remotely leftist, starting with screenwriters. So sure, there can't be an *official* blacklist, that would be unconstitutional. But word can go

76

around saying, 'Don't hire this person, don't hire that one,' and suddenly the hottest writers, directors, actors in town are as good as dead. No one dares defy the word — who knows what HUAC could do then."

Sidney shook his head. "We had actual Communist spies here — British men, educated at Cambridge, if you please — and we still believe in civil liberties."

"That's why there are Americans escaping the witch hunts living here," Hannah said.

He grinned at her shrewdly. "Are you hinting you're one such? I did wonder. They don't much cotton to leftist journalists, I hear."

"They don't," she agreed. "I saw the heat turning up and decided to get out before it got to me. Word is I've been forgotten in the midst of all the bigger fish."

Sidney had several choice words about the treatment of the bigger fish.

"I'm glad you feel that way," Hannah said. "Because I have to feed those fish, by which I mean I'd like to hire blacklisted screenwriters."

Sidney kept a stash of Walkers shortbread, which he nibbled when he was thinking, or worried, or both. He nibbled some now.

"I can't be the sort of person who shakes my fist from a safe distance," Hannah went on. "I've always been an activist. I have to do something strenuous."

He grinned. "You bonkers liberal do-gooder, you." Then he looked around the office, decorated with still photos from Sapphire's productions. He raised an eyebrow at Hannah. "You've been hiring blacklistees already, haven't you? That's why some of these writers have no other credits."

"Some of them are my friends," Hannah admitted. "All of them need help. I can't change what's happening in America, but I can continue to give these men a voice. And an income doing what they do best."

"I'm game," Sidney said. "And I understand the money end more than you, pardon my saying so. We'll need additional books and careful means of sending payments. And a stash of cash for legal fees if we're ever caught — they'd insist on you coming to America to testify, that's certain. Also, these writers get paid the same as any greenhorn."

Hannah could hardly argue.

So Sapphire developed the secret reputation as a place for blacklistees to submit work. Despite her determination, and bravado, Hannah was a little nervous. She had no friends in British politics, no one who could protect her if she needed it. She wasn't certain her status as a UK business owner would save her if the American Embassy requested she no longer be allowed residency, or refused to renew her passport. Or if a registered letter arrived containing a subpoena. Would she be forced to respond? She didn't want to find out. The fewer people who knew she hired blacklisted writers, the better. If there was one thing Hannah learned the day the HUAC hearings began, it was that even the person you least expected could turn out to be the one who betrayed you.

"If any of the men see you reading a script, they'll have a fit hoping it's one of theirs."

Hannah looked up from the script she thought was hidden in her capacious handbag and into the patrician face of Shirley LeGrand.

"Sorry, Shirley. Great gathering, of course, it's just —"

"You can't stop working, I know." Shirley nodded. "I wouldn't mind doing some composition myself, but I suspect it might look untoward for a hostess to work at her own party, radicals though we all are, *naturellement,*" she added, with a twirl of her long, slim fingers and slight eye roll at the men huddled in a circle talking politics, ignoring the women until they wanted fresh drinks.

"I thought I was being sneaky," Hannah confessed.

"But of course. Only don't forget I was taught to know what every white person in a room is doing at all times. Habits, don't you know."

Hannah knew. It was the same trick she'd employed as the only female journalist in a press room, and she had far fewer reasons than Shirley to be so vigilant.

The Morrisons arrived, accompanied by their sons — a teenager and a ten-year-old, both of whom looked as though they'd rather be hanged than here.

"Oh, strife," Shirley said, her only concession to cursing. "Why can't Charlie and Joan leave those boys in a barn? There goes the food."

"I'll put another few pounds in the kitty," Hannah promised. "It's nice for Joan to get out of that miserable flat. It's just not her, the poor dear."

These gatherings were nice for everyone, after a fashion. The American exiles in London met regularly to exchange news and leads on possible work, and quietly put any extra cash into a pot to help any of the group who needed it. Some of the blacklistees were in far more dire straits than others, though they put a good face on it. Surrounded by Americans, it was also a way to feel at home, even if many of them would never have been friends back in the States.

Joan sailed up to Hannah and Shirley with much rustling of her crinoline and kissed their cheeks. Hannah could smell half a bottle of hairspray.

"I hope you don't mind we brought the boys," Joan said to Shirley. "I know Bobby ought to be able to manage Alvie for a few hours, but he's really still a child himself, poor thing, and still in shock from the move. Besides, our neighborhood —"

"Will and I are always delighted to have the children here," Shirley assured Joan. Hannah sipped her drink to hide her expression. Will had once told her privately that Bobby reminded him of "the sort of white boy who can get carried away," which meant that, his Hollywood liberal upbringing notwithstanding, Bobby was not to be trusted in a group of white boys who spotted a lone black person. Or even a lone white woman.

Hannah agreed, though Bobby seemed too indolent for trouble. He was furious with his father for joining the Communist Party in the 1930s, sentencing them to the loss of their glamorous Hollywood life and, worse, his privileged American adolescence. He seized a whole plate of canapés and flung himself into a corner, hiding his face in a Superman comic book. Alvie parked himself near the table holding cookies, committed to an evening of sneaking the lot of them.

Charlie, armed with a drink, came to greet Shirley.

"Thanks for not minding the whole Morrison clan," he said, gesturing toward the boys. "Little monsters. I keep telling Bobby the blacklist will be over soon and we'll be back with the sunshine and starlets before he knows it."

Will joined them to top off everyone's drinks — he enjoyed being the host. "A teacher involved with the NAACP went to renew her US passport to visit her mother in Canada. The request was denied, which is how she found out she was accused of Communist sympathies. I shouldn't count on seeing that sunshine anytime soon." He kissed his wife's cheek and returned to the throng.

"It *must* be unconstitutional," Hannah grumbled. "And anyway, you'd think the government would want to be rid of all the Communists."

"I guess they figure, keep 'em at home, the pinkos turn yellow, then turn themselves in?" Charlie said. "It's a nutso time, all right. Better here than there, even with not much going on. You, ah, hear of anyone needing my sort of talent?"

Hannah looked at him. Joan had done an admirable job patching his clothes, so he looked distinguished rather than downtrodden.

"I'll let you know," she promised. "I'm always ready to read something," she added, though reluctantly. Charlie specialized in huge, sprawling Westerns, the sort that sent Hannah into a sleep not even gunfights could disturb.

"Yeah, I'm trying," he said. "I'm not much for television, though. Can't get myself to think that small."

Hannah suspected he meant no offense, though it was hard to tell with Charlie.

"Door's always open," she told him. He headed off to talk to the men with the air of a man who had done his duty and could now have fun.

"I bet he doesn't want to work for a woman," chimed in Olivia, whose husband Ben was writing a French film.

"Oh no, that's not the case at all," Joan cried. "He's just a movie man through and through. He practically lived at his local picture house in Williamsburg."

Olivia raised a brow and glided away — she was a minor actress and liked to circulate through rooms, reminding everyone of the character type she was.

"Why don't *you* write me something, Joanie?" Hannah asked. "You're so good with short stories."

"Those cream puff things?" Joan pealed with laughter. "Silly romantic nonsense. It was all right for *Woman's Day,* not the sort of television you want to do."

Hannah sighed. She'd attempted this tack with Joan before.

"What about trying for the magazines again?" Hannah suggested. "You could at least bring in something."

"No, no, no. The boys keep me far too busy."

Hannah knew Joan included Charlie in that grouping. Probably more than Bobby and Alvie.

"To London!" Will boomed from his corner, raising his glass. "To freedom from persecution!"

"Is it time for the toasts already?" Shirley glanced at her watch. "I'd better get another bottle."

"To telling HUAC and the FBI to stuff

it!" Charlie shouted.

"To getting to work without that damn Production Code!" Ben cried. This was met with huge cheers. Working abroad wasn't easy, but the screenwriters who got to write for the French and Italian industries waxed lyrical about the artistic freedom. The irony escaped no one.

"To better days ahead!" Will called again, and this was echoed several times.

"To London," Hannah whispered into her own drink. "To getting to call my own shots and fight back from exile." Her eyes wandered to her bag.

"No more scripts for you, young lady," Shirley scolded, flitting by.

"No, I'm behaving," Hannah said. "Though I almost forgot — Rhoda sent a drawing for you." She retrieved it — a startling likeness of Rhoda as a pirate, engaged in a sword fight. "She says she's fighting J. Edgar Hoover," Hannah explained.

"She's the one to do it," Shirley said, raising her own glass to the picture.

Joan admired Rhoda's work. "It must be lovely, having daughters, though don't you worry she doesn't play with dolls?"

"Paul's mother sent her a doll when she was three. Within a day, the head was floating in the sink and each limb was in a different room," Hannah said. "I much prefer her as a pirate."

"Oh my." Joan was horrified. "Though I suppose she's only little. I'm sure she'll grow up to be more like other girls."

Hannah and Shirley, who had never been like other girls, said nothing. Hannah felt sorry for Joan, struggling so hard to keep her family afloat. The Morrisons always needed more help than anyone else. Of course Joan craved conformity. It was so safe.

"Rhoda knows Hoover sees us as outlaws," Hannah said at last. "If kids didn't love the idea of that, the Saturday matinees and adventure books would go the way of the dodo."

She saw Joan restraining herself from insisting such things were for boys. Instead, she excused herself to minister to her own boys, assuring them the tedium would soon be at an end. Will waved Shirley over to join the conversation, and Paul raised his brows at Hannah and gave her a wink. Her heart zinged and she winked back. Years of marriage, two children, and still the sight of his eyes across a room made her want to dance.

She lit a fresh cigarette, thinking how much she enjoyed the word "outlaw." It made her think of highwaymen on horses, and pirates on the seas.

She looked again at Rhoda's drawing. Sometimes outlaws were really only outliers. Because sometimes it was the law that was wrong.

Hannah reeled and stopped breathing. The people, the room, all disappeared. She spun back through time, into the deep woods, where the pirate's sword became a bow and arrow. Where a group of outlaws were men fighting to restore justice in a world gone mad.

"That's the show," she whispered, stroking the picture like it was Rhoda or Julie's cheek. "Robin Hood. It's perfect."

She well remembered the Errol Flynn film — as though she could forget Errol Flynn in anything, especially tights — but as episodes tumbled through her head, she knew this would be better. *The Adventures of Robin Hood.* It would be intelligent, it would have a point of view, it would be like nothing else on television.

"And it will be terrific fun."

Shirley returned with the empty cookie plate and studied Hannah in bemusement.

"You look happier than a cat in a cream-filled birdbath."

Hannah gazed at her with shining eyes.

"I've got it. An idea so good it'll set television on fire."

"Well. I suppose I'd best stock up on long sticks and marshmallows."

Shirley didn't ask any questions and Hannah was grateful — the train of thought needed to build steam. The show must look like a film, with no expense spared on costumes and sets, to say nothing of the best actors they could hire.

And it would be the best-written show on television. Sweat pooled under Hannah's arms as she realized what she was going to do. This *Robin Hood* would be about a group of men unjustly labeled outlaws, chased from society, and their leader determined to create a more equal world, where the rich didn't get to eat everyone else. If anyone looked too closely, they would see just how subversive this was. If they really looked too closely, they would discover the entire writing staff comprised blacklisted writers. It was a huge risk, but Hannah wouldn't have the show written by anyone else.

She downed her drink in one gulp. Tomorrow she would begin to build a legacy, and, she hoped, salvage a lot of careers as she was truly launching her own.

CHAPTER FIVE

Phoebe sprawled across the top of the footed bathtub, reaching her hand through the space between the tub and the wall. She ran her fingers under the tub's curved rim, easing her way down to the end. Nothing untoward. She seized the mirror she'd tied to the broom handle, positioned Anne's big work light, and lay on the floor, double-checking the underside of the rim and scanning underneath the tub for anything that looked like a listening device.

Anne came in with coffee.

"Well?"

"Next apartment, I'm having a fitted bathtub," Phoebe announced from the floor. "Assuming the FBI can't disguise a microphone as a spiderweb, the bathroom is clean." She sat up and readjusted her bandanna. "They can't really bust in and plant something, can they?"

"That's what I've heard," Anne said,

wrinkling her nose. "Though I'd give something to see the agent who could sneak around Mrs. Pocatelli."

"You're right, no one would ever have come in here. I should stop looking," Phoebe said, going into the living room to scan under the love seat.

The phone rang. Phoebe's head snapped up, smacking the coffee table.

Anne answered. "Oh, hiya, Jimmy," she said, rolling her eyes. "Let me get you Phoebe . . . What? Oh, sure, things are super, you know me, work, work . . . No, I really don't have any free evenings until —"

"Just tell him I passed his stuff along and if the man likes it, he'll be the first to know!" Phoebe shouted, aiming the mirror above the wall sconce. Anne relayed the message and hung up before Jimmy could say more. The two women waited, watching the phone. It rang again. Anne glanced at Phoebe, picked it up, listened a moment, then put it back down.

"I don't know if there's anything listening to you in here, but the phone's definitely still being tapped." She put on the *Anything Goes* album and turned up the volume. "The important thing is not to get paranoid," she instructed Phoebe.

Phoebe stuck her head out from under

her lampshade. "Paranoia is the only thing keeping me going."

"You should try to work. You're always happiest when you're working."

Phoebe lit a cigarette and glanced at the typewriter. "Even if I could think, what would I write? What's the point? Who can I try to sell something to?"

Anne pulled her closer to the record player and lowered her voice. "You'll slap a fake name on it and submit to radio, just like you did back when."

" 'Back when' I used my own name." Phoebe sulked. She knew Anne was right. She should forget she'd been selling work as Phoebe Adler since the war and start all over as someone else. But every time she thought about it, fury and sadness balled her fingers into fists, and she couldn't bring herself to try typing, or even knitting. It was her name, and she was proud of it. She'd never wanted to be "P. B. Adler" to hide her gender in the hopes of more work. No, she was Phoebe Adler, and that was the name she was going to make big. But she had to do something, and soon. Maybe ask Floyd and Leo at the Coffee Nook if they needed a waitress. She knew what happened to women who ran out of money.

"What about Mona's suggestion?" Anne

whispered, then mouthed: "Going abroad?"

"I . . . I don't know. It seems so extreme. I don't even know how —"

"You should at least be packed. The rest we can handle."

Phoebe beckoned Anne into the bedroom and showed her the timetables and her ready passport. "But I can't. Even if I had the money."

"Tourist class is about a hundred bucks, we can get it," Anne said, ignoring Phoebe's snort. "So long as you keep your passport safe." She paused, lips pursed. Then she picked up Phoebe's leatherette handbag and examined the lining.

Phoebe heaved a gusty sigh. Anne was right, and anyway, it wasn't a very good bag. She took her manicure scissors, slit open the lining, and tucked her passport and the timetables behind the cheap satin. Anne glued the tear shut.

"Keep the scissors in there, so you can open it easily," Anne instructed.

"Assuming my passport's not on a list somewhere to be seized if I try to leave the country," Phoebe said. She had no idea if such a list existed, and didn't want to find out.

Phoebe looked into Anne's enormous dark eyes. They'd each always known what they were doing and where they were going. Being stripped of that knowledge was almost worse than being stripped of her good name.

Almost.

Much too early on Saturday, Phoebe got ready to meet Hank. She spent a long time patting the puffs under her eyes, using every trick she'd ever learned from a magazine to brighten her features. When she was fifteen she'd looked at her frizzy hair, doughy face, and glasses, and decided she was never going to blossom into a beauty. Right then, she also decided not to care. Today was different, though. She had to put a good face on things. She applied her makeup liberally, wrestled her hair into place, and put on her good suit. She concentrated on keeping her shoulders back and head high as she marched down Perry Street toward the restaurant.

Desiree's was as pretty as she hoped, and another time, Phoebe would have been thrilled to walk into such an elegant little room, with dark tables and flocked wallpaper. But she only had eyes for Hank, who pumped her hand with his usual force and pulled out a chair for her. She saw his gaze flit around the room.

"Worried you'll be seen with a Red?" she

asked, hoping it sounded like a joke. His smile was tepid, and she realized she might be closer to the truth than she thought. Her eyes went around the room as well, seeing only couples, which seemed a good sign. Though who could tell?

"Must be a good life, being a G-man," she said. "Spend your days hanging about, watching people do not much of anything, going to nice restaurants on the taxpayers' dime."

"Stop it, Phoebe," Hank scolded. "They work damn hard trying to keep the country safe."

She recoiled. It wasn't his words so much as his tone. He sounded rehearsed. Protecting himself, maybe? No, then he'd keep away from her altogether. So maybe he believed it.

He reached out and caught her wrist. She hadn't realized she was half standing, preparing to run out. She sat down again, sliding her hand away, resisting the urge to wipe it. Whatever game he was playing, she had to believe Hank was still her friend. She had to.

"Listen, Phoebe, do you know how to find someone who'd put their name on one of your scripts and take it for the rounds, pretending it's theirs?"

"They're called 'fronts,' Hank. I know the lingo," she said. "People mutter."

"So?" he pressed.

She considered. Perry Street was full of hungry writers who would take a percentage of a fee for performing that service. Jimmy, she was sure, would do it. The thought came and went. She couldn't. Not where she was known for being a produced writer. She knew the way they'd look at her. Better to scrub toilets.

"I thought I'd submit stuff directly, using a pseudonym," she said. It still galled her, but was better than anyone else knowing her shame.

"You can try," Hank said. "But you'd have to provide a body if that name gets called in for a meeting," Hank said. He poured wine. "No matter how it gets sliced, Phoebe, it won't be easy. People a lot bigger than you are all washed up, even if they never get subpoenaed."

"What part of this is meant to make me feel better?" she demanded.

"Phoebe, you're a nice girl, you've got a lot to offer. Wouldn't it be easier if you were married?"

"Well, my schedule has just opened up."

"I'm serious. Maybe this is a sign it's time to move on to the next stage of your life.

You should be able to find yourself a nice fellow."

"Even if that's true, it won't happen before I run out of money," she said, fiercely glad she'd ordered the most expensive item on the menu, even if she couldn't pronounce it and had no idea what she was eating.

"I know it won't be easy, but —"

Phoebe slapped down her knife and glared at him.

"Look, I could move into a fleabag room in a women's hotel, take a job cleaning up crime scenes. But you were the one who agreed with me back then, saying I had talent, and that I was going places. You meant up. Not down, and not out. This isn't right."

"No, it's not, but it could be worse. Most of the men on the blacklist, they've got wives, kids. People depending on them."

Phoebe bristled. Hank knew all about Mona.

He had the grace to look abashed. "All right, sure, but you know it's not the same thing. You said yourself Brookside would keep Mona just to study her. They're not going to boot her now. You can't compare your situation to a man with a wife and kids. You know that."

"Apparently I know all sorts of stuff," Phoebe said. "A miracle for a gal who never

96

got to college."

"Answer me straight, kid. Who've you been working for besides me?"

Phoebe looked down. Hank was the first man to ever hire her, and though she worked the rounds as dutifully as any other writer, her other radio bits never panned out into anything regular. She refused to believe it meant she wasn't good. Hank wouldn't use her so often if that were true. Possibly it was a woman's name on her scripts that kept her from getting ahead. Which was an argument for the front, if everything about it didn't make her want to tear apart the FBI headquarters with her bare hands.

"Look, if you're determined to keep on with writing, I've got a lead," Hank whispered. "No guarantees, though." He slid over a piece of paper: *Hannah Wolfson, Executive Producer, Sapphire Films. Cadogan Square, London.* Hannah. A woman. Hank smirked, seeing Phoebe's bemusement. "Used to be sort of a high-flying journalist, apparently. Married, if you can believe it, with two kids."

"Like all those men so much worse off than me," Phoebe said.

Hank narrowed his eyes but she could see a faint blush. "Anyway, word is she's bought some scripts from fellows on the blacklist.

97

You could contact her."

A married woman with children, running her own studio. Phoebe couldn't comprehend it. "Do you think she knows they're blacklisted?"

"That's the point. She's a New York lefty herself. You know, the type who cares."

Phoebe ran her fingers over Hannah's name. There was no shortage of New York lefties who weren't sticking their necks out to help anyone on the blacklist. Being in London must make it easier to take that risk, but it was still really something. She wondered what this Hannah Wolfson was like.

"I'll tell you this," Hank said expansively, pointing his cigarette at her for emphasis. "If you're still at it when I get that next job, the good one, I'm bringing you on, blacklist or no blacklist. That's how we can break this thing, you know."

Phoebe's spirits skyrocketed. It was like being in school, when she was the only one who knew the answer.

"Hank, that's it! If you do that now, if you tell Mr. Kelvin you're determined to keep me, and with my name, he'll have to agree, he can't afford to lose you. He's the type to play the hero angle. It'll be great for a small network like Adelphi, saying they're bucking the blacklist 'cause I'm okay. Sure, some sponsors will run, but there's always others who like to back a renegade. People will see the money, they'll see the Soviets aren't coming in with tanks, and then the blacklist will be broken by Howdy Doody time!"

Hank was shaking his head. "Phoebe, sweetheart, I'm in no position to do that now, you know that. You have to stay reasonable."

"But . . . but if . . ." She recognized his smile — the smile of a man about to pat a very silly girl on the head. "Right," she managed to say. "Of course. I understand." She did too. She understood that it was a hell of a lot easier to stay reasonable when everything you'd built up for years hadn't just been taken away from you, and there was nothing you could do to fight back.

"Good girl," he said, and slid over a fat brown envelope. Puzzled, she started to open it.

"Not here!" he yelped. "Wait till you get home, dummy."

"How very clandestine," she marveled. "Though I must say, if you're trying to keep yourself out of the soup and me looking innocent, this isn't the best course."

"You really can't keep your trap shut, can you?" Hank was actually raging at her. "I bet you mouthed off to the wrong person once and that's how you got yourself into this mess." He smacked the envelope. "Take it before I change my mind. It's only because of your Mona anyway."

Her heart chilled. He truly thought she had done something to deserve this. Phoebe tucked the envelope into her bag, wishing she had the courage to throw it in his face, wishing she didn't need his gift or his favor. But she did.

When they left the restaurant, Hank took Phoebe into the patisserie next door and ordered a dozen pastries. "Some nice breakfasts for a few days," he said, handing her the pretty pink box wrapped with white string.

"Thank you, Hank," she said. Her voice was stiff, but the thanks real.

He pumped her hand again. "Listen, honey, I always liked your work, but you oughta just get yourself married. I've never known a woman who wasn't happier when she was married."

Phoebe was tempted to ask how many women he actually knew, but only smiled and let him wring her hand till he felt he'd done the right thing. Now more than ever, her reputation mattered. She may be blacklisted, but she had to maintain a good name.

■ ■ ■ ■

Phoebe trudged home, wishing there was someplace else she had to be, something else she had to do. The pink box bumped rhythmically against her knee. She remembered being seven years old and understanding — sort of — just how serious Mona's condition was. Horatio took her to Gertel's Bakery and let her choose a dozen pastries. They didn't make her happier about Mona, but she treasured them anyway.

Perry Street was full of the usual denizens, pursuing art or anger or sex. Several acquaintances hailed Phoebe, and she vaguely registered their offense when she ignored them. She knew she should double her efforts to cultivate people — sneak her way to a job. But she didn't have the energy. Even the thought of climbing the steps to her building's front door made her tired.

Jimmy was in Mrs. Pocatelli's garden again. "Hey, Adler!" he yelled. "The fellow called, said I should come in for a meeting! Ain't that a beaut? You keen to celebrate? Maybe you and Anne —"

"Not right now, Jimmy, thanks," she said.

"Aw, come on, cut a guy a break, huh? How's about a cigarette, at least?"

101

"Sounds good, go get me one and I'll smoke it."

"Boy, Adler, what's eating you?"

He actually looked petulant. As she entertained lurid thoughts about the pruning shears in his hand, a vaguely familiar man with a green hat worn low over a handsome nose crossed her line of vision. He walked up to them purposefully.

"You're Phoebe Adler?"

She hesitated. The tiniest beginning of a thought entered her mind — the idea that a stranger seeking to confirm her identity might be a whole new menace.

"Boy, Adler, why does everyone want you all the time?" Jimmy demanded.

The man half smiled and thrust a pink envelope in Phoebe's hands.

"Phoebe Adler, you've been served. You're to report to the House Un-American Activities Committee for questioning on the date indicated." Both his tone and face were entirely without expression, and he moved quickly, disappearing almost before he completed the sentence.

Jimmy jerked away from Phoebe. "Adler!" he hollered. "You're a pinko!"

"I'm not —" Phoebe began, but the shadow of Mrs. Pocatelli loomed over her. Phoebe turned to see the landlady, the tendrils of her gray wig quivering as she glared at Phoebe.

"A Red!" she boomed. "A Red has been living in my apartment house! You dirty little minx, you made me trust you, filthy creature!"

Windows opened, heads peered out. Half the people enjoying this show would, if asked, insist they hated HUAC, the FBI, and all those seeking so aggressively to curtail every freedom and ideal on which the country had been founded. Plenty were likely in danger of the FBI themselves, but no one breathed a syllable of support for Phoebe.

I wouldn't either, would I? You can't risk looking like a sympathizer.

She despised them all anyway.

"You'll be out of my house this time next week, you hear?" Mrs. Pocatelli screamed, pointing a gnarled finger at Phoebe. "And you'll thank me for not tossing you out tonight."

Anne was in the doorway. Phoebe knew her friend was about to defend her, to say something that would compromise her own reputation and safety. Phoebe didn't dare shake her head with so many eyes on her, but Anne caught her eye and knew. She stood, radiating silent, impotent rage.

"I think it's against the law to evict me on those grounds," Phoebe told Mrs. Pocatelli. Not that she had any idea, but she couldn't bear not to say something. She couldn't bear anyone seeing her fear. She couldn't bear them enjoying it.

"Talk to a lawyer, then, but you'll see, my lawyer will say I'm allowed to keep my house clean of Commies," Mrs. Pocatelli snapped.

"I sure hope that fellow I'm meeting doesn't know I got referred to him by a stinking Red," Jimmy said. Phoebe wondered if he meant it or was angling for her apartment.

"Sheesh, 'innocent till proven guilty' really is yesterday's news, isn't it?" she snapped. She wanted to say that a person's politics was nothing to be guilty about, but didn't dare add fat to the fire.

She marched up the stairs. As she reached the front door, something soft and squishy pelted her on the back of the neck. She started and turned, dropping her bag and the pastry box. Another missile caught her square in the face. Tomatoes. Bright red ones. Dripping down, staining her best suit. She sensed a scuffle at her feet — two neighborhood dogs must have virtually sprung from under the steps to find the dropped box of pastries and tear it open. Normally, the specter of Mrs. Pocatelli was enough to keep the animals away, but even the dogs sensed open season.

Phoebe picked up her bag and shouted in the direction of the hurled tomatoes, "Lucky you, being able to waste food. Remember this when they come for you!"

She ran past Anne up to her apartment. It wasn't a sanctuary anymore, but she was damned if any of her persecutors were going to see her vomit up her delicious, expensive meal.

Anne woke Phoebe up a few hours later.

"I got the stains out," she said, handing Phoebe a cup of hot cocoa mixed with bourbon. "One thing about good wool, it's hard to ruin. Glad that scum didn't have a blueberry pie, though."

"No one on Perry Street would waste a blueberry pie," Phoebe muttered. "Besides, they wanted to throw something red. Subtle. Probably a failed poet retraining to go into banking."

"Here, smoke some of this." Anne handed Phoebe a rolled cigarette. Reefer. If Mrs. Pocatelli recognized the smell, she would skip eviction and just order Anne and Phoebe hanged.

Phoebe inhaled. The combination of booze, cocoa, drugs, and Anne's friendship steadied her. She took another hit and reached for the dreaded envelope.

The document was a stark form letter. BY AUTHORITY OF THE HOUSE OF REPRESENTATIVES OF THE CONGRESS OF THE UNITED STATES OF AMERICA was typed across the top. Her name written in a firm backhand after "TO." She skimmed the rest, allowing phrases like "you are hereby commanded" and "31 October" to wash straight through her.

"I suppose if I have to go to DC, autumn wouldn't be such a bad time," Phoebe said, letting the page drop. She hadn't expected this so soon. Maybe that was how they got people now. If it all happens fast, you don't have time to prepare, to master the tricks of survival. "Maybe this is good?" she ventured. "I go for the interview, I make it clear I'm perfectly innocent, and my name is cleared?"

Anne didn't need to do more than look sad, and Phoebe's hope swelled and subsided in the same breath. No one got out that easily. There was only one step to freedom now. Phoebe had to be willing to trade another person's name for her own.

So really, it wasn't any question at all.

"Anne's booked the passage for me," Phoebe whispered to Mona. "It should be all right. Hank still got me paid for the last script and gave me two hundred bucks cash besides. It's either friendship or a guilty conscience, you pick."

"That louse," Mona decided. "May he develop a chronic itch in a hard-to-reach place."

Phoebe smiled faintly, struggling not to feel the minutes slipping away. She could see Horatio Adler looming over her, arms folded, demanding to know what she was doing, leaving Mona and New York. Leaving her blood and her birthright.

She and Mona were in the sanitarium's conservatory, a cold, glass-encased room, guaranteed to be empty on a day that was, conveniently, pouring rain.

"Miss Adler, in the conservatory, with the rope," Phoebe said.

"The rope that's going to pull you to safety," Mona answered. "May as well start getting used to this weather. Though England's having a heat wave, can you believe it?"

Phoebe was going to London. She'd

decided not to mail Hannah a script, but rather take the chance of delivering it in person. Her funds were likely to disappear more quickly than she could imagine. Best to save pennies where she could.

"You're only doing what a lot of others have done," Mona said proudly. "I've read all about it, and overheard the Three Polios listening to that excrescence Hedda Hopper on the radio, carrying on about 'cowardly Runaway Reds' — like her mudslinging wasn't half of what drove them off. The blacklist is ridiculous. I'll bet once you start writing stuff for British television that wipes the American stuff's eyes, the big shots in Hollywood will call the whole thing off and that'll be that."

"Why aren't you running the world?" Phoebe wanted to know.

"No one's ready for another leader in a wheelchair," Mona said with a shrug. "Now, promise you won't come home too soon."

"Thanks a lot."

Mona tugged at Phoebe until they were nearly nose to nose.

"Don't be stupid. I'll miss you every second. You're my life, Phoebe-kins. But as my life, it's your duty to live. That was always our deal. You're not going to renege now, are you?" Phoebe didn't answer, and

Mona pinched her ear hard.

"Ow!" Phoebe yelped. "Sheesh, for someone who's supposed to be so frail, you've sure got an iron grip."

Mona didn't smile. "You have to explore, Phoebe. You have to see the world for me. And for the love of Pete, will you please at least go on a good date and then write me the sort of details that would be banned in Boston?"

"I'm on the run from the government, I've got no friends abroad, limited cash, almost no options to maintain my career, and my sister commands me to date." Phoebe rolled her eyes. "Because doesn't all that make me a very attractive package?"

"Oh, shut up," Mona advised. "You're smart, funny, and beautiful. What man doesn't want that?"

"The kind who are put off by smart and funny and think a beauty shouldn't wear glasses and should be able to control her hair."

Mona snorted. "British men will be more sensible, you'll see."

Phoebe sighed. There seemed a cosmic absurdity to Mona's getting all the family beauty, while Phoebe, who rarely even sneezed, was the one whose looks were usually labeled "interesting." Maybe prettiness made Brookside love Mona so much. She was a classic tragic beauty, with golden-blond curls and wide blue eyes. The effect wasn't even spoiled when she opened her mouth and swore like a sailor.

She could have set the world on fire.

Phoebe shook the thought away. It was hard enough not crying, and Mona hated tears almost as much as she hated anyone who didn't find Phoebe beautiful. Phoebe didn't worry about her looks, but she yearned for a life of glamour. An elegant room she could walk into and be part of a glittering circle. She'd thought she was getting close. Now she had no idea where she was going.

"Aw, sister, stop looking so sad," Mona said, tangling her fingers in a lock of Phoebe's hair.

"I'm scared," Phoebe blurted out, feeling like a five-year-old. "What if I get caught before I even get on the ship? What if I make it there and can't find a place to live, or any work? What if nobody likes me?"

Mona rubbed Phoebe's head. "You'll make it. You were always the luckiest Adler. You'll land on your feet. I promise. And anyone who doesn't like you isn't worth knowing."

Phoebe closed her eyes and rested her

head on her sister's lap till she was sure the threat of tears had subsided.

"All right, pull it together," Mona said at last, and the huskiness in her voice gave away her own emotion. "It's time for you to go. Now listen, don't slobber over me or look sentimental, that's the sort of thing that gets noticed. Everything is normal, okay? Just be yourself."

Phoebe slowly wheeled Mona back to the dayroom. "All right, all right, I'll arrange motorbike lessons," she said as soon as she was sure they could be heard. "But no lifting purses from little old ladies, you hear?"

"Spoil my fun, why don't you?"

Phoebe hugged her sister, inhaling her deeply. "See you in a few days, sis-terror."

"A few days after the end of the blacklist," Mona whispered.

It took all her self-control to saunter from the room in her usual gait.

"Don't you worry, Miss Adler," the head nurse, Nurse Brewster, said cheerfully. "Mona's our favorite, we take the best care of her."

If Mona heard that, she would say Nurse Brewster said that to all the relatives, but even Mona knew the staff really liked her, and not just because she was a living experiment. Phoebe trusted Nurse Brewster, though not enough to say anything now. She would leave money and a note for Anne to deliver next week when Phoebe, if she truly was the luckiest Adler, would be on a ship, steaming over the sea.

She felt eyes everywhere she went now. Was it the man with the green hat? Someone else? She hoped Anne was right and she was just imagining it. She hoped she looked like a timid mouse who would never dream of doing what she was about to do.

Anne opened the wardrobe Phoebe had lined with primrose wallpaper and filled with cedar chips. "Don't take more than you can manage," Anne advised as casually as if they were discussing dinner plans. "I'll scrape up some dough to send the rest once you're settled. Take the warmest stuff, London's damp."

For all her practicality, Anne couldn't hide the fever in her eyes. Like Mona, she saw it as an adventure. Phoebe scowled in resentment, but couldn't entirely resist the dark glamour of it all. She was no longer just a low-level writer trying to branch out from a grubby little TV show no one watched. She was a woman the government had marked as dangerous. She was being watched, followed. She was on the run. She was the stuff of movies.

Though, in a movie, she could pack a huge wardrobe into a tiny case. Instead, she could only manage her suitcase, handbag, and typewriter. The rest of her things would have to wait, who knew how long.

They worked methodically, laying things on the bed. Despite what Mona said about the current heat wave, London would be cold and damp most of the time. Phoebe packed her favorite knit sweaters and flecked wool skirt. A second blouse and her two summer dresses. The good suit would of course be her travel outfit. Hanging next to it was her plum dress. Plum for its color, plum for its status. The first cocktail dress she ever purchased; the first purchase that told the world, and herself, that she was on the rise. No more Klein's department store for her, this beauty was from Bonwit Teller. She fingered the silk, remembering the plush and hush of Bonwit's. The rustle as the dress settled around her. Gazing at her reflection in a three-way mirror. The saleslady's warm compliments. The string of fantasy wending its way through the places she would go wearing this dress, being seen, being somebody. There was no question. The dress was traveling with her.

Anne made no comment, instead rolling

the dress into a neat, tight ball, making space through force of will. Underclothes. Makeup. Toiletries.

"You'll need your knitting," Anne mused. "And you'd better take these," she added, packing Phoebe's low-heeled chunky walking shoes, a relic from the war.

"No, I've got the ballet flats," Phoebe protested, but Anne latched the case shut. Phoebe huffed, knowing Anne was right. She would need sturdy walking shoes.

She went through her keepsake box, removing her favorite snaps of Mona and Anne. She came to the photo of her first pay for writing.

"Remember this?" she said to Anne.

"Of course. Boy, did we all think you were a heck of a star that day. And we were right."

Phoebe gulped, and slipped the photos into her handbag. She ran her fingers over the passport and ticket, hidden behind the lining where they would stay till she arrived at the ship.

"I guess I'm about ready," she said, though it seemed impossible to be ready to leave your life.

Anne held out Phoebe's coat. "I borrowed fifty bucks and sewed it into the lining. Emergency stash," she said. She pulled a twenty-dollar bill from Phoebe's meager funds. "Here, keep this in your bra."

"Swell, now I'm a runaway and a cliché," Phoebe grumbled, complying.

She pinned on her hat, secured her silver watch, and slipped on her gloves. In the living room, she turned off the record player — she was done with Ethel Merman for a while. Suitcase in one hand, typewriter in the other, handbag over her shoulder. She took a last look at the pretty room. The hardcover books, the pictures, the records, the good crockery she'd been slowly accumulating. The phone that had been installed with such ceremony.

"I'll box it up, I'll keep it all for you," Anne promised.

"Thank you. But go ahead and sell the phone. Use the money to get yourself something nice." Phoebe shut the door with a firm click and handed Anne the key.

The predawn was overcast. Phoebe lurked in the dark doorway while Anne strolled to the corner to hail a cab. She thought there should be fog and strange shadows, but Perry Street was oppressively normal. The cab pulled up and the driver, already under Anne's spell, jumped out and hurried both of Phoebe's bags into the trunk.

A movement at Jimmy's window caught

Phoebe's eye as she got in the cab. Her throat constricted. What was he doing awake so early? She concentrated on forcing air into her lungs as they drove off.

"Does it look suspicious, you coming with me and having no bags?" Phoebe asked Anne. Anne ignored her. She had her hands full cultivating the driver, flirting with all her might to secure a swift journey where only one passenger would be remembered well enough to comment on.

Phoebe turned around to watch the Village disappear. Just another scene in a movie she might write someday. Or so she told herself.

"Can't say for sure, cookie," the driver said, answering a question Phoebe hadn't heard. "But it sure looks likely."

Her stomach dropped even before her brain caught up. Anne had persuaded the driver to keep an eye out for the possibility of their being followed. To Phoebe, all the sets of headlights looked the same. Studying the cars behind them, she began to see what the driver saw. The outline of another cab, keeping pace.

Anne leaned farther into the front seat, her cleavage spilling into the driver's shoulder as she directed him in a series of quick turns so well thought out and executed, it was like being in a Road Runner cartoon. It now looked as if they were headed for Idlewild Airport. The other cab still followed them.

Finally they caught a break. Their cab shot northward through an intersection as a slow-moving truck trundled through westward behind them, giving them enough leeway to make another two turns and lose their pursuer. Phoebe exhaled shakily and glanced at her watch. Her ship was boarding now, and they were farther from Chelsea Piers than when they started.

"Don't worry, cookie," the cabbie assured Anne. "I'll get you there just fine."

He sped up, swerving up and down side streets, giving the women a tour of city byways they didn't even know existed. Phoebe panted, willing the bile back down her throat, willing the fear to subside. She forced herself to be angry instead. Other people had gotten away. Why all this effort spent on her? She was no one, she'd done nothing. Who would bother to expend so much money, effort, and energy to keep her here, to force her to testify when she had nothing to say?

"All right, cookie, here we are," the cabbie cried. To his everlasting credit, he parked illegally and quickly found a cart for Phoebe's bags. Anne assured Phoebe she'd paid for the journey and the two dashed through the long building to the dock. Through the corner of her eye, Phoebe saw Anne cast the occasional look behind her. She didn't dare ask what was there.

The dock, the ship, the last few passengers embarking.

"Anne," Phoebe began, reaching for her friend, not wanting to say goodbye.

"Get the hell out of here!" Anne urged. She wasn't looking at Phoebe. She saw something else, something Phoebe knew she mustn't turn to look at. She ran for the ship, handing off her suitcase to a porter as she ripped her ticket and passport from her bag.

"I suppose someone has to be last," the agent said, hardly glancing at her passport as he stamped it. "Hurry on up, now."

She hurried. As soon as her feet touched the deck, she turned around. Anne was still there, leaning casually against a lamppost. She faced off against a man, a man hard to recognize at this distance, but Phoebe knew she knew him. She leaned forward, squinting. He looked up, scanning the decks. She'd seen that outline looking up from Mrs. Pocatelli's garden plenty of times. It was Jimmy. Jimmy! Was he working with the FBI for a few extra dollars, or did he see them leave and decide to chase them for an experience he could turn into a story? Or was he trying to find yet another way to bond with Anne, to catch them, to warn them? Phoebe gulped hard. Was Anne compromised now? There was no way to know, not for days at least. Phoebe wrapped her typewriter in her arms, clutching it like a baby. She understood now why someone might tell the FBI anything they wanted to hear. Paranoia was its own sort of parasite.

But Anne's head was thrown back in her classic defiance, and Phoebe swore she could hear her tinkling laugh over the engines. Even if she couldn't, the sound calmed her. She felt herself begin to laugh as well. She threaded her way through an unseen crowd, all the way to the bow. She was doing it. She was getting away. She was an adventuress, a wronged girl on the run. Barbara Stanwyck! Veronica Lake! She could manage it all!

Well of course you can, you idiot, Mona's voice sounded in her ears, laughing right along with her. *Haven't you always? Now get over there and make me prouder than ever.*

CHAPTER SIX

The *Queen Mary*'s rules were very clear. Tourist-class passengers were not allowed on the first-class deck. Phoebe, determined to pretend she was living the life she wanted, ignored the rules. After all she'd been through since the day she was fired, slipping onto the restricted deck was laughably easy. The Bonwit dress was for cocktails, not the dinner and dancing hours of this set, but she strolled about with confidence, and the porters and passengers ignored her. Except for the furniture, this deck wasn't so different from the lower ones. One could see and smell the sea just as clearly.

The smell was familiar, like a childhood memory, even though the only trip to the seaside she remembered was Fourth of July 1945, when the women of the airfield treated themselves to a holiday. The ship's deck was chilly, but Phoebe felt that hot sand burning her feet, heard the women screaming with laughter, tasting the final victory and peace to come, and with it all their good futures.

Had their parents taken her and Mona to the sea when she was too little to remember? Had some doctor ordered Mona be taken somewhere bracing, in that brief pocket of time when there was still hope of her becoming a healthy child? It seemed unlikely — Horatio could not have left the newsstand, and it was singular enough to give Mona fodder for dozens of jokes.

I'm never going to see her again, am I? A gasping sob escaped her, and she beat it down quickly, though no other passengers had bothered to brave the sharp wind tonight. Phoebe plunged her hand into her bag for her pad and pen. She wrote *A Memory of the Seaside* across the top of a fresh page and began to outline a script. A radio play, a bittersweet comedy about women at the end of the war, wondering about the men they loved, about the future, both secure and still as uncertain as ever. And then they happen upon a man, the last spy of the war. Germany's last hope, perhaps, surrounded by a group of vengeful young women in swimsuits. At which point . . .

Her thoughts were interrupted by a loud

moan. She looked up to see a man in a tailcoat lurching past her, weaving his way to the railing. He slammed into it and bent over, heaving and retching into the sea. Phoebe shook her head, wishing Anne and Mona were there to enjoy a good laugh at the excesses of the rich. She could never see the purpose of drinking so much expensive alcohol if that was where it ended up. The man bent over farther, and farther . . . he was falling.

Phoebe didn't know she could run so fast. She lunged, catching a fistful of bespoke wool that threatened to burst its seams. The weavers and tailors were worth every penny they'd been paid — the coat held firm enough for her to sling an arm around the man's middle and, despite his being so much larger and deadweight, ease him back onto the deck.

"My goodness!" he cried, sinking to his knees and flinging his arms around her legs. "My goodness gracious!"

"Just common decency, really," Phoebe muttered, attempting to disentangle herself. She pulled his silk handkerchief from his pocket and wiped his mouth. "We've got to get you some coffee."

"No, no, no, not just yet, I beg you," he gasped. He released her legs and wrapped his arms around his own knees, hanging his head between them. "Must . . . give me . . . let me have a moment. Must sit down."

Phoebe stopped herself from saying he was already sitting. She supposed she should ring for service, get the man proper help. Except that would mean drawing attention to herself. She patted the man's shoulder. He was shivering, murmuring, "Goodness gracious," over and over. His accent was British, a countryman of the nation she hoped was going to grant her asylum. This must make them allies of sorts, even if his clothes marked him as a man of immense wealth. He wasn't going to be the subject of the porters' derision and gossip, not if she could help it.

She glanced around to make sure there was still no one in sight, then slipped off her shoes, hoisted the Bonwit dress nearly to her thighs, and knelt beside him, slinging his arm over her shoulder. Panting and grunting, and agreeing with the sharp protest of every muscle in her body, she eased him to his feet. Together, they staggered back to the lounge chairs. His head lolled toward hers, and she could smell the brilliantine in his hair, the remnants of aftershave, and even a hint of powder from his armpit. It was a curiously intimate cluster of scents, and it made her feel shy and awkward about her rumpled skirts and stocking feet as she rolled him into a chair and ran back for her shoes. She crammed her cold feet into them as she sat opposite him, poised to jump clear should he be sick again. He was tall, and well built. He had a long, thin face that was mostly handsome, and his hair was so brushed and slicked, even his near tumble into the Atlantic hadn't put a strand out of place. As the shock faded from his features, he looked almost amused, as though this were already shaping into an anecdote to be told over more drinks.

"What about some ginger ale?" Phoebe suggested. "You need something to settle yourself."

"A brandy, I should think," he said. As his voice calmed, it became more commanding, his accent pure lord of the manor, straight out of an Ealing comedy.

"Well *I* should think you've had more than enough liquor for one night," Phoebe snapped. It was ruder than she intended, but her shoulders hurt, and her feet were clammy.

"Who on earth might you be?" he demanded, eyeing her up and down.

Phoebe put her nose in the air. "I be

Phoebe Adler, the woman who just saved your life and is still waiting for a thank-you. You don't know how lucky you are. That was the setting for quite the perfect little murder. You left the lounge drunk, there was no one else on the deck, one quick little push would have done it. The murderer would be clear on the other side of the ship in moments, and by the time anyone saw you were gone long enough to look for you, there would be no evidence to suggest anything other than an unfortunate accident. Very tricky case — you'd likely never be avenged."

He gaped at her, surprise, bewilderment, and nervousness intermingled on his face. He looked back at the scene of the crime, then into her twinkling eyes. A slow smile spread over his face. He chuckled and extended his hand.

"Nigel Elliott, and much obliged indeed."

"You're welcome."

He chuckled again and elbowed himself into a more upright position.

"And here I thought I'd have a nice change, not traveling by aeroplane. Glorious things, aeroplanes."

"They sure are," Phoebe agreed with reverence.

"You've flown, have you?"

"No," she said, suppressing a sigh. "But I helped build planes during the war."

"Ah! A Rosie!"

"No, Phoebe."

He chuckled again. Then he looked at her more closely, seemed to like what he saw, and leaned in confidentially.

"Please don't think I make a habit of getting roaring drunk and nearly making away with myself. I'd had a rotten evening and a row with my lady." He spat the word like it was an expletive. "Drinking was the only logical solution."

"Possibly you're with the wrong lady?" Phoebe was surprised at herself. She usually managed some restraint with strangers, especially ones so elegant. But there was an intimacy in having just saved someone's life.

His brows shot up.

"You modern American girls certainly do talk, don't you? Was it the war that made you so forthright?"

"I'm a New Yorker," Phoebe explained.

"Of course you are." He laughed. "And quite correct. A veritable gorgon, my fiancée, right only by rank and breeding. But there, it's unseemly for me to continue in bachelorhood — neither family nor career will stick it — and she is pleased enough with the trappings of the arrangement to

126

overlook . . . well. One must do one's duty."

Phoebe supposed it was the effects of the liquor that made him speak so unguardedly. Or perhaps he felt the same curious closeness she felt toward him. Probably anyone else might have taken all he said at face value — many Americans both mocked and coveted the British class system and claimed to understand its archaic ways. Phoebe, however, understood the world of Greenwich Village, home to reams of homosexuals who lived safely there but cultivated careful personas for the rest of the city. Floyd and Leo, the proprietors of the Coffee Nook, were well-known as a couple, though it wasn't much discussed. In quiet moments, they'd sat to enjoy coffee with her and Anne and offered tips on, as they put it, "how to weed out the ones looking for beards." There was nothing effeminate about Nigel, but Phoebe had learned her lessons well. She grimaced sympathetically.

"Family, career, duty, that's one ugly trifecta you're up against. And if you tried to bring home your real love, all three would very much rather you drop dead."

Nigel blinked, his face creased with faint alarm. Then he saw just how much she meant it and the expression changed to pleased surprise. "What a very perspicacious young lady you are! But there, let us move on from love and on to life. Tell me, my dear Miss Adler, what brings you on this particular journey?" He pulled out a silver cigarette case and offered her one. A Sobranie — Phoebe had never smoked anything so posh. She leaned back and crossed her ankles, hoping she looked like a femme fatale.

"I'm a writer," she said, attempting to sound airy. "But the censorship in America can make Victorians look like libertines. Really stifles the possibilities. So I thought, what the heck, I'll try my fortunes elsewhere."

Nigel blew a smoke ring and smiled a lazy, even sexy sort of smile that made her flush, in spite of what she knew of him.

"One of the blacklistees then."

Phoebe's back jerked upward of its own accord. "You know about the blacklist?"

"My dear girl!" He roared with laughter. "Everybody knows about it! I daresay crofters in the Outer Hebrides know about it. Even if I didn't read the papers, I travel to the States quite regularly and find the whole business most fascinating. The general British response is sheer bafflement. And some amusement, of course."

"Oh, sure, this whole thing is a barrel of laughs," Phoebe said.

"Now, now, I only meant people find it absurd to carry on like that." He winked and leaned in conspiratorially. "So! Are you a Communist then?"

Phoebe grinned, knowing she was about to disappoint him. She told him the story of the airfield and the union. He was easy to talk to, and despite his obvious wealth and status, he seemed understanding and genuinely interested. Even concerned.

"I say!" Nigel was impressed. "You don't look like a mutinous sort."

"I just wanted things to be fair," Phoebe said, shrugging. "Anyway, I'm assuming that's what got me fingered. That and voting for Roosevelt, probably."

Nigel considered. "Maybe you signed the wrong petition sometime."

"Sure," Phoebe rejoined. "Or checked the wrong book out of the library!"

They snickered, shaking their heads. Then they looked at each other and fell silent. Phoebe sighed. In thirty-six hours, they would dock at Southampton and she would officially be an exile.

"Curiouser and curiouser," Nigel murmured. He took a gold watch from his waistcoat pocket and grimaced at it. "I ought to return to the gorgon. I can't have her thinking I'm gallivanting during courtship." He stood and Phoebe stood as well.

"Well, pleasure saving your life and all," she said, extending her hand.

He laughed and produced a card, beautifully embossed in gold.

"Eternally grateful, dear girl, and truly charmed to meet you. If you land yourself on a television program in Britain, do drop a line and let me know. I can always receive post at my club."

Phoebe suppressed a laugh. It was the snobbiest version of "write if you get work" she'd ever heard. She told herself to make the scene funnier in a script.

He was still looking at her thoughtfully.

"I say, will you take some friendly advice?" he asked.

"I'll take almost anything, really."

He leaned in close, whispering in her ear.

"When you're interrogated by the border agents, don't tell them you're looking for work."

"What?"

He frowned at her and spoke in the tones one uses with a dimwit. "You're much more likely to get a decent residency permit if you're not planning to take a job from a Briton. Simply say you're doing research for a novel, and after that say as little as possible." He shook her hand again. "It has been my genuine pleasure, Miss Adler."

"Mine as well, Mr. Elliott," she said, her politeness masking the roiling within her. Only a few weeks before, she had been so proud of her honesty, saving her illusions for the page. Now she was someone who had to spin the truth around like a top, just in the hopes of keeping herself free and fed.

If there was any justice in the world, someone, someday, was going to pay for all this.

They docked during a dawn that was as misty and gray as she'd ever been promised England would be.

"Isn't there meant to be a heat wave on?" the man behind her grumbled. "Wouldn't know it's near-on August. Why did I come back?"

No one answered. Phoebe shuffled along, buffeted by the other blinking and bleary-eyed tourist-class passengers waiting to have their passports stamped. She held her head high and tried to look blank, even bored. Someone who was there on a lark, not on a desperate effort to save her life.

The queue moved at the sort of pace that made Phoebe certain the rest of her life would be spent standing right here. Everyone grew more cross, with some muttering gloomily about inefficiency and how none of this would be tolerated under some other sort of government. These were countered by strictures on not grumbling, which Phoebe was convinced were going to lead to broken bones. By the time she was next, she was past hunger, past exhaustion, past anything but her pounding heart and sweat-soaked hands. It wasn't impossible that the immigration agent would take one look at her paperwork and call someone to arrest her for immediate shipment back to America. Maybe they would handcuff her right there, in front of everyone, who would all have an excellent story to tell for the rest of their lives. As would she, when she got out of prison. She almost smiled, entranced by the drama.

"Oi, wake up!" a man behind her shouted, giving her a sharp prod in the back. "Waiting half forever and Little Miss Typewriter here hangs about like she's got all the time in the world."

The typewriter in Little Miss Typewriter's hand banged against her trembling legs as she walked the five short steps to the immigration agent, the longest part of her journey yet. She set the typewriter down between her legs, squeezing it tightly between her calves to stop their shaking. It was the last friend she had now, and its presence was reassuring as she watched the official open her passport. His lips were pursed in a manner that might have been disgust, boredom, or warding off a sneeze.

"Reason for traveling?" he barked.

"Well, they say it's very broadening," she said automatically. She could practically hear Mona and Anne's hands smacking their foreheads in unison.

Now he looked up at her, and his eyes were cold.

"This is rather a serious business, Miss Adler."

It was. She was appalled at herself for making a joke, though it seemed far preferable to telling a lie. But it was a time for lying.

"I'm writing a book. I came here to do research, and to write."

He grunted, rolling his eyes as if to say, "Oh, another of those."

"You have funds to live on for three months?" he asked.

"Yes," she lied again, hoping he wouldn't ask for proof. After the money she'd left for Mona and travel costs, she had barely a hundred dollars. It would yield maybe thirty-six pounds. She didn't dare wonder how long that would last.

He looked her over and shrugged. "All right, I'll grant you a residency permit of seven weeks —"

"Seven weeks! You just said three months!" Phoebe yelped.

The agent stamped her passport and handed it back.

"You may apply for an extension a week before expiry," he instructed her. "Next!"

Phoebe wended her way out in a daze. Seven weeks. And even three months wouldn't have been enough. Seven weeks. *But I'm here.* She was here! *I'm free, I'm safe, I can do my work. Provided someone wants to buy my work. And then, surely, I can get a longer residency.*

Here. Wherever "here" was. She gathered her suitcase along with the other admitted passengers and followed the throng into the main building, where everyone, whether preparing to sail or just arrived, looked a little lost.

Exhaustion swept over Phoebe. She gave herself a shake to dismiss the cobwebs, and followed the signs to the bureau de change, joining a snaking line of hunch-shouldered humans.

"All I've done since I've gotten here is wait in line," she chattered to a bleary-eyed young mother behind her, trying to calm herself. "Already I've gone native." The woman and her tiny daughter stared at her. "Tough crowd," Phoebe muttered.

When she reached the desk, she emptied the cash from her handbag. The money sewn into her coat, and the twenty-dollar bill in her bra, would stay put for now. A few moments later, she was presented with a small stack of notes and coins in a variety of funny shapes. She blinked down at it.

"I don't suppose you have some sort of a cipher that explains all this?"

"Move along, will you, we've not got all day!" someone snapped behind her.

Phoebe moved along, tucking the alien currency into her handbag. She didn't dare lock herself in a toilet stall to figure out the denominations she needed for train fare, as she couldn't risk leaving her suitcase unsupervised.

"I say, missus, I'd be honored to show you what coins are what, if you'd like?"

A young man, almost an adolescent, bobbed at her elbow. A round, sweet face that barely needed a razor. An accent like Laurence Olivier's in *Hamlet.* An easy, friendly, even admiring smile. Phoebe smiled in warm relief and reached into her handbag. Then she looked into his eyes. The friendliness was too practiced, too perfect.

"Oh, for Pete's sake!" she cried, snapping her bag shut. "I've just left New York and I almost don't recognize a shyster when I see one? Criminy. My father would turn in his grave if he hadn't been cremated."

She stormed off in search of a likely outlet for reporting confidence tricksters. By the time she found someone, there was no hope of finding the sweet-faced boy, and the officer scolded Phoebe for wasting his time.

Feeling betrayed by her supposed refuge only hours after arrival, Phoebe grudgingly trusted the ticket agent at the rail office to select the coins that added up to her fare to London.

"Got to just read them coins, hadn't you?" he said. Or what she thought he said, it was hard to tell.

Silly me, thinking I spoke English. Anyway, I'm too tired to read.

She was slightly heartened to successfully trade what they called "tuppence" for a cup of hot brown liquid they insisted was "coffee." Then she found a tobacconist. She scoured the shelves for Lucky Strikes.

"Not got them," the tobacconist said when she asked. Phoebe sighed. Of course they didn't. It was such a small thing, but she liked her brand. It tasted like New York. A taste diminishing by the minute.

"Want to try Woodbines, miss? Lots of ladies like them Woodbines."

It sounded like "laddies lick them woofies," which she would remember for Floyd and Leo when she got home. She selected a pack of Player's.

"Thems preferred by sailors, miss," the tobacconist said disapprovingly.

"Sailors, did you say?" Phoebe asked. "Well, we're all just sailing through life, aren't we?" The cost was "18d," whatever that meant. The tobacconist, still frowning, held up a coin and told her it was a shilling, worth twelvepence. Phoebe read "sixpence" on another coin and triumphantly paid for her cigarettes. She smoked one, decided it was only okay, and headed for the train.

There, she sat squeezed between a man dressed in fear of British weather, in a mackintosh, galoshes, and rain hat, and a woman who held out her newspaper so wide, Phoebe had to clutch her glasses lest they get knocked off when the woman turned the page.

Outside the window, the world turned green. Phoebe turned to stare at it, ignoring the mac man's harrumphs of protestation at being in her line of vision. It was so beautiful, so unlike anything she'd seen before. She looked harder and harder, until she could feel herself walking through that cool, rolling grass. She heard the hum of insects and the calls of birds, and a music that came from somewhere she couldn't see, something ancient, even primal.

As they neared London, the green gave way to rows and rows of redbrick houses, then a sea of gray stone. And amid it all, bomb damage. Phoebe had seen the newsreels after the Blitz, of course, but she hadn't expected in 1955 to still see whole streets of carved-out houses, portions of their fronts and backs still standing, interiors picked nearly clean. Homes. Full of busy, bustling life, now emptied and raw and cold. She owed it to those lives to look, but was relieved when the conductor called that they were arriving in Waterloo Station. She gathered her things and took a deep breath.

I am Wellington. Not Napoleon. She whispered it again and again as she made her way through the deafening crowd to the information desk.

Phoebe knew the names of some storied hotels in London. The Savoy. Claridge's. Brown's. The Ritz. Hotels for someday. For the person she would be when she had a velvet swing coat to slip over the Bonwit dress, a string of pearls, a diamanté comb in her hair. When she had a name that meant something, a name she was allowed to use without fear.

"Excuse me, could you recommend an inexpensive hotel near here?" Phoebe asked the uniformed man.

His tone was polite as he asked her a question, but Phoebe couldn't understand him. It was like trying to talk to someone underwater. Nigel's posh accent, and accents in the movies, were easy to grasp, but whether it was the rush of noise or her rumbling stomach and fuzzy head, she had to ask him to repeat himself, twice.

"Can you read?" he snapped at last, and she understood that all right. She gratefully accepted his scrawled directions and only got lost once before she stood before the Fairwood Arms. Phoebe saw no wood, no arms, and certainly nothing even remotely fair. Instead, she saw frayed curtains, cracked windows, and bricks nearly black with soot stains.

Don't be a snob, she scolded herself. She tried not to think of the cheerful redbrick building on Perry Street and the way Mrs. Pocatelli's glare would have scared off any soot that might have considered landing on those walls. *But her house didn't have to endure a war all around it,* Phoebe reminded herself. *And Mrs. Pocatelli is a lousy old bat.*

Except that's an insult to bats. Phoebe got a fresh grip on her bags, ignored her aching muscles, and marched up the steps. What could be a front garden was just a patch of cracked cement, but the front window boasted a window box filled with flowers. Its perch was precarious, but the flowers were cheery and bore all the signs of loving care. She regarded that as a good sign and rang the bell.

A round-faced woman with silver hair in a neat roll answered and showed Phoebe into a sitting room full of furniture that, though shabby, was clean and neatly patched. She introduced herself as Mrs. Bream and smiled pleasantly as she asked what sort of room Phoebe wanted.

"Honestly, the sort with a bed and maybe a door sounds super right now," Phoebe said, grinning. She bet Mrs. Bream was a wizard with a good thick soup.

"Oh, an American! Haven't had one of your lot in ever so long," Mrs. Bream said, smiling more broadly. "Now, I've got a room on the second floor, overlooking the garden, for nine-and-six a week, will that do?"

Phoebe had no idea what "nine-and-six" meant, but nodded fervently.

"Jolly good, jolly good," Mrs. Bream said, settling herself at the desk and opening a large book. "May I have your name, miss?"

"Phoebe Adler."

Mrs. Bream had gotten as far as writing a curvy *P.* Phoebe saw her fingers whiten around the pen. Her eyes shot up to meet Phoebe's.

"*Adler,* did you say? Is that Jewish, by any chance?"

"It's *my* name," Phoebe said, her neck tingling.

"I see. I'm afraid that room was actually booked yesterday, so we're full up."

Phoebe stared, the tingle running down her back, seizing her spine.

"You can't mean that?"

But Mrs. Bream very much did mean it. Her face was polite but closed. The flare of her nostrils said things Phoebe had thought she would never hear again. Not here. Not in what was supposed to be her sanctuary.

"Good afternoon," said Mrs. Bream — a dismissal, not a pleasantry.

Phoebe swore she could hear bones and muscles cracking as she bent to pick up her bags. Tears stung her eyes — the worst sort of tears. Shame. She wanted to be angry, and all she could feel was utter mortification. *Tell her you're relieved! Tell her this place is a dump! Tell her people who think they're better than anyone are usually lesser than everyone and they know it!*

Instead she gave the woman a long, hard look, then turned and walked out as steadily as she could manage. As soon as the door was shut behind her, she glanced to her left and, without another thought, reached out and gave the window box a firm shove. It came loose and shattered on the cement beneath it, drowning all the flowers in a heap of dirt and clay.

Once she was around the corner and sure no one was following with an intent to prosecute a foul window box attacker, Phoebe sat down on her suitcase, right in the middle of the sidewalk. She knew she should flag down a taxi, ask the driver to take her to the nearest hotel, and hang the cost. A bath and a rest and she would have the energy to make a better start tomorrow. But sitting there on her battered American Tourister, she couldn't make herself move. She was sweating, exhausted in the heat Mona had promised. Her head dropped into her hands. *I'll get up in a minute,* she told herself every minute for the next ten.

"I say, everything all right, miss?" A police officer was standing over her.

Phoebe blinked at him, and became aware of other people here and there around the street, most of them ignoring her just as she would probably have ignored herself, a few short weeks ago.

"Thank you, yes, I just needed to sit a minute," she said.

"Well, you can't stop here, miss, you need to be on your way."

"Yes, of course," she said, forcing herself upright. He wasn't warm, but he wasn't unfriendly either. "I've just arrived, and I'm a little lost. Can you find me a cab?"

The London constable lived up to the storied reputation. More quickly than she might have imagined, she was nestled in the plush seat of a black cab, and a few short minutes after that, the very decent cabbie deposited her at the door of a pub hotel and claimed, "This will do till you've found your way, miss."

Inside, a gangly man in shirtsleeves jumped to help her with her things.

"Is it a room you're needing, miss? Most certainly, miss. Call me Ernie, miss, everyone does. Mind the rough bits on the steps there, miss."

The bubbly monologue continued till he showed her into a pocket-sized room whose sloped ceiling and exposed beams immediately answered her dream of an old England.

"Oh, this is wonderful!" Phoebe cried.

The smile took up almost the whole of Ernie's thin face.

"All right, then, miss, very good, miss, glad to have you, very glad. No, no, no needs to pay now, miss, I'll sort your bill by the day or week, whichever you like. Bath just down that way and only four-pence for hot water. Be you wanting a spot of something?"

He brought her an enormous bowl of meat and potatoes, along with a steaming cup of tea. Even with the warm weather, they were soothing.

"There you are, miss, eat up and enjoy it now, and I do hope you sleep well."

The bed was narrow but the sheets were clean, and for the first time that never-ending day, Phoebe relaxed. She chuckled to herself as she fell asleep, thinking of how much Mona would enjoy this story of the adventure's beginning.

CHAPTER SEVEN

Sidney set down the script for the first episode of *The Adventures of Robin Hood* and gazed at Hannah, openmouthed.

"If all the scripts will be like this, it shall be a bonny brilliant show worth every penny it will cost." His brow knit, and he rubbed his hands in a way that made him look like a criminal mastermind, if he weren't so jolly. "And it's going to cost quite a heap of pennies, I should think." He whipped a pad from his jacket pocket and scribbled numbers furiously.

"I'm not worried," Hannah said. "Dollars to doughnuts it'll make a fortune, you'll see. You have to spend money to make money," she said, ignoring his baleful look. "This is going to look as good as any film. I want top cast, top crew, a historical consultant . . . and a woodland."

Sidney's pencil tip snapped off, smudging the page. "A what?"

"A bit of woodland. Robin Hood and the other outlaws are living rough in Sherwood Forest. We'll have the best sets anyone's seen, but we'll shoot as much outside as we can, and for that to look excellent, we need real woods."

"I well respect wanting to own good land," Sidney began. "But even assuming we could ever dream of raising such a sum, it's still England we live in. Been known to rain a wee mite, and no respecter of a shooting schedule, the weather is."

"We'll work around the weather and I'll find the money."

"Also a wee little lamp to rub, I should think."

Hannah grinned. "Bring on the best story editor you know. I'll order a few more scripts. Don't worry," she added with a wink. "They all work for scale."

"Scale" meant Screen Writers Guild minimums, suitable for either a green writer with no other credits or a blacklistee, whose involvement had to be hidden if Sapphire hoped for the cash cow that was American distribution. They would never pay less than scale, but until they knew they had more money and security, they wouldn't pay more. It hadn't stopped the Oscar-winning screenwriter Ring Lardner Jr. from enthusiastically agreeing to write the pilot, and he was going to be their chief writer. Ring had made waves during his HUAC hearing when he was asked, "Are you now or have you ever been a member of the Communist Party?" and he replied, "I could answer the question exactly the way you want, but if I did, I'd hate myself in the morning." And so one of Hollywood's top writers was soon sent to prison for contempt of Congress.

Ring was now free but, like too many others, struggling to find work. Robin Hood was a gift, and not just to his family's dinner table. He recognized the connection between the medieval Robin Hood and the modern blacklist just as clearly as Hannah did. The cruelties of a feudalistic world full of spies and turncoats, and a hero who sees that liberties, progressivism, and yes, a little wealth redistribution, would make for a healthier and happier society.

Ring lived up to his reputation, and had written a superb script. Hannah was especially pleased to see that the script wasn't polemical, or even overtly political. It was just an exciting story. Kids would watch the program wide-eyed, leaning as close to the screen as they could so as not to miss a moment. Adults would enjoy the interplay of relationships and the hint of romance, and it was little enough of a hint so as not to spur a universal eye rolling in the boys.

If this goes well, we can get a thirty-two-episode season. What a lot of hungry writers that could feed.

Hannah surprised Sidney by taking the presentation to the Independent Television network, so new it didn't yet have anything on the air.

"Why take the risk with ITV?" Sidney asked. "Surely the BBC is where to go. Haven't they aired more than one of our programs?"

Hannah waggled her eyebrows at him. "ITV is young, hungry, and eager for content. They want to make a mark, and the only way to do that is to be bold. We are the boldest show in town." She paused, watching him nod slowly, then moved in for the kill. "Also, they have capital and will have advertising, so they'll be willing to splash out on the budget."

"Let's be off like a loosed arrow!"

Two days later, they inked a deal with ITV. Their liaison, Mr. Pierce (whom Hannah thought looked all of sixteen), was nearly salivating.

"Robin Hood, brilliant! Crikey, I always

loved those stories. Who didn't? Thanks for bringing this to us, Miss Wolfson. Thanks a lot."

It wasn't an absolute yet. They had to see a pilot. But they were clear that a good pilot would mean an order of thirty-two episodes, to start as soon as possible. They wanted to change the face of television.

When Hannah and Sidney reached the street, Hannah threw out her arms and whirled around, not caring who saw her or what they thought. Sidney thought they should be cautious of tempting fate. Their venture could not stay so charmed forever.

"Caution is for tomorrow," Hannah said. Perhaps Sidney was right, but in this moment, Hannah was far too happy to care.

Paul took a long sip of the Tom Collins Hannah had mixed him.

"Ahhh. What a beauty. I don't know how you do it, sweetheart, but it always tastes like the Yankees winning the first game of the season."

"If I can get it to taste like a World Series win, I'll seek my fortune as a barkeep," Hannah promised.

Paul dropped a kiss into her curls. "Good god, I miss baseball."

Hannah didn't. They'd been to a rugby

match, a wild and violent spectacle that nearly made Paul faint. It was the first time Hannah saw the thrill of watching a sport. She knew what he meant, though. She knew he missed the crack of the bat, the wooden benches, hot dogs heavy with mustard, and bags of peanuts in the shell.

"You should write a story about British sport," she said. "There must be some rookie player on some team who had a dreadful war childhood and is now recapturing some joy in his life, realizing a dream and all that sort of thing."

Paul gazed at her in admiration. "I married a smart lady, didn't I?"

She ran her finger under his lower lip. All these years, and she still couldn't look into those eyes long enough.

"The smartest thing I ever did was say yes," she told him. They kissed for a long time and were still kissing as Rhoda marched into the room, singing, "Hurray for Captain Spaulding, the African explorer!"

They broke apart and Hannah marveled at her daughter doing a disturbingly good impression of Groucho Marx. "Did you teach her that?" she asked Paul.

"The film was on television, so that box is good for something, it seems."

Hannah laughed, but wished Paul wouldn't always criticize television.

"I'm glad you think so," she said, as he handed Rhoda an unlit cigarette to use as Groucho's cigar. "Because I've got an amazing chance. There's two acres of woodland right adjacent to the studio we're looking to rent for Robin Hood, and if Sapphire can buy it, we —"

"Woodland?" Paul sounded out the word as if he were trying to parse Aramaic. "You want to own woodland? What's next, a duchy?"

Rhoda was now mixing the lyrics of "Captain Spaulding" with those of "Lydia the Tattooed Lady," but Hannah stayed focused on her purpose.

"It'll work out much cheaper than renting, and far more practical. More importantly, it'll pay for itself by looking so evocative. It'll feel real because it is."

"Yes, men in tights dancing about castles and fires is what I call real, all right."

"Well, apparently if we went to Stonehenge on Midsummer Night . . ."

He guffawed. "Woodland. At least I know for sure this one is your idea, not that Scotch man's. Scottish." He wrinkled his nose, considering her. "A loan?"

"A loan." She kissed him. "Sapphire will

151

pay you back when we've got our American distribution deal."

"Oh, all right, so the twelfth of never."

Hannah laughed and smothered him in kisses, which made him laugh too. She was so happy, she jumped up to dance with Rhoda. Gemma brought in Julie, and Hannah swooped her up to dance as well. Paul shook his head, but joined in the merriment. Hannah swirled. All those Communist hunters were so sure they'd frightened everyone into behaving and that no one would dare try to defy them by thinking a thought they deemed dangerous. And here was Hannah, putting on a show that would defy them every week, and give work to those they said deserved neither liberty nor happiness, and probably not even life, if HUAC could get away with that.

Hannah spun harder, and Julie shrieked with joy.

The weeks of preproduction slid by like a dream through the spring and early summer, going so smoothly that Sidney organized vases of white heather to be displayed throughout the Sapphire offices. It was meant to be good luck and, he hoped, would ward off the bad fortune that must be waiting to rear its head and spoil everything.

"And here I thought the evil eye was a Jewish superstition," Hannah said.

"How can you be so calm?"

"Are you kidding?" she laughed. "I've never been so excited in my life!"

It was happening. The show had been cast, the costumes made, the sets built. They rented space at Nettlefold Studios in Surrey, and Hannah, thanks to Paul, bought the adjacent woodland. They shot a pilot, and ITV approved the full season virtually within hours of everyone viewing it. Ring had written three more scripts and had chosen his pen name: Lawrence McClellan. The filming schedule was locked. Hannah sent the pilot to various contacts in America. It wasn't just about the money they'd reap for ITV. She wanted *Robin Hood* seen by Americans. She wanted the children of Communist hunters to learn, however obliquely, that the hunt was wrong, that it went against every value meant to be American.

Ring spread the word among blacklistees at home, and Hannah whispered around the exiles in London. Five more blacklisted writers were given assignments. Then five more. A few grumbled about working for scale after having been so well paid, but as Sidney said, Sapphire was taking a risk hiring them. If word got out to the wrong people, that would be the end of American distribution — for *Robin Hood* and any other Sapphire production. It took a lot of work to keep the secret safe. That cost something.

Officially, every writer for *Robin Hood* was an unknown. Even Sidney didn't know all the details. Hannah shouldered that burden herself. There was one copy of the list of real names and their corresponding pen names, and Hannah kept that under the lining of her bottom desk drawer.

You couldn't be too careful.

"This is Miss Connolly," Sidney said, introducing the young woman he pronounced a "dead-clever up-and-comer."

"Best story editor there is to be," the young woman said before Sidney could say more. Her accent was even harder than Sidney's to grasp — higher and more sing-songy, and she spoke quickly. "I prefer just to be called Beryl, if you hire me. I was quite the roared-at 'Miss Connolly' all through school."

"You're Scottish as well?" Hannah said, hoping she was right.

Beryl's eyes crinkled in approval and she turned to Sidney. "Not 'Scotch,' like yon Yanks like to say. Ye've taught her finely."

"Miss Wolfson is a woman of understanding," Sidney protested. "You'll see. You two talk," he added, leaving Beryl in Hannah's office.

"You may as well know," Beryl said in a sharp, rushed tone. "I've not been to university. I came up through theater in Glasgow." She put an emphasis on it, and her button nose turned up proudly. "Rougher stuff than yon Sidney's Edinburgh."

To Hannah, these were just cities on a map, but she knew people from Brooklyn who would declare war on anyone who thought New York meant only Manhattan, so she nodded respectfully. Beryl had a pointy, intelligent face, and Hannah was impressed by how she'd flouted fashions and cut her dark red hair into a 1920s-style bob. She dressed like a Teddy Girl, in knickerbockers and a men's tweed jacket. Hannah noted a monocle tucked in her waistcoat and a pipe sticking out from her breast pocket.

"We're a small operation for now," Hannah told her. "It's really just us here in the offices, and Sidney and I will be going to the set quite a bit. I don't just need a story

155

editor, I need an assistant, someone who can manage what's going to be a lot of fast-moving business and never drop a ball —"

"Child's play. Done it all and more for Dickensian wages, 'tis the world of radical theater," Beryl interrupted. "I'm hoping for a challenge."

Hannah raised her brow and leaned forward. "All right, how's this for size? You can't ever accept any registered letters, especially if they've come from America."

"Jings!" Beryl cried, properly stunned. "Why not?"

"It's a precaution," Hannah explained. A registered letter could be a subpoena. It seemed unlikely, but who knew? "Prove yourself and I'll explain more later." She grinned and Beryl grinned back. Hannah was delighted. "Your desk is just outside. Read all the scripts we have by lunchtime. Check for character arcs, any inconsistencies, any language that's too modern. Our audience will be kids, but this show is going to be smart. No slacking. Let's pick this up again at two, and I want a full report and marks on anything of concern. No detail is too small."

"Nae, it shan't be," Beryl promised. "I'm known for being fierce on details. The Himmler of Proper Dialogue, I was once called, and I took it for a fair compliment."

"Good," Hannah said, standing. "One more thing. The scripts must be entertaining, whatever the content. You were a kid not so long ago, feel free to tweak as necessary to make sure each script is a humdinger."

Beryl grinned broadly. "May I smoke my pipe?"

Hannah tossed her a matchbook.

It took less than a week for the three of them to become a stellar team. Beryl asked no awkward questions about the scripts or possible registered letters and was promptly as passionate about *Robin Hood* as the others. Hannah was elated. Her only trouble was when Sidney and Beryl got into a spirited argument, which happened several times a day. Hannah had no idea how an English person would fare trying to understand their accents at top speed, but New Yorker though she was, it was hopeless. She felt curiously left out, a child trying to understand a grown-ups' conversation. She wouldn't dream of telling them, it would be far too embarrassing, but it made her more grateful than ever for her little circle of Americans in exile.

"Well, at least you understand Rhoda,"

Shirley said when Hannah confessed her trouble understanding her own employees. Now that Rhoda had started kindergarten, her accent had hardened into that of the native Briton Hannah was always startled to remember she was.

"Except when she says things like 'Aliens might live in hairbrushes,'" Hannah rejoined, and they laughed. Hannah needed that laughter, needed it to erase the loneliness she sometimes felt at work. Julie was talking more every day, and learning from Rhoda. Soon Hannah would be living with two foreigners.

Except that it was she who was the foreigner, and she knew it was critical she remember that. Britain gave her security and opportunity. The better she did by it, the more she might be able to rely on its protection if she ever really needed it.

Beryl came into Hannah's office with a pile of scripts.

"These are all revised and ready to go." She began ticking off her fingers. "We're still needing nine scripts to finish the first lot though, as you know; the historical consultant rang to moan about the men's hair not being medieval enough; and the girl engaged for script supervision says she's now engaged to be married, so she's skipping off to the land of satins and lace or some such rubbish."

Hannah removed her shoes and circled the office — these sorts of problems stimulated her. "Of course we want to be historically accurate, but remind Mr. Oliver we have to be reasonable." She picked up a photograph of Richard Greene, their Robin, in costume and makeup. "Sure looks handsome to me, and wouldn't with the medieval wig. I want the kids laughing at the jokes, not the hair."

"I'll be delighted to tell him," Beryl said, her eye glinting behind the monocle.

"I'm expecting more script submissions this week, and do please make some calls to get another script supervisor in. There must be dozens of sharp girls who'd love the job."

A few days later, Hannah and Sidney were arguing over possible guest actors and didn't hear the downstairs bell, or Beryl go to answer. They jumped, however, when Beryl stalked to Hannah's door and interrupted with a loud harrumph.

"There's an American come to call, says she's a television writer, wants to give you a script for consideration and even *see* you if she might and doesn't seem to have heard of such things as appointments and that

159

she'll wait."

"That sounds like an American, all right," Sidney said. "Or a Glaswegian," he added, winking at Beryl.

"Watch yon tongue!" she snapped.

A woman. A writer. It could be the perfect cover story for an FBI agent. Or it could be something novel. Hannah was intrigued.

"Did she give a name?" Hannah asked.

"Phoebe Adler," Beryl said. "Says she wrote for a tec show called *At Your Service*. On the Adelphi network. What the devil is that then?"

Hannah glanced at the American newspapers and industry trades strewn over her desk. The *Los Angeles Times* happened to be folded open to Hedda Hopper's latest screed about "Runaway Reds" that asked, "Are they now plotting from abroad?" Hedda Hopper was given to ridiculous hats and an excess of ruffles, but she was a woman with power. Hannah knew it was only a matter of time before she herself drew someone's attention. But if she knew anything about how Hoover's FBI worked, she knew none of his Hounds would try to gain entrance to her with such a feeble credit. *At Your Service* barely made the Nielsen charts. Phoebe Adler must be genuine. Hannah pondered. A female

Hound, if such existed, would carry a subpoena in her bag, or, at a stretch, a coat pocket.

"Take her bag, and coat if she's wearing one," Hannah ordered. "And don't be afraid of letting her know you mean business."

Hannah had never heard of a woman as an FBI agent — it sounded like the sort of notion J. Edgar Hoover would react to with a comment about his rotting corpse — but even such a woman would be no match for Beryl.

Beryl ushered in a young woman who followed her respectfully.

"Miss Wolfson, Miss Adler here to see you," Beryl said. "Even without an appointment," she added meaningfully, and Phoebe blushed.

"Thank you, Beryl, you may close the door," Hannah said.

Beryl gestured that Phoebe seemed trustworthy enough and was gone.

Phoebe thrust out her hand. "Thank you so much for seeing me, Miss Wolfson, really, thank you. I would have been happy just to leave the script but, well, I really wanted to meet you. This is swell of you, thanks."

Hannah shook Phoebe's hand, struggling not to smile. A Lower East Side girl, just like herself. That broad, booming twang was sweeter than a Bach concerto. Hannah herself had always spoken more softly, but she knew her people.

"Why exactly did you want to meet me, Miss Adler?" Hannah's voice was cold. It would be easy to feel an instant kinship with this young woman, but these were not the times to trust too readily. "Without an appointment?" she echoed Beryl.

Phoebe blushed again and took a breath. "I . . . well . . ."

Hannah saw all the marks of the recent leap into exile. Phoebe's big eyes behind her glasses were bright and intelligent, but they looked lost. There was that air about her — brazen, determined, hopeful, yet also anxious and at sea, swimming in disbelief. Twists of chestnut hair were winning a battle over the lacquer. She probably did a much better job controlling that hair when she had her bearings.

"Coffee?" Hannah asked.

"Oh jeepers, yes please," Phoebe gushed.

Hannah liked tea well enough, but kept a little hot plate in her office where a coffeepot warmed all day. She poured a cup for Phoebe, considered offering her a piece of the Walkers shortbread Sidney brought in by the kilo, and then decided to wait until Phoebe confessed to being blacklisted.

Newcomers hated admitting it.

Phoebe slurped greedily and Hannah studied her. A striking young woman, in her way, with a wide face and strong jaw. Freckles. A peasant face, one that could look heather pretty or potato plain depending on what light she'd happened to walk into. If she were an actress, she'd be the stuff of a cameraman's ulcer. She wore a career woman's suit — not new, but good quality and in good taste. Money had been spent to have it decently tailored to flatter her plumpish figure, big busted with wide hips. She took another big gulp, and Hannah noted her ringless fingers.

Phoebe set down her cup and took a breath. "I was told I could be straight with you. Is that true?"

"It's preferable, yes. Though you have no reason to believe me, I suppose."

"No," Phoebe said, nodding in agreement. "But I'd like to." She paused, looking hard at Hannah. "I . . . I'm on the blacklist. I've been writing for TV, not a great show, but I'm good. I wrote for radio too. Anyway, I've got some scripts — all crime stuff but I can do other things too. I was told you're a terrific producer and you can throw some bones to blacklisted writers. I know I should have written first, but I've never gotten anywhere without being pushy, so . . . well, I hope you'll look at my stuff."

"I might," Hannah said. She was impressed. The woman had gumption. "Who else do you know in London?"

"No one. Except Ernie, the fellow who runs the pub I'm staying in. He's awfully nice."

"If you don't mind my saying so, Miss Adler, half the industry is blacklisted, plus teachers, journalists, union workers — not everyone's skipped town. Why didn't you just scrounge underground with the others?"

Phoebe flushed. "I got a subpoena. I wouldn't have anything to say to Congress, and then they might cite me for contempt, put me in prison, and I've got a . . ." She paused, then threw back her shoulders. "I don't want to live scrunched up in a corner, being made to feel guilty just because I once spoke up for myself."

Hannah poured her more coffee. "What if you can't get any writing work?"

Phoebe set her jaw. "I'll ask Ernie if he can use a scrubwoman. But I've got to write. I'm good. All I'm going to do is get better. I've always had to push awfully hard. I'm used to it."

Hannah had often said much the same

thing herself. She decided to read Phoebe's work. If there was talent there, Hannah would recommend her for something, perhaps on the radio. *Woman's Hour* liked a bit of light drama, and the producer liked Hannah. It could be a start.

"Producers will expect other samples," Hannah warned. "A spec script for a British show will help you."

"Can't I write something for you?" Phoebe begged. "Just to consider? I'd really like to work for a — for you," she said quickly.

She'd been going to say "a woman." Hannah's eyes narrowed. Did Phoebe think she was softer, easier, because she was female? Countless men had thought that, and learned just how wrong they were. Hannah kicked off her shoes under her desk and leaned back. She had no intention of considering Phoebe for *Robin Hood*. Maybe she squeaked through on a low-rent detective drama, but this was a muscular adventure. There was no comparison. Besides, she couldn't compete with the top-drawer talent the show attracted. Still, women TV writers were a rare breed. A good sample of *Robin Hood* might get Phoebe far.

"I've got a TV show in production, *The Adventures of Robin Hood*. I assume you've heard of him?"

165

"Robs from the rich, gives to the poor?"

"That's the one," Hannah said. "Beryl will give you the specs if you'd like to try writing a sample. Maybe you can have it ready in two or three weeks?"

"Thank you. That sounds super," Phoebe said. Hannah saw the furrowed brow — Phoebe must be wondering how long she could manage without income.

"There are other Americans in London of the, shall we say, 'subversive persuasion,' " Hannah said. "Some of us are gathering Thursday. You ought to come, meet people. If you need help, we're there, which is to say here. It's what we do for each other."

Phoebe bit her lip. "I . . . no, that sounds great. I do want to meet people."

"But?"

A long, shuddering sigh. "I really stink at taking charity. I have to find work."

Hannah wiggled her toes, thinking hard. It went against her better judgment, but she decided to give it a try. "Listen, the show starts its full production schedule Monday. We need a new script supervisor. You know television scripts and you know something of how this all works. Are you game?"

Phoebe looked stunned but she sat up straighter. "Yes. Of course." Then her face clouded. "Though I guess my residency permit doesn't let me work, not if I'm not writing."

"A not-uncommon situation," Hannah said briskly. "So you won't mention it when you apply for renewal, and if you're found out, I never knew your status." She looked at Phoebe sternly, to be sure they were clear, then went on. "When you get to the set, say even less about yourself. Pay attention to the scripts and details like you've got five sets of eyes, and be sharp. I hear of one mistake and you're sacked, as they say. It's six pounds a week, which is pretty fair around here." In fact, Hannah had been planning to pay six pounds, twelve shillings, but she had to make some concession when everyone expected a Briton on the job.

"Thank you," breathed Phoebe. "Thanks a lot. Really."

"No mistakes. Oh, and listen, Miss Adler, if you don't mind my saying something personal, don't dress up for the job, all right? They're less likely to resent you if you look a little rough around the edges."

"Resent . . ." Phoebe began, but Hannah had no more time to spare.

"If you want to wear trousers, no one will mind."

"Trousers?" Phoebe's voice scaled upward, as though Hannah had just suggested she wear a bathing dress.

"And make sure you don't call them 'pants.' You may think you speak English, but you don't. I'll see you at the party on Thursday, Beryl will give you the information. And do start that script."

Phoebe seemed to relax. She smiled — a big, toothy grin that was really quite charming. She shook Hannah's hand.

"Thank you, Miss Wolfson. I'll strive to be a credit to you."

"Good," Hannah said, keeping her voice professional. She could determine soon enough if she could be friendly.

Beryl came in soon after, looking peevish. Hannah suspected she'd listened at the door.

"Say what you will about that one," Hannah said. "She's no delicate flower."

"No one will cotton to an American in a staff job," Beryl said bluntly.

"It's just temporary," Hannah assured her. "She needs help, we need a girl, we'll replace her once she's on her feet."

"She also said she's writing one of the scripts," Beryl said, adjusting her monocle.

"No, she's writing a sample," Hannah corrected her. "If it's any good, I'll use it to help her meet some other producers. Just till she's on her feet," she repeated.

Recognition crept across Beryl's face, magnified under the monocle.

"Jings," Beryl whispered. "She's one of those, isn't she? On yon blacklist?"

Hannah reached into her desk and produced a tin of Fortnum & Mason's best biscuits.

"Help yourself," she instructed Beryl.

"Jings," Beryl said again. She selected a biscuit with reverence. Like many Britons, she still wasn't used to treats after years of rationing.

"Sidney thought we could count on your discretion," Hannah said. "I've had every reason so far to think that's true."

"Beryl Maire Connolly is nobody's spy," Beryl said stoutly. "The very notion of that blacklist seems daft, sure, and all right to help along them who need it."

"But?"

Beryl set down the biscuit she'd been nibbling to make it last. "The themes in the plots, the concerns about registered post . . . ? Is it other Americans on that list, writing our scripts? Are you on the blacklist yourself?"

"I'm not," Hannah admitted. "But I knew I would be if I'd stayed. And I might yet be, one never knows." She took a biscuit and gestured for Beryl to finish hers and have another. "I have to help people, and I have to stick it to the men who force Americans like Phoebe Adler, like a lot of my friends, to run away from home."

Beryl smiled faintly. This was her language. But Hannah could see she was still upset.

"Robin Hood is our legend," Beryl said at last. "I suppose he's English, but he acted like every Scot I've known. It ought to be written by British writers."

"I know," Hannah admitted. "But this is something I have to do. If you would rather not be a part of it, I understand."

Beryl pursed her lips. She looked around Hannah's office, her eyes eventually coming to rest on the shooting script for *Robin Hood.*

"It's your job I want someday. There's nae better place for me to start getting it." She took out her monocle and polished it. "I respect what you're doing. I see now why Sidney thought I'd be ideal for Sapphire, and I expect I ought be flattered."

"You are very good," Hannah said. "I should think you'll have my job at your own company within five years."

Beryl selected a biscuit, iced with a delicate leaf pattern. She turned it over in her hand, admiring it. Then she looked up at Hannah and gave her a curt nod. " 'Tis your creation, this, I ken that very well. You can do as you like and good on you."

"What I like," Hannah said, "is to hire writers who can make this story sing. These writers on the blacklist, they know exactly what it is to suddenly be an outlaw in their own nation. They'll make everyone feel it, and that's what I want. That's when I'll call this show a success."

That afternoon, Hannah went to the film studio in Surrey to check that everything was ready for filming. A small crew was busy putting on finishing touches and getting things organized. They saw her and very nearly snapped to attention, making Hannah feel like a visiting general on an army base.

"Gentlemen, please, as you were," she said with a cheery laugh that made them all smile. It was peculiar, seeing herself viewed by all these young men with what couldn't be mistaken for anything other than admiration. Possibly this was what it was like to brim with sex appeal. Except this was better, because they were admiring her power as the creator of this make-believe kingdom they had built. She was so very unexpected — a woman, an American, a mother, and yet the queen of all this, the source of their income and their path to a long and great career.

"Good afternoon, Miss Wolfson" and "Can I have someone bring you some tea, Miss Wolfson?" and "Would you like to see how the tower stairs lock into the wall for an exterior swordfight?"

It was heady stuff.

Though it was Peter Proud, the art director, who was senior enough to take charge of her needs and show off the glory of the scenery, every man sought to have a word with her, and she made sure to address each one by name. The attention was almost unbearably flattering. This was, she realized, the sort of feeling that must lead some women into having affairs.

As much as she enjoyed the company, her true pleasure was in the creation, and the innovation. She had directed Peter Proud to let his fancy run free, and he had done himself as proud as his name.

"It's a whole new technique, like nothing anyone's seen in television production, Miss Wolfson," he gushed as he showed off the pieces of scenery that would be rooms in a castle, or a hut, or whatever was needed. "We don't need those sorts of massive sets where your fellas would spend ages lining up cameras. I told you I thought putting

172

these bits of scenery on wheels would work, and you see?" He pointed to the fat wheels under the castle and hut. "These will zip right in and out and then the rest dressed with bits as needed. We'll shoot scenes in a snap. And it'll look handsomer than any other program on the box, Miss Wolfson."

"That was the idea, Mr. Proud. You've done a brilliant job."

She left him to bask in the glory of her praise and walked alone to the stretch of woodland that would stand in for Sherwood Forest. In the middle, surrounded by trees and bracken and birdsong, she looked up through the leaves to the sky.

"What a long way from Orchard Street you've come, Miss Wolfson," she marveled.

A red squirrel, commencing upon its afternoon acorn, chittered at her. Hannah looked at it and it glared back, letting her know in no uncertain terms that the acorn was not for sharing.

Woods, though, woods should be for everyone, she decided with some mild guilt at Sapphire's exclusive ownership of these trees. Robin Hood would have disapproved.

When the time comes, Sapphire will gift these back to Surrey. They'll be a park, where anyone who ever loved this show can come and sit among the trees that transported them from their front rooms and into Sherwood Forest.

She hefted herself onto the low branch of an oak, something she was never allowed to do on rare childhood visits to Central Park, and let herself feel transported.

That night, after the Little Engine, along with vociferous support from Rhoda and Julie, thought it could, Hannah stroked the sleeping Julie and whispered an adventure to Rhoda. "The pirate queen befriends a wolf, and chases it all through the woods, swinging around the trees, on and on, into the Land of Dreams."

"Pirates and wolves," whispered Paul from the doorway. "She'll turn into an outlaw herself."

"A little wildness never hurt anyone," Hannah said fondly. She shut the bedroom door and joined Paul in the living room.

"I don't know, Hannah, people expect differently of girls now. We're back to living in more settled times."

"If these are such settled times, why aren't you and I back in New York?"

Paul poured a double whiskey and grinned at her.

"Because you want to be a career woman, and HUAC would be down on you like a ton of bricks."

Hannah laughed. "You make me sound like a gangster. Speaking of HUAC, there's another blacklistee in town. A young lady writer, for a wonder."

"Just what our group needs, another mouth to feed." Paul rolled his eyes.

"This one's got a smart mouth on her, she'll feed herself all right," Hannah said, not mentioning the job she'd handed out. Instead she fetched his pipe and asked about his day. He regaled her with his adventures in research and writing, and she snuggled beside him, feeling as warm and contented as Rhoda. She closed her eyes.

CHAPTER EIGHT

Phoebe inhaled two cigarettes in fifteen minutes as she walked away from the Sapphire offices. The Player's were growing on her. She hesitated by a sweetshop, longing for a Hershey's bar and gearing up for Dairy Milk instead, when she spotted a sign indicating she was near the Victoria & Albert Museum. Museums calmed her. She liked how they were clean and quiet, such respectful repositories of the past. They were always a good place to order her thoughts. Phoebe followed the sign to the doors and entered.

As she wandered, she thought about Hannah. She hadn't expected a woman with such a sweet face, soft curls, and motherly smile. She had, however, imagined someone firm and intimidating, and in this Hannah delivered in spades. *I sure hope I didn't seem weak, or silly. Or desperate.*

Phoebe plodded through a display of

dishes and silver. Beautiful things for beautiful lives. The sort of things she'd always wanted, for the sort of home she worked so hard for — now slipping further and further away. For all her talent, there was no certainty she would ever sell another script. Phoebe knew now how lucky she had been to start her career during the war, when so many male writers were off doing bigger things, and everyone was hungry for easy entertainment and good-enough writers willing to work cheap. Regular work, and guidance from Hank, made her better, and then she got better still. But if she wanted to sell something to Hannah, she was going to have to leap to the level she'd been striving for without passing Go one more time.

She followed signs to the medieval displays, realizing she had no idea what the medieval world even looked like. She'd visited the Metropolitan Museum of Art in New York a thousand times, but only wandered among the paintings. Phoebe liked looking into the eyes of the past. A vase wasn't the same thing at all.

The further back into history she walked, the more she grasped how little she knew about a lot. All her reading, and sneaking into movies, it wasn't the same as the sort of education she'd dreamed of before the war, before Mona went to Brookside. She read every newspaper Horatio sold at his little stand, and knew there were ways a bright, if poor, girl like herself might get into a women's college like Barnard, just a train ride away uptown. She went there once, and admired the handsome brick buildings and green courtyards where young women in tweed skirts and cardigans talked and read and drank coffee. She knew she would be one of them.

Even when she left high school for the airfield, she was sure she would reach Barnard after the war. But then her parents died, and she sold that script. She had to keep working for Mona's sake, and no longer minded. On a good day it was thrilling. Sketches written by her played on the radio throughout the war and on into the peace, and then television opened up a whole new vista, far larger than the walls surrounding Barnard. Anything she needed to know for work, she'd gotten from a quick trip to a library. Which was next on her list, but she still wanted to see this world. Feel it.

The displays of reliquaries and tapestries left her cold. The embroidery was exquisite, but she felt nothing of the intricacies of daily life in Robin Hood's time. Or death, for that matter, when it wasn't that of a saint or a stag.

"Is there someone here who can tell me about murder in the Middle Ages?" she asked at the information desk. The expressionless clerk ran a finger down a personnel list, rang a number, spoke to someone, and then turned to her in apology.

"I'm sorry, miss, there's no one free today. Perhaps next week."

Annoyed, Phoebe headed back to the pub for a supper Ernie had kindly kept warm. She asked him if he knew where she might find remnants of medieval London.

"Oh aye, now you ask, that's a good question there, miss, and a shame you weren't here before the war. But here, I think I know a few spots you might like." He dug around for a pencil and wrote a short list on the back of the day's menu. "Try the Tower first, miss, it's a good 'un."

As soon as she saw the Tower of London, she knew it wasn't going to draw her into the world of Robin Hood. It was too big, too grand, too far removed from Nottingham and the outlaws. She went in anyway.

"Here to see the Crown Jewels, miss?" she was asked.

"No, I'm for anything about torture and execution, please."

Phoebe studied the manacles and rack, disappointed to learn that these were only used in later centuries, when religious conflicts heated up. Things she'd never understood.

Another woman gazed at the rack in awe. Phoebe grinned at her. "Kind of nutty, isn't it, the way people acted like being Catholic or Protestant at any given time was enough to get your bones busted?"

The woman gaped at her, appalled. "You Yanks really are ignorant, ain't you?"

Phoebe decided she preferred the accents she couldn't understand. She began counting the hours until she met more of the American exiles in London.

The Bonwit dress was undoubtedly too grand for a gathering of supposed subversives, but Phoebe didn't care. If she had to go into this strange crowd alone, where people might think her in need of charity, she was damn well going to look her very best. She slipped her photos of Mona and Anne into her bag for company, then added the photo of that first check and snapped the bag shut.

There was a phone box by the Underground station. Phoebe glanced at her watch. It was just after lunch at Brookside.

Would her first letter have arrived with the morning mail? Now there was more to tell, and Mona's insistence that the other exiles were going to love her would help settle her nerves. Phoebe locked herself in the bright red box and picked up the receiver, then was caught short at the sight of two large buttons labeled "A" and "B." She tentatively pressed button A and called, "Hello?" She pressed it again. "Hello? Hello?"

"Yes, hello, miss, how can we help?" came the irritated voice of an operator.

"Oh, sorry, hi," Phoebe said. "I want to call New York, what's the charge?"

"A London to New York call is three pounds for three minutes, miss."

"You've got to be kidding me!"

"The telephone company does not make jokes, miss," the operator informed her crisply. "Do you wish to proceed with the connection?"

Phoebe slammed down the phone. Three pounds! For three rotten minutes. *First thing I'm doing when I get rich is buy shares in a phone company.* She closed her eyes to summon Mona, who demanded to know what the heck there was to be so nervous about.

Plenty. She had to make a good impression. She had to make friends. She had to make everyone there, especially Hannah, crave her company and, more importantly, her talents.

She hurried down the steps to find the train that would take her to the LeGrand house in the neighborhood of Islington.

She alighted at Angel and checked her directions. Having mastered the winding streets of Greenwich Village, Phoebe took to London with a confidence that quickly wilted when she discovered you could walk down Newcomen Street searching for an address and find the street name had changed to Snowsfields and you were no closer to your destination. She found Elia without too much trouble, though, and knocked smartly on the door of number eleven at five minutes past seven. A man in rolled-up shirtsleeves with a napkin tucked in his neckband flung open the door.

"Well, what is it?"

"I'm here for the party," Phoebe said stoutly, her back ramrod straight. "Hannah Wolfson sent me."

"Who?" His voice scaled upward as his face closed inward.

"This is number eleven Elia, isn't it?" Phoebe asked. The man slammed the door shut. "I didn't want to spend more time with you anyway," she told the door.

Phoebe headed back to the station and tucked herself in the corner of an adjacent pub to study her map and Beryl's scrawled directions. She ignored her thumping heart. There was no phone number. No one to call for help. If she couldn't find this house, she would have to go back home in abject failure.

She approached the publican. " 'Scuse me, can you help? I'm trying to find this address." She showed him the papers.

The man raised an eyebrow and laid a finger on the map. "Did you maybe go to Elia Mews, miss, when you were meant to go to Elia Street?"

"Oh," said Phoebe, staring at the name above the neatly pared fingernail. Beryl's writing was hard to read — possibly on purpose — but Phoebe should have at least noticed. Her ears were hot with mortification. "Oh, that must be it. Thanks," she said.

"Anything to drink?" he asked pointedly.

"Hm? Oh, no, I've got to get to this soiree," she said. "But thanks a lot, really."

She hurried out, pretty sure she heard him muttering about stupid and tightfisted Americans.

A few minutes later, she was at Eleven Elia Street, and a woman with a beehive hairdo and a wide, friendly smile opened the door.

"Hello there, you must be the new one. You're not alone, are you?"

Phoebe looked around herself. "I guess I must be," she said.

The woman laughed. "Hubby doesn't like going out, does he? Mine can be a bit of an old bear himself, but I can't blame him, he loves to just work, work, work."

"I'm not married," Phoebe said, ignoring the sinking feeling in her stomach. "It's just me."

"Oh!" The woman looked startled and studied Phoebe more closely. "Oh, maybe Hannah said . . . Well, anyway, do come on in! I'm Joan, by the way, Joan Morrison. It's not my house, I was just near the door. You're Fifi, is it?"

"Phoebe," Phoebe corrected her, thinking that Fifi could only be the name of a tiny spoiled dog, and why would anyone think her parents that cruel?

"Oh, of course, what was I thinking?" Joan laughed, seizing Phoebe's elbow and propelling her into a living room gray with cigarette smoke. Joan rattled off names, pointing at each man in the circle of men who saw no one but each other and then singling out a wife in the cluster of women across the room. Phoebe sighed. Being the only woman without a partner was nothing new, but she'd hoped that a gathering of black-listees abroad would be more like a Greenwich Village party, loud and boisterous and freewheeling. This looked more like the parties of television professionals Hank occasionally invited her to, where her status as an unmarried "gal writer" garnered mostly blank stares.

"So you're a gal writer?" the man Joan dotingly introduced as her husband Charlie said. "Huh. And you're all on your own? That seems a heckuva shame."

"Oh, I don't know, I like traveling light," Phoebe said.

His face puckered in confusion. "Oh," he said at last. "That's a joke?"

"The sort that'll keep me practicing a long time before I'm booked at Carnegie Hall," Phoebe said.

Several men heard this and laughed. Phoebe went to work introducing herself, but Joan soon steered her to the circle of women. Hannah greeted her politely and gestured to the serious-faced woman next to her.

"Meet Mrs. LeGrand, our hostess. I think I saw you speak to her husband, William LeGrand? You've heard of him, of course. Our Shirley herself is a composer and a biographer, and was field secretary for the

NAACP."

"That's the National Association for the Advancement of Colored People," Joan broke in.

"Yes, of course I know that," Phoebe said, hoping she didn't sound impatient as she shook Shirley's hand. Shirley was regal, her coffee-colored skin glistening, and she had the sort of effortless elegance Phoebe always aimed to create.

"I'm glad the organization still has name recognition," Shirley said. "Nearly all the officers were fingered by HUAC. We at the NAACP are the original blacklist."

Phoebe smiled, though Shirley's bone-dry delivery made it hard to be sure it was a joke.

"Of course, HUAC wasn't exactly incorrect," Shirley went on. "Will and I are proud party members. The Communists are the only party who think a societal racial divide is a ridiculous thing. We were keen to stay and fight, but there comes a point where reality must be faced. It's one thing to be silenced in prison, quite another to be silenced six feet under."

Phoebe hardly knew what to say. She felt frivolous. Shirley patted her arm.

"Those in power have never liked Negroes having a mouth. They would hate and fear

186

the NAACP irrespective of the odd Communist."

"I never get that. Aren't there more important things to hate?" Phoebe asked. "Like starving children, or unrepentant Nazis, or the last peanut in the bag being rotten?" The words burst from her before she could think. "Oh gosh, I'm sorry, that sounded so . . . I didn't mean to be disrespectful."

Shirley didn't smile, but her eyes had a small gleam. "That's the sort of joke that makes you sound like a party member yourself, *ma chère.*"

"You don't have to say what got you blacklisted," Joan piped in suddenly. "I mean, if you don't want to."

"Someone named my name," Phoebe said. "Isn't that how it goes?" She paused. "I don't know who, though."

"Ah, yes," Shirley said. "A not-uncommon predicament. Oscar Wilde was wrong — there are times when it's far better to not be talked about." The women exchanged grim smiles. "Well," Shirley said brightly. "A brief bit of housekeeping. If you require financial aid, we can help. If you're in good stead, please donate to the pool. We've formed a collective —"

"*You* formed it," Hannah said, nudging her. "*We* heartily agreed and wish we'd

187

thought of it first."

Shirley's eyes crinkled in amusement. "So," she went on. "We put what we can in the pot, which gets meted out to whomever needs it. No one's going hungry on my watch."

" 'Share and share alike,' " Hannah said. Shirley and Joan chuckled, and Hannah explained the joke to Phoebe. "During one of the HUAC dog and pony shows, Ginger Rogers's mother, of all people, decided she wanted her chance to come scream about Communism. Turns out she felt her baby was hard done by, because in *Tender Comrade,* old Ginger had the line 'Share and share alike. That's democracy.' The committee swallowed that like cream, especially 'cause it was a Dalton Trumbo script and he was one of their top Red devils."

Phoebe was dumbfounded. "*That's* the sort of writing that's supposed to trick Americans into picking up hammers and sickles?"

"Thank goodness HUAC exists to save us all," Hannah said.

"But it doesn't make sense," Phoebe insisted, ignoring the chorus of snickers. "Isn't democracy about people working together, the common good, that sort of thing?"

"That rather depends," Shirley said. "For my friends and family, democracy has meant white people extolling the glories of America while we pay taxes but are given strife for trying to vote, all while hoping today isn't the day we're lynched for crossing the road at the wrong corner. England's not perfect, but no one follows me through shops like I'm a thief, and I can sit wherever I please at the movies, so Will and I aren't overly minding life in exile."

Joan broke the silence that followed. "Anyway, are you all right for money?"

"Huh?" Phoebe snapped back to attention, guiltily relieved at the excuse to stop shuddering over lynchings. "Oh, yes, thanks."

"And where are you living, exactly?" Hannah asked.

"Oh. I'm in a room above a pub for now, but —"

"Well, how about that!" cried Joan. "The fellow across from us just moved out. We're in Soho. It's, well, it's affordable. Lively, lots of artists. Come over tomorrow at ten, the landlady will be there. I can get you the place, piece of cake!"

"Affordable," "lively," and "artists" were the sort of words that described Greenwich Village, perhaps euphemistically. Joan didn't look like the type who would choose to live in such an area, but Phoebe knew some of the blacklist's victims fell harder than others. She acidly congratulated herself on having been poor to start. It was an easier readjustment. Joan was a bit overwhelming, but she was also friendly. It would be nice, living near someone who understood her situation and could help her navigate this new terrain. Phoebe glanced at Hannah, now deep in conversation with Shirley and another woman, and wondered if Hannah had already known of the vacancy in Joan's building. She wouldn't be surprised.

Joan accompanied her to the buffet. "No run on the vittles tonight. Charlie packed my boys off to the movies," she said. She smiled and scanned the room. "What a shame there's no one single for you!"

"Ah well, maybe the next round of blacklisting will bring some more options," Phoebe said. Joan tittered, then rattled on about her children and living in London, not seeming to notice that Phoebe was watching Hannah loop her arm through her husband's and join his conversation. Extraordinary to think she was married, with children no less, and yet had such a career. Phoebe was pleased for her but had no illusions of such an arrangement for herself.

She didn't mind. Even Mona never understood that. Only Anne agreed there was safety in singledom, if one wanted to be sure of a career. Anne. *I wonder what she's doing right now.*

Hannah approached and handed her a fresh drink.

"Welcome to the club. I hope you'll make the best of it."

She seemed to mean it. Phoebe took the drink.

"Thanks," she said, meaning it in turn. "I intend to."

Joan's directions were so precise, Phoebe couldn't have missed Meard Street if she walked blindfolded. The "affordability" of Soho announced itself as soon as she turned the corner past the snug bookshops of Charing Cross Road. But if the streets were scruffy and dirty, they also buzzed with an energy that immediately put Phoebe at home. The characters outside the French Café looked like the same artists, writers, musicians, and probable criminals outside Floyd and Leo's place. As she walked, she smelled pizza, Chinese food, coffee. There were posters for shows and concerts. Then, as she neared number seven, the pure clear sounds of a saxophone sang out from a top floor somewhere and wafted around her head, pulling her lips into a dreamy smile.

Joan, standing at the door, saw the smile and beamed back, waving as exuberantly as if Phoebe were on a ship about to dock, rather than mere yards away.

"It's wonderful to see you!" Joan cried, pressing Phoebe's hand with the warmth of a longtime friendship. The warmth was real, though, and Phoebe found herself returning the friendly squeeze, which made Joan smile even more broadly. "Come and meet Mrs. Cotley!" she said. "She's waiting at the door of your new apartment, or 'flat' I should say! When in Rome, right?"

Joan practically dragged Phoebe to the top floor, where a careworn woman in an apron and headscarf leaned against a mop. She nodded perfunctorily.

"Mrs. Morrison says you're a decent young lady," she greeted Phoebe in a rough accent that was hard to follow.

"I had to explain that you being a working girl wasn't like what's usually meant around here," Joan said, giggling.

"I'm running a respectable place," Mrs. Cotley warned. "No funny business."

"There's nothing much funny about my business," Phoebe promised.

Mrs. Cotley nodded again and opened the

door. Phoebe swallowed her disappointment as she was overwhelmed by the smell of stale cigarettes and damp cloth. The two rooms with their severely sloping ceilings must have been servants' quarters once. Phoebe's eyes traveled from the chipped sink, tiny icebox, and two-burner hot plate to the sagging sofa and rickety coffee table, coming to rest on a parson's table and chair that fit perfectly under the window, bathed in light. A space made for a writer.

The table and chair made it easier to ignore the dark sliver of a bedroom, hooks in the wall instead of a wardrobe, and peeling wallpaper. She staggered a little when Mrs. Cotley explained that the shared bathroom was down the corridor and that this was a "coldwater flat." But Joan made it warmer, there was the light on the table, and there was music down the street.

Joan clapped gleefully as Phoebe and Mrs. Cotley shook hands. "I'll come help you get your things," Joan offered. But Phoebe thought of Ernie at the pub with sudden regret and said no, she'd like to do it herself. "Well, I'll keep lunch warm for you," Joan promised.

Ernie looked sorry as he settled her bill — and Phoebe was sure his charge of ten shillings was much less than what it ought to be — but he spoke cheerfully and insisted on carrying Phoebe's bags down to the street and hailing her a taxi.

"Of course you must have a proper home of your own, miss. No nice girl wants to stop in a pub for long, it's not right, miss," he said. "You'll be careful there in Soho, all right, miss, it's a bit rough. And if you're ever over this way, do be sure and stop in for a drop of something, miss."

He shut her into the cab and off she went, with only the lingering smell of ale in her coat to remind her of her first friend in London.

No. Not the first. That's Nigel. She half considered dropping him a note, but decided to wait until she had made a little money with this job on *Robin Hood* or, better, sold a script. She liked the idea of impressing him.

London's streets were dull and dusty, but Phoebe's eyes were drawn to flashes of color from flowers, either in window boxes or hanging from lampposts. A city coming back to life.

Phoebe had only just paid the driver when Joan appeared and seized her suitcase.

"You don't have to do that," Phoebe insisted, but Joan was already well ahead of her. Upstairs, they set down the suitcase and typewriter, and Joan looked around with satisfaction.

"Just needs a good cleaning and it'll be fine," she declared. "Come have lunch."

Joan and Charlie's flat was like the inside of a Victorian postcard, covered with tassels, frills, and doilies. A soft, steady hum of big band music emanated from a tiny radio. Joan swayed a little to the music as she set out bowls and cups. Phoebe surveyed the living room and kitchen, noting several photographs of two young boys in well-polished frames.

"My angels!" Joan said dotingly as she served soup and sandwiches. "The poor dears, off making the most of things before school starts. They hate the schools here. I keep telling them, if they got used to the weather, they'll get used to the school, and anyway it's better than being followed by G-men all the time."

"The FBI followed your sons?" Phoebe was disgusted.

"And me," Joan said. "I went lingerie shopping lots more than I usually would, just to embarrass them. But we were running out of money, and then we saw that they'd come in the house when we weren't there — apparently legal, if you can believe it — so it was time to leave. We had to sell our house, that broke my heart. And the IRS put a lien on Charlie's future earnings, which seemed a bit vindictive."

Phoebe burned with outrage for Joan, who went on as chattily as if she were discussing the weather.

"We're hoping Bobby, that's our eldest, will go to Harvard, Charlie's alma mater, but he really should be graduating from an American high school. We asked his grandparents to let him stay with them, but they were so appalled at Charlie being a Communist, they said they wanted nothing to do with any of us."

Phoebe stopped chewing. How could a blood relative behave like that?

"Still, other people have worse troubles," Joan said with a light laugh. "There are a few blacklisted directors here, doing all right, but they can't help worrying they'll get recognized. False names can't hide your face."

Phoebe sputtered. "I thought the whole point of being here was that we could work without worrying about that."

"Oh sure, sure, but you can't be careless. Word gets out a film has a blacklistee as writer or director, well, you can forget about American distribution."

Phoebe set down her spoon. Any script

she might write for a show distributed back home would have to have a different name on it. The hope she'd treasured in coming here, to keep writing as her own shining self, melted away.

Charlie stumped in from a back room, an unlit cigarette dangling from his lips.

"Any more coffee?"

"Darling, you remember Phoebe, she's just moved in across the hall."

"Oh." He looked at Phoebe and nodded, embarrassed. "Hello. Sorry, I haven't shaved or anything."

"That's all right, I didn't either," she said brightly. He blinked at her a moment, then gave a little bark that might have been a laugh.

"Your thing is funny, huh? Most girls don't do funny." He patted her shoulder. "Welcome to the shithole. I gotta get back to work."

He went back into his lair with a cup of coffee, cigarette still unlit.

Joan leaned in to Phoebe, her voice full of sisterly sympathy. "Did you lose a fellow in the war, is that why you're not married?"

It would be easy to lie. To be seen as comprehensible. Joan, Phoebe assumed, married at eighteen, had a baby a year later, and couldn't envision any other sort of life.

197

The day victory was declared in Japan, women were supposed to toss aside their tools and start having babies. The story went that they were now living exalted lives in suburbia, replete with appliances and convenience. Lives scrubbed as clean as the backs of their children's necks. But it was the ending of their movie, and Phoebe was sure she was still in the beginning of hers, and heading to a very different end.

"Just never met the right fellow," Phoebe said. "Probably I'm too busy being a career gal," she added, laughing because she was supposed to.

Joan laughed, too, shaking her head the way they always did. After lunch, Joan gave her a pile of clean linens — "Just until you get a few things of your own."

Phoebe went to her own flat. If Anne were here, she could draw a picture of the room for Mona. Then they'd get to work stripping the wallpaper and scrubbing the floor. Even without a penny, Anne could always acquire fabric and paint and cushions and turn a hovel into a home.

Phoebe made the bed and hung up her clothes. Tomorrow she would clean, buy groceries, get a proper coffeepot. For now, she set up her typewriter on the parson's table. Then she rolled in a sheet of paper.

She typed, *This isn't a shithole, it's a refuge.* She grinned. She was beginning to remember what it was to feel real.

CHAPTER NINE

"Oh, so that's the color the wood is meant to be!" Phoebe exclaimed as the floor was drying after its fourth scrub. "Not a bad shade of brown at all, I'd say."

Joan tucked some loose hair back under her scarf, smudging her nose. "No. These houses were well built. They have that going for them."

Phoebe continued scrubbing an unidentified sticky substance off the coffee table.

"This fellow who lived here before me, had he never heard of brooms?"

"He was a bachelor," Joan said, her voice warm and indulgent.

"And probably will be his whole life unless some girl is very, very unlucky," Phoebe said. "He could at least have hired Mrs. Cotley to do some cleaning. Or her son, didn't you say she has a son?"

"I'm sure he had no money to spare," said Joan.

"Could at least have bought a broom," Phoebe muttered darkly as she leaned out the window to beat a cushion, setting off clouds of dust.

As badly as Phoebe needed to get to the library and get her bearings on Robin Hood to start her script, the filth in the flat was simply too disgusting to bear. Joan had lent her an old dress and spent every spare minute that weekend helping her clean, only going home when one of her "angels" yowled from the door, "Maaaa, I'm hungry!" Phoebe didn't even see the boy — the call came and Joan scurried away.

On Sunday, Charlie pitched in and helped scrape off the worst of the peeling wallpaper. Phoebe had no money for paint, but they washed the dingy walls as best they could. As they worked, Charlie, who had been on plenty of film sets, gave Phoebe a quick lesson in the art of script supervision.

"You read along, let the assistant director know if the actor gummed anything up," he told her. "Don't let anything be inconsistent. If some fella falls in a mud pile in one scene, his clothes can't be clean what's supposed to be minutes later. Got it?"

"So, I pay attention to every detail and make a stink if one's off, even if it drives everyone nuts," Phoebe summed up.

"Bingo."

"No wonder it's mostly women who do this."

Despite Hannah's advice, Phoebe wore her suit to work. She liked the way it presented her as a serious woman, someone of substance. Professional.

The journey to Nettlefold Studios was easy enough — a short walk to the Underground, then a half hour train ride to Surrey and another short walk. Phoebe refused to think about whether or not she was nervous as she followed other arrivals to the main *Robin Hood* stage. Everyone rushed about with purpose and authority. Phoebe spotted a skinny young man in a Fair Isle sweater and bow tie carrying a large binder, every hallmark of an assistant director. She said, "Excuse me," three times, then finally tapped him on the shoulder.

"What is it?" he snapped.

"I'm Phoebe Adler, the new script supervisor," she said, holding out her hand.

He looked appalled, and Phoebe dropped her hand.

"Are you pure American?" he demanded.

Phoebe was baffled. "Do you mean like Seneca or Cherokee?" she asked.

He folded his arms. "Oh, wonderful, a bird who thinks she's clever, that's just what

I have time for. Did Miss Wolfson approve you?"

"I wouldn't be here otherwise," Phoebe said.

He frowned. "Are you British born, at least? Or Canadian?"

"I'm a New Yorker through and through."

"I see." His voice grew chilly. "Miss Wolfson wouldn't have engaged you if you weren't capable, but if I were you, dear, I'd tell everyone you're Canadian. I don't think they'll stick an American script girl."

"Well, I wasn't planning on getting stuck," Phoebe answered, but he sprang to attention on seeing a man in a tweed waistcoat and didn't hear her.

"Morning, Tommy," the man said. "Everything to schedule?"

"Nearly ready to roll, Mr. Bishop," Tommy assured the man, who was obviously the director.

"Good, have the cast called to the set."

He didn't notice Phoebe. She grinned at Tommy, a man who evidently knew when he had lost a battle.

"Oh, all right, come along. I've got the script girl's notebook on my table. I hope you're damn good at this job, is all I've got to say."

He wasn't expecting an answer, so Phoebe

made a few sounds she thought conveyed assent as he presented her with another fat binder. She pressed it to her chest as though she were donning armor, swiped a blue pencil, and scanned the table for a production schedule. Scene four was the first order of business, and she arranged the script in her binder accordingly. Then she returned to Tommy.

"Where would you like me to stand?"

"You can wait with the other girls for now, Miss . . . What was it again?"

"Adler. Phoebe Adler."

"Yes, all right," he said, as though giving her permission. "No need to stand too close to Mr. Bishop unless he wishes a consultation."

"Sure thing, Tommy," Phoebe said, unable to resist the urge to sound as New York as possible.

"The Other Girls" comprised the omnipresent wardrobe, hair, and makeup crew, imperious in their proficiency and savagely protective of their various charges. None of them wore a suit. As Phoebe approached them, she saw that their cardigans and skirts — and in one case, trousers — were carefully darned and patched. They stood a bit straighter on noticing her.

"Hullo," the trousered one greeted her.

"Are you with the producers?"

"Um, no. No, I'm Phoebe Adler. I'm the script sup . . . script girl." She hoped the term might indicate she was indeed just one of the girls. "And you are . . . ?"

"Dora, makeup," came the begrudging answer as all three women recoiled from Phoebe like she was wearing skunk cologne. "Are you an American?"

"Well, I'm from New York," Phoebe said, hoping to make them smile. It was well-known there were huge swathes of Americans who considered New York a country unto itself. New Yorkers, for a start.

"Oh," said Dora flatly. "Just fancy."

Phoebe had a funny feeling that "just fancy" was code for "this could not possibly be more ghastly."

"Miss Wolfson brought me on," Phoebe said, to establish her credentials. "Apparently they needed someone in short order and I was available."

"And I expect all the other local girls were booked," Dora said. "Awfully lucky for us you were so *available.*"

Phoebe was still struggling with accents, but sarcasm needed no translation.

Shooting began, and everyone snapped to attention. The scene was Robin and two other outlaws planning the rescue of a peasant falsely accused of theft. It was a small scene, simple, setting up the action, but the performances were so riveting, Phoebe couldn't breathe. She forced herself to concentrate on the page, relieved the actors said all the words correctly. She heard herself sigh when Mr. Bishop called, "Cut!"

Dora, readying her powder and base, heard the sigh. "I hope you're not fancying one of the actors," she said, her eyes glinting hopefully.

"Who me?" Phoebe said. "Not at all. I just like a good start to a show."

Dora was still suspicious, and as the scene was shot from different angles, Phoebe felt the Other Girls watching her, looking for ammunition in a battle she didn't understand. The scene wrapped and she made a mark in the book, watching in awe as scenery was wheeled away and another piece wheeled in. The next scene began just as smoothly. Before they shifted for alternate takes, someone called something Phoebe didn't understand but that the rest of the crew did. Everyone stopped work and trooped off to a large table at the edge of the stage.

Hannah was there suddenly, a guardian angel in tweeds.

"It's elevenses," Hannah explained. "Tea

break. The unions fought hard for it. Don't ask, just drink. You're managing all right?"

There was only one answer. Hannah was obviously on some cloud of her own, watching Robin Hood spring to life.

"It's swell," Phoebe said. "I really can't thank you enough."

"Don't bother with thanks," Hannah instructed. "Just do good work."

She disappeared again and Phoebe caught sight of Beryl in Hannah's wake. She could have sworn an eyebrow rose over the monocle, but it happened too fast for Phoebe to be sure. She went to get her tea, ignoring the whispers she was obviously meant to hear:

"Can't possibly need the work."

"Probably thinks she's about to meet the queen in that getup."

"Maybe thinks she *is* the queen."

Phoebe tucked her nose back in the binder to hide her burning cheeks. *They're just jealous,* came Mona's reassuring voice. *Sure,* Anne echoed. *They'd like to have a smart suit and good stockings. They can't even imagine affording such things.*

The Other Girls might have been gratified to know that by five o'clock, after standing nearly all day, Phoebe would trade every stocking she owned to be wearing their flat, ugly, and oh-so-practical shoes instead of her good, toe-pinching high heels. But she had done the job, and Tommy only grunted as she replaced the binder on the table. Tomorrow she would dress more simply. No one would forget, perhaps, but there was always the chance they might forgive.

From Hannah's perspective, this first day of filming was utterly perfect. Though it was Sidney's job as program producer to oversee the set, Hannah simply had to be there for this. She knew everyone could feel how good it was, that beneath their strict professionalism, they knew they were making something special. The energy on the set was so palpable, even the business-minded Beryl was swept away.

Hannah decided to stay through lunch to circulate among the more important cast and crew, offering congratulations and reminding them that she was the sort of executive producer who could be spoken to, should speaking ever be required. Being British, they wouldn't dream of it, but she still liked to make things clear.

As soon as the crew broke for lunch, she was surrounded by the director, Terry Bishop, as well as Peter Proud and several other men from the crew, none of whom could say enough about how pleased they were and hoped she was pleased too. Even though most of them had spent years working in theater and film, they still seemed so young, so fresh, so full of life. She felt guilty, enjoying this so much, but couldn't help it.

"Yon stunt doubles are making ready to rehearse!" Beryl broke in. Hannah caught the tone. Beryl was eager to see the sword fighting and archery, but also thought this fawning was going on too long. Hannah could not risk becoming too familiar. With some reluctance, she left the main stage.

She noted the few women of the crew chose not to approach. Phoebe sat alone in a corner, reading the script. That was smart. She should memorize the gold standard for an episode. It annoyed Hannah that Phoebe had worn her suit. It didn't matter that Hannah might have done the same thing, thinking it made a good impression. She didn't offer advice for young women to ignore. *Let her be friendless. That'll teach her.* Hannah would keep her in this job long enough to shore up some funds, then she'd let her go fend for herself. She'd do all right once she had the lay of the land. The detective show Phoebe had worked on was silly, but her script was good. Very good. Even Beryl, reading only out of curiosity, agreed.

"I'll be keen to see if she can write with any sort of a British voice," Beryl said. "Her dialogue reminds me of the GIs who roamed Glasgow like they owned it, and that's no great happy memory for me."

"If that's all she can do, her star won't shoot far," Hannah conceded.

Behind the main building was a lawn that must have pretended to be garden or grassland in hundreds of films since the studio was built in 1899. Today, it was a good place for stuntmen to parry and shoot. Every episode of *Robin Hood* would of course be full of derring-do. Most of the actors did their own fighting, a testament to the hard work of drama schools, but stuntmen were needed to allow the action to be as dangerous as possible. Hannah was determined to put hearts in throats every single episode.

The youngest crew member, a fourteen-year-old called Dennis who Hannah thought really ought to be in school, found an excuse to linger near the action. He was, at least, educating himself in the ways of the business, and Hannah smiled to see him cradle his transistor radio, no doubt a much-prized possession, under his ear as he gaped at the stuntmen — a Saturday kiddies' matinee in real life. Hannah felt his excitement as she watched the archer whose job it was to hit bull's-eyes. *Twang, twang, twang.* Its rhythm felt like the rock and roll that was becoming so popular. Paul preferred the soundtrack of the Depression, which reminded him of his youthful fire and fury. Hannah still loved that music, too, but found the new tunes irresistible. She liked the way they got under her skin.

"That stuff's for the kids, old girl," he once chided her gently.

"Now look, darling, if you want our children to like our music, you can't go about assigning who can listen to what," Hannah retorted. So now he was writing a story on the music of generations and how adults viewed the rise of the teenager.

Hannah congratulated the stunt choreographer and discussed his needs for an upcoming episode. As she passed Dennis on her way inside, a familiar voice emanated from his radio.

"It's a disgrace, the sort of films coming from France and Italy, and shows these countries have only descended further into degeneracy," Hedda Hopper fumed. *"If distributors won't stop showing them out of decency, their hand can at least be forced when good Americans refuse to patronize any picture house screening such muck. Furthermore, I am given to understand that some of these pictures are*

211

*being made by Reds! Not European pinkos,
no indeed, but the American traitors already
condemned by HUAC, now living cowardly
abroad so that they can continue to spread
their filth and attempt to corrupt impressionable minds. One way or another, these Runaway Reds* will be stopped."

Hannah's hand rose to strike the radio out of Dennis's grip. She balled it into a fist instead and strode over to the archery expert.

"Can you teach me to do this?" she asked.

The archer was astonished, but very pleased. He guided Hannah's hands, gently pushing her into position. She glared at the bright red bull's-eye, liking the feeling of the power in her fingers. Her eyes traveled the arrow to its point, the bowstring humming under her fingers as she pulled it back. She let loose per the archer's instruction and heard a delicious hiss as the arrow shot past her cheek and hit the bull's-eye with a hard thwack.

"Well done, Miss Wolfson, very well done indeed!" cried the archer as the other men cheered. Hannah felt better. A few more episodes to show the networks, and soon, she was sure, *Robin Hood* would hit the American airwaves.

I can hardly wait.

Joan waved out her front window when she saw Phoebe near their building.

"Coffee's just brewed!" Joan called.

Phoebe passed a twelve-year-old boy honing his skill with marbles. She vaguely recognized him as the landlady's son. He looked at her with interest.

"You've been at work, miss?"

"And returned in triumph," she said, hoping to make him smile. He only gazed at her with deep respect, which Phoebe found both flattering and unsettling.

"Goodness, have you befriended Freddie?" Joan was startled. "He seems a bit of a hooligan, though I suppose he'd be better off with a good education, poor fellow."

Joan's son Alvie, supposedly getting a good education, lay on his belly in front of a battered television, oblivious to company. *I've seen more animated piles of laundry,* Phoebe thought. Joan drew her attention to a stack of Hollywood magazines.

"Listen to this from Hedda Hopper: 'Readers will be delighted to know our vigilant efforts to rout out Reds in Hollywood have just this month seen five so-called Americans removed from influence. But we know there are still Reds among us, working to corrupt our most impressionable youth. Don't lose heart, good readers. Decent Americans can stop them, I'm even happy to shoulder the burden myself.' She certainly has a bee in her bonnet, doesn't she?"

"Isn't there something more important for a gossip columnist to worry about?" Phoebe asked. "Maybe Grace Kelly has a rash, or Lassie has worms?"

"You are funny, aren't you?" Joan smiled fondly.

"My sister's the real cutup," Phoebe said, then wished she hadn't. It was dangerous to think of Mona around other people. She took a huge gulp of coffee and offered Joan a cigarette. The big band music put her right back in the break room at the airfield. Where she'd worn coveralls and work boots. "I need to dress down for the set," she said. "Trousers, probably. I thought I was done with those after VJ Day. I haven't got a penny for clothes, not that those crew-shrews would believe it."

"Ooh, I can help!" Joan squealed, and dragged Phoebe into the bedroom. Phoebe hop-skipped right over Alvie as she followed Joan, and he didn't break rhythm as he blew a bubble. Joan opened a trunk and produced a pair of dark brown tweed trousers with a huge cuff. "I got these during the war — there was a stretch in '43 when we all wanted to look serious. They'll fit you fine, we've got the same hips." She thrust a matching brown-and-orange Pendleton jacket at Phoebe. "This will too. Then you'll knit a few things and buy something more modern when you can, though you'll still need a girdle for those slim trousers the girls wear."

"I think I'd rather just get another skirt," Phoebe said.

"You can wear socks with trousers," Joan explained. "Stockings are twelvepence a pair, socks are three. And cheaper still if you knit them yourself."

"Next I'll tie my hair up in a kerchief," Phoebe muttered. A timer buzzed in the kitchen, and Joan ran for the stove.

"The pot roast's done! If Charlie's in a good mood, would you like to join us?"

"That's all right, thanks," Phoebe said. "And thanks for all these, really."

"Share and share alike, right?" Joan grinned happily.

"Share and share alike, you said it."

Phoebe looked forward to having something to share soon.

The Other Girls barely glanced at Phoebe when she showed up in trousers and chunky shoes. She decided the isolation was just as well — fewer distractions meant she could focus. Besides, however lonely she might feel, being on set was exciting. She loved watching Mr. Bishop direct the actors, the actors act, and even the men arrange the lighting. She loved watching as the sets were wheeled in and out and dressed and undressed, coming to life and disappearing. Lunches she spent in a corner, eating a sandwich and reading the script, paying close attention to the construction and characterization. On Friday she was given a pay packet. Her ribs completely unlocked for the first time since Mr. Kelvin had told her she was blacklisted. She had income, she had a roof, she had a friend, and soon, very soon, she was going to have a script. She was not going to be stopped again.

The London Library was in St. James's Square, a short walk from Meard Street and a bastion of stately elegance, looking down its nose at the shabby collection of musicians and artists who flocked to the cheap rents and air of possibility. Phoebe felt shabby herself, wearing trousers and a Pendleton, but she'd had no time to wash her stockings and wasn't ready to part with twelvepence for more. She had less regret when she got inside — the marble was just as chilly as in her beloved Manhattan library.

"May I help you, miss?" the librarian asked, seeing Phoebe hover.

"Can we adjust the thermostat?" she asked. The librarian frowned. "Sorry," Phoebe hurried on. "I'm looking for anything there is on Robin Hood, please."

"How much do you already know about medieval history?"

"Nothing."

"Level four, H— England."

Phoebe looked around each room as she ascended, drinking them in. When she arrived at her destination, she ran her hand along the books, her mind thrilling to the reception of knowledge. As she made her way down the aisle, she gathered book after book, amassing a large stack. General history, a book about this king and that, a book on the plague, the peasants' revolt, witchcraft.

Progress down the aisle was hampered by a pair of legs that stretched nearly to Ancient

Rome and were attached to a young man whose long nose was buried in an anvil-sized book. He must have sensed her looming over him, but didn't move. Even a ladylike half cough, half "ahem" only resulted in his turning a page.

It would be unseemly to kick him, Phoebe decided, though she could say she tripped. She could go drop off her bounty at a free table and come back, at which point he might be gone.

But she felt as if she'd been drawn into a game, and was determined to win. She took another step so that her shoes just brushed his trousers, and stared down at his well-greased curls and the bridge of his nose.

After a pause, his eyes rolled up from under his glasses.

"I expect I'm blocking medieval basket weaving."

Phoebe forgot she was annoyed.

"Are there really books on that? Shove over, let me see." She nudged him hard with her foot — it might, indeed, have been classed a kick — and he was so astonished, he shoved over. There weren't any books on craft, but there was one on medieval manorial law — whatever that meant — and she added it to her pile.

"Are you a student?" he asked.

A "hah!" escaped Phoebe before she could stop it. It was a funny question for a woman who was twenty-nine. Though perhaps her clothes, loose ponytail, and mountain of books made her look the part. She hadn't even bothered with makeup, except lipstick. Just so she still felt like herself.

"After a fashion," she amended, selecting a book about medieval clothing and one on courtly love. A book of legends seemed misplaced next to one on battles, but she supposed it might depend on the nature of both. She laid them on the pile, which finally collapsed in a clatter to rival Jericho's walls. The din was followed by the hum of readers sighing in exasperation, letting her know she had interrupted something important and must now feel her shame.

The young man set aside his book and helped gather hers.

"You don't have to do that," she said. "I can make two trips."

He shrugged. "I've got time."

They deposited Phoebe's books at an empty table where she gloried over her bounty, pawing through the titles and choosing the shortest volumes to start with. When she remembered the man, she realized he'd disappeared, and she hadn't even thanked him. *Ah well, the stereotype of rude Americans lives on.* She put him out of her mind as she settled down to learn about the world that might have once contained a man called Robin Hood.

Like most legends, there were almost no facts. Phoebe liked facts. But she enjoyed the most popular tale — Robin of Locksley, a landowner loyal to Richard the Lionheart, became an enemy of Prince John and the local sheriff. His name besmirched, his estate stolen, he turned outlaw as he attempted to regain his name and fight for a more equal society, in the process becoming a one-man wealth redistribution system. *They might as well have called him Red Robin Hood.* Phoebe snickered out loud, engendering a chorus of angry "shhhs."

She read on. Discussions of village life were scattered, and many made it appear idyllic, a busy world of baking bread and brewing ale, of gardens and animals and weaving and dyeing and sewing and all the many tasks allotted to this day and that month. None of the books offered the sort of details Phoebe hungered for. Things like daily strife and conflict, and what sort of fun — and trouble — people got up to when they could. Because they did, they must. People didn't change that much. Whether swathed in tunics, kirtles, and doublets or dresses, jackets, and bucket hats, people were still people.

Phoebe put aside happy peasant life and turned to the plague. There was a pleasing democracy to the disease, as not all the stone houses, fine clothes, and certainty of superiority kept the rich from dying just as readily as the poor. Phoebe was just reading "The swollen tumours turned black and oozed pus, indicating imminent death," when a note dropped on the book: *Coffee? Cake?*

Phoebe blinked, returning from imminent death to the library. She looked up at the bespectacled, long-nosed fellow from the stacks. He grinned. A pleasant grin. Whether it was the peculiar experience of being asked, or the tumors and pus, Phoebe was too jumbled to do anything more than shake her head and plunge back into disease and misery.

An hour later, having at last obtained some useful knowledge of medieval crime and punishment, her thoughts turned to coffee. She followed the example of other patrons and wrote a large note instructing that her things be left in peace. Then she took the book on warfare and made her way to the basement canteen.

The beauty of the library gave her high

hopes for the canteen — squashy chairs and a rich aroma of coffee. Instead, she entered a chilly utilitarian room full of men, all wearing some shade of gray, buried in notes or books or newspapers. Phoebe sighed. She pictured her favorite Midtown diner, flossy, bright, loud. A fat red stool and a white-capped counterman asking her in a good-natured holler, "What'll it be, honey?" She'd sip hot coffee, strong enough to peel paint, and dunk two doughnuts as she listened to men in suits shout about this and that, swelling her full of hot air. Then she'd sail home to write, high for hours on the energy that was only New York.

"Yes, miss?" the barista snapped through her reverie.

"Coffee, please, and do you have any plain doughnuts?"

The barista raised an eyebrow and indicated the trays of refreshments under glass covers. Phoebe wondered how many days they'd been there.

"Try the Madeira cake," came a voice behind her.

She whirled around to face the man from the stacks, smiling crookedly.

"Did you follow me?" she demanded. Her fingers hurt and she saw her hand had curled into a tight fist.

The man didn't notice. "I was thirsty again, a happy coincidence. And I've secured the only empty table, so I hope you'll join me."

He really did look hopeful. His huge brown eyes sparkled under thick black eyebrows. He had a mole on his cheek and could fence with that nose. A detail Phoebe found rather appealing.

"I don't share tables with strangers," Phoebe informed him.

"I should hope not," he said, and laid a hand on his chest. "Reg Bassill. Allow me," he went on, handing a coin to the barista.

"No, thanks, I can manage," Phoebe said with some asperity. He was no aristocrat, nothing like Nigel Elliott, but he had a friendly voice and suaveness, plus that funny smile, which was in danger of disarming her. She couldn't cede an inch.

"All right then," he said easily. "But we are still partial strangers, you know."

She threw back her shoulders. "Phoebe Adler," she announced, watching to see if his expression changed. It didn't, and she decided to share the table. The sooner she sat, the sooner coffee would be over and she'd be back at work.

"So, Miss Adler, what brings you to

London?" Reg asked when they were settled.

"The weather, obviously," Phoebe said with an airy wave of her fork. The Madeira cake wasn't her usual sort of thing, but it wasn't bad.

"Obviously," he agreed. "You're a student, you said?"

"Yes, in the sense of being one who studies the world," she said, throwing out her arms. "By which I mean I'm a writer."

"Oh, terrific," he said, his eyes sparkling more than ever. "Have you written anything I might have read?"

"Only if you've got some questionable reading habits. I wrote for radio and a television show: not a great one, I'm not too proud to admit, but I'm trying —" She stopped before his interested eyes got her to reveal what she was trying. If loose lips sank ships, hers were on the verge of taking down an armada. "I'm working on a novel. Set in the Middle Ages. It's about a woman accused of a crime." Once she'd started, she couldn't stop. "She runs away but she's hunting the evidence that proves she's innocent."

"Cracking stuff," he complimented her. "Though might it be more dramatic if she stays and fights for her innocence? Surely running away indicates guilt?"

"Everyone's a critic," Phoebe said, rolling her eyes.

"Not at all," Reg hastened to assure her. "Only I think evidence would more likely be found on the scene, rather than abroad."

"I don't need help with the plot, thank you," Phoebe snapped, thinking it was a pretty good point and then feeling silly for getting enraged about a pretend project.

"Rotten habit, pax, pax," he said, holding up his hands in mock surrender. "Can't help myself, I'm a history chap."

"What does that mean?"

"It means I'm finishing a postgrad in history and working as a supply teacher, much to my family's chagrin."

"A supply teacher?" Phoebe was mystified. "You teach pens and pencils?"

He laughed. "No, it means I'm called in to teach in local secondary schools when the permanent teacher is off ill or something."

Phoebe drank this all in. It was like a free English lesson.

Reg continued. "What I'd really like is to get into politics. I'm doing some lowly work for the Labour Party now, and I've published a bit in broadsheets, but nothing so glamorous as yourself."

Phoebe didn't ask what a broadsheet was. She didn't want to encourage his talking about politics. In her long experience of Perry Street, once a man got started, he was unlikely to ever stop.

He offered her a cigarette. "So, your wronged woman. I assume she's wellborn?"

"I was actually thinking she was just ordinary," Phoebe said.

"It would be nearly impossible for a woman like that to get anywhere on her own. They wouldn't do it. What you have to understand about the medieval person is that there was no real sense of being an individual. You were bound by duty and community, and everyone had their role and knew what they had to do. An ordinary person wouldn't begin to know how to travel a larger world."

"I said this was a novel, not a history," Phoebe pointed out.

He laughed. "Quite right. But do bear in mind that only someone in a higher class would know how to read, which might prove useful."

"Because there were so many newspapers around?"

"No, but it's a fun way for a woman to confound people. Most didn't expect a woman to be clever, and it's much more fun when she is."

Something in his expression startled her. She'd seen men look at Anne this way, which suggested he was flirting. A light tingle ran through her, and she squashed it. Now was no time to trust strange men, however big and brown their eyes might be. She had work to do.

"Consider it borne in mind, thanks," she said, finishing her coffee. "I'd better get back and get her into more mischief."

She could hear Mona and Anne screaming at her to stay a little longer. She snapped back at them to let her focus on making a living.

"Oh, of course," he said, and she wondered if she saw disappointment flicker across his face. "But if I may, just one more thing. You should take your character through a forest."

"I wasn't planning on her being pursued by a bear."

He grinned. "Medieval legend is full of forests. People believed mythical creatures lived there, but if you could make it through to the other side, you were changed. Of course, that's all for knights, and you likely don't want to include magic, but anyway it's something to think on. Will you be back here on Monday?"

Phoebe was about to say she would be at work before she remembered she wasn't supposed to have a job. That Hannah had taken a risk for her, and until she went back to renew her residency permit and perhaps was granted some leniency, she had to tread carefully.

"That's up to the muse, not me."

"Of course. Well, I hope I see you again, Miss Adler," he said, extending his hand.

She gave it a firm shake. "Likewise, Mr. Bassill."

"Reg," he said. "Reggie occasionally, Reginald when it's official, but I prefer Reg."

"Mr. Bassill," Phoebe said with finality, and went back upstairs.

A forest. And Robin Hood took place in Sherwood Forest. There must be something to do with the idea of everyone believing in the frightening sorts of things that might be in the forest. Fear was a tremendous motivator for doing things, and also not doing things. Phoebe wrote the word "FOREST" in capital letters and circled it. She picked up the general history of kings, but was overcome by a sudden puckishness and instead opened the book on courtly love. Robin Hood and Maid Marian knew every trick in the book. She should learn them too. To write better scripts, obviously.

New patrons were allowed to check out only three books at a time. Phoebe bore hers home with great ceremony, feeling as if she'd ascended to a new rank. A student of history, in the service of her art. The evening sky was cool, with a soft sheen, and the air smelled of the salt and vinegar of early suppers eaten before theater, concerts, rehearsals, dances, cinema, all life's happy temptations. Anticipation, that's what she smelled, and it carried her home in a buzzy glow. She didn't care that she wasn't going out on the town. She was going somewhere better — deep inside her own head on a journey back through time. This script was going to be her best ever. It didn't matter that she said that about every new script she started. It was true.

A few working girls waited at the corner. Phoebe nodded respectfully. Everyone had to eat. As she reached number seven, she encountered Freddie, kicking a ball around with a few other boys.

"I say, miss," he hailed her. "Will you be reading them books?"

"And using them to create terrific adventures," Phoebe promised.

The other boys snorted in skepticism, but Freddie gave her a shy smile.

"Cor," he said respectfully. Phoebe didn't know the word, but the sentiment was clear and they exchanged conspiratorial grins. She made a mental note to herself to help him watch the show if he didn't have a television.

Upstairs, she hurried to her own door, trusting that the hum of big band music wafting from Joan's flat would silence her arrival. She couldn't talk, not when she was so ready to work.

She set down the books and took her knitting bag to the chair, where she conjured Sherwood Forest. Miles of huge trees, green and sweet-smelling. Soft bracken. The hum of insects and animals. There were spots of blue on the forest floor. Water, reflecting sky. But it wouldn't be square shaped.

Phoebe shook her head. There were two blue envelopes by the door. Mail! Joan must have brought it up and Phoebe hadn't even noticed.

She seized the envelopes, squealing on seeing Mona's firm, impatient backhand and Anne's generous handwriting with the loopy flourish. She opened Mona's first.

Well, sister, it's the usual here — nothing but parties and dancing all night. Trust you're the same, you flibbertigibbet, never did do an honest day's work, did you? Nor I neither, aren't we a shame to our name?

I caused quite the ruckus the other day — I organized wheelchair races all through our floor. I may have degenerating muscle function, but I beat everyone except Tommy Morton, who's fourteen. The little twerp just came out of an iron lung too. He says I look like Judy Holliday. I choose to think it's a compliment.

I'm proud of you, P. Do everything for me. If you don't, I'll ask Myrna Alsop to lick the next envelope and she's got syphilis.

Date some dashing Englishman and tell me all the details. Though I'm not sans opportunities. Tommy Morton's offered to take me on a midnight wheeling down the corridor. I could get arrested for corrupting a minor. Worth it just for the headlines.

Love you,
M

(It's 'cause Judy and I have the same nose and dimple. But my hair is prettier.)

231

Phoebe wiped her eyes. For the millionth time, she longed to trade places with Mona, just for a day. Give her sister a wild day of freedom. She'd no doubt create at least three international scandals. (*Darn tooting!* she heard Mona say.)

Anne's letter was a drawing — cartoons of Phoebe's things under her guard. The beloved chair, green Bakelite radio, Victorian glassware. And a tiny cartoon of what must be Anne's latest work, which Phoebe suspected wouldn't be intelligible even full size. On the back, Anne scrawled:

You're the word person, not me. My big news: teaching art one day a week at P.S. 3. Living end, huh? Village humming along, but a few more people spooked by the witch-hunting. So heigh-ho, you started a fad! Miss, love, hugs.

Well, of course. The Village was full of artists, writers, teachers, leftist activists, and homosexuals. Everything the Red hunters in Congress despised and feared. Anne as a teacher was a little astonishing, but good for her.

Phoebe noticed Anne hadn't mentioned Jimmy.

She stored the letters in the back of her

notebook. Monday she would buy some sticking gum so she could paste Anne's cartoons to the wall.

I'll have my treasures back again someday. I'll get everything back. We all will.

She worked all day Sunday. She read the new week's script twice during lunch on Monday, worked as late as she dared that night, then spent the rest of the week's lunches scribbling notes. The Other Girls overflowed with witticisms regarding people who must be taking correspondence courses, thought themselves clever, were writing fan letters to "them in Hollywood." Even Tommy caustically remarked that she had better not be using any of the show's paper or pencils to do whatever she was up to. Phoebe was just relieved no one would cross the line and peep in her bag to read her notebook. If they actually knew what she was up to, the taunts would become torments, and she'd be lucky to last on the job another week.

And she needed this job. Because even after another weekend spent writing and rewriting, she had to admit the script wasn't up to her standards. It was about a peasant found murdered and the outlaws accused of the crime.

She reread it Sunday night by the watchful gaze of Mona's photos and Anne's drawings, all tacked to the wall in pride of place, and sighed. It was just another detective story, with bows and arrows instead of revolvers.

"It's no good," she told the photos. "It's certainly not good enough, so it might as well be a trash barge floating out to Fresh Kills." A fresh kill was how she felt. Her great chance, and she was blowing it. She twisted up the pages and tossed them into the fire grate. To hell with it, she decided. She'd hatch another plot tomorrow. It didn't matter if Hannah was expecting something soon or not. It was better to wait and give her something excellent.

"Maybe I should try a love story," she suggested to Mona. "No one else seems to have done that and it works coming from a woman, especially if Hannah's going to send the script around."

Don't be ridiculous, Mona's reply snapped. *You have to write something you have at least* some *understanding of.*

Phoebe sighed and opened one of her library books to a chapter on medieval crime and punishment.

CHAPTER TEN

Rhoda stood in front of the television, waving a bottle and spoon.

" 'Are you tired, run-down, listless? Do you pop out at parties? Are you unpoopular?' " She stopped herself with a fit of giggles.

"What the heck is that child doing?" Paul asked, baffled.

Hannah and Gemma were wiping their eyes from laughter.

"It's from *I Love Lucy,*" Hannah explained. "ITV is airing it, so the British get to meet Lucy at last."

"Boy, they really are showing the best of American culture, huh?" Paul asked.

Gemma turned from Paul so he couldn't see her roll her eyes and picked up Julie, playing on the floor with an eggbeater. "Teatime for the cherubs," she announced. "Meat and vegetables, as is fitting for the Lucy advertisement."

"And pudding?" Rhoda wanted to know.

"Jamaican sweet potato pudding if you clean your plate," Gemma promised.

Rhoda shot into the kitchen, still carrying her bottle and spoon.

Paul shook his head and opened the latest delivery of the *New York Times*. Hannah lit a cigarette. It bothered her a bit, that Lucy Ricardo wanted to work and Ricky was determined to keep her home. But Lucy was funny, there was no denying it. Clever of ITV to pick up the show and start drawing eyes to their channel. She liked them. She was glad they were the ones who would air *Robin Hood.* Three more episodes were finished. She didn't risk saying so out loud, but she knew the show was good. Better than good. She curled up next to Paul and read along with him.

Monday afternoon, Beryl took a call and ran shrieking into Hannah's office.

"Miss Wolfson, Miss Wolfson! Oi, Sidney, get along, yon fellow from CBS is ringing through!"

"Keep the heid, keep the heid!" Sidney shouted, running into Hannah's office. He and Beryl folded their hands under their chins and watched, hardly breathing, as Hannah picked up the phone. She wasn't sure what "keep the heid" meant, but could take an educated guess. Her head was light and buzzy, but her voice perfectly calm.

"Miss Wolfson?" a secretary inquired. "I have Dale Winston, head of programming for CBS, long-distance."

"Miss Wolfson!" Dale boomed in a heavy Midwestern twang. Hannah tipped the phone away from her ear. "Listen, I just watched one and I don't need to see the rest, I know a winner when I see it. Boys will go nuts for this show."

"I'm hoping everyone will like it," Hannah said stoutly.

"Sure, sure," he said with a ringing laugh. "It's got 'huge hit' written all over it. We've moved some stuff so we can start it in a couple weeks — end of September. Lemme tell you, honey, that *never* happens." He sounded almost scolding. "The papers are already in the mail. Express, we're not kidding around."

Hannah was smiling too hard to speak. She felt tears coming on. It almost didn't matter what the terms of the deal were. *Robin Hood* would be on CBS, perhaps within days of its debut on ITV.

"This McClellan writer of yours," Dale began, and Hannah's smile tensed. McClellan was Ring Lardner Jr. "He's something, all right. Looks like he hasn't done much of anything before this. Is he some bright kid or something?"

"Keep the heid" indeed.

"Lots of bright hungry writers around," Hannah said airily. "He's done some theater and radio, really it was just a lucky —"

"Sure, sure, sure," Dale said. Hannah visualized him waving away theater and radio with a meaty hand. "Love to meet him if I get over there."

"I'm sure he'd be honored to meet you," Hannah said, casting a wild glance at Sidney, whose eyes went round. Beryl whispered, "Jings!" Sidney gestured at his watch and a production schedule. "We will certainly discuss this further," Hannah went on in a firm voice, "after the paperwork is finished. I'm afraid I'm meant to be heading up a production meeting now, but let's arrange —"

"Sure, sure, sure," he said again, chuckling. "Let's get the ball rolling. Seriously, honey, congratulations. It's gonna be huge. Believe me, I'm an expert."

"I believe you," Hannah said.

She hung up. Sidney and Beryl stared, looking like they were holding their breaths. Suddenly, Hannah whooped and upended her tin of Fortnum & Mason biscuits onto the desk for them all to devour. "Open the bottle of whatever's the best we've got!" she shouted. "Robin Hood is going to storm the beaches of America!"

As the day of the first broadcast grew closer, Hannah planned a home viewing party. Sidney, Beryl, any guests they wished to bring. Shirley and Will. She would like to invite Joan but didn't want Charlie.

"What about Olivia and Ben?" Paul suggested. "I like Ben, he's got a head on him, and not a big one like those other movie writers here."

"You just like looking at Olivia," Hannah teased. Instead, she invited the *Robin Hood* stars Richard Greene and Bernadette O'Farrell. She expected they would already have plans, but it was right to invite them.

"Oh swell, actors," was Paul's response when he heard this. "Just what we need to expose the kids to."

"Dear, you're talking about the children of a writer," Hannah said, laughing.

"What's that supposed to mean?" Paul demanded, no longer amused.

"It's a joke. For heaven's sake, you'd think you were the one who was about to have a debut."

"I'll be glad when it's over," Paul said. He

grinned in apology. "However it goes, at least you won't be bouncing around on your toes like a nervous cat."

Hannah looked down. She hadn't even realized she was barefoot and, indeed, on her toes.

"Jings," she said, giggling. "I'm starting to walk like Sidney. He bounces on his toes when he's excited," she explained.

"I'm sure he does," Paul said flatly. "What the heck does 'jings' mean anyway?"

"I don't know the etymology," Hannah said. "But I've come to like it."

What with the news of the American distribution deal and the upcoming premiere, the *Robin Hood* set blazed with excitement and chatter. When people started talking quickly, Phoebe still couldn't understand one word in ten, but she could tell people were organizing viewing parties. Everyone, it seemed, was going to one. Except her.

"Miss Wolfson's invited all the most important people," Dora told the rest of the Other Girls. Her voice rose when she was sure Phoebe could hear. "And some Americans, too, apparently."

Phoebe had to hand it to her. Whether or not her information was correct, she certainly knew how to time a line. And make it stick. Dora was right — Phoebe might have distracted herself wondering if all the exiles were invited to the party and she wasn't. She might have, except that she had something else to occupy her.

She was, for the first time in her life, suffering writer's block. Several drafts of a *Robin Hood* script later, and she had made little progress. It didn't help that all the scripts she'd read so far were not just excellent, they were little works of art. Hannah must have all the best blacklisted writers throughout America at her disposal. Phoebe believed in her own ability, but she couldn't help feeling she wasn't at this level, and that anything she handed in would be disappointing. There was suddenly nothing Phoebe wanted more than to impress Hannah. She felt certain that to accomplish that would open up a whole new world — one that would catapult her far beyond the world she knew with Hank.

If she could impress Hannah.

The phantom Mona and Anne were stubbornly silent on the topic. She still couldn't bring herself to confide in Joan. She had to solve the problem on her own. Under normal circumstances, she shook away cobwebs by walking up and down each New York street where she hoped to someday afford to live. There was nothing she wanted to own in what she saw on a Sunday stroll through London. And for all of Soho's grit and rebelliousness, it was nothing like Greenwich Village, where a quiet Sunday could still yield a coffee at Floyd and Leo's, a pizza, or chow mein. Some poky theater would be sure to have a performance. On a bright day, you could always troop over to Washington Square Park, where musicians were jamming and a few old men were willing to wipe the floor with you at chess.

Though Phoebe poked and prodded, she found nothing open on Sundays, in Soho or anywhere nearby. Some pubs did Sunday lunches, and she supposed there must be restaurants catering to tourists or the wealthy and entitled, but none of this interested her. Newspapers insisted Britain was on the rise again, that there would soon be no signs of bomb damage, that in fact life had never been better, but Phoebe, though grateful to feel free, couldn't shake the feeling that London was a city whose greatness was gone, and that she'd left the glittering future to enter a weary past.

Well, that's the attitude that's going to take you far, Mona scolded.

With help like that, Phoebe almost preferred the phantom stay silent.

■ ■ ■ ■

"I'm not so sure about this party," Paul teased as Hannah and Gemma prepared nibbles. "Everything's closed on Sunday nights. They'll stay till dawn."

"I can think of worse ways to mark the debut of the first TV show where I'm the sole executive producer," Hannah said. "Here, what do you think?" She popped a deviled egg into his mouth.

"More pepper," he said. "We should have said I'm the host tonight, so I look like a properly supportive husband."

"You *are* one, no one would think otherwise," Hannah said, reaching up to kiss his nose. "We support each other beautifully."

"We do," he agreed. "And listen, the timing isn't super, but my story needs your eagle eye. I'd like to get it in the mail tomorrow — can only hope the editor receives it by next week. God, I miss couriers. I hate to end the party early, but —"

"But of course!" Hannah cried, giving him a squeeze. "I'll clear the house by eight and bring out my biggest red pencil."

"You really don't mind, sweetheart?" He looked worried.

"Of course not, this is what we do, what

we've always done," she said.

He laughed and kissed her neck. "You're my best girl."

As soon as Paul's office door clicked shut, Gemma turned to Hannah.

"Mighty shame to end a party early," she said. "Have I not gone and made my special coconut drops?"

"It's Sunday," Hannah said. "Even subversives go to bed early on Sundays."

"Monday morn good enough to start changing the world again," Gemma murmured as she bore a tray of deviled eggs into the living room. Hannah stopped ladling cream cheese into celery and lit a cigarette. She didn't really want to end the party early.

In the living room, Gemma stacked the reviews Hannah had spent the morning poring over. Hannah took them up again and reveled in each one. "A remarkable entertainment." "Witty, adventurous, and great fun." "Sure to please the kiddies, and with intelligence enough to delight adults as well." On and on. Everyone knew good reviews didn't guarantee a hit; only actual audience response would tell her anything. But good reviews could pull a large audience. They were looking for numbers, the money people. If the show got them, it would go on. If it didn't . . .

"Mama, Mama, Mama, does it start soon?" Rhoda shouted, hurtling up to Hannah. She was wearing her pirate costume, the closest thing she had to looking like Robin Hood. "Can I have a pie and cheese?" Rhoda went on. "Can I open the door when they arrive?"

"You *may* open the door," Hannah granted. "As for snacks, you know the rules. Guests first."

Julie toddled in, helped by Gemma. "Eggy!" she hollered, pointing at the tower of deviled eggs.

"Guests first!" Rhoda shouted at her. "That's the rule, didn't you know?"

In the midst of this fracas, Shirley and Will LeGrand arrived. Shirley gave Hannah an enormous bouquet of cowslips. "Natives of Nottingham, like your hero," Shirley explained. Her smile was strained. Before Hannah could ask if she was all right, Will read Hannah's expression.

"The NAACP is purging suspected Communists from its rolls," he said.

"Oh strife," Shirley said. "We needn't discuss it here and now."

"We are living and working here and now because our own country won't allow us freedom of thought," Will said. "If we forget that, we are in danger of accepting it."

"Not a chance," Hannah said. "Not when Dashiell Hammett's in prison but Elia Kazan gets to keep directing movies." The name Elia Kazan always elicited a hiss from the exiles. Once a firebrand and member of the Group Theatre, he then readily named names before HUAC and was now going from strength to strength. And Hammett! The novelist behind the smash-hit Thin Man series was sent to prison for contempt because he refused to answer questions about the Civil Rights Congress, of which he was president. HUAC believed putting more famous people in prison served as a warning to anyone who thought they should be able to hold whatever views they wanted in a country that was supposed to be free.

Into this gloom burst Sidney, rubbing his hands and bouncing on his toes.

"I cannae stop reading the reviews! Brilliant, aren't they? Who knew the boys in the papers had such good taste? 'Tis as I say, give them quality and they'll appreciate it."

"Funny, I've never heard you say that," Hannah said good-naturedly, kissing his cheek. Rhoda pelted into the foyer and begged to hang up coats. Paul followed, laughing, and the others laughed too. Things might be bad in America, but this was, after all, a party.

Paul hefted Rhoda to the coatrack so she could hang things properly. She squealed with each lift, and Hannah watched fondly. Paul was always so busy with work, he rarely focused on his children. Hannah understood — his own upbringing was mostly by nannies, after all. But the thought stayed at the back of her mind as she greeted Beryl, Peter Proud, and Terry Bishop. Paul certainly adored the girls as much as she did, but she needed to find a way to free up more of his time so he could show it more. He was missing out on something special.

"Places, people!" Sidney cried, and Hannah's heart lurched. It was time. Paul turned on the television as Hannah gathered Julie into her lap and settled Rhoda next to her.

The *twannnnngggg!* of the loosed arrow that heralded the beginning and brought up the opening title was louder than she remembered from the screening room. She felt the little shiver of pleasure that went through the group.

As the show unfolded, she found herself looking not at the screen but at Rhoda. They'd had several long talks about how she was to sit quietly without interruptions, and remember questions for when the show was over, but as bright as Rhoda was, she was also still a child and, as Paul rightly said, a bit too young for *Robin Hood*. Yet she sat, utterly enraptured by the talk of intrigue and violence, and then actual swordplay. She emitted one small "oh!" of sorrow when a deer was killed, but clenched her hands together under her chin at the explanation that it was killed to feed starving children. Nothing either Gemma or Hannah had ever told her about starving children — and thus the importance of eating what was set before her — had ever stirred such emotion. Even the language Hannah was sure must be well beyond Rhoda, the talk of stealing a man's land when he was assumed dead, turned the little face red with indignation. A sneaky attempt by the sheriff to kill Robin made Rhoda's fists ball up in hot fury. Somehow, she seemed to understand that the outlaws were the ones who had been stolen from, and those who had done the stealing were the ones administering "justice," and this landed her firmly on the side of the outlaws. Robin's skill with a bow and arrow made her mouth drop open in pure, admiring awe. Then, as the episode ended and the credits rolled, there under the cast list read: "Executive Producer Hannah Wolfson." At this, Rhoda could not remain silent.

"That's you, Mama, that's you!" she cried, bouncing up and down.

And it was. Hannah hadn't realized Rhoda could read her name, but she did, and brimmed with ecstasy at the sight. All the hard work was worth it, just for that. She caught Paul's eye across the top of Rhoda's head. He gave her his special slow smile. Her heart leapt the way it had when they were first courting and he would look at her with warm desire, and take her hand. And the dancing, goodness the dancing. Neither of them could jitterbug, but oh, could they fox-trot. She'd called him a sly fox, and he'd called her a little vixen. How had she forgotten that? The dancing stopped after marriage. Work, political travails, escaping abroad, Rhoda and Julie. There was no space left for dancing.

Sidney pressed a glass of champagne into her hand. "Good work, Madam Executive Producer," he congratulated her.

"I couldn't have done it without you, Mr. Associate Producer," she said, clinking glasses. Then she turned to the group. "Thank you all so much for coming to share this moment with us tonight. I can't tell you what it means to me, truly."

There was a lot of talk then, brushing

aside her emotion, flooding her with congratulations. She had, it was agreed, created
something truly innovative.

"And yet it's one of the oldest stories we
know," Hannah said, laughing.

"Everything old is *nouveau* again," Shirley
said. "And in this case, better than ever."

Gemma reached for Julie. "Long past
bedtime for the babies," she observed.
Rhoda was sleepy enough to not fuss about
being called a baby and to accept a good-
night kiss. Suddenly she was wide-awake
and seized Hannah's hands.

"Mama!" she said, her voice heavy with
urgency. "I need a bow and arrows."

Everyone laughed except Paul. "Rhoda,
those aren't toys." He frowned.

"Oh, but they will be," Hannah said. "I've
already got the plans in place."

"Aye, that she has," said Sidney. "There
won't be a bairn in Britain not seeking to
be an archer."

Shirley snorted.

"This is how we know you're not Communists. You wouldn't be so set on taking
advantage of base commercial capitalism."

"The more money I earn, the more I can
share," Hannah said, laughing. "And the
better television I can make. And anyway,
money never hurts."

"No," Shirley said agreeably. "It really never does."

When the guests were gone and the plates stacked in the kitchen, Hannah climbed out of her good heels and collapsed next to Paul, wriggling her toes. She thought of Ring Lardner Jr., whose excellent script had so stirred her child, and wondered what it must be like to write something so good and not be able to put your own name on it.

Paul stroked her hair. "I might not think much of television, but this seems to be a very good show. I'm impressed, dear."

"Thank you, my darling!" she cried, and kissed him hard. A surge flew through her, like she could leap from roof to roof throughout London. "Do you know what we should do? We should go out dancing."

"It's Sunday," he said. "Can't you hear the tumbleweeds rolling by?"

"I bet there's somewhere, maybe in Soho," she persisted. "There's always somewhere. Let's chase adventure! What a story that would be."

"I've already got a story going, remember?" he said pointedly.

She'd forgotten her promise to read his story that night. Her guilt compounded as she realized it was the last thing she felt like doing. Her toes curled, eager to leap and twirl.

"Of course, darling, I'm longing to read your latest bit of genius," she said. "But first, let's put on a record and have a quick dance. Just one."

"Another time, all right?" He kissed her forehead. "I've got an early start tomorrow. I'll bring in the pages and head to bed. Thanks again, my girl."

She settled down with his work and a red pencil. She forced herself to read, but couldn't focus. All the words seemed to be in the wrong order. With a sigh, she poured another drink and leaned back, looking up at the ceiling. She was suddenly aware of the quiet, of her own solitude. There was something exhilarating about being the only one awake in a house. As though the night might last forever, spilling out in a sea of possibilities. She flipped through the records and put "In the Mood" on low to dance herself around the room.

"Well, look at you, my lady," she whispered. "You might be well past girlhood, with two babies to prove it, but you still dance like a little vixen."

As she whirled around, she thought they should add an episode of *Robin Hood* featuring one of the wives left behind to struggle on when a husband becomes an outlaw. Perhaps he sneaks home, and they look at each other, strangers now, she with resentment, he with guilt. But they remember something, the something that was between them when they first met. A village fete, a feast day, some sort of thing. Maid Marian would be the one to help them reconcile, though only briefly, because of course he must run off again soon or be killed by the sheriff. There might seem something romantic about being an outlaw, accused of a crime you didn't commit, but whatever it did for romance, it didn't do much for love.

The next afternoon, ITV sent her a gift basket the size of Rhoda. The numbers were stratospheric. The show was a smash hit. ITV was already keen to discuss a second thirty-two episode season. *I'm a hit!* Hannah thought. *A palpable hit!* She hugged herself. A classic New York "pinko" was poking her fingers in HUAC's eyes, and they had no idea.

"It's overwhelming, is what it is!" Beryl grumbled. Writers' agents were sending dozens of inquiries a day, offering their clients for consideration for a *Robin Hood* script, or another upcoming Sapphire project. "They seem to think we'll take just anyone." She cocked a brow. It was a joke no one could laugh at — according to the *Robin Hood* credits, Sapphire *did* take anyone, whether they had a credit or not, so long as they had talent.

Sidney was in his element. Hannah worried he might topple over from dancing on his toes so much. Everyone with any money was longing to do a deal with Sapphire. As soon as they had another show developed, they could run wild. "One company against the world!" Hannah cried, kicking off her shoes so she could concentrate. She had a new script to read. Not, she noted, from Phoebe. She was surprised. Even more surprising was that she was disappointed. Phoebe seemed to have a voice. Hannah couldn't help being curious to read her take on *Robin Hood.* Then again, maybe she wasn't surprised. Phoebe had likely realized that her voice wasn't right for the show. Not that Hannah had planned on using her anyway, but she *had* thought the younger woman would at least give it a good effort.

Oh well, there was plenty else to do. She tuned the radio, briefly getting the BBC announcing, "And in Washington, actor Zero Mostel is due to testify before the House Un-American Activities Committee . . ." Hannah flipped the dial until her irritation was soothed by Chuck Berry singing "May-bellene."

"Fellow's come calling," Beryl inter-rupted, scowling. "Says he's Frank Lang-ham."

"And is he?" Hannah asked, hairs on her arms rising.

"How can anyone prove anything?" Beryl asked, throwing up her hands.

Hannah went with Beryl down to the main door and peeked. It had been years, but she knew the face of the tall, lanky American. A bit more grizzled than she remembered, and the shock of salt-and-pepper hair was more salty, but it was him.

"Langham!" she cried, admitting him.

Frank Langham was one of the innovative firebrand directors in the Group Theatre in the 1930s. Hannah, as a radical, theater-loving young journalist, often mixed with the Group crowd. Success had taken Frank to Hollywood and the less firebrand but much more lucrative work as a midlevel film director. They'd lost touch, but Frank was unforgettable. Hannah grinned until she felt guilty, remembering one night at Bertolt Brecht's house, long before she met Paul, when she and Frank experimented first with reefer, then each other. The details were hazy, but Frank and his grin weren't.

"Tallyho, here I am in Blighty," he said in a two-pack-a-day rasp. "You'd think the Group would have gotten me here sooner. Kazan left me off his list, that old hangdog, but someone sang somewhere, and so hello, old pal."

Hannah smiled — Frank still talked like a Damon Runyon character — but the smile was sad, because of course he was black-listed. Elia Kazan, that turncoat of the Group, might have spared him, but Hoover's FBI and HUAC were damned if they'd let anyone once so radical get out alive.

"Well, what the heck was I doing with a six-bedroom house anyhow?" Frank demanded. "The old lady and I only have three kiddies. And a pool, cripes, remember when the pool was just chasing craps games? The French were warmer than that damn pool ever was, let me in to direct two films, how about that? But I was missing the sound of English. Or what passes for it here."

Gradually, he admitted that his wife, lonely and embarrassed by exile and worried for their children's future, had divorced him and returned to California. None of his easy jokes could hide that he was obviously in between jobs, and desperate.

Hannah's smile never cooled, but she was

annoyed at herself for being surprised and disappointed that this was why Frank was here. Of course he was calling on their old friendship in the hopes of a bone she could throw. Film directors thought television was a step down, but work was work, and anyway, *Robin Hood* was shot like a film itself, one of the reasons it looked so terrific on the small screen.

Frank was an excellent director. The crew might not love an American script supervisor, but a director with an Oscar nomination under his belt would be something else again. Likely they all harbored dreams of Hollywood, however much devotion they professed to the British industry. Just as likely, they wouldn't know, or care, that he was blacklisted. If they did, they certainly wouldn't try to jeopardize their plum jobs. But still. The writers were secret. This, this was visible, and memorable. This could be asking for trouble.

"Listen, don't worry," Frank assured her. "I've got a line on a film, if they can get the funding. I was just itching to keep my chops oiled."

"Of course," she said courteously. "Next year will probably be easier for us, hiring an American director." She knew she was right. But this was old Langham, with frays on his cuffs and patches on his jacket. "Then again, we've got an episode that's going to demand a lot of tight shots in dark places, and your noir expertise might be just the ticket."

She didn't imagine the hope that lit up his face, reminding her of the shiny young man he'd once been.

"Hannah, you're an A1 doll, and that's the truth."

She hoped Sidney and the others would agree. But "share and share alike," after all, and she wasn't having anyone suggest she'd become someone who wouldn't help out a friend.

"He will be good," Sidney agreed when he heard, rubbing his head. "Crikey, fancy an Oscar nominee willing to work for a television salary."

"Ah well," Hannah said. "If I have my way, a television salary will soon be nothing to sneeze at."

"And you always get your way," Sidney said, admiringly. "He'll have a pseudonym for a credit, of course, and if anyone on set even knows about his status, they won't think much of it. Not enough to question you, anyway. But maybe we only use him just this once."

"That's what I thought too," Hannah

agreed. "Just once. That can't possibly hurt anything."

CHAPTER ELEVEN

Neither reading the scripts nor watching the episodes being filmed prepared Phoebe for the effect of viewing *Robin Hood* on a television screen. She was relieved that Joan's son Alvie sat an inch from the screen and thought nothing of the adults behind him so he couldn't see her open mouth.

"Gosh!" he cried as the credits rolled. "Ain't that something?"

Charlie was too busy writing to watch the show, but Joan and Phoebe agreed with the young boy. It was something.

"Maybe next week you can have Freddie up to watch too?" Phoebe suggested.

"Maybe," Joan said evasively. Alvie, no longer interested now that adults were talking, disappeared into his bedroom. Phoebe knew he sometimes played with Freddie but was still obedient enough to his parents' interests to keep the boy from becoming a friend. A funny way of classing people from supposed leftists. Phoebe resolved to push the issue later in the week. Freddie ought to see the show. In the meantime, she got to the set early each day that week to paw through the trades in the publicity office, thrilling to the numbers. She was so excited, she even ventured to speak of it to the Other Girls.

"Get a load of these audiences, huh?" she said. "Heck, I know shows in New York that would have thrown a daylong party for just a tenth of those numbers."

"Didn't you just," Dora said wryly. "Very nice, I'm sure, but here we've got work to carry on with," Dora said with a sniff, leading the Other Girls away. It was just as well. In her exuberance, Phoebe might have forgotten herself enough to mention that she'd written for the show that would have thrown the party.

Her pride in being a small part of this production made writing a script even harder. What could she write that would capture the affection of a brat like Alvie? Or, better, an openhearted kid like Freddie?

I don't know what it is, she wrote to Mona. *It can't be that a person needs to be a fellow to write this sort of thing. It's just that something's missing.*

Phoebe sighed and looked out her window

at the endless peaks of sooty Victorian roofs. She knew exactly what was missing. Her fingers traced the photos of Mona and Anne. She thought of Perry Street, of Floyd and Leo, of all the people she might have said hello to on their various ways here and there. And she'd never gotten to say good-bye. She wondered if any of them ever asked about her. Anne wouldn't say. Probably just as well. It was dangerous to ask, and more so to tell.

As badly as she wanted to go home, she had to stay here. She'd ducked a subpoena. A real crime, more easily punishable than the accusation of Communism. She needed the refuge England offered, and had to hope that offer would be extended. It was time to renew her residency permit.

In her little box of important papers was the elegant card given to her by Nigel Elliot, the aristocrat — she presumed — whose life she had saved on the ship. It was tempting to contact him, to ask his good advice again. She sighed and put aside the card. Men like that didn't want to be asked too many favors. Better to save him for when she had something to exchange — news of real success, which he would enjoy. Or if she was desperate. That too.

■ ■ ■ ■

"You'll be fine," Joan encouraged her. "Just don't tell them the truth."

Phoebe grumbled over these instructions as she followed Joan's usual meticulous directions to the tiny office squirreled away in a large building in Whitehall. Here was where she would tell more lies, all to buy more time in safety. As she opened the door, a young woman in a wooden chair burst into tears. A man embraced her, gazing imploringly up at another man in a uniform.

"We have been here a year. We have work, we are Jamaican, that is part of Britain, all is in order."

"You did not declare a criminal record," the official said in a cool voice.

"I am no criminal!" the woman wailed. "It was a lie! My missus here swears by me, only read this letter, please!"

"*You* may stay," the official said to the man. "But your wife must be deported, pending investigation."

"This is not acceptable!" the man cried.

"I must ask you to remain orderly," the official said. "You may seek counsel."

Phoebe tore her eyes from the miserable couple to see a pert young woman with ferocious red curls behind the desk, eyeing her unsmilingly.

"I'm here to renew my residency, please," Phoebe stammered. She was aware of the couple leaving and couldn't bear turning around to see if they were under escort.

"Passport," the redhead said, extending her hand.

I should have looked. I should have given them one look of real sympathy. Let them know there was a friend in this cold room. Is this how it happens, then? One mistake, or someone's lie, and off you go?

She surrendered her little green passport with a trembling hand. ("The American embassy really puts the screws in the Brits, trying to get them not to give us residency," Joan had chirped over coffee. "Shirley and Will got a letter from the embassy, asking them to send in their passports for 'checking.' They didn't, of course, but you do wonder.") Phoebe stood there, wondering. Could the embassy have instructed the British to seize her passport? Would the British comply? And then what would happen? The redhead bore her passport away, leaving Phoebe to stand and sweat. Her toes ached. It had been a while since she'd worn her good heels.

The redhead returned, her face still

closed. She came near enough to the desk that Phoebe could read her discreet name badge: Miss C. Smith.

"What does the *C* stand for?" Phoebe asked, wanting to pretend friendliness. It must be harder, surely, to hurt someone you felt vague kinship with? Then again, she remembered Jimmy's face after he'd followed her and Anne to the docks. Nothing she'd ever done for him mattered. Who had promised him what, if he could stop her?

The redhead kept her fingers on Phoebe's passport. Phoebe felt the sharp eyes assessing her, noting the suit, hat, watch, pearls lent by Joan.

"Cassie," the redhead said, after some deliberation. A nickname. Phoebe had passed one test.

"Reason for extending your stay?" Cassie asked.

"I'm writing a novel," Phoebe announced. "A real corker" — since when did she use that word? — "about a woman in medieval England. Being here is great for research and atmosphere, you see."

She knew she didn't imagine the flicker of interest in Cassie's eyes.

"And how far along are you?"

"I've barely scratched the surface, I'd think."

"And you have funds enough to live on?"

"I do," Phoebe answered stoutly.

Cassie nodded and stamped Phoebe's passport. Six months.

"Gosh, really?" Phoebe yelped.

Cassie rolled her eyes up to Phoebe.

"You expected something different?"

Phoebe could have kicked herself. Why, why did she have to lose control of her mouth now? Six months was such a gift, compared to seven weeks. Though a year would have been better. Or five. Time she hoped she didn't need, but would be grateful for, just in case. She didn't want to end up like that couple. As much as she wanted to go home, she didn't want to go like that.

"No, no, that's great, thanks," Phoebe said. Her reward came as Cassie slid the passport back to her. She tucked it in her bag, keeping her fingers on it. "Thank you, Miss Smith," she said in a tone she hoped combined British formality and American friendliness. "Good afternoon." She was out before there was any hope of a mind being changed.

Six months. A lot could happen in six months. Eisenhower could insist the persecutions by HUAC be suspended. Hollywood could decide the maintenance of the blacklist was too much trouble. The ACLU could

266

start pushing back at last. J. Edgar Hoover and the whole of HUAC could have a pool party that was struck by lightning. One just never knew.

Her feet skipped of their own accord as she swung herself onto the bus.

Freddie was outside with his group of cohorts.

"I see you more often than your mother," Phoebe greeted him. "I'm starting to wonder if you're the one who really runs this show."

His face flushed with pleasure, and Phoebe was rather touched. She reached into her purse and pulled out the first coin she laid hands on — a sixpence.

"Here," she said, handing it to the overwhelmed Freddie. "For doing such good work. Have a chocolate or something."

Freddie was promptly surrounded by his pals, all offering their considered opinions on what he should buy, and any thanks were lost in the scrum. Phoebe chuckled as she went upstairs to see Joan.

"Sixpence, really?" Joan scolded. Of course she'd seen the exchange — the woman was the Mata Hari of Meard Street. "A penny would have been enough to transport that poor child."

"So six puts him in seventh heaven," Phoebe said with a shrug. "Anyway, it's a celebration. Residency renewed for six months."

"Golly!" Joan was impressed. "Last time I only got thirty days."

She laughed at Phoebe's stunned face, and silenced questions with envelopes. Mail! She couldn't wait to dive into Mona's words and Anne's drawings.

"Open that one!" Joan cried, pointing to an envelope that only bore her name, Miss Phoebe Adler, in a disciplined handwriting she didn't recognize.

Dear Miss Adler,

It has been my grave misfortune not to meet you again at the library, and hear more about your novel, or indeed learn anything further about you. Maybe we can arrange a meeting somewhere else? If you're amenable, I do hope I hear from you.

Reg Bassill

An address was at the bottom, but Phoebe was too shaken to read it.

The man from the library. He had followed her! Was he a spy? Or worse? Every crime story she'd ever read scrolled through her brain. There was this sort of man, the quiet, unassuming type, attractive without being so handsome as to be suspicious, who lured his victims slowly, with a gentle sweetness. He enjoyed the surprise in their eyes when he finally revealed his true intentions. Phoebe burned with rage. So this Reg thought she, a friendless, rudderless American, was an easy target, did he? Well, he'd have to try a lot harder to catch Phoebe Adler unawares.

"He was so charming," Joan said, unable to contain herself. "You have to admit, the English have a way about them. So well-spoken."

So he had charmed Joan, had he? Enough to convince her to pass on this note. Well, didn't he think he was smart.

"He can have his way somewhere else," Phoebe said. "The only man in my life right now is Robin Hood, and he's already more than I can handle."

She ignored Joan's disappointment. If it was romance Joan wanted to experience, there was no shortage of it in the afternoon radio plays.

"What a hit we are in America!" Hannah marveled, drinking in the numbers. "And these reviews. 'A real asset to the airwaves.'

'One of the first truly great new entertainments of the television age geared toward kids.' "

" 'Tis still impressive even after a fourth read," Sidney agreed, grinning.

Hannah grinned too. She knew she was carrying on to excess, but she couldn't help it and didn't want to. To Sidney, being a hit in America was gratifying, and meant more money. To Hannah, it meant she had done all she'd aimed to do and more. She'd made a mark, landing a solid hit to the jaw of everyone who ever tried to stop her, especially the madmen who had hounded so many out of their work, reputations, and country. Those men would never guess a costume adventure beloved by kids would defy them, tell them how wrong, wicked, cowardly they were. Smack them back for every time they demanded, "Are you now or have you ever been a member of the Communist Party?"

The phone rang — Beryl announced it was Shirley.

"Hannah, thank goodness!" Hannah hardly recognized the voice of Shirley LeGrand, usually so deep and measured. Now she spoke in a squeak. "Hedda Hopper's here, in London. Officially, she's just doing a publicity tour, but it's whispered she's got information, she's looking for blacklistees on sets! Hannah, she may be heading straight for *Robin Hood*! And Langham's directing this week. Strife!"

Hannah's heart chilled. Hedda Hopper. The crisp little voice on the radio, the poison pen in the papers, was here, as she promised, hunting "Runaway Reds." And no doubt getting an expenses-paid holiday. Someone had given her information. Someone had betrayed them.

Shirley continued, her voice higher and tighter. "You've got to get Langham off that set, now!"

Hannah hung up and dialed the publicity office at the studio. Hedda Hopper, who gleefully ruined the careers of anyone she hated, heading for *Robin Hood.* It certainly would make a terrific story, this shiny new success, aimed straight at kids, made by blacklistees. Hedda Hopper wouldn't be able to uncover the real names of the writers, but she knew Frank Langham on sight. Reporting him as a director on *Robin Hood,* even for one episode, could be lethal.

"Publicity, Miss Brown!" a chirpy voice answered the phone.

"Hello . . ." Hannah glanced at the staff roster. "Pamela dear, this is Miss Wolfson."

She could almost hear the girl's spine

straighten.

"Yes, Miss Wolfson, how can I help?" she asked reverentially.

"Is Miss Smithson there, or soon back?" Ena Smithson was the senior publicist, with a long career in theater. This girl, fresh out of school, was her assistant. "Sharp as a tack and eager to learn," Ena had told Hannah.

"No, I'm sorry," Pamela said. "She's out all day meeting with the people from ITV and the toymakers, arranging for the debut of the merchandise."

"Yes, of course," Hannah said. "Okay, listen carefully, dear, this is urgent. A woman called Hedda Hopper may wish to visit the set —"

"Not really? *The* Hedda Hopper?" Hannah had never laid eyes on Pamela but pictured a sudden blonde who carried three movie magazines on her person at all times. "How simply marvelous!"

"No, dear, it's very important that Miss Hopper *not* be allowed on the set — you'll be polite of course but explain the set is closed to guests, do you understand?"

"But why?" Pamela protested. "Adults are watching the show too. A story about the show like this could double their viewership."

Give the magazines some credit — they'd

taught Pamela something.

"Just do as I say, Pamela dear," Hannah ordered. She knew that most British women this age responded reflexively to the tones and words that brought them straight back under the firm gaze of a headmistress. Likewise, a certain breed of man could be brought to heel if reminded of his nanny. There was something to be said for this aspect of the class system. "Miss Hopper is not to be allowed on the set, and should she ask any questions, the only people you are to mention are the actors. Every last one of them and no one else. Is that clear?"

"But, Miss Wolfson, I've seen the sort of things she writes when she feels she's been hard done by. It could do us far more damage."

Hannah was caught short. The girl had a point. But Langham had to get away, shooting be damned. Telling Pamela as much could cause suspicion, and who knew how discreet this girl was? But insisting Langham be asked to drop everything and come to the phone would be worse — much though she respected Frank, she knew he could be irrational when panicked. No, she needed someone to quietly get rid of him, someone who truly understood the danger and could remain calm. "Can you find Miss

Adler and have her call me?"

"Who?"

"The script supervisor." Hannah hung up and faced a wild-eyed Sidney, who had obviously heard her on the phone. He was actually clenching his hair.

"We have to go down there," Hannah insisted.

"We cannae!" Sidney howled. "The Americans are ringing us in twenty minutes' time, and then only a wee interview with the *Radio* bleeding *Times*! We'll look goons to cancel them. Our only excuse could be that one of us died."

Hannah hesitated. "No, we'd never be able to keep that one up. I shouldn't have hired Langham. I knew that all along. I'm sorry, Sidney."

He popped a Walkers shortbread into his mouth. Hannah watched the effect of butter and sugar turn him affable again.

"Nae your fault, 'tis the foolishness of the circumstances. That Hopper creature doesn't know your history, does she?"

"If she did, believe me, we'd already know. No, she's looking for people actually named, and we've got a huge one all ready for her." Hannah reminded herself that her own status was fine. It must be. She would indeed know by now if it wasn't. She shoved

274

a piece of shortbread into her mouth, chewing hard to banish the wave of paranoia she'd come to London to escape. *This is how the Red hunters win. Get inside you, wherever you are.*

"Our people will manage it," Hannah insisted.

"They will," Sidney agreed.

They quelled their anxiety with another piece of shortbread each and prepared for their phone meeting. Hannah kept one ear cocked for the other line, willing Phoebe to call and say she would help keep Hedda Hopper at bay. It was unfair, perhaps, throwing the obviously and suspiciously American Phoebe into Hedda Hopper's path, but Hedda wouldn't know Phoebe from Adam. And Phoebe, more than anyone else on the set, knew the danger the woman represented. She was clever. She would know how to warn Langham, how to keep the evil woman from securing the prize she wanted so badly.

Within an hour of his beginning work the day before, the *Robin Hood* set labeled Langham "an interesting experience."

He had a speed and gruffness that the crew delightedly assured each other was the American style of direction. The Other

Girls, having ascertained that Langham was divorced, engaged in a silent rivalry to attract his attention. His scruffiness was excused as "eccentricity." He was Oscar nominated, not unattractive, and might go back to Hollywood at any time. Who was to say that return wouldn't be enhanced by a pretty English girl on his arm?

Phoebe, not wanting to remind people there were now two Americans on set, willed everything to go more smoothly than usual so she didn't have to open her mouth. By Tuesday the strain was getting to her. At lunch she hid her face behind her notebook, thinking dark thoughts about Langham and everyone who had anything nice to say about him.

Tommy found her and tapped her shoulder.

"I think Miss Brown was looking for you."

"Oh, was she?" She couldn't say she had no idea who Miss Brown was. Tommy would tell her — with that marvelously English polite condescension — but it would get around that the American hadn't bothered to learn people's names, and who did she think she was, anyway? So Phoebe chose her words carefully. "Did you happen to see where she got to?"

He shrugged — anything to do with

Phoebe was of no interest to him. "Back to her desk, I expect."

There were desks everywhere. Phoebe pondered. "Miss Brown" did her little good; half the crew were called Brown. Not that a given name would help. Nearly every woman but Dora was called some variation of Priscilla or Camilla . . . Vanilla, Flotilla, Chinchilla, who could keep track? They all just sniffed when she walked by anyway.

"Hey, script gal!" Langham barked. "Lemme have a gander at scene eight." He seized her notebook and ran through the script. "Uh-huh, uh-huh, uh-huh. All right, Tommy, let's set 'er up." He snapped the binder shut and strode off with it before Phoebe could say anything. She tagged after him, clearing her throat politely. No one was going to accuse her of being so impertinent as to actually request her binder back. She was too focused to register the unusual buzz building at the edge of the studio floor.

The chatter rose to a crescendo and Tommy hurried to Langham, eyes bright with the pleasure of important information to deliver.

"There's a Miss Hedda Hopper here, sir, wanting to tour the set for a *Photoplay* story."

Langham staggered backward. His hair

seemed to visibly whiten. It was like watching a film cut to half speed, the stricken face of Langham and the perplexed face of Tommy flickering in and out before Phoebe's disbelieving eyes. Hedda Hopper, here. A joke. A joke that would bomb before the drunkest audience at the grubbiest Village club. Because as much as Hedda Hopper ranted about "Runaway Reds," her world was the mansions and hotel poolsides and palatial film studios of Los Angeles. Not gray, battered England, and not snug little Nettlefold Studios. Impossible.

"Oh God, why did Hannah hire me?" Langham said, looking around the set with wild eyes, as if he were watching it burn.

Hannah . . . Robin Hood! Phoebe was no great shakes at mathematics, but she could add one and one.

"Tommy, get rid of her!" she cried. "Say it's a closed set."

"That won't fly, the broad's got a nose for blood like Dracula," Langham moaned.

Phoebe looked back and forth between the two men. Langham was completely ashen. Tommy was openmouthed.

"Mr. Langham, you've got to hide!" Phoebe said. "Hide in the set!" she ordered, snatching back her binder. "In the sheriff's tower! You can watch through the arrow slits. We'll pretend Tommy's the director. I'll sneak over to you for directions and pass them to him. She won't notice me, and once she doesn't find what she's looking for, she'll get bored and leave."

Langham locked eyes with Phoebe. They both knew what Hedda Hopper was looking for. He ran for the tower, Tommy ran to spread the word, and Phoebe ran for the lion's den. Ignoring the flustered young woman she recognized from around the studio, Phoebe extended her hand to the devil in a flowered hat.

"Welcome to the set, Miss Hopper, though I'm afraid it's a very busy day. How long are you in town, maybe we can arrange a more convenient visit?" Phoebe wasn't deliberately trying to put on a British accent, but she softened her *R*s and *A*s. The studio woman glared, but Miss Hopper didn't seem to notice anything untoward. Phoebe guessed she was the sort who assumed that a few softer tones meant one had been born and raised in the shadow of Big Ben.

"Well now, that is funny," Miss Hopper answered in the patrician voice Phoebe knew only too well from the radio. A voice Phoebe also knew had replaced a rural Pennsylvania twang. "Miss Brown here says it's a great honor to have me. Publicity department having a bit of a civil war, eh?" Miss Hopper's eyes glinted.

The Miss Brown who'd looked for her? Phoebe had no leisure to ruminate.

"Not at all, Miss Hopper! Miss Brown undoubtedly didn't realize. But tomorrow should work very well — our whole principal cast will be here."

"Who are you?" Miss Hopper demanded.

"Me? Just the script girl, the director sent me over to apologize, he's so busy," Phoebe said with a deprecating titter. Her fingers were nearly pushing through the binder. She wished someone would alert her that the set was ready to keep Langham safe, and that she might get away from this woman.

Miss Hopper's face was magnetic. Phoebe saw both the prettiness that had once helped her gain a toehold and the stately beauty she still possessed, even into her sixties. But what really drew attention was the woman's hat. She was famous for outlandish hats, and this one was quite the conversation piece, though Phoebe suspected Miss Hopper wouldn't like the conversation. A replica of the Statue of Liberty was built into the hat, pointing due north amid a sea of red, white, and blue silk flowers in brilliant Technicolor. No one would ever accuse Hedda

Hopper of subtlety, but this open proclamation of her nationality was a miscalculation. The crew knew condescension when they saw it. Even the most Hollywood-obsessed Other Girl wanted to see the back of her.

"Well, Little Miss Script Girl," Hedda Hopper snapped at Phoebe, "it just so happens that today is *my* most convenient day. And Miss Brown here knows the value of Hedda Hopper, so here I am. I'm sure no one can object to my having a little look around." She waved a green Mont Blanc like a baton. Let other columnists do their reporting in pencil. Hedda Hopper would of course use a fountain pen.

Phoebe kept pace beside Miss Hopper, ready to create more distraction if she had to, trying not to swivel her head, searching for a sign that they were safe. She went hot and cold. No doubt Miss Hopper looked at her only to see a pale, square-faced creature with glasses, barely controlled hair, and an outfit that Miss Hopper would consider appropriate for hoboes. How hard would she have to scratch, though, to find Phoebe Adler, one of the very Runaway Reds she was here to expose?

"I'll chat with the actors," Miss Hopper announced. "They probably don't get much of a chance to mingle with anyone from

Hollywood, poor things."

A ruse. It had to be. Hedda Hopper must know that Richard Greene, their Robin, had acted in Hollywood for several years. She was hoping actors, rarely unwilling to talk, would reveal something damning. Bernadette O'Farrell, resplendent in her Maid Marian costume, sailed up to the gossip-monger. Phoebe tried to catch her eye, but Bernadette was busy playing up every stereotype of Irish charm as she took Hedda Hopper's hand. "Top of the day to you, Miss Hopper!" she cried, her voice dripping with shamrocks.

Tommy materialized at Phoebe's elbow and smoothly backed her away, his face splendidly unruffled. Phoebe had to admire him. One thing about having grown up amid regular bombing raids, nothing much fazed you after that.

"Everyone knows," he whispered. "Miss O'Farrell's softening the bat up, Mr. Greene will move in next. Go get instructions from Langham, I'll keep guard."

Phoebe moved with a studied casualness to the enormous dolly that held the high tower exterior — imposing even though its stone bricks were only painted. Behind it was a staircase that served as the interior of any given castle. When used during a shoot, this portion of the set had a lot of padding underneath it. Right now, though, the only thing on the other side of the stairs was the light safety rail. Phoebe thought the actors had nerves of steel, staging swordfights on these steps. Between the stairs and the situation, her own nerves had all the strength of a rotting banana.

Langham knelt by the arrow slit so he could look out the thin strip but avoid being seen from outside. Phoebe hunched over and padded up the steps to him, where he whispered in her ear.

"Tell Tommy to arrange them in a triangle — he'll know what that means. Sharp pacing, this is a tense scene."

No kidding, Phoebe thought as she wended her way back to Tommy. She muttered instructions over her open binder, pointing with her pencil. Tommy nodded, looking exactly like a bright young director who recognized an error in continuity, and shouted out directions.

Hedda Hopper's face flushed purple with rage. That confirmed it. The woman had been told Langham was directing this week. Someone had whispered something. There must be good money in revealing secrets.

As the take ended, Phoebe speed-drifted back to the tower and scaled the steps with more confidence. Langham gave instructions: another filter on B light, and Malcolm, the guest actor playing a peasant accused of stealing a cow, was being too hesitant. Phoebe wasn't surprised. It was hard enough being a guest, but downright head-splitting when your director changed midstream with no explanation.

Tommy followed through to perfection, spoke bracingly to Malcolm, and the scene went well. Langham approved and was ready for reaction shots, which required some shifting. This was done with a lot more shouting and fuss than usual, in the hopes of irritating Miss Hopper. She cast a cold look around the set — Phoebe thought of a snake looking for the most likely mouse to swallow.

"Don't look!" Tommy hissed. It was too late. The snake eyes were on Phoebe.

"You!" Hedda Hopper bellowed, sharp heels click-click-clicking over. "I saw you walking hither and yon. Why would a script girl wander so much?"

"They give us a lot of nice food on this set," Phoebe said. "Walking helps keep the weight off."

Miss Hopper hooted with laughter. "Nice food? Only someone who's never had a decent meal in her life would call English food nice." She gave Phoebe's hips a very deliberate assessment. "And you, dearie, seem to like eating. You know, all the Hollywood girls wear girdles with every outfit."

Phoebe bit her inner cheek to keep from laughing. The woman certainly had no qualms about insulting everyone and everything around her. Phoebe hoped the conventional truth was true, and that such pride would go before a fall. Preferably off a high cliff.

Tommy interrupted. "So sorry, Miss Hopper, but we really must get this next shot before wrap. I do apologize, it's inconvenient I know. Miss Marrow, come along now." He propelled Phoebe to her usual perch, leaving no moment for her to forget herself and utter a fateful "huh?"

He didn't know she was blacklisted. He didn't even know she was a writer. Maybe he had guessed and was protecting her? Names of blacklistees might well be accompanied by photographs. Phoebe wouldn't be a fine catch like Frank Langham, but anything was better than nothing. However, it was more likely Tommy was protecting her from any attempt Hedda Hopper might make to blackball her as a script supervisor. That, or he knew the woman hated Jews, and the name "Adler" might set her off. Either way, it was clever . . . and kind.

The next take went off perfectly, and Miss Brown, finally doing her job, told Miss Hopper they were preparing to wrap and if she'd like to schedule another visit, that would be lovely. Miss Hopper cast a withering glance around the set.

"This is a very silly show for very silly children. I wouldn't waste another minute here." She flounced away; Miss Brown had to skip to keep up with her.

Phoebe held out until she could no longer see the bobbing red, white, and blue flowers and sank straight into the director's chair. She didn't get up until the director himself came out of hiding and patted her shoulder.

"Those are some good brains you've got, doll. Consider me grateful."

Whispers went around the set, little fireworks of surprise on learning it was Phoebe who had saved the day. Even the most vapid of the Other Girls knew a report of a blacklistee involved could derail their American deal. As admirable as Hannah was to give her compatriots assistance, it would have to end.

That particular whisper unnerved Phoebe all over again. Would her own job disappear before she'd sold a script? She reminded

286

herself no one on the set knew she was blacklisted. *I wonder if it would make me more interesting or more ostracized?*

After they wrapped, Langham shot off to the nearest pub. Phoebe shrugged on her coat and hat.

"Good night, Miss Adler, or should I say Marrow," Tommy said, bopping her lightly on the shoulder.

"Marrow, like that stuff in bones?" Phoebe asked.

"I suppose so," he said. "Our air raid wardress was called Mrs. Marrow — made of steel, she was. Here, have a choc," he said, handing her a Rolo.

Phoebe was so stunned that by the time she remembered to thank him, he'd disappeared.

That typical London rain — light and misty, just enough to get under the skin and make a person realize why tea and scones were such a dietary staple — beat down on Phoebe as she walked home from the Charing Cross station. She couldn't be bothered to tie her scarf around her head, letting her hair frizz into a beehive some women paid good money for. Rounding the corner on Meard Street, she heard a mournful saxophone wail from a back window.

Oh, Mona. You were so right, but you had no idea. Even here, where I came for safety, I'm not safe. None of us are.

She kicked a stone, wishing she could be one of the street kids. It must be schoolwork keeping Freddie and his pals inside, as they usually didn't mind the weather. The street felt dark and deserted without them, except for the music that wound its way inside Phoebe's nerves.

Not deserted, though. A lanky figure leaned against the jutting wall by number seven, twirling an umbrella. He lurched forward on seeing her.

"Gosh, that's me lucky!" he exclaimed.

It was Reg.

CHAPTER TWELVE

The intelligent brown eyes behind the glasses were as sparkling as Phoebe realized she remembered. Which didn't stop her from jerking a knitting needle from her bag and wielding it like a dagger.

"Stay back, or you'll have a very embarrassing hospital visit," she warned.

"Pax, pax," he said, holding up his hands. "Charming to see you again too."

She tightened her grip on the needle.

"You've been following me. You know what we call that in New York? Creepy! And that's when we're being polite."

"Pax," he said again. "Fair cop, I did follow you after we met, but it was an accident, I swear. I live one road over. I could hardly believe the chances. That's the honest truth. This isn't some Jack the Ripper sort of thing."

"It would be pretty sorry if it were," she said. "Murderers are never as sharp as they think they are. You may have suckered one of my neighbors into thinking you're a charming Englishman, but if you've been down here more than ten minutes, there's no way she hasn't seen you. She knows your face if I disappear. And the landlady's son is twelve years old, misses nothing that happens on this road, and likes me — those sorts of boys get more murderers hanged than Miss Marple."

She would have handed over a week's salary for a snapshot of his expression. *So that's what they mean by "gobsmacked."*

"Are you a detective?" he asked with a nervous smile.

"Don't try and be cute," she snapped. "What the hell are you doing here?"

"I thought I would drop off another note. Mrs. Morrison wasn't in but she said you're usually expected around now."

Phoebe made a mental note to throttle Joan.

"Did you think that maybe my not responding to your last note might have meant something?" she asked, raising an eyebrow.

"I did. But I couldn't resist trying once again," he said with a deprecating smile.

Phoebe's heart gave a strange and very uncomfortable leap. She gripped the knitting needle harder, liking the feel of the metal burning into her skin. Liking anything that distracted her from wondering what this man's game was.

"Oh, hello!" Joan's voice boomed from the corner. Phoebe gritted her teeth. If only Anne were here. Anne was a whiz at ascertaining a situation and acting accordingly. She could send a man packing with a half-flared nostril. Joan smiled the smile of a would-be matchmaker. "So lovely to see you again," Joan trilled to Reg. "Won't you pop up for some tea?"

Phoebe rolled her eyes. Joan sounded more British than the queen.

"Oh, I don't want to intrude on evening plans," Reg said, and Phoebe almost softened to him.

"Nonsense, it's a celebration!" cried Joan, shaking a pink bakery box.

"Wow, did Charlie sell something?" Phoebe asked, forgetting her irritation and how rain soaked she was getting.

"No, silly, we're celebrating you saving the day!" Joan squealed with laughter. "Come in, come in, you're wet, you'll catch cold. Hannah sent a telegram. I've bought a cake! Come in! And put that knitting needle away before it rusts."

Phoebe was half-inside when she realized

Reg was joining them, buffeted by Joan and her desire to make things merrier with more.

"Don't take this the wrong way," Phoebe told him, "but I think this should be an Americans-only evening."

"Don't be ridiculous!" Joan snapped.

Phoebe stood firm. Reg looked harmless, even — yes — charming, but she had enough on her plate without a stranger demanding her attention. Joan should know better, especially after the Hedda Hopper catastrophe. He could be anybody. He could be dangerous.

"Quite right," Reg said. "Americans only. If I could just have one more word, Miss Adler?"

Joan harrumphed but went upstairs, leaving Phoebe and Reg in the tiny vestibule. Phoebe had never lingered there long enough to determine the exact smell. Pea soup, she decided. With a hint of long-dead mouse.

"All right," Phoebe said bluntly. "One more word. I recommend 'goodbye.' It's succinct, and works as a sentence."

"True," he said with a grave nod that she was pretty sure was half-joking. "But it has an air of finality that seems so, well, final."

At home, he might be amusing her to gain entrée to television, or Anne. Showing off cleverness because he knew how she valued it. Here, she was thrown. Phoebe had lost any taste she'd ever had for being thrown. Besides, she was impatient to know what exactly Hannah had said. That she'd saved the day! She, Phoebe, was a hero. Extraordinary. Maybe that was what was holding her here, feeding her curiosity to hear what this not-unattractive stranger wanted to say to her. This was a story, anyway. Something to work into a script, or just something to please Mona. Who would be furious if Phoebe didn't see this through to its end.

"I know you're a busy woman, Miss Adler," Reg said. "I respect that. And no doubt you've an abundance of reasons for not having another coffee with me. But I'm hoping you might find some time anyway."

"Why?" she asked. She was playing no game. She was genuinely puzzled.

He ran a hand through his lightly greased mop of dark curls.

"You seem like the sort of person who, the more one gets to know her, the more intriguing she becomes," he said. His eyes were huge and serious.

The comment might be a line, but Phoebe had to hand it to him, it was a good one. She pushed her glasses farther up her nose. It was possible this man found her interesting enough to want to know her better. Or maybe he took pleasure from getting close enough to get a good poke in the eye.

"Of course, mystery lingers more from a distance," she said, because it was the sort of thing she would say. Not that she had any usual line for a situation like this. The boys at school had respected and been terrified of her. Then came the war, and no men. After the war, her focus had been on winning and retaining an independence that would hold her and Mona afloat. She always told herself that, once she was secure, that might be the moment to consider romance, if such a thing were to present itself. She didn't want to need a man. Wanting was one thing. Needing was something very different.

"Have you been to the Seven Stars?" Reg asked.

"Are you trying to recruit me into some pagan worship circle?"

He grinned. "It's a pub. Very nearly medieval — it actually survived the Great Fire. If you're disinclined towards a pint, we can have a coffee. After lunch, when it's quiet enough to let you feel the ghosts."

"I don't believe in ghosts," she informed him tartly.

"Ah, and they say such delightful things

about you."

She could control her smile, but not her eyes, which she knew were dancing.

"I'll think about it," she promised. "And check my schedule. If I can manage something, I'll let you know."

"You are a most unyielding businesswoman, Miss Adler," Reg said in admiration. "That's all quite fair, and you know how to reach me."

"Not exactly," she said, remembering there was an address on the note she'd crumpled.

"Fortunately, I was prepared for just such an occurrence," he said, handing over another envelope with her name on it. "I think you've got a willing messenger there" — he pointed behind her — "so you needn't put yourself out with delivery. I hope to hear from you, Miss Adler." He gave her a funny little salute and loped out the door, a whirl of duffle coat, trailing scarf, and cheerfulness.

Phoebe turned and saw Freddie's round eyes peering through a slit in the broom cupboard. The willing messenger. Reg was even cleverer than she'd thought. She grinned and beckoned Freddie as she opened the note.

Dear Miss Adler, I daresay a reasonable man would accept your silence as polite refusal, but I am choosing to be an unreasonable man on the chance you've lost my address or changed your mind. If either of these things are true, please send word.

"Bourchier Street, that really is the next one over, isn't it?" she asked Freddie, pointing to the address.

"It is, indeed, miss," he told her, proud to have his good information sought.

"Did that fellow look all right to you?"

Freddie threw back his shoulders. "I think he might be, miss, him being well-spoken and seeming like a right gent, despite not having posh clothes. He had a sort of . . . good humor, I'd say, miss."

This was a deeply considered opinion, and Phoebe nodded gravely.

"I think you might be right," she agreed. "If I may secure your services, when it's convenient," she continued, dropping a penny into his hand.

"Right you are, miss, and most pleased," he said in his most refined tone. Then he couldn't resist, looking at her with shining eyes. "Is it true, miss, you were a heroine today? I heard Mrs. Morrison shouting about it when the telegram come."

"A nasty old bat is trying to chase some of us into prison for crimes we didn't commit," Phoebe confided. "I was able to thwart her."

Freddie gazed on her with the sort of worship that once preceded sacrificial offerings. Phoebe had to admit, it was gratifying.

Even more gratifying was the telegram from Hannah:

SHOWER PHOEBE WITH PRAISE SHE'S SAVED US FROM HURRICANE HOPPER = TELL HER TO COME FOR LUNCH SATURDAY = AND I HOPE TO SEE A SCRIPT AS CREATIVE AS HER QUICK THINKING +

"I went out to ring Shirley and she told me the rest," Joan explained.

The whole thing was suddenly hilarious. Phoebe plunged into the story, the details of which needed no embellishment. They pealed with laughter, Phoebe struggling to catch her breath in between descriptions of Hedda Hopper's hat, voice, nose, pen, and fury. Their shrieks summoned the family: Bobby, the teenager, stormed out of the flat, casting his mother and Phoebe the look of disdain so endemic to adolescent boys, making Phoebe laugh harder. Alvie ran to the table, comic book dangling from his hands, his curiosity about the joke forgotten when he registered the presence of cake. Then came Charlie, his face thunderous.

"I'm right in the middle of . . . oh, Phoebe, hello," he said reluctantly.

"Hiya, Charlie," Phoebe said, nodding respectfully. He had circles under his eyes, and she discerned subtle patches in his trousers. His face grew admiring as he heard the tale. But there was fear in his eyes too. That was the problem. They could laugh all they wanted. They still needed to be afraid.

Charlie handed off his share of cake to the eager Alvie, who couldn't believe his luck. Joan's indulgent smile was melancholy, and Phoebe made a note to herself to bring the Morrisons another cake, another time. Under the guise of coffee, lest anyone think it was charity.

"Gosh," Alvie said, his eyes round like Freddie's. "Imagine a lady being the hero of the day."

"Your mother's one every day," Phoebe said, annoyed that Charlie and Joan laughed at their son's remark. "Besides, haven't you ever read *Wonder Woman*?"

The boy rolled his eyes. "Borrrr-ing," he pronounced, and grinned at his father's laughter. He was less pleased to be told the last piece of cake was Bobby's, and retreated back into his room.

"Yours is a heck of a story though," Charlie assured Phoebe. Phoebe, buoyed with cake, laughter, and, she had to admit, Reg, swelled with contentment. She was a heroine, beating the would-be conquering army from the castle. What couldn't she do now?

Her eyes glazed. She felt herself murmur something as she crossed to her own door. Within seconds, she was typing. She didn't even need to start knitting first. She was Maid Marian, seeking out Robin and the outlaws in their most recent hideaway — an abandoned house — to tell them of a village being terrorized by the sheriff's men because it was suspected of harboring an outlaw. As Robin and his men plan to save the village, there is a shout from the watchman — a surprise attack is coming! They're surrounded. One very young, nervous outlaw believes the attackers' assurance that anyone who gives himself up will be granted clemency. He rushes out and is immediately killed. All hope seems lost, but Marian was in this house once and knows there is a secret passageway. She leads them all to safety, and while the attackers are busy burning down the house, the outlaws conduct a sneak attack on the village, setting all the people free.

Phoebe flexed her fingers. The secret passageway wasn't a brilliant choice — it was a Gothic idea and a contrivance. But how much would she have loved such an adventure when she was twelve? The kids watching the show would be enthralled. And it would look awfully exciting. With suspenseful music and the shadows playing off the dark walls of the passage, viewers' hearts would be happily in their throats. Plus, there were deaths! All good clean fun.

She typed a title page: *The Sneak Attack by Phoebe Adler.* It was not the name that was going to end up in the credits, but it was hers. She was going to write it wherever she could.

The change at the set of *Robin Hood* was instant. Dora, head of the Other Girls, greeted Phoebe with a cigarette and a compliment on her excellent knitting. The actors said, "Good morning, Miss Adler," as they came to the set. Langham shook her hand. Miss Brown had been packed off. And there was a handwritten note from Hannah, asking again that she come to lunch on Saturday. The set became a fun place to be, and her nights were energetic as she wrote and rewrote the script. If she could only have sat down with Mona and Anne in person to tell them about her coup, life would be almost perfect.

Hannah answered the door herself, and Phoebe immediately extended her hand.

Hannah seized it and tugged Phoebe into her arms. She smelled of Shalimar, the same "grown-up scent" Phoebe had sneaked to Mona. Phoebe hugged Hannah tighter, then pulled back in case she was about to sniffle.

Hannah laid two hands on Phoebe's shoulders.

"I wanted to come to the set to congratulate you right away," she said. "But I thought it best not to make a fuss over you in front of the others. And I was going to invite you to a very posh dinner in town, but in the end I decided we'd be at our most leisurely right here, where we can really chat."

Rhoda, wearing a prototype of the Robin Hood costume that was about to hit shops, charged into the hall, brandishing a toy bow and arrows with an unsettling menace.

"State your business!" she cried, her eyes narrowed.

"I come in peace," Phoebe promised her. "And hope not to leave in pieces."

The girl giggled and aimed instead at a painting of a hunting scene.

"Want to see me hit that deer?" she offered.

"Rhoda, darling, go and help Gemma with Julie," Hannah ordered. "Later, we'll go out into the garden."

Hannah watched fondly as Rhoda galloped away on a pretend horse.

"Her school has asked I send along some manacles," she confided. "I'm not sure they're joking."

"My school asked my parents much the same thing," Phoebe said.

"And if you and Rhoda had been boys, they'd have called you scamps," said Hannah.

"Oh, I got called things." Phoebe laughed. "But never that."

"What about a word that rhymes with 'scamp'?" Hannah asked.

Phoebe laughed again. "You'd think once I grew this huge bust that might have done it, but no. Everyone knew I wasn't interested in anything except making something of myself."

Reg popped into her mind, and she wondered if her bust was part of the attraction. She hoped not. Anyway, he'd only seen her swathed in layers of tweed.

"I was never interested in boys either until I married one," Hannah said with a giggle, pouring them champagne.

"Excuse me?" Paul, walking by on his way out, stopped and raised a brow.

Hannah laughed harder and waved a hand toward Phoebe. "Paul, darling, you remember Phoebe Adler, who —"

"Yes, yes, the name Phoebe has become legendary the last few days," Paul said, nodding pleasantly. "Congratulations, dear, we're all safe to fight another day. Or, at least, Frank Langham is."

There was something in his tone that made Phoebe uneasy, and she was glad to see Paul leave.

If Phoebe was disappointed not to be taken to one of the posh restaurants, Hannah more than compensated by setting out a scrumptious lunch ordered from Fortnum & Mason. The dishes threatened to overrun the table.

"Did you leave any cheese in the shop?" Phoebe asked.

Hannah explained that Shirley was joining them later, and Rhoda and Julie were promised a bit of "elegant lady time." Phoebe knew Shirley's presence was a high compliment. Shirley LeGrand did not spare either her time or her friendship indiscriminately.

Hannah, too, was no easy friend, but

Phoebe's handling of Hedda Hopper had evidently upgraded Phoebe to the category of someone to be trusted. They ate with gusto and laughed, and Hannah told stories.

"I'd been in journalism since college, but I was thinking I wanted to go on to greener pastures," she said, spooning half a carton of stuffed mushrooms onto her plate. "Once you've been in the muck reporting on the brilliance of the New Deal, and then the war, everything else pales. I went into political speechwriting, and then once the Red-hunting started, I knew my New Deal–loving, socialist self would get a target on her back before long. So we left. Paul liked the idea of the adventure." Her eyes twinkled. "There aren't many chances in life, I think, to get in on something wholly new," Hannah continued, suffused with the rosiness of nostalgia for herself of barely six years ago. "Television seemed like a great chance to tell a lot of stories. A friend of a friend gave me a leg up — not that anyone wanted me, of course, but I was a quick study and willing to work for peanuts, so they embraced me soon enough. I made them laugh, that helped."

"Were you working on a comedy?" Phoebe asked.

"No, no, I'm far too serious," Hannah

said. "But I was a junior producer, and the one ladies' toilet in the building was for the secretaries and cleaner, in the basement. My respect for secretaries and cleaners aside, I knew this was a battle I had to fight and win. So I went to the junior executive washroom on my floor and hung my handbag outside, on the door handle. The fellows thought it funny, thank goodness, and converted another gents' loo into a ladies' soon enough."

This was how it went, Phoebe thought, as Hannah continued to tell stories of her quick rise to head her own company — a rise helped by her husband's money, but plenty of men rose in life via family money. If Hannah hadn't had Paul, she'd have found another way. Phoebe wondered how many handbags would have to be hung on how many doors before a ladies' toilet was a given.

"So I see you have something for me," Hannah said, pointing to the blue-bound script peeking out of Phoebe's bag. Phoebe took it out and stroked it.

"Took longer than we discussed, but it's worth it," she said.

"Not very modest." Hannah grinned. "Excellent. Well, hand it over."

Phoebe did, and Hannah opened it.

"You're not going to read it now?" Phoebe was eager, but didn't want to sit and watch Hannah read what she hoped was, at last, her ticket back to her career.

"We don't take days off, you know that," Hannah said. "A few hours here and there, but never a whole day."

It was true. The weeks Phoebe had spent escaping America and resettling herself in London were the longest time she'd gone without properly writing since she started, back at the airfield, snatching a few hours here and there when she was supposed to be asleep. She could still hear Dolores Goldstein shouting at her to get off that damn typewriter before she pitched the thing out the window.

Good old Dolores. She should have gotten her chance to do everything she wanted. Of course, maybe something had stopped her. It wasn't easy. Phoebe, Hannah, Anne, they were the lucky ones. And luck was sometimes known to run out.

Shirley came in as Phoebe was thinking this — another mostly lucky woman, with another husband who cheered on her work. She and Will were on the forefront together, fighting for civil rights, which had ended up getting them a one-way ticket out of the country. Better than prison, though. Plenty of the accused sat in prison, and no one yet seemed to think that maybe the government was being a touch unreasonable in its pursuit of possible Communists.

Shirley was impeccable in a cream-colored suit with navy trim, a cream-and-navy petal hat hugging a lightly pressed hairdo. The sort of easy elegance that only real style could buy. She was everything Phoebe had always striven to be, and Phoebe couldn't help feeling shy of her as she held out her hand.

Shirley raised a knowing brow and leaned in to peck Phoebe on the cheek. Phoebe recognized Joy perfume.

"You're clever," Shirley pronounced. "I thought you might be."

Hannah served Shirley a martini. "You two talk, I'll just be reading."

If Shirley noticed that Phoebe was jumpy, with one eye wandering toward Hannah and her progress through the script, she made no comment, instead engaging Phoebe in gossip about the ongoing efforts of the FBI to undermine the National Association for the Advancement of Colored People.

"They underestimate Negroes, that's their problem. They think because we seem to behave it means we're compliant. But by segregating us, they've put us all together where we can organize. It's going to surprise them, sooner or later."

If the NAACP was full of people like Shirley, Phoebe suspected that surprise would come sooner.

"I suppose it's not been so easy for you either," Shirley said generously. "No one expects a writer to be a *femme*. Has being Jewish helped or hurt?"

"Funny thing," Phoebe said. "It's good for the men. For me, who knows? Honestly, I'm not even sure I *am* Jewish — my father screamed the place down if anyone mentioned religion. If I am, I'm only half, Mama being a Quaker. We always thought we were so ironic for hating oatmeal."

" 'We'?"

"Me and my sister, Mona." She bit back her emotion. What was Mona doing right this minute? Phoebe saw Hannah glance up at her and then return to the script. "She and I were quite the ones for making up stories," she said, forcing a laugh.

"Here's to making up stories," Shirley said, and they clinked glasses.

"Funny, isn't it, the way it's always 'half-Jewish'?" Phoebe mused. "No one ever says 'half-Gentile' or 'half-Protestant,' do they?"

"It's often 'half-black' too," Shirley said. "Though that can depend. Funny, indeed, how certain folk enjoy pointing out how someone deviates from the 'norm.' "

" 'Certain folk' meaning WASPs? Are we saying they're the norm?"

"They've certainly arranged things to appear that way."

"I've seen them in action," Phoebe said. "They may be all sorts of things, but normal isn't one of them."

"Will you tell them or shall I?"

Hannah closed the script and joined Phoebe in laughter. She opened a little box that contained a Victoria sponge.

"Quick, let's finish the cake before Rhoda sees it. I've got chocolate fingers for her and Julie."

Phoebe twisted her own fingers together, watching Hannah's face. She was rewarded with a grin as Hannah tapped the script.

"This is what I hoped you could do."

"Really?" Phoebe was louder than she intended. "You mean it?"

Hannah gave Phoebe a gargantuan slice of cake.

"Not entirely," she said. "Because in fact it's better than I expected." She grinned at Phoebe's surprised blush. "It's good enough for the show. I had no intention of bringing you on *Robin Hood,* I was going to use your sample to recommend you for *Woman's*

Hour. Which I still will, because you'll need more work. But this is *Robin Hood,* Phoebe. It really is."

"You sound surprised," Shirley said, her tone sly.

Phoebe swore she could detect a faint blush on Hannah's cheek.

"I suppose I didn't think Phoebe was the sort who could write this kind of script. Not that it's perfect," she insisted. "Some of the language is too modern, too American, but Beryl will fix that. Anyway, it's obvious you've paid attention." She reached into a drawer in the sideboard, produced a pen, and crossed out Phoebe's name on the script. "Who will you be?"

Phoebe sighed. "I'd hoped coming here meant I could keep my name."

"Write a play then," Hannah told her briskly. "Meantime, be grateful you're not sharing your fee with a front."

"I suppose you'd rather I not be a woman in the credits," Phoebe said, looking Hannah right in the eye.

Hannah smiled, and Phoebe knew she'd stepped up just a bit further.

"I was wrong. Be a woman. It suits you. If anyone even notices the name of a writer, it's good they know women can do this sort of thing."

Phoebe nodded. "Ivy," she decided. "Like poison ivy. Ivy Marrow."

"Not bad. You might consider 'Morrow.' "

"Why?"

"Because some morrow or other, you'll be Phoebe Adler again."

All three women laughed, though none of them thought it was very funny.

"It pays seventy pounds," Hannah said. "Do you still need the script girl job?"

Phoebe considered. It would be nice, having more time to write. But seventy pounds, though a lot at once, would disappear quickly, especially after she'd sent thirty-five of it to Mona.

"I do. If that's all right."

"Is your sister the only one to call on, should you need help?" Shirley asked.

Phoebe looked at each interested, sympathetic face and felt a rush of real friendship. Out came the story of a family so insular, it comprised solely of the four of them. And a beloved sister born without any immune system and yet somehow surviving, a curiosity to doctors, a devastation to the foursome, which fractured further with each near-death illness, until Mama and Horatio folded into ashes. It was only the last of the funds they'd accumulated, the agreement with Brookside that Mona be a subject of study, and Phoebe's contributions that kept her out of the poor ward.

"I should be there," Phoebe said at last. "Whatever she said, I should be there." Tears rose, hot and angry. Shirley passed her a handkerchief.

"She was right," Hannah said softly. "You got a subpoena. You were marked."

"I know, I know that," Phoebe choked out. "But any day could be it, and I won't be there. She deserves to have me there."

"Even if you were in New York, and not in prison, you might not get there in time when the end comes." Shirley said.

"I'd stand a better chance than from here."

"You should phone her, have regular chats," Hannah announced.

"It's three pounds for three minutes," Phoebe said savagely. "I know that staff, it takes them three minutes just to get Mona to the phone."

Hannah smiled and lit a cigarette.

"I'll contact them and arrange for you to speak to your sister every Sunday."

"But . . ."

Hannah held up her hand. "Phone calls are cheaper on Sundays. Today's a celebration so we'll push the boat out."

She led Phoebe into the living room, to

the black telephone on a marble table. Phoebe could hardly believe it as Hannah first demanded the operator connect her to the Brookside Sanitarium in Manhattan, and then that Miss Adler be brought to the phone at once. She still didn't believe it, even when Mona's voice — that dear, dear voice — came down the line.

"Phoebe, you idiot, can't you telegram first? I was in the middle of my tap class."

Phoebe was so happy she could do nothing but squeak.

"Oh God, Mona, I miss you."

"Don't sound so drippy, you'll spoil my sangfroid. Tell me everything."

Despite Mona's talking like Mona, Phoebe could hear the delight in her voice, the happy surprise, the longing. She told her a swift version of the Hedda Hopper story and was rewarded with her sister's huge, ringing laugh. She told her Hannah had just accepted a script. And to make her extra happy, she told her about Reg.

"Oh, Phoebe! Are you at last deflowered?"

"Mona! Geez, I'm not even sure I want to see him again. He might be a creep."

"Not if he likes you, he's not. See him again and find out, that's an order. Now tell me the truth, kiddo. Are you happy?"

Phoebe glanced around the room. It was

just the sort of room she had always envisioned for her home. High ceiling, two huge bay windows. Squashy sofa and chairs, perfect for curling up to read or knit and think of new ideas. Bookcases stuffed to the brim. The hi-fi and the television. Alone in this room, as a favor bestowed, Phoebe felt a stab of longing. A life like this was so very far out of her reach. She ran her fingers over an ornate cut glass ashtray on the telephone table, the exact color of the Victorian tumblers she had bought with such pride. All she had given up, left further and further behind, because she, who'd always been brave, was afraid.

And yet, she was doing it. She was making a life here. Hannah might have granted favors, but Phoebe had kept that job on her own merit, and sold this script because it was good. Joan, and now Hannah and Shirley, were her friends. And Reg, well, maybe he wasn't anyone to be cautious of. Look at Hannah and Shirley, after all, whose careers were done no harm with husbands and even, in Hannah's case, children. So what was one coffee date? She'd enjoyed their impromptu one, after all, and might well enjoy another.

"I am," she told Mona. "I'm happy." And she meant it.

"I'm proud of you," Mona said. "I knew you could do it, of course, but I'm proud of you. Don't let them scare you, all right?"

Phoebe's eyes fell on a copy of the *New York Times,* open to a story about another HUAC hearing, another round of questioning, another opening salvo: "Are you now, or have you ever been, a member of the Communist Party?" More names demanded, more given. More refusals, more imprisonments. *More dog, more pony.*

"No," she said to Mona. "I won't let them scare me."

She knew she should hang up, but couldn't bring herself to say so. Mona, as usual, guessed as much.

"Listen, I'm off to the races today, so I need to go get my hat on," Mona said briskly. "Love you, four-eyes."

Phoebe willed her voice to be steady. "Love you, two-wheels."

She was rewarded with one more laugh before the click. She set down the phone and kept her hand on it until Hannah came back in, followed by Rhoda.

"Come to the garden!" Rhoda ordered. "I'll teach you archery."

Hannah laughed. "Paul says her hope chest will be filled with a bail fund."

"I've always had a 'hope-not chest' myself," Phoebe said.

Hannah laughed again and hooked arms with her to take her outside.

"Listen, I've got so much to thank you for —" Phoebe began.

Hannah waved this aside.

"I am buying the script because it's excellent, period. And I'm glad to help keep you in touch with your family. Too many others have lost theirs."

The day was cold but bright. The women smoked and drank and watched Rhoda shoot arrows. Phoebe decided it didn't matter what had brought them all here. They'd made a new life, and all things considered, it wasn't a bad one.

Hannah sent Phoebe home with a small basket of cheese and fruit. She swung it as she strolled, looking forward to sharing it with Joan. Saturday evening in Soho was full of Teddy Boys — and girls too — lounging in the coffeehouses that seemed to multiply by the week. They drank, talked, read aloud from newspapers and magazines, and fiercely assured each other they were going to change the world. Phoebe smiled on them lovingly, in their oversized Edwardian-style velvet jackets with flouncy handkerchiefs, and thought they might just do it. They'd grown up amid bombings and terror and death. They were afraid of nothing now. What couldn't they do?

Besides, they had music. Soho felt more like the Village every day, or maybe she was only just starting to notice it, with music pouring out of so many windows. The weather was chilly, but the music found its way through the glass anyway, wanting to be heard. It wasn't just the musicians, practicing for clubs that must exist behind some of these quiet doors. The music also streamed from record shops, all packed with young people eager for what was new. From America, from around Britain, from Europe. Music, coffee, change in the air. They worried about the H-bomb, but there was plenty of fun to keep worry at bay.

Phoebe swelled with nostalgia, remembering dancing at break times with Anne and Dolores Goldstein and the other girls, dreaming of a better time to come. And here it was, for some, anyway.

No, for me too, she thought, pushing her shoulders back. She was a hero. She had sold a script. She had friends. She lived on a street full of artists and musicians, just like she always had. Mona was only as far away as Hannah's telephone. And she was going to have coffee with Reg, if only to have a story for Mona next Sunday.

Inspired, she hurried upstairs, eager to write to Anne and Mona and turn that storytelling into something else, maybe a short play for *Woman's Hour.* She could wait to speak to Joan — a decision more easily made when she heard wafts of a family argument rising above the big band music. She shut her door quietly.

Joan — or Freddie, but most likely Joan — had once again slipped mail under her door. A drawing of the Chrysler Building from Anne, which gave Phoebe a pang. London was full of majestic buildings, even after the Blitz, but oh, the Chrysler Building. That was New York. Phoebe sighed, and tacked up the drawing next to the others. Two other envelopes. She recognized Reg's refined handwriting and smiled. The note was short, saying only how much he'd enjoyed their chat and looked forward to buying a heroine coffee. The address on the other envelope was typed. Intrigued, she tore it open. Her grip went slack, and the stiff yellow page fell to the floor, where the words blazed up at her:

Your subpoena is still outstanding. You might run, but you cannot hide.

Chapter Thirteen

"Pure dead brilliant," Beryl pronounced, tapping Phoebe's script with the new title page. "Who's this Ivy Morrow lass?"

"She's pretty good, isn't she?" Hannah said agreeably.

"Too much to hope she's Scottish," Beryl muttered, wielding her red pencil. Hannah wasn't deliberately keeping Beryl in the dark about Phoebe, not exactly, because of course Beryl knew the script was from a blacklistee. But Beryl knew very few of the actual names behind the scripts. She liked Phoebe well enough, Hannah supposed, but it seemed more prudent than ever to keep Phoebe's name a secret. One piece of news was out: Hedda Hopper had uncovered a blacklisted director working on a French film. Its American distribution deal had been canceled.

"Everyone ought be relieved," Sidney said, trying to cheer them. "A subtitled drama about farm workers — would have been reams of empty cinemas anyway."

"We need to hit even harder," Hannah said. "Use our success to go darker. I want a story about an innocent man tortured for a crime he didn't commit, all orchestrated by the sheriff to consolidate some power."

"The bairns will love that," Sidney said with his barking laugh, rubbing his hands together. "Speaking of consolidating power, let's be pressing on with getting a deal for another show."

Another show. When no one ever expected her to have one, she would have another. An expanding empire. And a chance to give more work to blacklisted writers, cocking a snook at both HUAC and its Hollywood toadies. There was so much to do, so much to make happen, and never enough time. Yesterday, she'd spent her script-reading time editing Paul's latest story for the *New Yorker*. He rewrote it all afternoon while she played Robin Hood with Rhoda and Julie in the garden. Gemma reported a call from Phoebe, which was odd, but Hannah was in the middle of being interrogated by the sheriff, and instructed she would come to the set to see Phoebe tomorrow. She never had enough time with her family, and this moment was too important to interrupt. Robin Hood was about to rescue her.

"It must have been horrible for the wives and children of the outlaws," she mused, looking over the *Robin Hood* schedule. "So much time apart, never knowing if you'd be a family again."

" 'Tis ever the way," Sidney said. "Men go off and women keep the home fires burning best they can."

"Ever the way indeed," Beryl snarled. "Men have the adventures and women the grief."

"Marriage can be a great adventure," Hannah said. "It's a huge mistake in stories, thinking marriage is the end. Really, it can be just the beginning."

"Aye, right." Beryl rolled her eyes. "I reckon I'm the only person on earth who sees *I Love Lucy* as a tragedy of an energetic woman bored out of her mind and trying to have a bit of life in her life."

"Talking of adventure," Sidney said, "let's do another one for telly. Build on what we've got. We can well afford it now."

"If a Scotsman says so, it must be true," Hannah teased. She was impressed Sidney wanted to do another expensive show. By television standards, *The Adventures of Robin Hood* was lavish, with a ten-thousand-pound budget per episode. Hannah secured the love of the camera crew by insisting it be shot like a film, using a 35-millimeter camera. The rest of the crew loved her for sparing no expense on the other details: the sets, props, costumes, and hairstyles had all been vetted, mulled, and designed with only slightly more care than a baker might apply to a birthday cake for the queen. The critics agreed it was one of the finest-looking shows on air.

"Another adventure it is," Hannah agreed. "One that uses woodland."

"Talking of adventure," Beryl echoed Sidney, with a grim expression, "your lass Phoebe rang, saying she needs to speak to you rather immediately. And there's this, sent last night." She handed Hannah a telex from Dale Winston of CBS.

MISS WOLFSON. REALLY MUST MEET MCCLELLAN. OR ANY NY-BASED WRITERS? SOME SCRIPTS ORIGINATING FROM AMERICA? GENIUSES, ALL! DALE.

McClellan. That was Ring Lardner Jr. Not that it mattered. None of the writers could meet with anyone, ever.

"This is what we get for being such a roaring success," Hannah grumbled. "Why can't the top brass pretend writers don't exist? They'd certainly like to pay them that way."

"We have to put him off," Sidney insisted.

"I know."

"Or have a front pretend to be McClellan."

"I'm not allowing any such meeting I don't oversee," Hannah barked.

"Hannah." Sidney touched her hand. "We can't let ourselves look suspicious."

"Too late," Hannah said. "We're the most suspicious game in town."

She glanced at the other message. Phoebe. Needing her immediately. That was suspicious too. Hannah took a long drag on a cigarette, shoved some shortbread in her bag, and grabbed her hat and coat.

There was, at least, nothing suspicious about Hannah arriving at the set shortly before lunch and watching a scene being filmed. Prince John was in Nottingham, giving the sheriff instructions.

"It's simple enough, Sheriff," the prince hissed. "Spread the word that clemency will be offered to any outlaw who is willing to come forward and give the names of at least ten others. The man who names names will not only be spared, he will be given a reward for his loyalty to the Crown, his true English patriotism. Or rather, he will be given that reward in full when he also directs you to the whereabouts of said outlaws. You can keep that part quiet until they've been caught."

"They move a great deal," the sheriff complained. "And there are many who are happy to shield them."

"That matters not," the prince countered. "There is always one whose anxiety for the welfare of his family, and his good name, will step forward. We need Robin. He's obviously too clever for you to capture, so instead sweeten the pot, and lure away one of his friends. You capture one, who gives up ten, you sully more names, you break the glamour of the rebellion."

The director cut, and that was a wrap for lunch. Peter Proud descended on Hannah to gush about a new innovation in set design he was eager to try, and the other admiring men of the crew gathered to admire. They couldn't say enough about her discernment, taste, genius, and their own delight in their work and the show. And she couldn't help a twinge of guilt, because she could never get enough of this. That morning, she'd spanked Rhoda for breaking the lusterware lamp, then attempted to calm Paul after Julie projectile vomited onto his Harris Tweed blazer. Here she was an object of adoration — a brilliant, generous executive, somehow also made to feel like a desirable beauty, far above the hassles of a wife and mother, or a semicriminal hiring blacklisted writers and dodging Dale Winston's demands to meet them. It was easy to forget all those worries, to forget why she was really here, to forget Phoebe's phone calls.

The thought snapped her back to herself. Phoebe wasn't someone to waste pennies on a social call. So Hannah smiled and small-talked her way through the circle of men she loved so much, edging toward the doors that led out into the main corridor. If Phoebe had any sense at all, she was tagging behind, waiting for the moment to catch up to her. By the time Hannah urged Peter Proud to go and get his lunch, she was at the rear door that led toward the wood. Phoebe stepped up to her, buttoning her coat. At first, Hannah thought she was fine. Then she saw the panic in Phoebe's eyes. She opened the door and led them out into the woods.

"It's not the best idea, but here," Hannah said, handing Phoebe a cigarette.

"I've been through two packs today already," Phoebe rasped. Hannah looked at her more closely. Her hair was working its way out of the fat ponytail, spiraling upward along with her voice. Her eyes were wide and anxious, and tinged with something like fury. She looked like a woman freshly blacklisted. She plunged her hand into her pocket and held out an envelope to Hannah with two tobacco-stained fingers, her lips curled as though she were handing over a freshly plucked bowel.

Hannah slipped the plain piece of paper from the envelope and read the typed message, her lips mashed together. She shoved letter and envelope into her breast pocket and stepped closer to Phoebe.

"Do you think it's someone trying to scare you?" Hannah whispered.

"And doing a pretty damn good job of it," Phoebe snapped, biting her nail.

"I meant someone with a personal gripe, not the FBI," Hannah said.

"What sort of world is this, where that's supposed to make me feel better?" Phoebe slumped down into the bracken and wrapped her arms around her knees.

Hannah examined the envelope. The postage stamp was London, and there was no return address.

"Who besides the exiles know you were subpoenaed?"

"In London? No one. It's not exactly an

opening gambit." Phoebe paused, thinking. "There was this fella I met, coming over on the ship. I told him. Or anyway, he guessed and I confirmed. I saved him from drowning, that's the sort of encounter that leads to an exchange of confidences."

"Does he know how to find you?"

"I don't see how, but he seemed sort of important. The kind of man who can track people if he puts his mind to it."

Hannah knew the sort of man Phoebe meant. The sort she'd always found amusing to track herself, back in her journalism days.

"We can at least find out if it's him," she promised.

"How do you figure?" Phoebe was skeptical.

"You don't get where I've got without picking up a few tricks," Hannah said. "Though you don't have to wait for me. If you have the means, you should contact him yourself. Might throw him off guard."

A slow grin spread over Phoebe's face.

"I was looking for a reason to be in touch with him. This could make it a lot more interesting."

Hannah couldn't resist tucking Phoebe's hair back into place.

"Well, exactly. If nothing else, you'll get

yourself a story."

"Or a whole lot more trouble," Phoebe pointed out.

Hannah looked hard into Phoebe's eyes. "They can keep trying to hurt the show all they want, but they can't hurt you any further, not here. So don't let them think they're getting the best of you."

She wondered later, though, if she'd spoken the truth. Who was to say they couldn't keep finding new ways to hurt you?

Nigel Elliott was an easy man to trace, even without Hannah's long experience.

"He's involved in diplomacy, though he doesn't need to work," she told Shirley and Will, who had come over for drinks and discussion. "He's an actual baronet, with a 'sir' before his name and everything."

"But you say he didn't tell Phoebe that?" Shirley asked.

"I suppose if someone's just saved your life, you're inclined to dispense with such formalities," Hannah said.

"Oh, come on!" Paul laughed. "You don't really believe that story?"

"Why would Phoebe lie?" Hannah was baffled. Paul usually loved such tales.

"My dear, you've been working in fiction too long," he said, shaking his head.

"Not at all," Will said. "I, for one, am more than inclined to believe a sturdy young woman like Phoebe could rescue a drunk about to topple off a ship."

"You have a point," Paul said with a smile. "These so-called aristocrats are so soft, even a girl could save one. Especially if she hoped there'd be marriage in it."

Hannah forced a smile, because of course Paul was joking, but it bothered her that he would agree with Will after dismissing her and Phoebe. Perhaps he wanted to look deferential — the good white man who recognized the intellectual and professional superiority that Will LeGrand wore so lightly on his shoulders.

Could he be jealous? Will was a famous exile, Shirley targeted, and Hannah essentially operating an illegal writing ring to keep people working. Paul was barely less innocent than Rhoda, granted leniency to stay up past her bedtime to listen, building a model plane meant for much older children to make. Julie was privileged to drowse in Shirley's lap. Hannah wondered what the girls were absorbing from this conversation. That Phoebe was fearless and Hannah an able producer, that's what she hoped was being heard.

How come Paul doesn't want to hold Julie?

I got his blazer clean.

She sipped her drink and grinned, ready to drop a bomb. "The real fun is Sir Nigel's diplomacy work might be just a cover. From what I gather, he seems to be connected with MI5 in some way," Hannah said, pleased to see her guests' surprise.

"I know you're good," Shirley said, her face disbelieving. "But how can you possibly have discovered that?"

Hannah shrugged. "Well, I could be wrong. But I put a few things together and made a guess. Now we'll just have to hope that if I'm right, he's on our side."

"Should Phoebe meet with him?" Shirley was dubious. "MI5 may not be the FBI, but they aren't exactly pro-Communist."

"She wants to see him, to let him know she's not scared," Hannah said admiringly. "I think he's all right, though. He gives a lot of money to radical theater groups. Not that he uses his own name." She topped up her drink. "Hard to believe the FBI would make such an effort to come to London, and for Phoebe of all people. What about you?" she asked the LeGrands. "Have you gotten harassed here?"

"Not here," Will said. "But my agent keeps me apprised of the mail his office receives. People are quite happy to put pen to paper and let me know they think I'm a dirty Red as well as a dirty . . . Well, I don't think it's what Stendhal meant by *The Red and the Black,* do you?"

"In our NAACP office, we got nasty letters by the truckload," Shirley said, sounding almost nostalgic as she rocked Julie. "On Fridays, we liked to have a contest for which was the most offensive. Also the most illiterate."

"Ha! My lady journo pals and I used to do the same thing!" Hannah cried. "Of course, we were just happy to have our work given attention."

"Here's to our work getting attention," Will said, raising his glass again.

Hannah drank to that. At the office, she pinned copies of *Robin Hood*'s best reviews on all her noticeboards. When Sidney saw them, he bellowed: "Ye nae wan anyone t' think your eggs are double-yoakit!" It took some while for him to cop to a translation — that people might think her boastful. Hannah saw no real harm in being pleased with her accomplishments, though. And anyway, the reviews were a spur, more than a laurel, reminding her she could never relax, that the show's quality must always be at this level. Hannah liked pressure. It kept her sharp.

"Of course, if you keep getting attention, you might hear from the FBI in some way as well," Shirley warned. "Has anyone else heard anything?"

"If they have, they've kept it quiet, and name me one of our group who'd keep something like that quiet," Hannah said. Since there were no names, she went on. "I suppose someone looks at Phoebe and thinks she's a woman alone, vulnerable, she might be easy to break. HUAC gives the red-carpet treatment to any bird who decides to sing."

"If they have names to name," Shirley pointed out. "Best to stay where we're safe."

"Safe so far," Will warned. "And Britain could refuse to renew our residency. Only a fool lets himself get too comfortable."

"Strife," Shirley said. "Though there is Canada. Or France. Or Africa." She glanced at her husband, who nodded, and she explained, "We've been talking about going to Ghana, perhaps taking a page out of the book of Hannah Wolfson and helping launch their television industry. You're an inspiration to us all, *ma chère.*"

Hannah smiled, but her heart lurched. She hated to think of Shirley leaving. London had become home. The Americans had formed a community. She'd already lost one of those. She didn't want to lose another.

She pulled a sleepy Rhoda onto her lap.

"I suppose we'll just have to keep our guard up. We've gotten along this far. The odd threat can't stop us."

She took Paul's hand and he squeezed her fingers. There was this, at least. Paul, the children, their home, their work. She had never been a superstitious woman, but she gave the polished wood end table a light knock anyway.

Just in case.

Phoebe sent Nigel a typed note. She wavered a long time before deciding to sign her name, hoping it couldn't be used for handwriting analysis.

I wonder how much more paranoid I'll become before any of this is over?

She also wondered if it would ever be over. Hoover and the FBI and HUAC all believed this was permanent. The new order. Everyone in America was to be tracked, or at least think they were. That would keep them toeing the line.

Phoebe propped her chin on her fists and looked out at the rooftops over Soho. She tried not to remember her window over Perry Street, where she could watch the Village go by. Anne had sent a drawing of

333

Floyd and Leo's, where a sign was posted for submissions to the Christmas Eve Cabaret. Phoebe heaved a long, shuddery sigh. This was the year she had planned to audition her ability to guess how people had gotten their facial scars.

It was the day of the Macy's Thanksgiving Day Parade, she realized. It was an event she'd rolled her eyes at since she was thirteen, and she was now bereft to think it was happening when she wasn't in New York. On the first of December, Greenwich Village lit up like a kaleidoscope, with all the shopkeepers stringing colored lights in their windows, often hanging tinsel and garlands too. The Italian market on Bleecker Street attempted to outdo all the department store windows on Fifth Avenue, with a little toy train going around and around, carrying cheeses and sausages in its cars. And now here it was, nearly December, and there would be no tree in Rockefeller Center, no ice skating, no carts selling chestnuts, no Radio City Christmas Spectacular, no department store windows, no cabaret, and no Chinese food and a double feature on Christmas Day.

Phoebe glared at her typewriter. She couldn't sit and write, not when she felt like running wild in the streets. She tore a page out of her notebook, scribbled *So let's finally have that coffee why don't we?* and went out to find Freddie. Within five minutes, he returned from Reg's flat on Bourchier Street with a note (and, Phoebe suspected, another penny in his pocket) suggesting they meet that afternoon. Another penny sent Freddie away to agree, and Phoebe went to tackle her hair.

It occurred to her as she was finagling the comb through her frizz that this was a date. Her first date. How the heck did a woman get to be almost thirty and never have a date? Because there was Mona to worry about, and then the war, and then work to get, she reminded herself. So this wasn't a date, really, because she still had to focus on work, had to focus on Mona. This was just a break, a story to please her sister. So no dressing up, no effort, only a bit of lipstick to maintain standards.

Reg was leaning on the post outside number seven. He smiled that funny crooked smile as she emerged. Again, she felt her heart give a little leap and she spoke more loudly than usual, because she didn't want to encourage him. Or herself.

"You oughta watch yourself, hanging around like this. You look like you're casing the joint."

"Thank goodness I've seen American films," he said. "I'm not sure I'd understand you otherwise."

"I never understand half of what I hear around here! And I can't say anything, it being your country and all."

"Plus we invented the language," he pointed out.

"But we made it fun," she countered.

"Ha! We can match you slang for slang."

"A likely story."

All the way to the Underground station at Tottenham Court Road and then the ride to Bishopsgate, they compared their respective lingos. Phoebe, though she'd eavesdropped on conversations when traveling to work, and on the set, realized she hadn't learned much of the language that was both so familiar and so foreign. Reg explained that he'd grown up in North London ("Not the nicest part, but we kept things up well") and that the language there was as different from the Cockney rhymes that were considered the common tongue of London as English was from French.

"As kids, we were fascinated when we heard it, of course, not that we often did," he said. "My parents had notions, wanting us to go to university and make something of ourselves. If I ever called the stairs 'the

336

old apples and pears,' I'd get my ears boxed."

Which, Phoebe learned, had nothing to do with boxing.

"It's a great step down, my being in Soho," Reg said in mock sorrow, shaking his head for emphasis as they ascended the stairs at the Bank stop. "Such a disappointment to my family. A veritable black sheep, I am." Then he reverted to earnestness. "But the war changed all our plans. First I was too young and then too asthmatic to serve, so I took up my place at Oxford after all. They liked to assure us we were doing our own sort of duty by carrying on the tradition of fine education. Guilt, a wonderful motivator. There were more starred first degrees in my year than the place ever saw before or since, I should think."

" 'Starred first'?" Phoebe asked. "We stopped getting stars after kindergarten."

Reg laughed. "In a British university, it's a top degree. Good luck ever meeting a chap who got one and doesn't work it into the conversation."

"I notice you haven't actually said you got one," Phoebe observed.

"Well, my people might have notions, but they still uphold modesty as a valuable trait," Reg said, and winked. "And if you'll look to your left, Miss Adler, you'll see a fine example of medieval London." He gestured like a museum docent.

"It's a church," Phoebe said. "I thought we were going to that Seven Stars pub."

"I thought you'd enjoy the detour," he said simply.

Mild annoyance swirled up Phoebe's spine, but Reg's smile was very sweet, and the small stone church very handsome. The annoyance dissipated by the time her gaze landed on the spire.

"It doesn't look that old," she said at last.

"Like many buildings, St. Helen's has received some tweaks over the years," Reg conceded, guiding her inside. "But give the old girl some credit, she's survived the Great Fire and the Blitz and still puts on a fine face, doesn't she?"

"Probably uses Elizabeth Arden," Phoebe said. She fell silent, though, on seeing the mostly Gothic interior, with arches far more majestic than the small exterior would have suggested. It felt like a place Robin Hood might have gone to worship. It must have offered such peace, in the midst of so much fear. She lay a hand on a plastered wall. It was cool. Calm rolled over her, reminding her how very not calm she had been for such a long time.

"How many people must have sat in here over the centuries," she said, surprising herself by whispering. "The clothes changed, but the prayers stayed the same, didn't they? Asking for health, for comfort, for a better day tomorrow."

"It's all most of us ever want," Reg agreed.

She looked at him then, and felt like she was looking at this man for the first time. The huge brown eyes behind the glasses were warm and intelligent, and had a snap that made her smile. Her smile encouraged his own crooked smile, and he ran a hand through his mop of brown curls.

"Actually, most of us want a heck of a lot more," Phoebe said. "They'll say all the right things in church, even think them, but given half the chance, plenty of New Yorkers would pray for a penthouse apartment with a view of Central Park."

"And what about you, Miss Adler? What would you pray for?"

"Well now, that's a personal question," she said, grinning. "And it presumes I'm a praying sort of gal, besides."

"How perfect, then, for me to ask forgiveness inside a church," Reg said.

"Aw, that's swell of you. And tell you what, just for being an all right fella, you can call me Phoebe."

"I'm honored."

"I should hope so."

Something in his smile unnerved her and made her sweep her eyes back up to the ceiling, admiring the dark beams, so stark against the white paint.

"Funny, isn't it?" she murmured. "The outlaws and their pursuers would both have come to church, looking for what amounts to the same thing, and certain they were both right. Both sides always think they're right. Hoover and HUAC think they're right, and there isn't a single person on the blacklist or in prison who doesn't think they're the ones who are right."

She caught herself then, realizing she shouldn't have said that out loud. Not yet. Because who really knew who could be trusted? And yet, she wanted to trust this man. She wasn't sure Joan was the best judge, but Freddie thought Reg was all right, and she felt confident in the boy's assessment.

Reg looked like he wanted to ask a question. Instead, he joined her in staring at the ceiling.

"I thought I'd become a professor, something to land me properly in the middle class. Make a name for myself writing a new sort of history, about the real people. Bring the excitement of history to life so everyone can discover it, not just the lucky ones who get the chance to look for it. I'm quite sure, you know, that the more people know about the past, the better we can all be. Though I wonder now if I shouldn't focus on being an ordinary teacher, working on the ground with the sort of kids I was. Things are changing here, you know, and in ways we couldn't have imagined before the war. I even fancy the idea of getting involved in politics a bit. It's worth dodging any mud that might be slung to help make better things keep on happening, don't you reckon?"

He was younger than herself, she realized, and full of an idealism she didn't remember ever having. It made her nostalgic for someone she'd never had the luxury to be. Even Hannah had once been that person, as a fiery young journalist. Heck, she still was, and she was more than ten years older than Phoebe.

"Do you really think better things are happening?" she asked him.

He extended an arm to her, an extravagant, Victorian sort of gesture that nonetheless felt exactly right, and she looped her arm in his. He escorted her out of the church and on a crawl through London.

"Loads of us missed the war soon after it finished, if you can believe that, because the peace wasn't much fun. Rationing's only finally finished, and I expect you've seen what remains of a lot of people's homes. But I'm a Londoner, and I know who we are. We are on the rise again, and in a way that will do far more for the real people."

"Oh, those real people. They get so many promises," Phoebe said.

"They were promised National Health and got it. More is coming, you'll see."

She wondered vaguely if she would see. How long would she be here? She had to get a Christmas present for Mona, and all she wanted was to be there in person to give her a hug. And some oil to slick her wheels so she could embarrass Tommy Morton in the corridor races.

"Phoebe?"

"Except she might crash into a wall," Phoebe said.

"Sorry?"

She looked at Reg. His expression was bemused, but interested.

"I have a sister," she began. All along Holborn (where, it pleased her to learn, criminals used to pass on their way to be hanged), she told him about Mona, the airfield, the parents who'd kept so much from her and

342

died so soon, leaving her to make her way and eventually become a television writer.

"And yet you left it all behind to come here and write a novel," he said.

"It's the obvious trajectory," she said bitterly.

His voice dropped to a whisper. "Or perhaps you *had* to get away?"

"You make it sound so nefarious," she said. "Careful. If I'm someone who committed one crime, I might commit another."

"But you didn't commit a crime, did you?" he pressed. "Quite the opposite."

His eyes were too intense. She backed away from him.

"I don't like where this is going. It's not your business, none of this."

"Pax, pax," he said, reaching for her arm again. She jerked it away from him. "Phoebe, do you really think I'm not on your side?"

"Right now you're in front and at an angle," she pointed out.

"Clown all you like, but good luck finding anyone in Britain who thinks the blacklist is sensible." At the word "blacklist," she jumped and glanced around. He moved closer and took her hand. "I'm an historian, Phoebe, and haven't we just had a war that shows the madness of persecuting people

343

for their beliefs? I can show you my Labour Party card, if you like. I promise, I'm for you."

She stared at her hand, wrapped in his. His thumb stroked hers.

"I should scram," she said quickly. "I need to work, I need the money. Mona needs the best Christmas I can give her."

"She'll get it," Reg promised. "She'll also want you to have a cup of tea." He gestured to the pretty black-and-white exterior of the Seven Stars.

Phoebe wasn't sure she wanted to go in with him now. Those eyes were a little too magnetic. The sort of eyes a person could get lost in. Phoebe didn't want to get lost. What guarantee was there of ever being found again?

"Think of how many centuries of tavern fights have been in here," he said.

His powers of persuasion were strong. "I hope people were killed," she warned.

The pub was dark and poky, and Phoebe couldn't help smiling, because it definitely felt like a place Robin and the other outlaws would go for clandestine meetings. If she squinted, she could sweep away the leather and shine, turning it all into rough wood and barrels of ale, served in pewter tankards. She let Reg order them tea from the unimpressed publican, imagining the shouts of a brawl, the drawing of daggers, the serving boy in the corner gearing up for another evening of scrubbing blood off the floor.

"Rather bloodthirsty, aren't you?" Reg marveled as she shared her thoughts.

"Thirsty, anyway," she conceded, reaching for a cup.

"Not yet!" he remonstrated. "It's not ready."

"It's tea," Phoebe protested. "What do you add, parsley?"

Reg ignored this, swirling the pot in a steady rhythm. At last, he poured it out, adding milk with the exactitude of a chemist measuring arsenic doses.

Phoebe took a sip. The tea was strong enough to peel paint. Reg grinned.

"I'm a North Londoner by way of the true north, in York. If you want a proper cup of tea, it's got to be done by a northerner. Also fish and chips."

"I should go north sometime," Phoebe said.

"You should." He smiled again, and it wasn't just the tea that warmed her through.

He walked her back to Meard Street, where Freddie and the other boys were kicking a ball about under the streetlights.

"Kids never get cold, do they?" Phoebe

said. "It's like it's a job manifest."

"Can I see you again next weekend?" Reg asked. He suddenly seemed not much older than Freddie.

"I . . . I don't know," Phoebe said. "I have to write, I need more work."

"I know," he said. "But there's a lot of London out there, and I'd love to show you more of it."

"I'll let you know," she promised.

He kissed her hand so quickly, he was nearly to the corner when she realized it. She shouted after him, "Hey! So did you get a starred first?"

He called back, "An ordinary first. But I got the star today."

Phoebe had to laugh, both at the line and the chorus of "ewwwwwws" the street boys harmonized. She beckoned Freddie to her.

"You're still sure about that one?" she asked.

"Yes indeed, miss. Only there was another man I saw a few days ago, miss, and I didn't cotton to his look at all."

"Who? What? Why haven't you said?" Phoebe yelped.

"I've not seen you, miss, and Mum's most particular about me not knocking on the tenants' doors. He was tall, dressed like a toff, not one of us at all."

Phoebe chilled. That sounded like Nigel.

"Looked down his big nose at all of us, but didn't say nothing," Freddie continued, his voice heavy with scorn. "Walked with a swagger, just like in them American copper films. Tilted that big green hat of his, like he thought he was so posh and swank."

On Meard Street, a man's thinking he was "posh and swank" was a great sin, and Phoebe cradled that tiny bit of comfort in her clenched fist, the sure knowledge that her pursuer had made the denizens scoff. Because it was him, of course it was. The man in the green hat. The FBI Hound who had handed her a subpoena. There was no chance he was just coincidentally in London on vacation and had taken a wrong turn.

"Look at me, suddenly inspiring all these men to follow me about. Ain't I the vixen, though?" Phoebe rolled her eyes. Freddie, perhaps understanding adult sarcasm for the first time in his life, was emboldened to pat her arm. Phoebe thought of something. "He didn't drop off a letter or anything, did he?"

"No, miss, only walked about slowly, and asked me if I'd seen any Americans. I told him certainly I had, aren't they in all the films?"

Phoebe could have kissed the boy. Instead,

she gave him a sixpence, and he looked at her with deep adoration.

"A letter did come for you today, though, miss. Mrs. Morrison was a-cooing over it because it was engraved, she said."

Engraved? The FBI might waste money chasing political leftists, but they wouldn't bother with fancy stationery.

The envelope was a heavy vellum, sent by someone who didn't even know the cost of postage, let alone care. Nigel's handwriting was a florid calligraphy that seemed more suited to the previous century, along with his language. He was delighted, et cetera, and would she join him for a spot of something at his club?

Nigel. In league with the FBI, or a man who might be a friend? Maybe she would find out. She hoped, if the man in the green hat was following her, he'd see her going to a posh club in her Bonwit Teller dress. If her peace was going to be shattered, she might as well look fabulous.

CHAPTER FOURTEEN

"A kiss on the hand?" Mona shrieked. "The song says that's Continental. I expect something else from an Englishman."

"A tip of the hat, maybe?" Phoebe asked. "A polite wave?"

"I'm thinking something way more impolite. What did it feel like?"

"Mostly just lips on my hand," Phoebe admitted. "But, um . . ."

"Speak up!" Mona boomed.

"I don't know. It was . . . nice."

"There's the power with words that makes you a writer of such note."

Phoebe had no retort. She wanted to describe the little twirl of her spirits when Reg touched her, but it all felt like a cliché, not anything real. Mona deserved better than that.

"You're quiet," Mona accused. "You must like him."

"I do," Phoebe admitted. "But it's so hard

to know who to trust."

"Very few people are really double agents," Mona said. "If I were you, I'd assume he sees you're one swell cookie. So go ahead and toss him a crumb or two."

"I'll have to ask if that's legal here."

She wished she could tell Mona how scared she felt. Scared that Mona was going to die soon, scared that she would live on and Phoebe couldn't send her enough money for good care. Scared that Reg would be a distraction from the work she needed to do to keep her and Mona comfortable. Scared she might think he was someone to trust, and then be wrong. Scared she wasn't as safe as she thought she was. But she couldn't upset Mona. She owed Mona a life well lived. So long as Mona believed she was thriving, even happy, pesky details like the truth didn't matter. Mona didn't even have to believe it. Pretending was good enough.

Saturday, Phoebe and Reg went to the British Museum. They sat in front of the Rosetta Stone for a long time.

"It unlocked history," Reg said reverentially. "So much we wouldn't understand without it. Not just language, but part of who we were."

"Yes," Phoebe agreed. "Though how much do people change, really?"

"You're a cynic, Phoebe Adler," he teased.

"I'm a realist," she corrected him. "People have always been scared of stupid stuff, and done stupider stuff to try and make themselves feel better."

"Maybe it's you who should be teaching history, rather than me."

"Let's go look at medieval weapons," Phoebe urged.

He was fun. He was easy to talk to. She liked the way their arms linked. He guided her through Bloomsbury, still teeming with writers and artists, and they shared an eel pie and mash at the Lamb, listening to locals arguing about politics and plays. Phoebe luxuriated in the cacophony so like that at Floyd and Leo's. She and Reg joined in the general conversation and people listened to her, and laughed at her jokes. And when Reg asked if she'd like to go to a club in Soho that night, she was sorry to decline, even though she was excited for her Nigel adventure. She had to work, she said.

Better not to tell him the truth yet. Not until after she'd looked Nigel Elliott in the eye and decided for herself whether or not he was an enemy.

■ ■ ■ ■

The Egotists' Club was in Park Place, a street even richer than Park Avenue. Phoebe felt both thrilled and alien as she stood before the white Georgian building, readying herself to go in. Hannah had told her that Nigel seemed to be all right, and indeed might be worth cultivating, but to be on her guard and see if she could outsmart or unnerve him. Phoebe took a deep breath, fighting the girdle that dug into her stomach. There was no mistaking her for someone who belonged here. But so long as she told herself she didn't care, she had power. She threw back her shoulders and strutted inside.

"May I help you, madam?" the concierge greeted her. Politely, but with a chill, waiting to see if she merited deference. The name Nigel Elliott produced the right response, and her coat was taken with the same regard as if it were a mink, rather than a tired bouclé wool from an end-of-season sale at Saks. Phoebe caught a glimpse of herself in a full-length mirror, no doubt strategically placed so female guests could make sure they were ready to enter in style. From her piled and slicked updo to her good stockings and heels, she looked like the self she barely remembered. The vision of the lady she'd always striven to be. The successful career woman, who was invited to all the best places. She touched her watch, wishing she could tell her parents who she was tonight. Suddenly Nigel was there, leaning in to kiss her cheek in a rush of brilliantine and expensive aftershave.

"Lovely to see you again, my dear, do come in."

"I have it on good authority that I'm to call you 'Sir Nigel,' " she said as they traversed a room as grand as a palace.

"My friends are allowed to call me Nigel," he said with a laugh and a pat on her hand. "Especially the ones to whom I owe my life."

He looked like a friend. He spoke like a friend. Not that one could always tell. She'd thought Hank, Geraldine, and even Jimmy were friends, after a fashion. Nigel seated her in an enormous leather chair by a fireplace, handed her a glass of champagne and one of those delectable Sobranie cigarettes. If he was out to cause her grief, he was certainly making the journey pleasant.

"Your note suggested that things are going rather swimmingly," Nigel said. "I couldn't be more delighted. I do hope that means you are liking London."

"As a hideout goes, it's pretty swell," Phoebe said.

Nigel laughed. "One envisages you lurking in the cellar of a safe house."

"No, I landed on the top floor."

He laughed again. "So, are you able to divulge the nature of your work, or is it all terribly clandestine?"

"Clandestine is my middle name," she said, tapping her nose. "Actually it's Berneice, isn't that cruel?"

"My charming wife's Christian name is Hortense. At least you have 'Phoebe,' a truly lovely name for a truly lovely young woman."

It was real, then, the bond she'd felt on the ship. She could read his tones perfectly. He was a man living a lie, trying not to get caught. He was more unhappy than not. And he let her, a near stranger, know all this, because her own situation was so similar. He was someone she could trust. He was a friend.

"I've sold a script," she said in a low voice. "To a terrific television show. Now I'm working on another, trying to make lightning strike twice."

"As though you were Zeus himself," Nigel pronounced. He waved his hand and a waiter descended, set up a tray full of covered silver dishes, and in seconds presented Phoebe with a small plate piled with meats and vol-au-vents.

"I do hope you don't mind a bit of informal nibbling," Nigel said. "Women aren't permitted in the dining room except for luncheon and afternoon tea, though I had a bit of a hunch you would enjoy this arrangement more anyway."

It was as though he knew that, certain she could trust him, she wanted to ask him more. Though perhaps it did his reputation no harm to be seen whispering to another woman by a fire. People might remember that, and not notice if his toe tapped against the toe of another man.

"So this is a safe space to talk?" she asked. "And you're a safe pair of hands?"

"Nothing gets heard here. As for me, well . . ." He displayed a pair of well-manicured hands. "Soft, I suppose, but beneath the supple surface, overflowing with capability. I like to think you can put yourself in them with assurance."

Phoebe didn't say the words "Robin Hood," but she told him Hedda Hopper had come to London, sniffing out blacklistees.

"Yes," he said grimly. "Your country is brimming with wealth and glory, and yet it cannot abide the idea of those it disapproves of getting on with their lives."

"Do you think that extends so far as sending anonymous threats by mail?"

"That seems a bit extreme," Nigel said, looking closely to see if she was joking.

"What about sending an actual FBI Hound to London?"

Now he laughed. "For you? Darling, forgive me, but you're of far too little consequence to warrant such bother."

"How do you know?"

"I've got a lot of friends in a lot of places, including various stages of trouble. I know things."

Another wave of his hand brought a tray of cakes. "Take one of each," he urged. "We're only recently off the sugar rationing, we ought to indulge." He ate a few cakes, clearly relishing every mouthful. "I met that head of the FBI once. Hoover. Rather Dickensian sort of name, when you think of him hoovering people up into his traps and prisons. I'd have thought a nation so powerful would be a bit more fearless, but such are the times in which we find ourselves. They're afraid of the Soviets; they think you might be in league with the Soviets; and so want *you* afraid of *them*. Socratic dialogue at its most inane."

"If American Communists were really in cahoots with the Soviets and the FBI's pounding them so hard, you'd think it'd prove the Soviets are all talk, no trousers."

"Ah, you've picked up some local lingo! My congratulations," Nigel toasted her.

"Doesn't much help me if it turns out I'm not really safe here," Phoebe said.

"You are safe," he assured her. "But they want to keep you all worried. They hope that you might ultimately give yourself up, just for the relief of that worry." He drained his glass. "Though I daresay it's not impossible they might find a way to prevent your residency being renewed. Bit anticlimactic, compared to stopping a film from being distributed, I should think."

"So they *can* touch me?" Phoebe hated the fear in her voice. Hated how much Hoover would love it.

"My dear girl, try not to fret." Nigel took her hand. "I'll cast a few stones, see if I can learn something of real use for you. Maybe someone once sang a song about you that made you sound like more than you are. Or, of course, it could be personal."

"I never saw the man in the green hat till he started hounding me."

"Rotten Hound, if he let himself be seen. Hoover ought to whip him." He tipped the

357

last of the champagne into her glass. "They may think they have power here, but they don't know what Britain is still capable of. Don't forget that."

Phoebe asked one more favor — if he could find out for her if Reg was who he said he was, or a spy. Nigel laughed.

"My goodness! You have picked up a host of admirers! You had best hope they never find out you're asking to have them vetted."

"I had you vetted before I came here," Phoebe said slyly.

He threw back his head and laughed.

"Of course you did, pet, I would hope for nothing less." He squeezed her hand. "You're a clever and resourceful young woman. I have great faith in you. Look how splendidly you've managed already."

"I've only managed because I've had help," she admitted.

"The person who claims they've done everything all on their own is usually deluded or a liar," he told her in a tone that brooked no arguments. "Now then, I've got another engagement, but you and I shall rendezvous again soon. I enjoy your company, my dear Phoebe."

"Likewise," she said. "So really, how much of a Red can that possibly make me?"

He laughed and walked her to the entrance, waving his hand to have her coat fetched and then helping her into it. "If I don't see you before, have a very happy Christmas and New Year's, my dear girl." He kissed her cheek and whispered, "If you run into real trouble, ring the number in your pocket." He kissed her other cheek with exuberance. "Charming to see you again, my dear, utterly charming!"

Phoebe was halfway to Soho before she reached into her coat pocket and found a small card with a number and an address for telegrams. She hadn't seen or felt him go anywhere near her pockets. *Neat trick. I'll have to work that into a script.*

Despite the threats, the man in the green hat, Hedda Hopper, and all of it, she felt better. Someone might be watching her, but far more people were looking after her. There was safety in all those numbers. She held her head high as she walked down the middle of Meard Street.

"I can look after myself too," she said aloud. "Don't make the mistake of thinking otherwise."

Atta girl, she heard Mona's voice in her head. *These bastards don't deserve the pleasure of thinking you're scared. You be their Scrooge for Christmas.*

The holidays passed quickly. A party at Hannah's, a party at the LeGrands', a ten-minute phone call with Mona on Boxing Day. Phoebe told her more about Reg and their ongoing adventures — forays to the National Gallery, St. Paul's, the remains of the London Wall.

"Yes, yes, yes, but what about the kissing?" Mona demanded.

"Still nonexistent," Phoebe said. "We talk a lot about violent history, it doesn't lend itself to romance."

She could hear Mona's eyes rolling.

"Step on it, kiddo," Mona scolded. "Time's a-wasting."

Phoebe knew it. Each phone call, Mona's voice was just a bit weaker. Weaker, but angrier. Mona wasn't going gently into the good night.

"I think he's got something special planned for New Year's," Phoebe said.

"That only keeps him meeting expectations, not exceeding them," Mona said.

The Bonwit dress came out again on New Year's Eve. Reg was right. Hope was coming alive in London — all England, if the papers were to be believed. Everyone, even the toughest Teddy Girls, who sported knickerbockers and workingmen's boots, would put on the style tonight. Phoebe suspected even Beryl would concede enough to the celebratory mood to put on her finest pair of trousers.

Freddie was practicing marbles in the vestibule.

"Gosh, but you look smart, miss," he greeted her. "Are you off somewhere posh?"

"Seeing as it's Mr. Bassill, I doubt it, but I thought I'd dress the part."

It felt alien, not wanting to go "somewhere posh." She thought of Nigel, who had sent her a short note to say that Reg was a Labour Party member and socialist through and through, but these were no great impediments to his general decency, and besides, he went to Oxford so he probably knew how to behave. Nigel would be in the poshest of places tonight, counting the minutes until he could escape and go where he really wanted to be. "Somewhere posh" was not, perhaps, such an ideal.

Mrs. Cotley opened her door from the dim back of the building and glared at her son. "Not troubling you, is he, miss?" she asked in a warning tone. Freddie looked down.

"Not at all, Mrs. Cotley," Phoebe told her.

"He's my best pal in the building."

She realized as she said it that it wasn't such a compliment to Joan, but she wouldn't trade Freddie's shining eyes for anything.

"All right then," Mrs. Cotley said, resigned if unconvinced. She left the door ajar. The sounds of Nat King Cole singing "Unforgettable" poured into the vestibule.

"Will you be dancing, do you think?" Freddie asked Phoebe.

"I hope so, though I'm awfully out of practice," she admitted.

"They're making us dance at school," Freddie grumbled. "It's stupid."

"I always thought so too," Phoebe agreed. "But I like it now." She impulsively took Freddie's hand and spun him around. He laughed and let her be the lead as they goofed about with exaggerated gestures and silly faces.

"This is how dancing should be," Freddie said in approval.

"I'm inclined to agree," Reg said behind them.

Phoebe grinned and held out a hand to him to join their circle. He stared at her a moment, his mouth open, then joined them for the rest of the song. They bid a disappointed Freddie good night and headed off.

Meard Street was packed with people

heading to parties, or at parties, chaos blaring through windows. Reg said nothing. True, he would have to raise his voice to be heard, but that had never stopped him before. His silence unsettled Phoebe.

"Take a breath, Reg, and let a girl get a word in edgewise, won't you?" Phoebe said at last.

Reg smiled and ran a hand through his hair. "I do apologize," he said. "I find myself rather taken aback by your appearance."

"It's New Year's Eve, I wasn't going to dress for digging ditches," Phoebe said.

"You'd still be lovely if you had," he said.

Now it was Phoebe's turn to be wordless. Lovely? She knew she wasn't the funny-looking kid she once was, but no one except Mona had ever called her lovely. And here was Reg, implying he saw her that way even when she wasn't wearing makeup and her best dress.

He took her to one of Soho's jazz clubs, a place they accessed via a tiny alley and several imposing doors. Inside, it was just like a movie — with plumes of smoke and sweaty revelers drinking and dancing. Reg proved to be a good dancer. Phoebe was her usual self, making jokes and banter, but all she could think was that this was the story Mona wanted. This was a real gift for her sister, and better for that realness. Phoebe could have spun fanciful scenarios for Mona, but even over the phone, Mona knew when Phoebe was lying.

She had a sudden jolt. *Who else? Who else can read me and know what's true?*

No one, she decided, except Anne. Her sister and her oldest friend. She relaxed and looked up into the brown eyes that were smiling at her. Without her noticing, Reg had turned handsome. Phoebe blinked away from his eyes to take a breath.

"Happy New Year!" someone shouted. The room burst into "Auld Lang Syne."

"I thought that was an American thing," Phoebe said.

"It's a Scottish song," Reg reminded her.

"The Scottish don't get enough credit," Phoebe said. "They invented television, the telephone, and the refrigerator. Also bicycle pedals and the mackintosh. So they made staying in comfortable, getting around fun, and going out in the rain tolerable. Not sure if they gain or lose points for inventing golf, though."

"It's subjective," Reg said. "Any English inventions that impress you?"

"Fingerprint classification!" Phoebe cried. "A crime writer's best friend."

"Do you reckon yourself a crime writer still?"

"I'll never not be interested in people behaving badly. And getting punished for it," she finished with relish, her fist clenched.

"I say, you look fierce," Reg said. "Remind me never to cross you."

"Hey, Reg," she said, poking a finger into his chest. "Don't ever cross me."

He laughed and wound his hand around her finger, taking her hand and guiding it to his lips. He kissed it once, twice, and folded his other hand over it. "I won't ever cross you," he promised.

It was as if they were alone in the room. Phoebe felt herself gulp.

"Good," she said, but her voice was husky. " 'Cause then I'd have to . . . do something," she finished lamely. Her brain was refusing to function. Her only consolation was that he looked as flustered as she felt.

They took a long, circuitous path home, and Reg's hand stayed curled around hers. Parties were winding down — the music flooding the streets was quieter. People were still outside — some shouting, some dancing, some fighting, some kissing. Phoebe noticed none of them. She didn't notice anything until Reg stopped.

"Listen," he said. The strain of a saxophone playing "Unforgettable" wafted down from a window. "It's our song tonight." Reg drew her to him in a slow dance. His other hand was under her coat, pressing into the plum silk. Even with the din around them, she could hear the swish-crush of the fabric against the small of her back. Heat moved up her spine and down her legs as her body involuntarily pressed closer to his. The hand holding hers went to her face and tilted it upward, and there were those enormous brown eyes again. In a film, she supposed one of them might have taken off their glasses. Then he was kissing her and she was kissing him and she forgot everything else until he drew back just enough to raise her glasses to the top of her head.

"Those eyes," he murmured. "How well can you see me?"

"Up close everything is clear," she said. She slipped off his own glasses, folded them, and tucked them into his coat pocket. "And yourself, Mr. Bassill? Am I just a shadow now, all rough around the edges? How many fingers am I holding up?"

He took the fingers and kissed each one.

"Three," he told her.

"Actually, it was four," she teased.

He laughed and hugged her to him. Then he tilted her head up again, his eyes close to hers. "How much . . . ?" he whispered. "How much do you have to love about a person before you simply love the person?"

Phoebe was glad he was holding her so tightly. Otherwise, she'd slip straight to the ground. The cleaning bill would be astronomical.

"I . . . don't know," she croaked. Love? How was that possible? Surely he hardly knew her?

"Well, allow me to take a quick inventory," he said. "Intelligent, charismatic, funny, fearless, talented. A fighter for justice, a cocker of snooks to all who would thwart her. And under it all, a tender and generous heart. I've never said it to anyone before, but I love you, Phoebe Adler."

Phoebe decided now was not the time to confirm if cocking a snook meant thumbing a nose. She hoped it was a touch more rude.

"You don't have to say anything," he said. "I know it's awfully soon. I just had to tell you."

"I think I've just found one advantage to being blacklisted," Phoebe said. "You can't possibly be cadging for a free ride to America."

He laughed and kissed her temple, then her cheek, then her lips again. "This is what I love about you."

It was, perhaps, something about her Americanness — or specifically, her New Yorkerness — but Phoebe knew, quite suddenly, that it was really just her. This man running his finger along her cheek saw *her* — and loved her.

"I hope you don't mind my saying I'm not sorry you were blacklisted," Reg said, his eyes twinkling.

"That makes one of us," she said. "Though things haven't been going so badly, all things considered."

"I'm glad."

The song ended, and a nearby fight heated up. Someone threw a bottle and shouted, "Go to hell, you bastard!" Phoebe couldn't help smirking a little at this example of how love could turn sour. It wasn't a bad thing to remember. It kept a person from losing their head.

"I guess that's our cue to head home," Phoebe said, with a twinge of relief. This was all too much, too fast, too heady. She wanted to keep kissing him, and she wanted to put a door between them. She wanted to write all this down for Mona, and Anne too. Also herself. She wanted to keep this moment.

"Next Saturday night, if not sooner?" he asked at her door, the way he always did.

"I'll check my calendar," she promised with her customary wink.

She stood by the door, watching him until he turned the corner. She wrapped her arms around herself and squealed, something she hadn't remembered doing since 1943, when she opened the letter saying she had sold a script for a radio play.

As she unlocked the door, something caught her eye. Meard Street was full of people going and coming home. But she was almost sure, just for a moment, that she saw the cut of a flashy suit, the shadow of a hat that was just a bit too familiar. Familiar enough to make her shiver.

"Is anyone there?" she shouted into the darkness.

"Who bloody wants to know?" someone shouted back. Several people laughed at this, and other shouts and catcalls followed.

"Happy bloody New Year to you too!" Phoebe called, and was rewarded by laughter as she went upstairs. It almost warmed her back up again.

As far as Hannah was concerned, the holidays weren't over until the third Monday in January, when *Robin Hood* resumed filming. She bounded out of bed at five.

"We're back! A new year, more scripts,

more episodes!" She danced around the room as she dressed.

"Wish you had that sort of energy to help me with a new idea," Paul muttered, glaring at the clock. He was always irascible between stories.

"The rebuilding of the East End!" she cried. "A day in the life of a London librarian! The underground clubs in Soho — find a good one and take me!"

"How about a day on the set of *Robin Hood*?" he asked, sitting up.

"Don't be silly, darling, you're not an entertainment writer."

He flopped back down and rolled over. "You just don't want me interfering with all your admirers."

She froze, her hairbrush halfway through a wave. She'd never told him about enjoying the attention of the men on the set. She'd told no one, not even Shirley. It was a tiny pleasure for her alone.

"All I meant, darling, is you're a serious writer," she said soothingly. "And it might look a little odd if my husband writes a story about my show. Anyway, there might be a big profile on us soon. Sidney's been liaising with a reporter from —"

"Of course he has," Paul interrupted. "*I* was joking. I don't know what his excuse is, besides giving you more to do. Isn't it dangerous, putting your name more out there?"

"It'll be about the show, not me."

"A show that needs no publicity. You're hardly underdogs."

Rhoda, attracted by the sound of her parents' voices, burst into the room and jumped on the bed.

"Can we get an underdog?" she shouted.

Julie, drawn like a magnet by the word "dog," ran to Hannah. "Want dog, want dog!" she demanded, clinging to Hannah's legs.

"Good morning to you too," Hannah said, hefting her daughter to her hip.

"A dog, just what we need," Paul grumbled, reaching for his robe. "What's the point in having help if we can't even keep the kids out of the bedroom till we're dressed? We could have been sleeping. Or something."

Hannah waggled her brows at him and he chuckled. There was never as much time for "or something" as she wished.

"How about we get home early and steal a bit of 'or something' time this evening?" she suggested.

"Only if I've got a new story to celebrate," he said, laughing. "You know me, can't sit around twirling my thumbs for long."

She did know him, and she remembered it wasn't so long ago that the only reason they needed for lovemaking was that they were in love. She couldn't say that, not when he was tired and casting about for a new idea. Not when the children needed breakfast and she needed to consult with Gemma about groceries for the week and then get to the office.

What do I expect? We're not kids. We never were. I'm a plump, middle-aged mama with a demanding job, and he's a middle-aged daddy fighting to stay competitive in a field that would as soon kill him as look at him. We're lucky to get a half night's sleep.

"When can we get the underdog?" Rhoda insisted.

"When things settle down a bit," Hannah promised.

Gemma wrangled the girls off to the kitchen amid demands to know when things would settle down, and Hannah followed, keeping her shoes off so she could think. It wasn't just a demanding job. It was, by the standards of people like Hedda Hopper, HUAC, and J. Edgar Hoover, a criminal operation. She looked around the cheerful, pale green kitchen, where coffee was percolating, eggs were boiling, and Rhoda was shoveling porridge into her mouth. Hannah helped Julie manage her own spoon, thinking she must look like a mother straight out of *Good Housekeeping,* not a master of the underworld. It was heady stuff. She was ready to go back to the bedroom and engage in all manner of "or something."

Paul, shaven and shiny, came whistling into the kitchen. Hannah leapt up, but he gave her only a chaste peck on the cheek — he always said children shouldn't see more than that — then dropped kisses on each daughter's head. He accepted toast from Gemma, took the newspaper, and strode away whistling.

"I hope that means an idea is starting to take shape," Hannah said. "He's like a wounded tiger when he's between stories."

"So he be," Gemma said. "But little different from any other man I've seen."

"I suppose they can be a bit ridiculous, really," Hannah said.

"Not much supposing there," Gemma agreed.

Everyone was excited to be back at work. Hannah had convinced Sidney to dole out handsome Christmas bonuses rather than tins of Walkers shortbread, but the money wasn't the incentive. Articles about the show appeared in every important entertainment publication, and every department was praised. Everyone had a story about friends or relatives who, over Christmas, had expressed pride, pleasure, and a touch of envy for their being so exalted as to be connected with such a program. Nearly all of them had once been assured that television was a fad that wouldn't last, that pursuing work in the arts was a certain path to penury. Now they worked on what the papers called "the most entertaining and well-made programme for children on television." Such adulation guaranteed longtime employment. The joy on the set was palpable, and every time Hannah visited it, she swelled with pride.

Though Phoebe had mentioned a suspicious man around her street, there were no further sightings or letters, and the man she spoke of the most was Reg. She sparkled like a Christmas tree when she talked about him, and Hannah remembered the early days with Paul, that feeling of love being so powerful, you could spread your arms and float to the stars. Even Shirley was charmed by Phoebe's happiness, and Joan insisted on taking personal credit for it, having delivered Reg's letters.

Not that Phoebe didn't have her fears.

She'd sold — with Hannah's help — a short play to *Woman's Hour* and was working on another, plus another *Robin Hood* script, but no amount of money she sent home would change the fact that Mona would soon need help breathing.

"I knew this was coming," Phoebe admitted on Sunday. "But it's still a surprise."

Hannah made a mental note to tell Phoebe to use the line in a script sometime. Scripts continued to pour into the Sapphire offices by the sackful, and she and Sidney were bombarded with requests to coproduce television films. "I like this one," Hannah announced. "It's about the Peasants' Revolt."

"No money in it," Sidney complained.

"Nonsense. We've got people excited about watching medieval stories. This fits right in with our manifest."

"We maybe ought to show we can do other things," Sidney suggested.

"We maybe have another problem," Beryl cut into the argument. "Your man Dale Winston is on the telephone. He says he's in London for a week and insists he's meeting with you, and a writer for *Robin Hood*. He won't take no for an answer and says this afternoon is most convenient for him if there's someone based in London."

Sidney exhaled a ream of language that Hannah was sure was appalling, but his speech was so fast and his accent so heavy, she heard none of it. All she heard was Shirley in her head, saying, *Strife.*

"Fine," she announced at last. "He wants a writer, we'll give him one, and today is as good as any other."

"Are ye off yer heid?" Sidney bellowed.

"We'll give him Ivy Morrow. Beryl, that's going to have to be you."

A concoction of pride, outrage, excitement, and pure horror danced across Beryl's face.

"Go on, tell him to swing on by and we'll give him tea," Hannah ordered. "Don't worry about him recognizing your voice later, he'll likely think all Scottish women sound the same."

Beryl was too flustered to argue. She stalked back to the phone.

"How can this possibly work?" Sidney asked.

"He'll find her fascinating," Hannah said, in the tone of one who knew. "Plus, he'll only understand one word in ten."

"Hannah —"

"Beryl's the story editor, she can talk about writing till the man wishes we'd never gotten past hieroglyphics. And she's smarter than Socrates, he'll believe anything she says."

"I suspect that'd be far more effective if he found her pretty," Sidney said.

"He'll find her enchanting," Hannah insisted. "Beryl looks just like anyone's idea of a British female writer."

Beryl stumped back into the office, frowning. "This will work best if he thinks me bonny," she complained. "We likely ought get me a skirt, he won't cotton to me breeks," she said, gesturing to her knickerbockers.

"Writers can get away with all sorts of eccentricities," Hannah said. She thrust her makeup bag into Beryl's hand. "Do yourself up and the rest will all be charm."

"Oh, fantastic," Sidney said, shoving a chunk of Walkers into his mouth.

Dale Winston arrived promptly at three. He was a big man with a ready laugh, but the set of his jaw and glint in his eye bespoke him as a man who was all business. He'd risen to power on a combination of charisma and ruthlessness. Hannah knew the type well.

"Quite the shoestring operation you have here!' he boomed, casting an approving glance around the small offices. "Keeps expenses low, very smart. Where's the rest of the staff?"

"Sidney is at the set," Hannah answered truthfully. He'd needed to go, but equally they thought it best he not be seen. It was one thing for a man like Dale to know Hannah was Sidney's superior; it was another for him to see it in action. "And my girl had a family emergency, so I let her go home. I can manage a few hours."

"Now that is something!" Dale pumped Hannah's hand again. "That is something. You ladies sure can run things, I've always said so."

"Well, we certainly try!" Hannah said brightly. "Do chat with Miss M—"

"Miss McGough," Beryl said, sticking out her hand. Hannah bit back a "who?" Howard McGough was another of Ring Lardner Jr.'s fake names. His episode about a lord informing on the outlaws and attempting to lynch his own serfs had just aired. Beryl, rather fetching with her hair combed into curls and her face made up, did not look like a Howard. Hannah could see Dale Winston taking in the well-shaped legs in thick stockings and breeches, the men's jacket and waistcoat, the strawberry-blond curls. As Hannah suspected, Beryl answered his idea of what a young female writer in London might look like, and he was pleased.

"McGough?" Dale frowned in confusion. "I thought you were a man."

"People do, that's how I'm able to do all right for myself," Beryl said cheerfully. "It's actually Horatia, and who mightn't go for Howard instead, be frank now."

Even without Scottish Gaelic, her burr was still a mighty thing, and Hannah bit the inside of her cheek as she watched Dale's face screw up in concentration, listening. "I do say, I didn't think I'd be so lucky as to land myself on a show like this," Beryl went on. "I'm looking forward to writing several more episodes for the next season, and hopefully more after that, should there be yet another. I know it's not really the sort of thing anyone thinks ought be written by women, but I like to think I bring something extra to it."

"I'd never have guessed!" Dale laughed. "Sorta makes you wonder how many other writers out there aren't who they say they are."

"We're worse than actors, and no mistake," Beryl agreed. She went on to dazzle him with an array of projects she was working on — combined plots from several recently submitted scripts — and Dale nodded and made notes.

"You're a very clever young woman, Miss

McGough," he congratulated her. "I'm glad Miss Wolfson plans on keeping you busy, though she shouldn't be surprised if I steal you for something else."

"At a price!" Beryl warned him. "I'm a Scot, after all." There was a lot of shaking of hands and agreements that they must all meet again, and he was gone.

Beryl seized her handkerchief and wiped her face clean.

"McGough?" Hannah said, eyebrows nearly in her hairline.

"I decided that if I'm going to play at being one of the writers, it's going to be one of the tops. And a Scot, obviously."

"Obviously," Hannah said. "I'll never be able to repay you." Her hands were damp — she hadn't realized how much she was sweating.

"All part of the game," Beryl said cheerfully. "Though I daresay your original plan means that 'Ivy Morrow' is also one of the blacklisted."

"Ah. Yes. Yes, she is." Hannah held her gaze. "But you knew that."

"I suppose," Beryl admitted. "Is she at least a woman?"

"She is."

Beryl nodded slowly. "Well, there's me having mine hat for tea. All right then. All right. 'Tis how it has to be. And I reckon 'tis good for him to see a British writer."

She looked ready to say more, but stopped. They both knew what she was going to say. Believing there was a British writer on the show would give Dale Winston ammunition to vouch for them, should they ever need it. Hannah was glad Beryl didn't say anything. Bad enough to think it. No one needed to hear it out loud.

A few weeks later, Rhoda had a half term, and Hannah decided to answer a barrage of questions about her work by bringing Rhoda in for an afternoon. She suspected Rhoda would be bored, but Beryl recognized a kindred spirit.

"Aren't you a brilliant wee bairn?" Beryl said an hour after they'd become acquainted. Hannah thought "bairn" sounded like "barn," an odd thing to call a child. "I hear you're a great hand with a bow and arrows," Beryl pressed. "No sheriff's men will storm our castle, eh? I may pelt them with stones, myself."

"And boiling water!" Rhoda shouted, dragging Beryl to the window, where the enemy must be encroaching. "We'll pour boiling water all over them!"

"Won't we just!"

The battle became more grisly. The faster they talked, the less Hannah could follow the action. She bit her lip. It was one thing to feel foreign surrounded by her Scottish employees. It was quite another to suddenly, genuinely, not comprehend the language of her own child. Rhoda had been born in London, and it was right that her accent was British, but Hannah hadn't realized the extent of the separation it would create between them. Rhoda was able to understand various accents, while Hannah, who had always prided herself on her ability, still had so many moments of being just a little behind. She was only forgiven, she was sure, because she was a woman of some small power and substance. Rage swelled up inside her. She despised being forgiven. It was too close to condescension.

The feeling subsided as quickly as it had risen. London was the only home Rhoda knew, and her assimilation proved Hannah had done everything right. Besides, it was Hannah's home now, too, and possibly would be forever. She just had to keep on claiming it. She joined the fighters at the window, and the three of them laid waste to an entire invading army.

It was after four when Hannah and Rhoda headed home, and the afternoon was dark.

But it was cool and pleasant, and they were happy to walk a little while.

"Mama, I have a very important question," Rhoda said.

It was rare, this moment of seriousness. Something that only happened when they were alone. Less influenced by Beryl's speed and force, Rhoda's accent was pure central London, and Hannah had no trouble understanding her. Its little pipe, so lilting and earnest, reminded Hannah that she had made a whole separate person. A small miracle. Hannah had to catch her breath before she answered.

"Yes, Rhoda, ask me."

"Am I going to be a television producer when I grow up?"

Hannah smiled down at the round face with the shortbread crumbs stubbornly clinging to the corners of her lips. It was both thrilling and awful to imagine her grown, with a clean face and a hairdo and suit, running an office. The idea of Rhoda and Julie growing up only made Hannah want to cuddle them more.

"You might be, if it's what you want to do and you're good at it," Hannah told her. "Or perhaps you'll do something completely different. You'd like that too."

Rhoda nodded, thinking it over.

"Daddy says it's important for a girl to be a good wife and mother."

"Does he now?" Hannah kept her voice light. So Paul had found time to talk with his children when she wasn't around. And say things she would never have believed came from him, if Rhoda hadn't told her.

"But you're a good wife and mother," Rhoda puzzled, frowning. "And you're also a television producer, so I don't quite see what he means."

Hannah fought the urge to sweep her daughter into her arms and smother her with kisses. Rhoda deserved a real answer.

"I think he means for you to not worry, that you can do whatever feels right," Hannah assured her. "You do as you wish, and don't let anyone tell you otherwise."

Rhoda nodded again, satisfied, and skipped along beside Hannah, singing a pitch-free version of "What Shall We Do with a Drunken Sailor."

It was quiet, and the air smelled fresh. Hannah looked at her daughter fondly, wishing Julie were here too. And Paul, even though she was disappointed in him. Maybe if he saw more of Rhoda's buoyancy, he wouldn't feel he needed to guide her into a box her mother eschewed. Hannah resolved to convince Paul to spend more time with all of them as a family. He owed them that.

As they turned the corner, Hannah saw the long shadow of a man behind them. She stopped suddenly, and the shadow did as well.

"What is it, Mama? Do you see a bat?" Rhoda was full of hope.

"Maybe. We ought to go to the zoo and learn all about bats, shouldn't we?"

"Yes, please!" Rhoda was overjoyed. "They eat bugs," she added, proud of her vast knowledge.

The shadow had gone but footsteps continued all the way to Chelsea. Hannah thought of all the monsters she adored as a horror-loving adolescent, monsters she now wished were real. The Mummy, the Golem, Dracula. Instead, here she was stuck with the Invisible Man. Because there was no way around the truth. They were being followed.

CHAPTER FIFTEEN

"And you're sure?" Shirley asked.

"Of course I'm not sure, who's sure of anything?" Hannah lit a second cigarette from the one she'd just finished. "I'm not even sure I should be on the phone." She'd said nothing to Paul, pretended everything was normal, and waited until this quiet moment in her office to call Shirley.

"The British may feel they owe the Americans for finally helping win the war, but they wouldn't hold with bugging the phones of a production company," Shirley said. "Not unless they thought you were colluding with the French."

Hannah snorted.

"Anyway," Shirley went on, her mellow voice more honeyed than usual, "if our fellow Americans are going to waste taxpayer dollars having men follow us around in London, the joke is on them. What can they possibly deduce? That your office is in Cadogan Square and your home is in Chelsea. Whatever else I might think of the FBI, I like to assume they'd have already figured out that much without a great deal of effort."

"So you *do* think it was someone from the FBI?" Hannah said.

Shirley was silent. Hannah heard the click of a cigarette lighter.

"Hedda Hopper came to your set. That means someone tipped her off. You don't exactly know who, do you?"

"I couldn't begin to guess."

"No indeed, and the likelihood is you never will. In the meanwhile, I'd hardly put it past that Hopper creature to spend some of her own ill-gotten fortune and hire someone to upset you as punishment for the set treating her so disrespectfully. Ludicrous and spiteful, yes, but is it implausible?"

Hannah's eyes traveled over the American newspapers on her side table. There was some mention of Communists, Communism, or hearings on every front page. Buried in the bottom corner, perhaps, but there. It remained red-hot news.

"I'd put nothing past that woman," Hannah said.

"Well, precisely."

Though it didn't explain Phoebe's harassment. But what point was there, really, in trying to make sense of so much absurdity?

"I don't even mind them trying to make me squirm," Hannah said. "I've always done my best work when someone's trying to give me grief. But tailing me when I'm with Rhoda, that's a different matter. That's a killing offense."

"Keep your head," Shirley advised. "They want a reason to escalate. Don't give them one."

"No. Though they say a woman's provocation knows no bounds." Hannah sighed. "What are the odds we're in for it now just having had this conversation?"

"Oh, strife," said Shirley, this time sounding impish. "We may have to flee our country to retain our freedom."

The conversation wasn't exactly comforting, but Hannah had too much work to do to wallow. She slipped off her shoes under her desk and turned to a list of production requirements for upcoming episodes.

A sharp knock and Beryl stuck her head around the door.

"Pardon, boss, but there's a bloke to see you, says you're one of his comrades. Aye, that's the word he used." She paused. "He looks like what we'd call a keelie."

"Explain," Hannah said.

Beryl shrugged. "A bit of a rough. Though too old for it, really. Says he's called Charlie Morrison."

It was tempting to ask Beryl to send him away. She was busy, and it was just like Charlie to think he could drop in without calling. But she thought of Joan, and allowed Beryl to let him in. She shoved her feet back in her shoes.

"Hiya, Hannah, sorry to barge in," Charlie said. He had undergone extensive ministrations — Joan must have had him steam cleaned — but Hannah promptly understood the meaning of "keelie." There was an inherent roughness, even in his shaven face, that was stronger since she'd last seen him. Something in him had never escaped the tenements of Brooklyn, and anxiety enhanced it. Hannah greeted him more warmly than she'd intended and offered him coffee.

"Last few times I've seen you, we haven't had much chance to talk." Charlie smiled uneasily. "How about that new guy, huh, from DC, the fairy who used to work for Social Security?"

Hannah sighed inwardly. Charlie was a card-carrying Communist who would have sworn up, down, and sideways that he believed in the equality of all men. Yet here he was, insulting a new exile escaping a government purge.

"The sweeps continue," Hannah said. "That lawyer working for Hoover, Roy Cohn, has some bee in his bonnet about homosexuality. They'll clear out a good bit of the federal government if they keep this up."

"Seems so, yeah. So the thing was, it got me thinking, and I landed on a story for *Robin Hood.* I figured, what the hell, I should write it and the worst you'll say is no, right? But I'm hoping you'll say yes." He pulled a folded script from his jacket.

Hannah took the script. She would read it, of course. She knew that for him, this was the lowest he could go — casting his retrimmed hat in the ring for television, the mule created when film, radio, and theater came together in an unnatural act. Not only television, but a show created and run by a woman. Who had already bought a script from his neighbor, who herself had the gall to be younger, single, and female. Hannah wondered which of these was Phoebe's greatest sin.

"I wanted to dig into Robin's feelings about living in exile," Charlie said enthusiastically. "It's the classic fall from grace, and his fight back to where he belongs."

"Is it?" Hannah asked. She knew Charlie's youngest son watched the show, and wondered how many episodes Charlie had seen.

"The age-old story, huh?" he continued. "A man trying to reclaim his honor. It's the stuff of all the Great American Novels."

"You should certainly try writing the next one of those," Hannah encouraged him. None, she decided. Possibly he'd asked Alvie to summarize.

"Funny you say, I've been writing a book too," he confided. "It's a doozy, though finding a publisher with the balls to take it on won't be easy. But once that's done, it'll make a million, and then the film version will knock it out of the park."

"I look forward to it," Hannah said. "Meantime, I look forward to reading this. I'll get back to you by the end of the week."

Charlie nodded nervously. "Sure. Great. Thanks a million, Hannah, really."

After he left, Hannah lit a cigarette and skimmed the first few pages of the script. They confirmed what she'd suspected — that he hadn't bothered to watch a full episode of the show. He had no sense of the characters or their voices, let alone their hopes and actions. The script was one of Charlie's Westerns about a tough guy battling an enemy, but with bows and arrows rather than guns. It might be a tidy B movie, but it wasn't an episode of *Robin Hood.*

She waited three days before sending Charlie a warm note, thanking him and asking if she could send the sample to some other producers she knew. Maybe it would raise his hopes. She sent a separate note to Joan, enclosing ten pounds. A gift, she said, to give the boys a surprise. She couldn't think of any way to suggest it was best not to let Charlie know about it, and hoped Joan would make the connection on her own. However she spent it, there was some truth to the note. It wasn't their children's fault that they were caught up in all this turmoil. There was nothing any of them wouldn't do to try to make things easier for their children.

Phoebe's fingers, red and swollen from exertion, galloped mercilessly over the typewriter. Her body was in her tiny flat, a cigarette dangling from her lips, knitting needles stuck in her uncombed hair. Her mind was deep in Sherwood Forest, where a newlywed peasant named Alisoun wept to Maid Marian, hoping this important woman might save her from a terrible fate. Alisoun's husband was one of the outlaws and she pined for him, but they could only exchange secret messages left in a tree. Not notes, because neither of them could write. Instead, they had to draw their desires on leaves.

But before all the adolescent boys who worshipped the show were moved to vomit, enter Alisoun's neighbors, a couple who coveted her garden, her chickens, her cow. Her escapades into the woods must mean she was in collusion with the outlaws, aiding and abetting. And if abetting, why not also a-bedding? She must be committing adultery, no doubt giving succor to Robin Hood himself, committing all the crimes meriting imprisonment and torture, and so the property made forfeit and up for grabs. Pesky details like evidence were easily dismissed, but Alisoun must destroy the leaves — real proof of communicating with an outlaw. And yet, they were all she had of her husband, so would Marian hide them? Though the real problem was clearing Alisoun's good name and keeping her small property safe.

Marian would succeed, of course, but even the most hardened boys would chew off half their nails waiting to see what would happen. They'd never guess Marian's real motivation — her own long love for Robin, which might only ever be that damn courtly love. Phoebe thought "courtly love" read like a prude's imagining of medieval life — full of tourneys and roses and tapestries and scrubbed clean of plague and wars and bloody deaths in childbirth. Courtly love, reserved for unrequited longing in the upper classes, saw flirtations dragged out for years, with nothing but dropped handkerchiefs and exchanged roses to keep the flames going. A story worth a thousand eye rolls. Then again, it could be far more erotic to pine for a single embrace than to deal with someone day in and day out, and ask them if, just once, they could manage to drop their dirty socks in the hamper rather than leave them on the floor.

There was a sharp rap at the door, and Phoebe cursed. She couldn't pretend not to be home, not when she'd been typing so hard. She stubbed out the last of the cigarette and went to open the door.

Reg leaned against the jamb, holding a white rose. "I am devastated to interrupt the flow of genius, but if our date is to be postponed in the wake of creation, I imagine I must still be required to provide sustenance."

"But you're so early," she said. Since New Year's, their outings were in the evenings, rather than the afternoons, giving her an uninterrupted day to work. Nothing was quite enough. Not enough time with Reg, not enough time earning more for Mona.

"It's past seven," Reg informed her. "I've been waiting outside, having quite the chat with Freddie till he was called in for supper. Then I thought I'd best risk breaching the battlements."

Phoebe glanced at her watch, then at the window, which had turned dark without her realizing. A small portion of her was still both Alisoun and Marian, attempting to navigate a world so very stacked against them. She ran a hand through her hair and found the knitting needles, attached to a half-finished scarf dangling around her neck. She became aware that she had no makeup on, hadn't even washed her face, and was wearing the cardigan with moth holes, covered in crumbs from breakfast — whenever that was.

"I suppose you'll have to come in, because there's no way I'm going out," she said, standing aside to admit him for the first time. She watched him look around with interest.

"It's exactly the home a writer should have," he pronounced.

"Smoky, poky, and dark," Phoebe said in

agreement.

"Not at all," Reg said, taking her hand. "It radiates energy."

"I have to stay warm somehow." She put the knitting needles and scarf back in the basket and tried to comb her hair with her fingers. "I wish you could have seen my place in the Village. That was a beautiful home. Here, look." She pointed to the photos and drawings on the wall. "All done by Anne, my best friend. That's her there."

"It does look lovely," he agreed. "But I'm happy you're here, circumstances notwithstanding." He put his arms around her, and she leaned her head on his chest. There'd been no word from Anne for nearly two weeks, which meant she was so deep inside a series of paintings, she'd forgotten time. Phoebe heaved a sigh.

"And that's your sister." Reg smiled, pointing to Phoebe's favorite photo of Mona, the one with Groucho Marx paper eyebrows taped to her face. "She looks just like you."

"Except that she's pale and blond and slim," Phoebe said.

"Details," Reg said with a wave of his hand. "She has the exact same sparkle in her eyes as you do. There's no mistaking it."

Phoebe's heart tangoed around her chest.

She wished she could introduce Reg to Mona, not just tell them both stories about each other. Her fingers twined through his and she tugged at him, but was suddenly aware of how alone they were, how it could be possible to stay here for a long, long time. She backed away and nodded to the rose.

"It's funny you bring that by. I was just thinking about roses in medieval life. Why did you get a white one?"

"I told you, my people are from York," he explained. "Red roses are still associated with the House of Lancaster."

"Wasn't the War of the Roses five hundred years ago? I think you can move on."

"Is this your way of saying you'd prefer a red rose?"

"No," she said, taking it and touching the petals. "Considering the reason I'm living in this hovel, I'm inclined to steer clear of anything red."

"Is it too late for me to say that's why I opted for white?"

"You're the Oxford man, find a way to make it clever."

Phoebe poured out the last of her gin for them and used the bottle as a vase for the rose. They sat on the sagging sofa.

"So," he said, sipping his gin. "What

397

spurred you to read about roses?"

"Oh, that courtly love baloney," said Phoebe. "I have to make reference to it."

"Is that a requirement for *Robin Hood*?"

Phoebe choked on her gin. She sputtered as half of it came up her nose.

"What are you talking about?" she demanded.

"Pax, pax," he said, rubbing her back. "I saw the page in your typewriter. You're an obvious writer for *Robin Hood*. I'm over the moon for you."

"Look, no one's supposed to know, all right? Hannah can't be seen hiring blacklisted writers. It would bring down the show in America."

Reg looked surprised and hurt. "You don't think I would tell anyone, do you?"

"Not on purpose, no," Phoebe admitted.

"Fair play," Reg chuckled. "I could see myself boasting about my girlfriend being a writer on a fine television program, but amazing though it may seem, I'm actually capable of keeping quiet when warranted. I'd never jeopardize you."

He reached for her hand again. She pressed his fingers but pulled away.

"It's not really a love story I'm writing, anyway. Most of the kids who watch *Robin Hood* would feel betrayed. But they're not opposed to a damsel in distress if they think she's going to be tortured. I don't blame them — violence, murder, and treachery make for great entertainment."

"My hard-boiled heroine," Reg said, kissing her on the nose. "If we aren't going out for supper, shall I play the conquering warrior and fetch us a takeaway?"

"Great. I'd like chop suey and egg rolls from Wu's on Bayard Street."

"That's New York's Chinatown, isn't it?"

"I'll settle for fish and chips from that place around the corner."

"Hardly settling, when it's the spot the tops-and-tails crowd descend on after the theater if they fancy feeling Bohemian." He kissed her cheek and left.

Phoebe leaned against the door, suddenly starving for battered cod and fat chipped potatoes with the oil and vinegar drizzled over them. Those, and something more.

"You're doing well, aren't you?" Charlie said from his own door.

Phoebe jumped. She hadn't heard the door open. Charlie smiled and raised a glass to her.

"Joan took the boys out, letting me have the evening to work in peace. I came for a refill, heard you, figured I'd say hello."

"Hello," Phoebe said. "Work going all right?"

"Sure, sure. What about you?"

"Oh, it's fine. I never have as much time as I want for writing, but it's fine."

"All the time in the world is never enough, is it?" He shook his head, chuckling. "Listen, you got a smoke? I'm out."

"Coming right up," she said, and went to get one. Charlie followed her, nodding in approval as he gazed around the flat.

"Haven't been in here since we helped you do up the place. Looks all right. You're doing all right. Good for you."

Phoebe handed him the cigarette, hoping he wouldn't ask for a light. She wondered how long it would take Reg to return. On a Saturday night, the local chippy could have a queue outside the door. Reg hadn't exaggerated — it was hugely popular. She didn't want to ask Charlie to leave, but she wanted to wash her face and comb her hair. Or write another scene. Anything but take care of this man who always seemed to need so much caretaking.

"Word is you sold a script to Hannah," Charlie said. "Joan heard from Shirley it's a good one."

"That's awfully swell of her," Phoebe said. "Now I don't feel too crazy trying my luck with another." She didn't mention writing for *Woman's Hour.* Something told her to play down her successes.

"Always gotta try for another," he said, nodding sagely. "The first one could be a fluke, you never know. It's all right, though. It's all right. It's all right."

She was tempted to offer him a shilling to stop saying "all right."

"Especially all right for a gal," he went on. His expression and tone were perfectly pleasant, but the back of Phoebe's neck began to tingle. "Not married. No one's counting on you. Depending on you. And you're selling scripts. You've written what, five things ever? And you're selling scripts."

"Look, Charlie —" Phoebe began.

"Why don't you get that fellow to marry you, huh? You're starting kinda late as it is. Get on with what you should do and leave space for the rest of us who need it."

Nothing but consideration for Joan kept Phoebe from ordering Charlie out at knitting-needle point.

"Sure, Charlie, I'll ask him about that toot sweet."

Charlie moved with the speed of a practiced murderer. His hand seized the back of her hair, and his breath told her he'd drunk the better part of a bottle of bourbon.

"It's not right, you hear me? It's not right. Do you know who I am, what I've done? And you, you're the one getting everything."

Phoebe forced herself to breathe steadily. The detectives in *At Your Service* always said men like this became more agitated when they saw they were having an effect on their victims. Stay calm and they might lose some steam. Might.

"You're right, Charlie. It's not right, Charlie." Keep using their name, that was another tactic to avoid getting murdered. Not that it ever helped the women who were already dead. "I'm sorry, Charlie. I didn't mean to upset you."

Tears welled up in his eyes. She decided he probably had two bottles of bourbon in him. His hand shook, but he didn't let go of her.

"Single . . . a gal . . . it's not fair . . ." he muttered, digging his fingers in tighter. It hurt, but Phoebe didn't dare even gulp.

"What the devil is going on here?"

Reg was back at last, just in time to get the wrong idea.

Charlie looked around at Reg and seemed to come back to himself. He released Phoebe and backed away sheepishly, not meeting either of their eyes.

"Reg, this is my neighbor, Charlie Morrison. No doubt you've seen a few of the movies he's written. He was just asking me about a scene and forgot I'm not one for acting things out. But he'll get it just fine, won't you, Charlie?"

Charlie's face was still full of contempt, but he gave a small grunt and ducked past Reg back to his own apartment. The door slammed.

Phoebe pulled Reg inside, shut her own door quietly, and locked it.

"Tell me the truth, Phoebe, what was that?" Reg demanded.

"What did it look like?" she snapped, taking several deep breaths. "My drunken neighbor being a drunken creep."

"I didn't see you fighting him off." Reg looked at her evenly, his eyes narrow over two heaping servings of fish and chips wrapped in newspaper.

"What was I supposed to do? He's my neighbor, I'm friends with his wife. If I'd kicked him how and where I wanted, I'd bring my whole home life crashing down around me. He's completely stinko, he won't remember any of it in the morning."

Reg looked unconvinced. "In vino veritas, you know. A man who makes a pass when he's drunk would like to make one when he's sober."

Phoebe snorted. "That wasn't a pass. That was him wanting to rip my head off. He's upset 'cause I sold a script and that seems to mean I'm taking food from his kids' mouths. He's upset 'cause I'm working and not married."

Reg's eyebrows rose over his glasses. "But that seems absurd."

"Does it? I'll turn thirty this spring. I'm supposed to have married and cranked out some apple-cheeked children by now. I've broken all the rules."

"I should think a creative person would appreciate that. Anyway, surely your being blacklisted makes you more admirable in his eyes?"

"Oh, Reg, who knows? Can we please eat now, or do you have any more accusations to throw at me first?"

He handed her a packet of fish and chips. "Pax, pax," he said with his most crooked smile. She could tell he was still troubled but was being very English and choosing not to press the subject further.

Phoebe shoved hot chips in her mouth. "Pax" was Latin for "peace." She wondered when — or if ever — she would know real peace again.

"Have you picked me out a hat from Harrods?" Mona asked on the phone. "I want to look my best for Ascot." She spoke between raspy breaths. Phoebe closed her eyes. Nurse Brewster had written to her. Mona's functions were declining rapidly. It was a matter of weeks now, if that.

"Maybe I'd better come and escort you over," Phoebe suggested.

"Don't think I don't know you mean half of that," Mona warned.

Phoebe sighed. Mona's mental functions were as sharp as ever.

"Anyway," Mona continued, "I'd like to get to London on a rocket ship. I need to meet Reg and Hannah and see an episode of *Robin Hood* being filmed."

"I'll start making the calls," Phoebe said, annoyed at the crack in her voice.

"Geez, kiddo, your voice sounds as bad as mine. Hold it together. At least one of us needs to be able to complete a sentence in under a minute. What's new with Reg? Has he deflowered you yet?"

"No, but he brought me a rose," Phoebe said. She twisted her fingers around the telephone cord. "It's great, but it's so confusing," she said, a baby sister again. "I don't really know how I feel, or what I want."

"You know you want to spend your Saturday evenings with him, instead of working," Mona said, her voice stronger and more like itself. And making Phoebe feel guilty for not working Saturday evenings. "You know he's bright and fun and funny and considerate. He loves you, which means he's smart and has high standards. What goes through your mind when you're with him?"

"The work I should be doing instead to try and keep you in the style to which you've become accustomed."

"Phoebe."

Phoebe looked down. "I guess . . . I guess I think that I'm happy. He makes me happy," she whispered.

"Happier than a good plot, right?"

"Let's not get ridiculous," Phoebe countered, but her heart wasn't in it. "So, what do you think? Is this love?"

"I hope so, little sister," Mona said, without a hint of sarcasm. "No one deserves it more than you."

Hannah came into the room as Phoebe hung up, bringing her a cup of tea and a slice of strawberry cake.

"Not to be a busybody, but your voice carries into the kitchen, so I heard the last of that."

"I'm a New Yorker, my voice can carry into the next county when I get going,"

Phoebe said.

Hannah put a hand on Phoebe's shoulder. "I hope you told your sister the truth, not just what she wants to hear. It's a wonderful thing, being in love."

Rhoda ran into the room and jumped on Phoebe. "Come play with us, come play!" she ordered. "I'm Robin, Mummy's Little John, Gemma's King Richard, so you can be Will Scarlet or Friar Tuck."

"What about Julie and Daddy, who are they playing?" Hannah asked.

"Daddy was s'posed to be the sheriff, but he had to go out," Rhoda reported. "And Julie doesn't understand the game. She's stupid."

"She's little," Hannah corrected Rhoda. Phoebe had seen a shadow cross Hannah's face at the mention of Paul being out, but her voice was perfectly cheerful. "Why not have her be Maid Marian?"

"All right," Rhoda said agreeably. "She's the only one who won't mind wearing a stupid dress. What about you?" she finished, rounding on Phoebe.

Phoebe would not have dared say she liked dresses. "I'll be the sheriff."

Rhoda narrowed her eyes. "Can you be properly evil?" she asked skeptically.

Phoebe squatted to be level with Rhoda.

"Try me," she said in her most menacing tone, designed to make small children cry.

Rhoda beamed in delight. "Super! Now come on, let's play."

Phoebe hoped to tell Hannah about the incident with Charlie and get her advice. But the game became so involved, and thrilling, she didn't get the chance. She didn't entirely mind. She'd had more than enough talk about men for one day.

Four days passed before Joan tapped at Phoebe's door. She presented Phoebe with an apple pie.

"A taste of home. Can you believe they don't ever seem to do it here? Meat pies as far as the eye can see, and no good old apple pie."

Phoebe was uncomfortable. Joan shouldn't be baking for her as an obvious apology when her sons would happily reduce a pie to crumbs within five minutes.

"I'd love a slice," she said. "But the kids should have the rest. You want them bragging to their classmates what a terrific cook their mother is."

Joan laughed faintly. "I think they believe food is conjured from thin air, nothing to do with me."

"Eh, that's just the face they put on,"

Phoebe assured her, starting water for coffee and getting two plates. "Join me."

Joan automatically took over, measuring out the coffee and serving them pie. She sat down and stared at her slice. Phoebe slid the pack of cigarettes across the table to her, but Joan waved them aside.

"I'm so embarrassed," she said, clutching at her neck.

"It's okay," Phoebe said automatically. Though it wasn't.

"He told me yesterday. He's embarrassed too. He didn't mean to lose his temper with you, I hope you know that."

Phoebe wondered what exactly Charlie had told Joan.

"He's not like this, not really," Joan went on. "He's just under so much pressure. The boys, you know."

"I know," Phoebe said. She wished Joan would stop, would let them both pretend it had never happened. That would be the British way of doing things, and Phoebe decided it was seriously underrated.

"He certainly has no objection to single women working. After all, you have to do what you have to do. Not everyone can land a husband, or has family to help."

"That's good of him," Phoebe said, inwardly seeching. How could men who were so dedicated to Marxist ideals of equality be so Cro-Magnon when it came to women? "Family to help," indeed — as though she should be the spinster aunt in a spare room, whom everyone would love more if she could be considerate enough to promptly drop dead.

"No, I mean it," Joan insisted. "Honestly, I don't think he would have minded if I were still writing stories and sold one. Money is money. Of course, I don't have time, much less any ideas these days."

Stories? Joan was dismissive, waving away her own work of another life ago, stories in women's magazines, silly fluff that bought her little luxuries like more hats than she reasonably needed and, on at least one momentous occasion, was sold as an option to one of the studios. That had helped buy their bungalow in Los Feliz. "I wish you could have seen it." Joan sighed. "The trees! Orange, peach, avocado. Can you imagine? I hope whoever lives there now didn't cut them down."

"I bet you could come up with a good idea easily enough," Phoebe said encouragingly. "Start with a woman baking an apple pie in London, you'll have something great before the oven timer pings. It already sounds like a winner for *Good Housekeeping*. And money is money, as you say."

"No, no, I'm far too busy helping Charlie," Joan said. "And the boys, you wouldn't know it, but they really do take an enormous amount of time and energy."

No, Phoebe wouldn't have known. Neither boy ever seemed to be around much, even Alvie, who was only eleven. But then again, Phoebe didn't know what went on behind closed doors — except big band music. She wondered if Charlie ever grabbed Joan's hair as he had hers. Her fist clenched around her fork.

"What about your families?" Phoebe asked, making her voice bright to hide her rage. "Can't they help a bit?"

"Oh, well, I suppose they'd like to in their way," Joan said, not meeting Phoebe's eye.

"I don't like to take charity either," Phoebe said comfortingly. "But if you're so worried . . ."

"It's different for you, all right?" Joan said with a sudden snap that made Phoebe jump. "Charlie was in the party, lots of our friends were. And then they all ended up on the blacklist. You only got a taste of it, what the FBI Hounds get up to. Your phone was bugged, right? So, sure, we could only talk in code, and even that was dangerous. Still is. Everyone wants to keep the heat off everyone else, and themselves too. So it's easier not to talk at all. As for family, well, you're the exception. Most of us abroad, family stops writing. It's not that people think you've done anything wrong. But it's hard to accept, a family member living like this. It's embarrassing. The blacklist, all of it. And they've got their own circles, their kids, their work, they can't risk it getting tainted. My father's a high school principal — if someone calls him a subversive, or finds out his daughter and son-in-law are blacklisted Reds, he'd likely be tossed out on his can. He's got six years till retirement, he's not taking any chances, and why should he?"

Joan looked away, and Phoebe wished she could hide the photographs of Mona and Anne, and Anne's cartoons, so proudly displayed on her wall. All that proof of the love she still received from home. Her arms hurt, wanting to hug Mona and Anne. She would have liked to hug Joan, but for once Joan's body was cold and aloof, unwilling to be warmed back into cheerfulness.

"Those men, at the FBI, in Congress, they all extol the American family," Phoebe said at last. It made Joan laugh. A bitter laugh, but a laugh.

"Yes, and the home, and good, hard

work," she added. "What a terrific joke."

Now she allowed Phoebe to take her hand.

"We have each other," Joan said, meaning Charlie and the boys. "And everyone here is our family now. Don't think we don't value that."

"I wouldn't dream of it," said Phoebe. "I swear."

Joan still wouldn't meet her eye.

413

CHAPTER SIXTEEN

Sidney bounced into Hannah's office, rubbing his hands.

"Spring has sprung!" he cried. "Haven't I just gotten off the phone with a fine lad at the *Spectator,* of all the things, and whom do they wish to interview but your own fine self! Marvelous way to trick us into buying copies."

"Those devils!" Hannah laughed, but shared Sidney's enthusiasm. The *Spectator* was an important magazine. Its politics were too conservative for her or Sidney's taste, but it was known for witty essays and meaty discussions of culture and literature. If they wanted to interview her, it meant they considered *Robin Hood* to be of real cultural significance. And her to be respectable. "Who else do they want to interview?"

"Just you, boss!" Sidney bounced harder.

Hannah was surprised. Magazines usually liked to interview stars.

"Why me?" she asked.

"Same reason *Sight and Sound* wanted an exclusive with you," Sidney said, surprised in turn. "You're a bit of a wonder. American, a woman, creator of the most popular show on telly and that's mostly for boys. You are a star, my dear!"

Hannah scoffed, but she couldn't help feeling pleased. *Sight and Sound,* after all, was a magazine for the industry. The *Spectator* would capture far more readers. She really was becoming somebody.

Which could be why she was being followed.

Hannah came home early to tell Paul the news. He was far more cheerful these days, having sold an idea to *Harper's Magazine* about performers at the edges of London's nightclub scene. Neither she nor Paul were so petty as to mention that this had been one of Hannah's off-the-cuff suggestions. It was useful, having good news. It was an excuse for a glass or two of champagne before dinner, which could ease the way into mentioning the man who had tagged after her and Rhoda. Paul would be upset, of course, but he would also have something helpful to say. He liked getting outraged — it made him feel young.

"The *Spectator*? Wants to interview you?" Paul studied her to be sure she wasn't joking.

"It's the novelty of it all," Hannah said. "I'm American and a woman and yet making a success here. Perhaps I'm a cautionary tale!"

"I won't be surprised if that's how they frame it," Paul said, in the tones of the wise old journalist who Knows How These Things Are. Hannah didn't remind him that she'd been a journalist too.

"Oh well, most of our audience are *Beano* readers anyway," she said airily.

"Sure, it might offer a free packet of Jelly Babies," Paul agreed. "Anyway, good work, honey. And I hate to skip out on you like this, but I've got to conduct my own interview with these sad sacks. I'm buying the drinks, obviously. Probably dinner too. I'll be late, don't wait up." He kissed her on the forehead and left.

Hannah glanced at the clock. Not quite four. Gemma had taken Julie to pick up Rhoda at school and then go shopping for supper things. Here was Hannah, home early to have a drink with her husband, and there he was, off for drinks with someone else. She was glad for him to be busy and productive. She knew it made him feel

416

important. She just wished she could re-arrange time.

The children's bedroom was clean — Gemma deserved a raise — and Hannah moved around it with the same respectful quiet she might a medieval cathedral. Without them in it, it felt like a place where time stopped, waiting for real life to begin again. She ran a hand over the stuffed bookshelves, the overflowing toy chest. On the little craft table was a cartoon of Rhoda as Robin Hood, saving a man from the noose. She'd written in her laborious printing: *Rhoda loves Daddy!*

Hannah pressed her hand to her mouth, bursting with love for her family. Usually, she would ask Rhoda what she wanted to share and how, but she decided Paul had to see this as soon as he came home tonight. On the way to their bedroom, she changed course. Paul would go to his office first.

The mess in Paul's office was comfortingly familiar. Hannah straightened a pile of papers covered with red and blue corrections and notes, and set the cartoon down on top of them. She hadn't been in this room in a while. It got the best light in the flat. Had he noticed that when they moved in, or had she? It didn't matter. He had claimed it, expressed his desire, and he had already agreed to upend their lives. She would never have denied him this, even though it would have made a lovely playroom.

The room was dusty — he didn't trust anyone else to clean, but did little himself. Hannah should be tending to that. She looked around at the piles of papers and books on the shelves, facing all different directions. Dog-eared, or scribbled in the margins. Paul was no great respecter of things. Hannah hoped the girls wouldn't inherit this trait.

There was one small blank patch on the windowsill, a space covered in dust but not detritus. Hannah wrote, *Love you, Sloppy* with her finger. She grinned, feeling adolescent and illicit.

A flicker of blue and red caught her eye. She knelt to look under the shabby footstool, sagging with the weight of magazines, and found Rhoda's kazoo. She blew into it — the *bzzrt!* that blared from it echoed in a sort of rustle, as though the books were offended by the noise. Paul certainly had been. Hannah suspected he had confiscated the kazoo during one of Rhoda's rare permitted visits to the sanctum. She scanned the shelves, looking for where it must have been laid before it dropped. A box filled with matchbooks seemed the likely spot. She pulled out a few matchbooks so she could hide the kazoo — time without listening to a kazoo was good time, indeed — and started to replace the matchbooks when she noticed the painting on one. It was for an establishment called Elysium Gardens, and if the illustration was anything to go by, it had nothing to do with Greek mythology. Paul hadn't mentioned that this was the sort of nightclub included in his story. Hannah laughed. How many men would give how many eyeteeth to insist that watching women dance in various states of undress was all part of their work?

Well, there's no harm in looking, she thought as she idly opened the matchbook. As she expected, the matches inside were illustrated with painted women, who wore little more than beckoning smiles. What Hannah hadn't expected to see was the name Doris written in a woman's loopy handwriting, with a phone number underneath. She could just be an interview subject, telling Paul how to contact her for a long meeting before a show. Innocent, aboveboard, completely professional, and Hannah had no business snooping anyway.

But her own journalist senses tingled with a near radioactivity. Whatever Paul felt, about her, about the children, about their lives together, she couldn't say and wouldn't try. But Doris was more than a source, or a story, and it wasn't just the little heart that she used to dot the *i* that gave her away. She was someone knitted into a private corner of Paul's life, a place Hannah wasn't meant to venture.

She replaced all the matchbooks. She crossed to the note she'd written in the dust and wiped it off with her handkerchief. He wouldn't notice it was clean any more than he'd noticed the dust.

In their bedroom, she studied herself in the mirror. As a young woman, she'd been called attractive. "Pretty" was the wrong word — she'd been far too pugnacious for that, and it showed even in her resting face. What was she now? She hadn't bothered to think about it for a long time. She supposed that, with makeup and a cheerful expression, she might be considered "handsome." That was the word for women who had achieved a sort of stateliness, which might itself be a polite word for having grown plump but being able to dress well enough to turn it to some advantage. Her hair was faded but her good haircut and shampoo kept it looking nice enough. Her skin was paler and drier than she remembered, but it really wasn't bad at all. Her eyes, she was pleased to note, still sparkled and snapped.

She turned away from her eyes and considered what to do. What was the best course for a woman on discovering her husband might be wandering? Some would say to do nothing, that this was what men were and it was to be expected. Some would suggest suing for divorce, taking him for every last farthing. Maid Marian might suggest arranging an accident. Simpler times.

Hannah stalked out of the bedroom, snatched her coat, and went out. Gemma and the girls wouldn't be back for half an hour. She didn't want to stay in their home, festering, letting her shock and rage and hurt leak from her pores and seep into every corner, where the girls might find it.

She walked with her arms wrapped around herself, hands digging into her elbows. She was vaguely aware of the pain and liked it. The afternoon was drizzly and she liked that too. The chill stung her eyes, air-drying the tears she didn't want to shed in public, but couldn't allow anywhere else either. A woman didn't just need a room of her own for work; she needed it for all the emotions she couldn't afford to let anyone see.

She came to a park far enough away from her square that she was in no danger of being seen by any of her neighbors. She sat in the middle of a bench to discourage anyone from joining her and scrunched down into her coat.

Another time, Hannah would have enjoyed observing how many people lingered around a park in such weather. Frazzled nannies, desperately hoping to wear children out enough so that they'd sleep through the night. Teenage couples, seizing a moment of pretending to be sophisticated adults swept up in a romance before returning to their parents' homes. And men. Two elderly men played chess, their only concession to the weather a large umbrella that covered the chessboard, rather than themselves. It was their day to play and they were going to do so and that was that. They had probably played through the Blitz too. Those were the sort of men who made Britain what it was.

These others, though, the younger men, Hannah wasn't sure about them. Some were smoking, bored expressions on their faces, no doubt killing time until they couldn't avoid going home. Hannah despised them. Even if home meant a snappish, weary wife, and squalling children, the wife might be less snappish and the children less squally if the man spent more time there. Other men might have been looking for company, and Hannah hoped for the sake of her rage they were unmarried. Possibly they were trying to settle their troubled souls, just like her. One or two looked sad, lost. She hoped that wasn't the look on her own face. If so, the man with his hat tilted like Bogart's, gazing at her through the corner of what looked to be a very handsome eye, was being most inappropriate. Those few dangerous years, when she was fifteen, sixteen, seventeen, she would have been thrilled to be looked at by someone like him. Now she saw the way his gaze slid from her and lingered instead on the prettiest of the nannies, wrapping up her charges and packing the smallest into a pram. A man of leisure, who came just to look. Nothing unusual in that. It was very likely all the men looking and lingering meant no more harm than an overfed cat lolling before the locked henhouse. Nevertheless, at the moment she would have been very pleased to break their noses, one after the other.

By the time she returned home, with windblown hair and a nose pink with cold, she was weary and thirsty, and still had no idea what she wanted to say to Paul, if anything. But she was able to sit down to supper with the girls and laugh when they expected her to. For now, it would have to be enough.

Over the next few days, Hannah forced herself to decide she was imagining things.

Doris was one of the featured characters in Paul's story, and it was exactly his style to tell the simple truth of the life of a woman society dismissed as disreputable. Assuming anything else must be the effect of reading scripts every day. Hannah was immersed in drama. Of course she would leap to the most dramatic conclusion when faced with something so inherently dramatic in her actual life.

"Are you well, boss?" Sidney asked. "You seem a wee down in the mouth."

"Oh, it's nothing," she said. "Just the news from America — more prosecutions, more former radicals deciding to name names and protect themselves and go on to bigger successes. It's discouraging."

"Hardly 'news' anymore now, is it?"

Hannah flared up. "Maybe not, but the day I stop feeling something about it is the day I shrug it off as 'normal,' and it's not, it can't be, it mustn't ever be."

"Didn't mean to vex you," Sidney said, looking wounded. Hannah so rarely showed temper, certainly not at her staff. "So long as you're all right to do the interview with your fellow from the *Spectator* today."

"Yes, of course, looking forward to it," Hannah said automatically. She knew she ought to apologize for snapping, but wasn't in the mood. The blacklist and Communist witch hunt weren't the cause of today's temper, but they always lurked somewhere. It was the witch-hunting that had sent her family abroad. *And Paul into the arms of a broad? No, no, don't think about it. Not here, not now.* The day any of them shrugged over the stories of the American government persecuting its citizens in this way was the day they might as well say it was right. Any number of Americans agreed with it, but any number of Germans had once agreed that Germany should persecute Jewish people. "Oh, but Communists are different," came the argument. "It's a dangerous political movement. They're aligned with Soviets, they're determined to quash democracy." But the Nazis had said the Jews wanted to rule the world. Facts, evidence, reason — none of that mattered. Hannah stabbed her pen into the blotter. She had to stay vigilant.

"We'll do the interview in the outer office," Hannah announced.

"Why not in your office?" Sidney was

surprised.

"I don't want journalists in there." She didn't elaborate, and Sidney asked nothing further. A good journalist had a way of seeing things in a space you didn't realize were visible. Everything that had happened since *Robin Hood* began — Hedda Hopper, Phoebe's threatening letter, being followed — none of it was a coincidence. Her own name was safe because she'd been prescient and lucky, but who knew if that could change? The less anyone saw of her private space, the better.

The journalist from the *Spectator* had a round face, round glasses, and shy smile. He looked like he could be an adolescent fan playing a ruse, but Hannah, ever the watchful journalist herself, knew from some sleuthing that he'd gone to Queen Mary's Grammar School and Cambridge University, interned at the *Express,* and had come up reviewing theater. They spent a very happy twenty minutes discussing the intelligence of the scripts and the way some episodes seemed to include pleas for social justice and warnings about a world without it. Hannah was almost relaxed when he flipped to a fresh sheet in his pad.

"I'm given to understand you are not only married, but have children," he said, smiling brightly. "Two little girls?"

"That's right," Hannah said, her scalp tingling.

"Awfully unusual, isn't it, a wife with two small children working such a monumental job? What does your husband say?"

"If you like, I can arrange for you to interview him directly," Hannah offered in a generous, helpful tone, grinning so it looked like a joke. She couldn't decide if she was more outraged or disappointed by this man's presumption. She would deputize Sidney to view a draft of the article before it was printed and make sure it didn't paint her as some monster who neglected her family.

"Oh, gosh no," he said. "That's all right."

Hannah nodded and flashed her most disarming smile — the one that had worked so effectively when she herself conducted interviews. It was an easy way of changing the course of the story, because wasn't it surprising that such a soft, sweet mama was also the mother of this adventure program so beloved by young boys?

"I've been given to understand that a good deal of the scripts originate in America," he said. "Is that down to you being American yourself?"

"Your information isn't entirely accurate,"

427

Hannah said, smiling as sweetly as ever. "Some scripts do come from abroad, but that's because I like to guarantee a wide range of views."

"And it certainly gets you a wide range of viewers," he said admiringly before returning to protocol. "What's your favorite part of the job?"

Now Hannah's smile was real.

"Whatever part I'm working on the moment I'm doing it."

The journalist smiled too. He knew a top-drawer quote when he heard it.

"Beg pardon, Miss Wolfson." Beryl was suddenly looming. "Only it's time to go out for the table read."

It wasn't, but the attentive Beryl sensed the interview had gone on long enough and wanted no further forays into dangerous waters, however adept Hannah might be at navigating them. Besides, they all knew that a mention of the Glaswegian story editor in the menswear and monocle would add color to the piece.

But Hannah still told Sidney to follow up. She wasn't taking any chances.

She knew Beryl and Sidney were discussing her, comparing notes as to whether she was quite herself this week. She frowned out the window. "Herself" was, among so many things, a woman beloved and respected by her husband. But maybe that part of her had slipped away, had been slipping away for a long time, possibly since the day she'd realized she was likely to be targeted by the FBI and HUAC, and it was better to clear out from their line of sight. Maybe she'd known it for years now, and had been too busy becoming other people — a mother, a producer, a savior (or lawbreaker, depending on how you looked at it) — to pay attention to what was happening within the relationship with the man she loved.

Her eye landed on a man in the square, reading a newspaper. Only he wasn't, was he? He glanced up at her window under his hat. Didn't he?

If only Rhoda were here. She could nail that eye with an arrow.

Hannah turned from the eye and reached for her hat. She might not be able to stop anyone spying on her, or her family, or her show. She couldn't stop her friends from being harassed, abused, imprisoned. But she could go to her husband and ask for his honesty. He had taken plenty. He could give her that.

It was funny, Hannah thought, the things

you remember. She'd forgotten the pain of giving birth, but she remembered the first meal she'd ever made for Paul as a married couple. Roast chicken with potatoes and gravy, creamed spinach, strawberry short-cake. She made it now.

Paul ate without seeming to notice any of it, and Hannah thought she might as well have served him cardboard and bird drop-pings. He talked on and on about his work, stopping only when Gemma brought the girls in to say good night. Julie was already asleep in Gemma's arms, but Rhoda clasped her arms around Paul's legs.

"Daddy, snakes are the only true carni-vores because they eat nothing but meat, not plants, not ever."

"Is that so?" Paul asked, patting her head. "And what can you tell me about flowers, or princesses?"

Rhoda pulled a face. "Princesses don't *do* anything, Daddy!" She considered. "But there's supposed to be a flower somewhere that smells really, really bad. Really, really bad. Can we go and smell it?"

"Maybe," Paul said dismissively. Hannah hated the disappointment on Rhoda's face.

"The corpse flower," Hannah said. "We'll go smell it next time it's in bloom."

Gemma took the girls off to bed, and

Hannah served Paul coffee and cake. He reached for a newspaper. Hannah sighed. He might not always give Rhoda the answers she wanted, or anything like enough attention, but he was there. Rhoda loved him with the beautiful simplicity of a child's love. Hannah wondered if that love gave him the same pang it gave her, if it ever took his breath away, seized him up with so much emotion, his skin swelled, because his body could never be big enough to hold all that feeling. She had never seen him look at the girls as though he could never look long enough, never memorize every feature and keep it inside him forever. He might look that way when she couldn't see. She hoped so. For their sake, and for his.

She slipped off her shoes and wiggled her toes. "Paul," she began. He looked at her over the paper, but the phone rang. His eyes lowered again, and Hannah took the hint and went to answer.

"Hello?"

There was no response. She heard something, though, she was sure. That wasn't so unusual. The British telephone service often had a way of making one nostalgic for the reliability of passenger pigeons. "Can I help you?" Hannah said into the phone. But there was still nothing. After a moment, she hung up, but kept her eyes on the phone. Paul still sat, smoking and reading.

"Anyone in particular?" he roused himself to ask.

"Not really," she answered, drumming her fingers on the table.

"Oh good."

"Paul." He looked up at her again. She didn't have to do this. The pot didn't need stirring. But she knew the question would gnaw at her till she had nothing left.

"What about Doris? Is she anyone in particular?"

His expression didn't change, but he methodically folded the paper.

"What did you do?" A grim smile teased his lips. "Track me like you did that man Phoebe was wondering about?"

"So she's not just someone you're profiling for your story."

"She started that way," Paul admitted. "And then we got to know each other."

"Or rather, you watched her take her clothes off, again and again and again," Hannah couldn't resist pointing out.

"She listens," Paul snapped. "She listens, and she cares. She's interested. When was the last time you paid real attention to me? It's always the girls, or the group, or of course your *work*. When was the last time you actually needed me?"

Hannah was thunderstruck.

"What on earth do you mean? Of course I need you. How can you doubt that?"

"You needed my money," he spat. "To get us here, to get your damn company set up. What do you need now? The man you talk about most is Sidney, not me."

She might have laughed, but it was so absurd. Sidney! She would almost feel more guilty if he mentioned her admirers on the set. But Sidney?

"Paul. I love you. Just you. You're the only one I've ever loved." She paused, letting that sink in. Then she moved closer, and asked, "Do you still love me?"

The question hung too long for there to be any real doubt. Finally he said, "I don't know. Yes, sure, but it's different now. It's you everyone seeks out, for anything and everything. We started off as partners, but now no one even sees me in this marriage. You've become this, this paragon, larger than life. Where do I fit?"

"Some paragon!" Hannah burst out. "Let me tell you what being so visible gets me. I was followed, actually followed, by what I'm sure was a Hound, and I was with Rhoda, no less —"

"Damn it!" Paul smacked the table. "Now

you've got the children involved."

"It wasn't my fault!" she protested. "People have been through worse, just ask Joan and —"

"No! No. I'm sick of dealing with all your Red friends, trying to eke out something here when I could be high-flying at home." He looked at her a long time as he reached for his pipe and lit it. "I was going to tell you. I've been offered an editorial job in Toronto, building up a magazine —"

"Toronto!" Hannah almost laughed. "That's what you're calling high-flying? Or home?" She snatched up a cigarette and lit it with a shaky hand.

"No, but I had thought it was a place you could live safely without worrying about the feds touching you," he said, sucking on his pipe.

"And I was supposed to just leave everything?"

"That's what wives and mothers do, you know."

Hannah's jaw dropped. "But . . . you love that I work. You always did."

"We have girls, girls who think it's normal to have a part-time mother. Look at Rhoda! She keeps on like this, she'll be completely unmarriageable. You want her to be like that ridiculous Phoebe, scratching around for whatever work someone's willing to throw her?"

"Independent and following her dreams? I can think of worse things," Hannah said.

"No one wants to hire a girl for anything unless they're desperate," Paul told her. "Even you didn't want to hire Phoebe, you only did because you can't turn any of the damn blacklistees away. You could lose it all, end up with so many counts of abetting Reds, you'll be in jail till Julie's kids graduate from high school, you want that?"

Hannah shook so hard, she dropped her cigarette.

"I'm doing the right thing," she insisted, grinding ash into the carpet. "You used to be proud of me for that."

"Except now our kids are targets," he said.

"They can't touch me here, they can just try to scare me. I won't be scared."

"No," he said softly, almost lovingly. "No, you won't. Never were, never will be. And maybe that's it. Maybe I'm the sort of fellow who wants a woman who gets a little scared sometimes, and needs me there for her. So there we are."

Hannah ran her eyes hungrily over his face. The pale skin, the dark stubble along the prominent jawline, the large eyes. She still wanted to stroke that cheek, kiss his forehead, his mouth. In a film, she would. Then he'd remember how much he loved her and why. And they'd melt into their bedroom, and into each other's bodies, and all this would be forgotten. Later they'd lie together, making assurances, so that when the spell lifted and they got up, got dressed, went back to being themselves, something new was forged and they would go on, stronger than ever.

She felt as though someone had opened her up and scooped out all her insides. When she didn't say anything, he took her hand.

"I need something for myself, Hannah. I can't keep feeling forced into being here, because of you. This is a heck of an opportunity and I'm not turning it down. I'll let you keep the girls, I'll even give you a settlement, not that you need it."

It was all so casual. Ten years. Two children. Reduced to a shrug. In a way, this admission of how little he cared about the girls was a relief. It would make the business of falling out of love that much easier.

He went to a hotel for the night. Or so he told her. The tears held until he left, then rolled silently down her face with no effort, as if a spigot had been flipped on behind her eyes. Still weeping, she went into the girls' room and sat on the floor between their beds, listening to her daughters' breathing. She was lucky, she told herself. She had wonderful children who needed her, and she had work. So many people depended on her, she couldn't curl up inside herself and nurse any unhappiness. She just had to get on with it.

She sighed, leaning her head against a bookcase full of stories. Grown-up stories all said love should cost something. She wondered if she might be a fool after all, because she had never imagined she would have to pay for one love with another.

CHAPTER SEVENTEEN

Music poured from Joan's open door. She pounced as soon as she saw Phoebe.

"Did you hear? Has the news spread to the set yet?" Joan cried eagerly.

"Is the blacklist defunct?" Phoebe asked.

"Silly! Paul's got a mistress," Joan said, her eyes glittering. "He's actually leaving Hannah and the girls, moving to Canada of all places. Can you believe it?"

Phoebe couldn't. She believed in Hannah and Paul. It was beyond sense that they should come apart.

"That's awful," she said. "Are you sure?"

"Oh yes!" Joan warmed to her tale, regaling Phoebe with details she couldn't possibly know. Which meant the story had gone around already, gaining steam. Phoebe's chest contracted with sadness for Hannah.

"It just goes to show, just like Charlie's always said," Joan finished triumphantly. "It's all right for a woman to work before she's married, if she has to, but anything else is unnatural. It won't end well."

Phoebe was appalled. "How can you say that? Hannah's your friend. She's been nothing but wonderful to you."

"I didn't say I'm ungrateful," Joan explained. "Of course it's a shame. But honestly, think of those poor girls. Rhoda's so strange already. Take away her father, and what chance does she have to grow up healthfully?"

"There was just a big war," Phoebe pointed out. "Lots of kids are growing up without a father. Freddie downstairs, for one, and he's fine."

"But he'll never amount to anything," Joan insisted. "He'll leave school at sixteen, get some lousy job, and that'll be it for him. And that's if he's lucky."

Phoebe stepped up to Joan, so they were nearly nose to nose.

"You have no right to be such a snob. If your husband was so concerned with providing for his family, he could have found extra work cleaning toilets. As for Hannah's kids, I'll lay dollars to doughnuts they at least continue to respect their mother over the years, which is a heck of a lot more than can be said for your boys."

Joan's eyes flooded with tears. They might

have been tears of anger, rather than re-
morse, but Phoebe had no patience for
either. She flounced into her flat and
slammed the door behind her. After a moment, she heard Joan's door close too.

All three of the Other Girls bounded over
to Phoebe when she arrived at the set the
next day.

"Is it true? Is Miss Wolfson actually getting a divorce? Who would ever have
thought?"

Phoebe looked at them without pleasure.
Once they'd achieved détente after the
Hedda Hopper incident, everyone returned
to their corners. The Other Girls did their
jobs, took their breaks, and clustered about
together, and Phoebe was "the peculiar
American" whose head was constantly
buried in a script. It was comforting.

"You'll have to ask Miss Wolfson," Phoebe
informed them. Dora, ever the leader,
wrinkled her nose and stalked away, and the
others tagged behind. Phoebe didn't care.
At least it meant no one else would dare
think she was one to tell tales.

"Of course they know," was Hannah's
untroubled comment that evening. She had
summoned Phoebe for a drink after work in
a quiet pub. "I told Beryl and Sidney,

440

because I'll have some dealings with lawyers in the next few weeks and it might be disruptive. They obviously found a way to let everyone else know not to try ruffling my feathers. So now everyone's being wonderfully English and pretending to be more respectful of me than ever. It's quaint, really."

She seemed almost serene, except that she swallowed her gin and tonic in three gulps and ordered another.

"I'm so sor—" Phoebe began, but Hannah held up her hand.

"Don't give me sympathy. God, I hate sympathy. Give me something to read. Don't you have another script by now?"

"I do," Phoebe said. "I'm finishing it up. But it's . . ." She was about to say it was about a married couple, and did Hannah really want to read that right now, but she couldn't manage the words.

"It's what? Let me tell you something, Phoebe — if you're going to succeed, you've got to be quicker, okay? Most people don't want to hire women, you know that. You have to be better than all the others."

Phoebe was stung. Hannah knew how hard she worked, how she was balancing her day job with writing. Then she thought about the time spent with Reg and became subdued.

"I am better than all the others," she said. "I'll drop the new script in the mail tomorrow."

"Good," Hannah said, knocking back another drink. "And listen, I know Joan's a bit much, but she called me up bawling today, and that'll continue till you make up with her — there's no chance she'll come to you," Hannah pressed on, quelling Phoebe's protest. "Please, for me? I can't take care of her on top of everything."

For Hannah. Of course she would do it for Hannah. Hannah, who was now fiddling with the bar mat, staring into her glass as though she were a medium.

"Listen," Hannah muttered. "I owe you an apology. I thought you were being nutty when you said a fellow was maybe spying on you. But I saw a man watching me at least once, and I'm guessing it's not because he was struck by my beauty."

"So what do we do?" Phoebe whispered. She felt a twinge of alarm but also excitement. If she was right and someone was here, trying to — what? Capture them? — then fighting back with Hannah was sure to be satisfying. Add in Shirley and Will, and the so-called subversives were guaranteed to score a decisive win.

"We pay attention," Hannah instructed. "Don't give anyone a reason to look at us again. Do your work, Phoebe. Make your money. And don't trust anyone if you can help it."

It hardly sounded like Hannah at all, she was so bitter. They pressed hands quickly but that was all. There was nothing left to say.

Phoebe headed for the bus stop. She was so deep in thought, she didn't feel the prickles at the back of her neck. By the time she was aroused enough to whip her head around, she saw only a sea of ordinary men, heading home after the drinks they felt so entitled to enjoy before settling to their dinners.

"You can't touch me!" she shouted into the throng. Men actually jumped back, they were so startled. Phoebe laughed, not caring how she looked. Just at the moment, she wanted someone to try to give her some grief. She was done being afraid. All she wanted to do now was hit back.

Phoebe read over her script, then walked to the phone booth on Charing Cross Road to call Shirley.

"If you have a script ready and you think it's right for *Robin Hood,* why on earth would you hesitate in giving it to Hannah?" Shirley was perplexed, and her honeyed voice was laced with mild contempt. It unnerved Phoebe, but she persisted.

"It's about love and marriage, in part," she explained. "Hannah's not going to want to read about that right now, is she?"

"Oh, strife," Shirley snapped. "Hannah is a professional. She won't let anything in her personal life interfere with her work. But you might ask yourself whether a story about love and marriage is right for a kiddies' adventure show."

"It also involves conspiracy and torture," Phoebe clarified.

"Then you'll just have to see if that's enough, won't you?"

Phoebe sent the script. Three days later, Hannah summoned her to the office after work and presented her with seventy pounds.

"It's the best work of yours I've read yet. Beryl will toughen up the soft parts."

"Soft parts?"

Hannah smiled. "Just a few lines here and there. It's obviously written by someone newly in love."

Phoebe went hot and blinked away from Hannah's intent gaze.

"Love happens," Hannah said, sounding

genuinely pleased for Phoebe. "And usually when we least expect it. You might as well enjoy it while it lasts."

"Except it's getting in the way of my writing time."

"Maybe." Hannah shrugged. "But you're also writing with new warmth. Might as well enjoy that too. And Phoebe . . . make up with Joan already, will you?"

Joy wrapped in a reprimand. Phoebe had far more important worries on her mind than Joan — Mona, for one, who was declining fast, and Anne, who hadn't written in too many weeks to ignore. And, of course, whoever was following them around London, and why, and what they might do. But the joy overtook her. A single script could just be luck. Two meant she was a professional, to be taken seriously. She smiled. She was a real writer again.

As she approached number seven, Freddie lunged forward to greet her, his face solemn with duty.

"This telegram come for you, miss, marked urgent. They didn't like to leave it, but I told them I'd get it right to you, miss."

Phoebe took it with shaking hands, absently thrusting a coin into Freddie's palm. He hovered beside her, brimming with

445

anxiety. She read the contents three times before any words began to sink in. *Come to Southampton, meet at the tea shop, as soon as possible.* Southampton, where the ships came in from New York. An hour by train at least, and this had been waiting. She warned Freddie to sound the alarm if she wasn't there in the morning, but there was no time to contact anyone else, or to check if the telegram was legit. There was no question of going, going at once, because the telegram was signed "Anne."

Even when she arrived, breathless, glancing around wildly, she knew it could be a trap. Why anyone would go to such efforts, she couldn't imagine, but one thing was always clear from crime reports: logic was rarely a criminal's hallmark.

But there, hunched at a table, looking small and lost, was indeed Anne. Phoebe walked to her in a daze, hardly believing it.

"Hi," Anne said softly. She was pale and drawn, looking down into an empty teacup. "Do you have a cigarette?"

Phoebe handed her a pack. She didn't know what to say. Anne's voice was low and furtive, her expression nervous and wary. She didn't seem like Anne at all.

"Stop looking at me like that," she ordered

Phoebe. "I was sick the whole time on the ship, but I'm not a ghost yet." The words were more like Anne, but the tone was so sad.

Phoebe hailed a waitress and ordered coffee and sandwiches.

"Look at you, all trousers and tweeds," Anne said, perking up with the arrival of the food. "And bright-eyed. England is agreeing with you."

"Sometimes I don't recognize myself without a skirt and heels," Phoebe admitted. "It's like being incognito."

"Good way to commit a crime," Anne said.

"Not me, I'd rather catch the criminal," Phoebe replied.

They laughed, and it almost felt like no time had passed at all. They could be holding court at their favorite table in Floyd and Leo's, eating cheesecake with cherries and whispering over which man at the counter was most likely to be a murderer, a confidence trickster, or just a garden-variety creep. Anne drew police sketches while Phoebe made notes, and their targets glared at them as they laughed. A lump rose in Phoebe's throat. There was a lot of fun to be had while you were waiting for your real life to begin.

"Please tell me you're here for a long trip," Phoebe said. "You can stay as long as you want. Maybe between us we can spruce my place up a bit."

Anne gave her a rueful look.

"I'm headed for Paris. A second cousin lives there, she can spare me a room. It's a good place for artists, you know, especially when one is trying to be a cliché."

"The last thing you are is a cliché."

"Well, we'll see," Anne said with a shrug.

Phoebe knew she wasn't imagining the discouragement in Anne's face. Or the nervous, guilty looks that slipped out from under her banter. If she had a sketch of herself amid their old selection, she'd be an obvious culprit.

"Why didn't you sail to France directly?"

"Oh, you know, beggars, choosers — this ship left first." Anne lit another cigarette.

Phoebe exhaled in a low whistle as realization hit her. Anne must have fallen prey to the FBI and HUAC herself. Anne saw the understanding in Phoebe's eyes and nodded sadly.

"Good old HUAC, keeping us all safe from the big, bad Reds like me."

Phoebe's cup paused halfway to her mouth.

"You . . . you're actually a Communist?"

Anne shrugged. "I joined the party when I turned eighteen. It wasn't illegal. And it made a lot of sense for someone like me. It still does. You know the Communist Party is completely against any form of racial discrimination? Not only that, they think the whole concept of classing people by race is hogwash. What reasonable person wouldn't want to be a part of that?"

Phoebe knew this, because of Shirley and Will. She knew that a lot of the members of the NAACP were, or had been, members of the Communist Party, and that white members of the party were active in the South, trying to help black people gain voting rights. Dolores Goldstein used to rave about the absurdity of Jim Crow, and point out that the north wasn't without its biases and bigotry, too, but Anne never joined in that conversation. Like Phoebe, she never seemed very interested in politics, beyond winning the war.

"Anyway," said Anne with a toss of her curls. "I prefer to call myself a Marxist. I still like to believe we can build a fairer society, ain't that a joke?"

"But you were always so busy with art." Phoebe was confused. This wasn't the way Anne talked.

"Oh, look, I know I could have told you,

but you were always so uninterested in politics and busy with your own stuff."

"What does that mean?" Phoebe was hurt. Was Anne suggesting she hadn't been a supportive friend?

"It was good, it was right," Anne consoled her, putting her hand on Phoebe's. "You had to take care of Mona. Why burden you with secrets?"

"Dolores Goldstein didn't keep it a secret."

Anne gave her a long look, then lowered her voice. "I didn't care about racism because I'm a crusader. I cared — care — because I'm what they call a mulatto."

Phoebe felt her mouth drop open. She wished she could control it, because she didn't want to make Anne uncomfortable. But she couldn't help being surprised. They'd been friends so long, and here was something so important to who Anne was, yet she'd never felt she could tell Phoebe.

"So, what with that and the party, I was five kinds of an idiot for taking a teaching job," Anne said, stabbing a sandwich with a knife.

"Oh, Anne, you had to sign a loyalty oath, didn't you?"

"I did." Anne scooped up sugar and let it snow back into the bowl. "Hell, I'm lucky they caught me on the party membership, not my race. Old Dolores Goldstein was right — even New York wouldn't have loved learning that."

"For the love of Pete, what were you thinking?" Phoebe scolded. "You knew what they could find and you became a teacher? Signed that damn oath? Why didn't you just skip Go and ask for a stint in the Women's House of Detention?"

"I needed the money, all right?" Anne snapped. "I figured if I signed the damn oath, it would be fine. It's not perjury, I *am* a loyal citizen. More so 'cause I want to make the country better." She went back to fiddling with the sugar spoon. "Look, it came down even faster than it did for you. I was able to sell some stuff, the rest I asked a friend to take, but who knows? Anyway, I'm sorry. Here's your share." She slid folded bills across the table to Phoebe.

Phoebe fingered the little wad like it was an ancient relic, brushing over the glare of Andrew Jackson. The paper felt foreign. She clutched it, trying to remember having such items in her handbag, using it to buy groceries, stockings, pay installments on her furniture and treasures.

Which were all gone now. Phoebe closed her eyes, willing her rage back down her throat. That rage wasn't for Anne. Phoebe knew exactly whose fault it was that she no longer owned any of the things she'd bought with her own money.

"Do you think it was Jimmy who ratted on you?"

Another shrug. "Even if he was, so what? The end is the same." She bit into the last sandwich. "I guess I wouldn't be surprised. He didn't bawl to see the back of you. Vindictive little worm."

"He'll get his," Phoebe insisted. Anne shrugged again. Phoebe slid the wad of bills back to her. "You'll need this more than I do. I'm getting by all right."

Surprise and faint hope filled Anne's eyes, but she shook her head.

"You should have it, I'm . . . I'll be fine. I didn't want to . . . It was just all so quick . . ." Her voice cracked and she gulped down more coffee. "They tapped my phone, of course. Broke in, too, not that they needed to by then."

Phoebe remembered Joan telling a similar story. She gaped at Anne.

"It's legal," Anne growled. "Completely legal, 'cause I'm supposed to be so danger- ous. Just because I think people should be treated equally. Land of the free. So deter- mined not to be like the Soviets and treating citizens like this. What a joke."

Phoebe ordered more sandwiches, wishing the place sold gin. "You were with me pushing for a union, they could have nailed you on that."

"You're right. Nice of us, giving them options."

"Listen," Phoebe said. "I don't know about Paris, but it's not all peaches and cream in London." Her voice dropped to a whisper a bat would have strained to catch. "The Hounds are still baying at us here."

She'd never seen Anne look incredulous before. It was a novelty she could have done without. A man at the next table coughed, and both women jumped.

This is HUAC's real legacy, isn't it? There are plenty of ways to destroy a person without ever laying a finger on them.

"I should be heading to the ferry," Anne said at last.

"Can't you stay a few days at least? We can run wild, like old times."

"Old times are called that because they're gone," Anne said with finality. Then she sighed. "I'm sorry. It's great to see you. But I've got to get there and get started."

She was still so beautiful, with all those red curls and freckles. But the thing that made her so magnetic was missing.

"Look, take this, really," Phoebe said, thrusting the bills into Anne's hand. "I just sold another script, I'm in clover." She took her key from her bag and used it to cut open the stitches in her coat lining, retrieving the fifty dollars Anne had sewn there. "And I can pay you back this too."

Phoebe knew she didn't imagine the look of stunned relief on Anne's face.

"But . . . Mona?" Anne asked.

Phoebe hesitated. But Mona was dying, and her friend needed this. She flung her arms around Anne, squeezing her tight, as if she could hug her memory of her friend back into her living body. Anne clung to her a minute, then pulled away and looked around nervously.

"We should be careful. Can't have anyone saying we're dykes on top of all of it."

Phoebe laughed. "There's a story that would fall apart in two seconds."

Anne gave her another pitying look. "You can't be too careful." Then she softened, clutching Phoebe's hand. "Thanks. So much. Really. I better go. I'll write, I promise."

"See you in the funny papers," Phoebe said. They turned away. A moment later, Phoebe turned back to call to Anne, to make their old gesture, pointing at each other, acknowledging their mutual greatness. But Anne had already disappeared.

Phoebe could see Reg pacing in a circle under the streetlight outside number seven as she trudged down Meard Street. She sighed, not sure if she wanted company or some quiet time alone, and wished she had the option to decide. He pounced on her.

"What the devil happened to you?" he demanded.

"Where do you want me to start?" she asked.

He ran his hand through his hair several times, looking wild. "I came round to see you, and young Freddie tells me you got an urgent telegram and ran off and might be in danger. I've been half out of my mind for ages!" He actually glared at her.

"Oh, I am sorry!" Phoebe blazed in a sudden temper. "How awful for you to have to stand around and fret while I'm getting dragged off to the Tower of London for a lovely afternoon's beheading."

She heard a passerby giggle.

"How was I to know what to do?" Reg asked. "Your neighbor wasn't home, and you haven't introduced me to any of your friends. How was I meant to try to find you?"

"Oh, for crying out loud." Phoebe threw up her hands. "You've heard me mention Miss Wolfson. You might have tried going to a phone box and asking an operator to find her number — there aren't that many Wolfsons in London."

"She's got you there, mate," a man who'd stopped to watch chimed in.

Phoebe rounded on him. "Hey, aren't you meant to be British? I'm a stranger here, and even I know you're supposed to ignore other people's arguments."

The man shrugged and headed off, saying only to Reg, "Hope you're getting some value for money with this one."

"What am I, chattel?" Phoebe bellowed after him.

Reg took her hand and stroked it. For a moment, she was ready to sink against his chest. She snapped back suddenly, half turning from him. "I can't. I can't have anyone else worrying, can't have more people to worry about. I can't love you right now, I can't, I just can't, it's too hard, all of this is too hard."

The words made no sense, but they wouldn't stop coming. Every contraction of his face made her hurt more, when wave after wave of pain was already washing over her. She wanted to push him away. She wanted to grab him tight and never let him go. She'd lost Anne. She was losing Mona. She'd lost a home, and now the last of the things that had made it home. She'd even lost her name. She didn't want to lose Reg just as she was starting to find him.

But she couldn't stop seeing Anne's face, so beaten down and anxious. She couldn't stop seeing Hannah's face, sad and bitter. The blacklist broke love everywhere. Phoebe couldn't bear to let it happen to her, when she'd already lost so much.

"I have to be alone right now," she said. "Please, I just need to be alone."

"Of course, if that's what you want," he began, "But . . ."

"Stop, stop, stop!" she cried. "If you want company, go to the library, see if there's another woman willing to give you a kicking."

As soon as she said it, she was sorry, but her throat was too tight to say anything more. She slammed the door behind her and ran upstairs, wiping her eyes. She pulled out her key, then turned and looked at Joan's door. Hannah was right. They needed each other. It was what kept them all going here on Mars. And she missed Joan. Missed her terribly.

Even before she knocked, her scalp tingled, telling her something was wrong. She knocked and listened, waiting, wondering. A shiver went right down her spine as she realized what she was hearing. Nothing. Not a single note of big band music.

She knocked again, harder. "Joan!" she yelled, giving the door one big pound and then wiggling the handle. To her shock, it gave way to her touch and the door opened.

It was like walking through a house in a dream, where nothing was quite as it usually was. The furniture was there, but stripped of tablecloth, throws, doilies. Phoebe's eyes adjusted further, seeing no photographs, no magazines, no vases, no radio. She crept through the two small bedrooms, seeing the surfaces empty of toys, books, the sewing box, and Charlie's typewriter. Seeing the vast expanse of nothing, but unable to believe what she knew was right before her eyes.

She didn't need Hannah or Shirley to tell her there was no way the family had gone to a cheaper place in London. Because they hadn't. Because Charlie was a man at the end of his rope, and he would sooner reach for the cushiest lifeline than compromise his pride.

He'd contacted the FBI, contacted HUAC, and agreed to name names in exchange for a golden ticket back to America and his professional life.

He was going to point a finger at *Robin Hood,* and every last one of them here in London.

CHAPTER EIGHTEEN

After she'd talked Phoebe back from the
brink, Hannah debated what to say to
Sidney. He believed in Sapphire's unwritten
mission, and even incidents like Beryl's pos-
ing as a writer he found little more than
shrug-worthy — a quirk of doing business
with Americans and their peculiarities. The
show was such a hit, it was impossible
anything so absurd as the blacklist could
touch it.

"But it can, can't it?" Hannah mused to
Shirley that afternoon. "HUAC could insist
CBS stop airing the show. CBS could say
no, but would they? I don't know."

"One 'no' like that might bring about an
end to the blacklist," Shirley said, pouring
Hannah tea and adding a few splashes of
gin, for "flavoring." "I expect you know
something of Denmark's actions during the
war, yes?"

Hannah smiled. "Yes. They helped their

Jewish population escape, rather than agree to hand them over to the Nazis. Hitler must have yowled about it for weeks."

" 'No' can be a mighty word," Shirley said. "Imagine if more people used it."

History rolled over Hannah. People might have said no to allowing slavery, or the racial laws, or keeping women from voting. It was a risk, but what wasn't?

"People don't have much stomach for risk," Hannah said.

"They do not," Shirley agreed. *Quel dommage.*"

Hannah knocked back her tea and didn't need to ask for a refill.

Shirley lit a cigarette. "Charlie's likely to testify any day. I'll ask Will to send a mindfully worded telegram to some select friends so we get an early report."

"Thanks. I suppose it won't be broadcast."

"He's not famous enough to warrant a major broadcast, no, but HUAC does like its doings known. We'll find a way to know what we need to know and when."

Hannah sipped her tea, which was mostly gin.

"It could get bad. Sapphire's reputation could be harmed. Am I even safe? What if they find a way to aim both barrels at me? Never mind blacklisting, they could insist my passport be seized, issue a subpoena, maybe even extradite me. What would happen to the girls? Paul certainly doesn't want them."

"Strife," Shirley snarled. For all Paul's condemnation of Hannah's influence, his new life didn't include his daughters. He had settled a large chunk of his family's money on the girls, stipulating that the solicitor, not Hannah, was to manage it.

"Then again," Shirley went on, "the Hannah I know finds a crisis stimulating, rather than daunting." One side of her lips curled upward.

Hannah smiled ruefully. "That may have been before the love of her life turned out to be a toad. But you're right. I'd better shore up one hell of a deal on the next show, and shake down Paul for my own settlement before anyone turns my name to mud. If I have to hire a lawyer to rep me before HUAC, I want the best."

"Hardly a point in doing things any other way," Shirley said, pouring out the last of the gin.

Will's contacts acted with admirable speed and thoroughness. Charlie was to testify next week. It would not be broadcast, but it was to be recorded, and a copy of that recording could be sent to England. There were two problems: timing and discretion.

Phoebe was invited to discuss the problem and, to Hannah's delight, came up with a solution. "Nigel Elliott! He flies back and forth all the time. Or sails, but mostly flies. He might help if it isn't too illegal."

"Just for now, I can be a reporter again," Hannah decided. "We'll call it a leak to the press." Phoebe composed the telegram then and there. Nigel's response came to the Sapphire offices the next morning:

```
HOW  GLORIOUSLY  CLANDESTINE  =
WILL  ARRANGE  TO  BE  IN  DC  NEXT
WEEK  =  LOOKING  FORWARD  TO  MEET-
ING  THE  ENTERPRISING  MISS  WOLF-
SON  SHOULD  SUCH  BE  POSSIBLE  +
```

Good to his word, Nigel Elliott brought the recording back two days after Charlie's testimony. He came to the Sapphire offices to deliver it to Hannah.

"Aren't these premises simply charming?" he marveled as he was shown into the main office, where Beryl regarded him without pleasure. "So this is how a business is run. What an extraordinary thing. Very charmed to meet you," he said, extending a warm hand to Hannah. "I enjoyed reading your interview in the *Spectator.* I've not seen the program myself, I've really not got time for television, but I deeply admire you, creating such a success. Quite a thing for a woman! I daresay it's your American spirit that does it, and very admirable too."

"The British could do more if those with money would provide funding," Beryl said to the script she was editing, in her broadest Glaswegian.

"Ah, a lady of Caledonia!" Nigel said with a laugh, turning approvingly to Beryl. "Quite right of you, dear, I'm sure, and indeed something that ought to be done. Now then, I mustn't linger, my car is waiting — I came directly from the airport to make sure you received this properly. You have the means of listening?"

"Oh yes, I'm quite established with all the latest equipment," Hannah said drily. She was grateful to this man, but while she found his patronizing tone amusing, and knew he didn't intend it as such, she sensed Beryl was barely restraining herself from throwing him through the window.

"Jolly good, jolly good, I thought you might," Nigel said cheerfully. "Americans do like to buy all the latest gadgets, and it's mighty fine of them. Well, I was unable to attend the event and know nothing of what's in it, but I hope it's of use to you. Most glad to have been of service in such a scrumptious cause, do call on me again should you wish, though of course I hope you won't have need. Perhaps someday I might come and view the program being filmed? I should so enjoy that."

"Of course," Hannah said, taking his card. He bowed and, with many "cheerios," headed back to his car. Hannah and Beryl went to the window and saw a massive black Bentley idling, taking up most of the road.

"I think less than nocht of the French," Beryl raged, "but they surely had the right idea in thwacking off the heads of all their namby-pamby blue-blooded bastards. He's the type who thought the Great War a damn fine idea and sat back during the last one and never suffered for rationing and would nae think to put sixpence into a production started by one of his own countrymen."

She was too enraged to ask how Hannah knew him, or what he'd brought her.

"The whole concept of aristocracy is ridiculous," Hannah agreed, conveniently setting Beryl off on another long tear. Somewhere in the middle of it, Hannah said she would go home to give Julie lunch — she was stealing as much time as she could for her children now — and Beryl hardly noticed. When Hannah left ten minutes later, Beryl was giving her thoughts on a script for *Robin Hood* in which the peasants marched into a nobleman's home and demanded they be given an education just like his, so that they might prove he was no more special than they.

That's a start, Hannah thought as she hailed a taxi. *The more real information people have, the more power they can wield.* She glanced at the bulge the recording made in her bag, hoping it would give her the information to help her retain her power.

She'd called Shirley from the office and found her friend already at the flat with Gemma and Julie, readying the reel-to-reel player that Hannah did indeed possess. She liked to listen to completed episodes of *Robin Hood* before they were locked, to make sure every word was clear. She couldn't have American audiences struggling to understand anyone.

"I never liked that Mr. Morrison," Gemma said with a sniff as she handed Julie to Hannah. "One eye larger than the other, and both of them twitchy. His wife means well enough, I'm sure, but I always thought her a bit of a pretty dunce, if I'm speaking plain."

Hannah said nothing. She didn't know what she thought of Joan right now.

"Here we go," Shirley said as the tape began to play. Hannah stroked Julie's hair and concentrated on breathing.

"Charles Alvin Morrison," a crackly voice began. *"Are you now, or have you ever been, a member of the Communist Party?"*

"Sir, I regret to say that I was. I joined in 1937 and remained a member until 1946."

"You attended meetings?"

"I did, and I can give you names of people in my chapter . . ."

Names. Names, names, names. Hannah recognized one or two. A fellow screenwriter. A B-movie director. A press photographer. She closed her eyes, imagining what was about to befall these men. The end of comfort, the end of security. All so Charlie could pick up his Hollywood life again.

"And when you were in England, you met with other Communists?"

The listeners exchanged glances.

"I did, there's a good number of them there, a lot of them working under different names on movies and television shows."

"Can you tell us who they are?"

"Fred Langham. The director, he's there, he's shooting a film right now."

Hannah's heart stopped. Charlie knew all

about Langham hiding from Hedda Hopper on the set of *Robin Hood,* and it would make one heck of a story.

"Can you tell us the name of the film?"

"No, I don't know it. I just heard about it through the grapevine."

"Mr. Morrison," the voice scolded, *"we agreed to your arrangement on the grounds that you provide us with solid information about Communist activity on the part of Americans at home and abroad. If you are not able . . ."*

"Wait!" Charlie cried. *"I can. I know for a fact that at least one confirmed Red has written for that television show* The Adventures of Robin Hood!"

"No!" Hannah cried, sinking her teeth into her fist so hard, she tasted blood. Shirley emitted one ferocious cry of *"Merde!"* before recovering herself and putting a hand on Hannah's arm as Julie gazed up at her with big, worried eyes. Hannah leaned her head against Julie's, waiting for names. But they didn't come. To her astonishment, Charlie admitted that this was all he had heard. He had no names.

"They won't let that stand, they can't possibly," Shirley said, her voice full of doubtful hope.

The committee asked a few more questions, but seemed pleased. They thanked him and promised that this television show would be investigated. The recording ended.

"Joan," Hannah said at last. "She begged him not to give us all away directly, and the show only as a last resort. He hates us but loves her. Good for him."

"So," Shirley said. "How will you proceed?"

Hannah took off her shoes, summoning the Hannah who indeed found crises stimulating. Then she grinned and lit a cigarette. "Easy as pie. Anyone who asks, I'll show them my list of writers. Most of them have only written for me and some other British and European programs, and they've never been anywhere near a blacklist. If anyone asks, well, I'm sorry but I've simply no idea what Mr. Morrison is talking about! He must certainly have heard wrong. You know how rumors can be."

There was her own private list, of course. A truly enterprising investigator could find that a check sent to Howard McGough, or Eugene Hale, or Roger Ehrlich all ended up at Ring Lardner Jr.'s house. But what were these men's banking arrangements to her? The questions would come, she would plead ignorance, promise punishment and future diligence, and that would, she hoped, be

469

good enough for CBS. No one wanted to lose a hit television series.

Life as a young reporter had taught Hannah that there were some things best kept even from an editor until they absolutely had to know. For now, she held off telling Sidney about Charlie's testimony. She did tell Phoebe, though, when she came to have her weekly talk with Mona.

"That louse!" was Phoebe's blunt assessment. "Of all the times for me to be right about something."

"Nothing wrong with being right," Hannah complimented her. "You've got good instincts, you know, you'd make a fine producer yourself."

"If my instincts were so good, I'd know what we should do now."

"Nothing yet," Hannah said. Phoebe frowned, but Hannah dug in. "You have to trust me. First, I'm officially not supposed to know anything, so it would be awfully funny to defend myself before an accusation's been made. Second, loose lips sink ships. No point worrying anyone till there's reason to worry."

Phoebe shook her head, confused. "But you left home when you weren't even targeted yet."

470

Hannah's eyes narrowed. "That's different. I knew how the tide was turning and who my enemies were. I had to get out of sight to be out of mind, so the choices were to come here and reinvent myself, or flit off to Connecticut or some damn thing and be a housewife . . ." She trailed off. If she'd done that, she might still be married. Her eyes traveled the room, seeing Paul's old records next to hers, his favorite ashtray, his print of New York in the 1920s. It was as if he were just on a trip, due back any day. Maybe he *would* return. Then she could decide if he was forgiven.

"I'm glad you came here," Phoebe said.

Hannah snapped back to attention. "Me too," she said. Meaning it, despite everything. "We'll be all right. Our official list of writers is squeaky clean, and Dale Winston loves Howard McGough."

"What did you think of Nigel?" Phoebe wanted to know.

"He's definitely the sort of person I want on my side in a jam," Hannah said. "Though I'd rather meet your fellow Reg."

Phoebe's face clouded. "We . . . aren't quite talking just at the moment. It's . . . he's taking up time when I really need to be writing."

Hannah lost patience.

"Didn't I also say something about love? For Pete's sake, Phoebe, the man makes you happy. And you can't ever have too many friends."

Phoebe looked away. "The more time I spend with him, the more I'll want to spend with him. What's the point, when the minute the blacklist is over I'll move back to New York?"

Hannah poured herself a drink. "This blacklist isn't going anywhere anytime soon. Live your life. And anyway, London's not so bad, is it?" She squeezed Phoebe's shoulder. "Make your phone call, then come join me and the girls. We're building a castle out of matchsticks, and then we'll put it in the fireplace and pretend Genghis Khan's come to call. Invite Reg over. If he doesn't behave, we'll toss him in the fire too."

"He doesn't have a phone," Phoebe explained.

"Another time then." Hannah headed for the playroom. It had been ages since she'd thought about life after the blacklist. It had stopped mattering, because this was home now. She might still not understand all the accents, and hated the class system, but this was her city now, and even the freedom to go back and reclaim New York had no pull on her heart.

Or perhaps she didn't believe that the persecution of anyone who had ever challenged the status quo would ever be over.

The call from CBS came a few days later.

"Hiya, Miss Wolfson." Dale Winston's voice boomed. She sat up straighter. "Listen, it's the nuttiest thing, but can you have your girl send over the list of writers for the show?"

"Don't you already have it?" Hannah carefully sounded surprised.

"They want to see all the names connected with the episodes that haven't aired yet," Dale said apologetically. "Look, don't feel bad, they'd do it for *Lucy*, too, except it's only ever the same pair of writers."

"Shall I send it via telex?" Hannah asked. "You can have it in an hour."

"Nah, it's not that urgent." She could hear him sucking at his cigar. "Them crackpots with the feds, they're always trying to throw their weight around. You know what they're like, trying to keep a hand in like they think they know better than us how to run our business. Trying to tell us what we should do, like we don't already have production codes. I tell you, it's damn Soviet of them, pardon my French."

Hannah smiled. There were still some men

who thought they shouldn't sully a lady's ear with "such language." As if she hadn't heard — and spoken — any amount of language herself. She wanted to use some now. She wanted to shout that CBS didn't have to comply, that they could push back, that they could tell the FBI they would hire whomever they wanted as long as they were good and it was indeed damn Soviet of the government to think it had anything to say about the matter. If *Robin Hood* could openly hire blacklisted writers and succeed, and democracy was still standing just fine, wouldn't everyone see that the FBI and HUAC had no clothes?

"Oh well, I'm sure there's no harm in it," Hannah said lightly. "I'll send it by the next post."

"Just so they know we're playing ball," Dale agreed. "We don't have to jump right when they say 'jump,' though. They can cool their heels a bit. We fought a war against the folks who expected that sort of jumping, ain't that right?"

"We certainly did," Hannah said, wondering if he could hear her teeth grinding.

"You'd better believe it," Dale said again, sounding pleased. "Hey, is Miss McGough writing one of the upcoming scripts? Boy, is that one ever a pistol."

"Isn't she just? She's one of our favorites. I think you'll love her next one."

There was a lot of good-natured joking and laughter, and a warm goodbye. The smile slipped from Hannah's face the second she hung up, and she reached for the list of writers. She would type a copy at home and mail it herself. In a way, it was a relief. CBS would confirm the names were clean, and the FBI would think Charlie had made up the story to sound impressive. He wouldn't be the first to do that. *Or the last,* Hannah assumed, heading home early once again.

There were two men's umbrellas in the stand when Hannah arrived, two hats on the rack, two overcoats. One set belonged to Paul. Hannah's heart swooped up and down. Gemma was pacing the hallway and looked at Hannah in horror and alarm.

"I'd put a curse on him if I could, and I don't even believe that nonsense," she said in a low voice.

"What's happening?" Hannah asked, but she pushed past Gemma to find Paul.

He was with another man in his office. A room she didn't recognize. It was empty of absolutely everything. Except dust.

"Ah, Hannah," he greeted her. "Home

475

early. Trying to make time for the kids?"

"I might ask you the same," she said evenly, turning to the other man. "Who the hell are you and what are you doing in my house?"

The man gave her a pleasant nod and turned to Paul. "I think I have enough to be getting on with. I shall wait in the vestibule."

Hannah ignored him as he stepped around her and left the room.

"Your lawyer?" she asked Paul.

"No, don't be silly. A real estate appraiser. Our little place here has gained in value since we moved in, and should be in some demand."

His words were more incomprehensible than Beryl's broadest dialect.

"What are you saying?" she gasped. "You can't sell our flat."

"*My* flat," he reminded her. "I paid for this place myself, and it's my name on all the papers. Of course, you can probably afford it now if you wanted to carry a mortgage, and I don't see any reason why you can't put in an offer."

It was lucky for him he'd had the office cleared out. If his letter opener were on his desk, she'd have slit his throat with it.

"You're really doing this? You're taking your own daughters' home?"

"They'll be fine. I want my business here done. It's my place and I'm selling. Do you want to buy it from me?"

Hannah loved the flat, their garden, their square. The last thing she wanted was to move. But she wasn't going to let him humiliate her like this, and she knew she couldn't stay in the home they'd moved into together when she had thought they were embarking on an exciting new adventure and he, she now realized, was perhaps already well down the long road from resentment to contempt.

"No, you do what you want to do, I'll find us a new home," Hannah told him. She searched his face for guilt, but saw only resignation.

"So you will. I'd wish you luck, old girl, but you don't need it. You never did. You might be one of the few women on earth who doesn't."

It wasn't the worst thing he could have said.

"Good luck to you too," she said acidly. Paul left without waiting to see the girls. Hannah's solicitor had told her she could "accrue a rather handsome personal settlement" if she wanted to get vicious. As soon as the door closed, she went to the phone and called the solicitor's office, authorizing him to get as vicious as he liked.

"Was Daddy here?" Rhoda asked when Gemma brought her back from school. Hannah was surprised — Gemma wouldn't have told Rhoda anything. Then she realized the smell of his aftershave lingered in the hall. Hannah opened her typewriter on the dining room table, biting her lips.

"He was," she said, laying down the list of *Robin Hood* episodes with the fake names attached and rolling paper into the typewriter.

"Why doesn't he want to play with me?"

Hannah looked at Rhoda. She looked tiny and plaintive. Hannah pulled her into her lap.

"He does, he's just having a difficult time right now. It's hard to explain."

"Oh. May I type?" Rhoda asked, tapping keys before Hannah could stop her.

"No!" Hannah shouted. Two of the keys had gotten entwined. She set Rhoda back on the floor. "Mama has work to do, you know better than to interfere with it."

"I'm sorry," Rhoda said, starting to cry. "I just wanted to play."

Hannah blinked back her own tears. "Darling, I'm sorry I was short with you. Please, go and play with Gemma and Julie. I'll be in as soon as this is done."

Rhoda gave her a look that was part reproachful, part sorrowful. Her shoulders slumped as she trudged away.

Hannah dropped her head in her hands. Soon she would have to explain to Rhoda that Daddy had gone away and they weren't going to see him for a while. It was far easier when they died, Gemma assured her, but that wasn't much help. Who knew what Rhoda's classmates would repeat from what they'd heard at home about this unnatural thing: a divorce. She just had to hope that Rhoda was indeed enough of her mother's daughter to let insults roll off her back, and that they could band together to teach Julie to be the same way. How much more, though, how much more would they all have to suffer before any of this was over?

She rubbed her face hard and rolled in a new sheet of paper.

CHAPTER NINETEEN

Freddie was dawdling outside, in no great hurry to get to school. He looked at Phoebe in open admiration.

"Cor, you look smart today, miss!"

Phoebe wore a cardigan knitted in the new nip-waist style. It was dark green, which she knew was her best color, edged in burgundy. She wore it over a fitted lilac pullover, which just peeked out from between the lapels and under her light green scarf. She'd brushed her trousers, shined her shoes, and tied her hair back with a green and burgundy bow. Today was an important day, though only she and Hannah knew it. Today began filming on the episode written by Ivy Morrow. Which was to say Phoebe Adler.

The Other Girls cooed over her cardigan and asked for the pattern.

"It really gives you a nice figure," Dora said in admiration. "I hadn't realized."

"You're lucky, being so curvy," said another girl wistfully. "It's very fashionable."

Phoebe tried to ascertain what they thought of the week's story, but all her time on the show had taught her that most of the crew paid no real attention to the actual plot or words — everyone focused hard on their own duties, which to their mind was the most important detail.

Filming began, and Phoebe forced herself to concentrate on being a script supervisor, rather than getting caught up in the script. Her words! Her words, being filmed at last, readied for broadcast! She could hardly contain herself, and knew she was smiling as each scene was filmed, as the words — lightly altered in the edits by Beryl, but still Phoebe's own — were given life by the actors. Bernadette O'Farrell's Maid Marian gave a line such a particularly smart spin that Phoebe bounced on her toes just like Sidney. Bernadette saw it and smiled at Phoebe when the scene finished.

"You're in a lively mood, Miss Adler!" she sang in her beautifully trained voice. "Are you in love?"

"Only with our program," Phoebe said. "That was a super scene."

"We are special, aren't we?" Bernadette agreed, and sailed away to be powdered.

Phoebe tried her luck with Tommy. "It's a

good script, isn't it? We just keep getting better."

Tommy was watching the director and cameraman argue over the angle for shooting a castle wall. "I suppose," he said absently. "Though we're the best already, so we have to stay tops."

It was better, really, that no one would be drawn into a discussion. It made her look less suspicious. At lunch, she was called to the phone. She thought it must be Hannah, with some pleasant thing to say. Instead she was greeted by the florid tones of Beryl.

"Ye'd best be able to manage that script without making any sort of spectacle of yourself. I'll nae have you giving Miss Wolfson anything to fret over this week of all weeks, else you'll answer good and proper, is that clear?"

Beryl might not always be comprehensible, but she was certainly clear. It didn't stop Phoebe's feeling excellent, so good that by the end of the day, she changed course on the way home and went to the next road — where Reg lived. She rang the bell of number eleven.

A woman in an apron and curlers answered and gestured Phoebe to the top floor. The smell of cooking wafted out — something Italian — and suddenly Phoebe was back on Bleecker Street outside John's Pizzeria, where she and Anne were prepared to feel worldly as they devoured an entire pie between them, with a bottle of red wine, so exotic in its straw-bottom holder. She closed her eyes, remembering the bliss of the melted cheese and tomato sauce singeing the roof of her mouth.

"Phoebe?" Reg was standing in an open door, staring at her.

"Let's get a pizza. The best one you know of."

"Is this your way of saying you're sorry?" he asked, but he looked amused.

"Pax, pax," Phoebe said. "There, that's your way. Let's go. My script started filming today, we have to celebrate."

He took her to Brusa's, in St. Martin's Lane, and the pizza was better than John's. Or perhaps she didn't remember. Or perhaps, as she finished her second slice, wiped her mouth, then leaned across the table to kiss Reg in full view of astonished diners, it was just that she was in love.

"Must be actual Italians," someone muttered.

"Isn't there some way I can come visit you on the set?" Reg begged. "I'd love to see your work being made immortal."

"I wish you could," Phoebe said mournfully. "But we're not allowed."

He walked her home.

"So. All the crises are averted?" He looked at her hopefully.

"No," she said, shaking her head. "Not in the slightest. But I'm having a terrific week and you're the person I wanted to share it with."

He kissed her, right below what had been Joan's window. Phoebe wanted so much to tell Mona about this. And she wanted to give some of this joy to Hannah, the woman who was her benefactor, and now also her friend. The woman whose life was coming to pieces. It was unfair for Phoebe to be so happy when Hannah was so sad. Had Hannah really meant it, when she told Phoebe to choose Reg if she wanted him? Wasn't Hannah proving, however unintentionally, that a woman who wanted a career mustn't also try to have love in her life? Then Reg's hand ran down her back, and Phoebe made up her mind. She took his hand and led him upstairs.

"Still bouncy and bright, I see," Dora commented to Phoebe the next day. "All right for some, I suppose."

Phoebe only smiled. This week marked her life's beginning again. She was well on her way back to being that curious creature — the career girl, the gal writer, whatever they might call her. Once she could reclaim her name, nothing would stop her.

She was also officially, without question, head over heels in love. She'd whispered it into Reg's hair at one point, and they'd spent half the night saying it back and forth.

"I can't sleep," he'd murmured. "I keep looking over and it's like there's a present for me under the Christmas tree."

"Should I go put on a bow?" Phoebe had asked.

"I say," Dora gasped, cutting across Phoebe's reverie, "that's never who I think it is."

"It's Hannah," Phoebe said, nonplussed but pleased to see her.

"Beside her, you plonker," Dora snapped.

"I'll be damned," Phoebe breathed, following Dora's gaze.

It was Nigel Elliott.

He stayed most of the day and was a very flattering audience. A lot of the cast and crew recognized him from society photos, and Phoebe had the curious experience of watching the actors, who were no great strangers to the papers themselves, being deferential and even fawning to someone who was only famous because of his family connections. Phoebe tended to forget he had a title, and in her own little life in London, further forgot that nobility still traveled in a rarefied air, and were considered special people, to be treated as such. She noticed not everyone did so, especially Bernadette O'Farrell.

"That's because she's Irish, rightly not impressed with the crumbling classes," Tommy confided to her. "More and more like that now. The old days are done. We're not going to bow and scrape and jump for the aristocracy as though they're somebody."

But Nigel Elliott *was* somebody, at least to Phoebe, and she couldn't help but be pleased when, doing the rounds, he shook her hand warmly. She was impressed with his slyness — no one would have guessed they already knew each other.

"What a fine job you seem to be doing here, very fine indeed," he said, much as he'd said to everyone else. But he pressed her hand and winked.

It wasn't until near the end of the afternoon tea break, when Nigel was ready to leave, that Hannah had a few seconds to speak to Phoebe.

"It's a treat for him, he made that clear,

though it might have been a command. Anyway, it was an easy enough thing to do and why not? We're in his debt and this is barely repayment as it is." Her face softened as she watched him asking the cameraman to explain his work, paying close and fascinated attention. "He's a bit much, but I think at heart he's all right."

"Well, you found that out back when you had him checked out, didn't you?"

Hannah looked at Phoebe unsmilingly.

"All I knew then was that he seemed to not be a danger to you. And to us. Now I know his intent is to be a good man. It improves him."

"He's very firmly on our side," Phoebe said.

"Which improves him even more."

Though Nigel was an easy and even enjoyable guest at the set, Hannah was exhausted when she returned to the Sapphire offices. She wouldn't have come back except she and Sidney were preparing the final presentation for their new show: *The Adventures of Sir Lancelot.*

As soon as she saw Beryl's face, she knew something was wrong. Her mind raced, trying to remember if Paul's name was still on the lease for the premises. Then she saw him.

He was posed in the window, smoking, watching the city below. He turned and nudged his green hat upward, a gesture straight out of a Western film. Hannah wanted to laugh.

"The skinny malinky longlegs is nae welcome," Beryl exploded. "I'd gie him a skelpit lug, only he seems to be connected with the coppers."

Hannah could only assume the man understood as little of that as she did. She turned to Sidney, whose face was thunderous.

"I did say we don't allow visitors to wait unless they have an appointment."

"It's all right," Hannah said, looking the man straight in his bright blue eyes. "I'll see him now."

"Good idea," the man said in a lazy twang she placed somewhere in Brooklyn. She waved him into her office. May as well pretend there was nothing to hide. She exchanged one quick glance with Sidney and Beryl before she stepped in and closed the door. She could at least feel confident they were readying weapons.

"Make yourself comfortable, Mr . . . ?"

"Oh, you can just call me Mr. G." He

winked, twirling his hat on his finger.

"If I didn't know better," Hannah said, eyeing him carefully, "I'd say you were a very misguided actor attempting an audition."

"Heh. No, no pansy work for me, thanks. All right, so Agent Glynn if you want it that way, Miss Wolfson."

"Glynn," Hannah said conversationally. "Your people were Welsh."

"Some time ago. We're true-blue Americans now."

"That must be gratifying."

He looked at her steadily and she looked back, refusing to break gaze first. She realized she recognized him. He was the one she'd seen outside the window, looking up. He might even be the one she'd seen in the park that day, the day she discovered her marriage was over. He certainly was having quite an extended stay at the taxpayers' expense.

"There's some mighty funny stories told about this little show of yours," he said, grinning. "Some folks say it's being written by men on the blacklist. Now that's a funny thing, ain't it? Because everyone knows that someone on the blacklist isn't fit to write stuff for American audiences, especially kids."

"I've heard that said, certainly," Hannah said.

"I bet you have. So the folks at CBS have a list of names of all the writers, and they all check out. Nice and clean."

"Clean? You obviously haven't met too many writers."

"Joke. That's cute. But there's other stories I've heard. I hear some Red writers give themselves a fake name and go on writing."

"How very shocking."

"Ain't it? Some people can't help themselves, gotta keep trying to turn the kids Commie."

"Fortunately, America has an excellent educational system that should help inoculate young minds against anything so untoward," Hannah said, enjoying his moment of confusion. He'd probably not heard the word "inoculate" before.

"Listen, sweetheart," he said in a colder voice. "It's my job to protect the public. Don't think we don't know what you were like as a reporter. Maybe some Reds change as they get older, but you don't look the type."

"I changed from a reporter into a producer," she pointed out.

"Still being cute, huh? But I know what I

know. For example, I know you've got a gal named Phoebe Adler working for you on your little show. Sure, just as a script girl, but should she be near scripts?"

Hannah put her head to one side. "I wish I understood you, Agent Glynn."

"Sure you do. Or maybe you didn't know she ducked a subpoena."

"What I do know is that she's officially an employee of a Sapphire production, and Sapphire is a British company, so it's of little concern to the FBI, isn't it?"

"Maybe. But I don't think the folks at CBS would like knowing there's a known Red anywhere near the *Robin Hood* set, would they?"

"Is she a proven Communist, then? That might be a different matter."

He didn't answer, and Hannah studied him without pleasure. Sharply dressed. A better suit than he could likely afford on an FBI Hound's salary, though it might be his only suit. Did he know Phoebe, or someone she knew? Or was he one of those Hounds who couldn't stand it when prey got away? Those were legendary, and everyone in the exile community said they were the most dangerous Hounds of all. They couldn't rest until they'd caught their quarry again, and broken its neck.

He helped himself to one of her cigarettes and lit a match on her desk.

"I've heard lotsa stories. I wonder what I'd find if I had a look at the addresses some of your writers' checks get sent to? Might make for some interesting reading."

"Well, I'd be happy to help you prove a point, but that's the sort of confidential information I'm not at liberty to share," she informed him.

"Maybe you'd prefer I come back with a warrant."

"I think you'll find it has to be the British authorities who would handle that. The police are Scotland Yard, if that's useful."

"British authority, there's a joke. Listen, sweetheart, you think anyone in America will be impressed you didn't play ball when asked nicely?"

"I did as the executives at CBS asked, but I'm not going to breach confidentiality without proper cause," Hannah said, folding her arms. "I also think the British government and press would be most interested to learn that such an act was asked of me under these circumstances."

He gave her a long, sardonic look. "Play it your way, sweetheart, but no one would say this show has Reds on staff if it wasn't true."

"People often say all sorts of things, and

don't make too much effort to determine whether or not any of it is true," Hannah said.

He smirked and put on his hat, tilting it in a raffish gesture she guessed he'd learned from Humphrey Bogart.

"Ballsy, ain't you? I bet you can be a lot of fun when you let your hair down."

"I guess we'll never know," she said brightly, grinning.

He laughed good-naturedly. It was like playing a game of being friends.

"Just between us, sweetheart, I'd make sure your house is clean. Find some little English honey to be a script girl. Bet your crew would like that too."

"I appreciate that, thanks."

He showed himself out, raising his hat to Beryl as he left. Hannah turned from Beryl's questions and lit a cigarette. Dale had said everything was fine and as far as he was concerned, the matter was closed, and heck, even Lucille Ball had apparently been a Communist at one point and he'd like to see anyone try to push *I Love Lucy* off the air. The feds, Dale had suggested, were free to go shove it.

"I don't suppose you might tell a person what the devil's going on here?" Sidney demanded.

"My countrymen can't seem to resist trying to frighten me," Hannah told him ruefully. "They can't bear someone they don't like being productive. So much for the puritan work ethic."

"Miss Wolfson," Beryl said, her voice shaking. "You know I've nocht but total support for you, and I've never asked, but are any of the writers *not* blacklisted?"

"Would it matter, when one is all it takes to hurt us?"

Beryl stared at Hannah and Sidney a long moment.

"It's all of them, isn't it? Every last one. I suppose I've always known."

"Well, of course you did. Everyone does. We're the biggest open secret in the whole damn industry. There's a coterie that admires us for it."

Beryl snorted. "Oh, admire, aye, but do they do anything like the same? They do not."

"It's not easy," Hannah said, with feeling.

"Oh no?" Beryl went on acidly. "You carry on quite easily, jeopardizing our whole company by continuing to hire these Americans."

Hannah reeled. She was used to Beryl's sharpness. She had never experienced it quite so directly, and at the expense of

Beryl's even stronger loyalty.

"Beryl, that's hardly —" Sidney began.

"Nae, I willna hear it!" she snapped. "How can you be sure this man cannae stop the program airing in America? And if he does, then what happens to the message of it all?"

"He wants that power, but he doesn't have it," Hannah replied. "They've got their guesses, let them guess. They can blacklist someone because someone else points a finger, but they can't shut down a show without proof of what they'd call a crime. And we're not going to give them any. Are we?"

Beryl gave her a mulish, mutinous look that chilled Hannah's heart. She knew Beryl wasn't the sort to squeal. She was, however, the sort to decide she'd had enough and move on to less treacherous pastures. No one could blame her, but Hannah knew she couldn't let Beryl go, not yet.

She looked at the staff she considered friends. "Sidney, you always knew what we might be up against. Beryl, you knew the day I said not to accept registered letters. Because they might be a subpoena. I wasn't sure what they could do to us from here, and never wanted to find out. You both are the best I could ever hope for, but if you've got cold feet, I won't stop you from letting them walk you on out. I'll be sorry as hell, but I won't stop what I'm doing till they make me, or till the blacklist is dead."

Beryl and Sidney exchanged looks. Something seemed decided between them, and Sidney held up a large folder.

"We'll never have more opportunity for hiring hungry writers if we don't get *The Adventures of Sir Lancelot* on the air."

So it was back to work. Hannah hoped this particular storm really had blown over. She couldn't bear to worry about any more of the people in her world. Bad enough it was time to remove Phoebe as script supervisor. Quickly. She hated it, it felt weak, like giving in. But she'd said all along the job was only temporary. If there was one thing Hannah was certain of, it was that Phoebe would be fine.

The telegram came as Phoebe was combing her hair. It said only:

DON'T GO IN TODAY = TALK LATER +

The last thing Phoebe was prepared to do was wait. She stormed into the Sapphire offices half an hour later, her hair still mostly uncombed.

"Oi, you canna barge in like ye have any right here," Beryl snapped, looming in front of Phoebe. "Who d'you think you are?"

Phoebe hesitated, remembering that she had to maintain professionalism. Besides, Beryl had at least six inches and fifteen pounds on her.

"She told me not to go in today. I want to know why."

"Because we found a local girl with a lot of previous experience who needs the work. Miss Wolfson can explain the whole of it to you," Beryl said in a clipped tone. Then she leaned in and whispered, "You ought to be grateful, in fact."

Before Phoebe could ask anything more, Hannah opened her door. She was wearing her coat and hat and looked sorrowful.

"I was coming to get you, as it happens," she said in a leaden voice.

"Miss Wolfson, you're nae leaving?" Beryl was stunned. "The meeting —"

Hannah shook her head. "Gemma just called. Come along, Phoebe."

Suddenly Phoebe knew.

Hannah gave the cabdriver an extra shilling, and he got them to Chelsea in record time, where Phoebe ran straight to the phone. Gemma held out the receiver.

"I saw you a-getting out of the taxi, the operator is connecting you."

"Brookside," the receptionist answered.

"It's Phoebe Adler," she said.

"Of course," the receptionist said, her tone suddenly breathy as she clicked away, arranging the connection to the room that had been set up just for this.

"Hey, girl wonder," came Mona's voice. A shadow of Mona's voice, sounding farther away than ever. An oxygen tent, Phoebe realized. "Would you believe it's pneumonia? Heck, it's not even cold here. I think they ought to give you a refund." Phoebe could hear how every word was an effort. And she was still Mona. Tears streamed down Phoebe's face. She should be there, holding her sister's hand. Mona should not be surrounded by strangers, with only a black Bakelite phone to represent her family.

"It's monstrously unfair," Mona wheezed. "All this time without any immune system to speak of, I should be taken out by something much more glamorous. Do me a favor, bribe them to put something better on the death certificate, will you?"

"Mona, I'm so sorry," Phoebe said in a squeak.

"Me too," Mona said. "But it's all right.

498

We didn't do too badly. I love you a lot, little sister. You've been the best part of my life."

Phoebe was crying too hard to answer.

"You keep making a spectacle of yourself, okay? Otherwise I'll find a way to punish you."

"You would too."

"Of course." The words were getting softer, with more wheezes between them. Phoebe could hear low voices in the background, rustling.

"I love you!" she shouted, desperate for Mona to hear that before she stopped hearing anything else. "Mona, I love you!"

She could hear some vague mumbling, but nothing coherent.

"Mona? Mona?"

After a moment, another woman's voice answered. Nurse Brewster.

"I think she said, 'I'm not deaf,' Miss Adler."

Of course she did.

"We've given her morphine," Nurse Brewster continued. "She's in no pain."

"Put the phone by her, let me say something else," Phoebe ordered.

"I'm so sorry, Miss Adler, but she's not conscious anymore."

"She'll still know I'm there. Hell, at least

let me hear her breathing!"

"Here's the doctor to speak to you, Miss Adler," the nurse said sadly.

Phoebe shook her head, choking on sobs. Hannah took the phone and Phoebe vaguely heard some words, but her head was pounding and she thought she was going to be sick. She pressed her forehead to the cold marble table.

"Phoebe?" Hannah whispered. "It's a morphine-induced coma. The doctor thinks it'll be over within a few hours at the most. He'll call back himself when she's gone, he's promised."

Phoebe looked at the receiver, lying in the cradle, and scowled at Hannah.

"I wanted to at least hear her breathing till then."

Hannah's eyes filled. Somewhere in her muddled mind, Phoebe remembered that Hannah was in the midst of a divorce, that things might be uncertain, that she might not feel comfortable spending a pound a minute for what could be hours of silence. Phoebe wanted to spend the money herself, not that she had it, though she knew Mona would call it a waste and it would be the first thing she'd come back from the dead to punish her for.

Dead. Nearly all Phoebe's life, Mona was

supposed to be dead any day now. It didn't make any sense that the day should be today.

"I never even got to tell her I slept with Reg," she whispered, and started crying again.

The phone rang, and Phoebe snatched it up, forgetting it wasn't hers. She heard the receptionist say, "Brookside."

"Mona!" Phoebe cried. That made sense. If anyone could figure out how to die and come back, it would be Mona.

Her own voice saying, "It's Phoebe Adler," sounded so little like what she thought she sounded like, she thought it must be Mona, making one of her weirder jokes.

"Mona?" she called through the endless clicking.

"Hey, girl wonder." A shower of ice encased Phoebe's body. The recording went on. "Would you believe it's pneumonia? Heck, it's not even cold here . . ."

"Give her back!" Phoebe screamed into the phone, over Mona's voice. "Give her back, give me back my sister!"

"It's monstrously unfair," Mona wheezed.

"Give me back my sister!" She hardly noticed Hannah, wide-eyed and pale, attempting to wrestle the phone from her. "At least give me something!"

". . . much more glamorous."

Hannah wrenched the phone away and slammed it down. She and Phoebe stared at each other in horror.

"How the hell are they tapping my phone? Unless they've gotten MI5 involved, it's illegal. I'll slaughter them." Hannah was red with fury.

"I want them to give me my sister," Phoebe wept.

"I'm sorry. I'm so sorry." Hannah hugged her a long time. "I suppose at least it's lucky you weren't at the set when we got the call."

Phoebe had forgotten why she'd come to Sapphire that morning in the first place. "Why am I off *Robin Hood*?"

Hannah guided Phoebe to the sofa and poured them brandies. "Your pal, the man with the green hat, he knew you were working there. He knows you're a writer, he at least guesses I hire blacklisted writers, and he's desperate not to leave London without a juicy souvenir. We can't feed the fire. If you need more work —"

"I don't though, do I?" Phoebe's voice was flat and hollow. "I don't have anyone to support anymore, except myself." She gulped her brandy. It was warming. After another sip, she could almost breathe. "He can't really hurt us, can he?"

"Not if he knows what's good for him," Hannah snarled. "I'm not one to go down too easily."

Hannah offered to make up the guest bed, but Phoebe said she would go home.

"I just want to be alone. Thank you. Thank you for letting me say goodbye to my sister."

Hannah hugged her again, and Phoebe rested her head on her shoulder. Mona used to hug her just like this. It was hard to believe she never would again.

She walked home. No more phone calls. No more letters. No more Mona. And she hadn't been there.

What if I'd just answered that damn subpoena? What would they have asked me, about the union? Heck, they had all our names anyway, so what would have been the difference? I'd have answered, looked like a squealer, and they'd have let me go.

Maybe. She wondered idly if it was in fact Dolores Goldstein, wherever she was, who'd been caught somewhere and given them all up. It didn't matter, and that was the devil of it. As much as she'd have wanted to be there with Mona when she finally left the world, it didn't matter. This was where she was, and this was the life she was living.

Without really thinking about it, she ended up at Reg's door.

"Mona died," she said.

"Oh, darling," he said, taking her into his arms. They just stood there in his doorway, holding each other.

"I'm glad she's not in pain anymore, I am, and I'm glad she's out of that damn place." Phoebe wept. "But she should have gotten to live. Really live."

"I know," he whispered, stroking her hair. "I would have loved to meet her." He kissed Phoebe's brow. "She's still in you. She always will be."

"She'd compare herself to a tapeworm," Phoebe said.

Reg smiled. "Naturally. But you'd try and beat her to it, wouldn't you?"

"I'd lose."

"You're not alone, Phoebe," he said, taking her hands and kissing them. "I promise. You're not alone."

She didn't want to be. She nudged him inside and closed the door behind them.

Reg got up early to run to the huckster's for groceries so he could make her what he called "a proper northern breakfast." He insisted it had great curing powers. Phoebe stared as he filled her plate with eggs, bacon, sausage, crisp potatoes, beans, fried mushrooms, and tomatoes. He toasted half a loaf of bread and poured her a cup of tea so strong, she suspected she wouldn't blink the rest of the day.

"Stay here," he urged. "I have to go and teach, but stay, read, listen to records, do whatever you like."

"I want to write," she said.

"I've got any amount of paper and a typewriter," he said. "A good one."

Phoebe finished a third cup of tea.

"I want *my* typewriter. And a change of clothes. Don't offer me yours," she warned. "I'd be afraid they'd fit."

He smiled and took her hand. "I'll see you tonight?"

"Yes, please."

She went home, munching on a piece of the toast he'd insisted she take with her. It was Friday, the last day of filming her script. She wondered if any of the crew missed her. Or would remember her by next week.

The building was quiet — everyone was at work or school. She still missed the music from Joan's flat.

I should get a radio, she thought, opening her door.

"Well, there you are, Miss Adler," the man greeted her. "Apparently also known as

505

Miss Morrow."

Phoebe couldn't speak. Couldn't scream. Could hardly think. She knew him at once, even with the green hat sitting on her coffee table rather than his head. He had all her finished work stacked beside him and was reading a copy she'd kept of the script that was wrapping in a few hours. The one that still bore the title page with her own name on it.

CHAPTER TWENTY

"It's the nuttiest thing," the man said in his pleasant voice. "Hannah Wolfson swears there are no Reds writing for *Robin Hood*. I wonder what she meant by that."

"She didn't know," Phoebe said quickly. "I put my name on my copy for me, but I changed it and mailed it in to her as a blind submission. I'd been reading the scripts so long, I knew how the show went. I just wanted to be a writer again."

"Aw, that sort of gets me," he said, tapping his chest. "Gotta love a gal's sob story, and you're not a bad looker if you lost the glasses and dressed like a woman. Hell of a picture, I'd say: the little lady who wanted to make something of herself."

Phoebe said nothing as he nattered on. She kept her face as still as she could while her brain whirred and spun. She was a fast runner, but didn't trust herself to be fast enough to keep ahead of him and get a bus or cab to get to Hannah — especially not with that giant breakfast inside her — and anyway, running would just add more fat to the fire. Even if Freddie came home for lunch, he would only come upstairs if there was mail. He couldn't get to Hannah, but he could try to find Reg.

"This is illegal," she said in sudden realization. "You don't have jurisdiction here, you've broken into my flat illegally. Even at home you're not supposed to be seen snooping." Was that true? She couldn't remember. This all felt too much like a bad dream. She looked down to check she was wearing clothes.

"Oh, honey, don't get worked up," he scolded her. "I've got a warrant." He waved a piece of paper at her. She snatched it and read it through, shaking her head.

"This can't be right," she insisted. "You're not with the British police. I don't even know you're really with the FBI." Though she did.

He showed her his badge. Glynn. It looked official, not that she knew for sure.

"But you're still not with the British police," she said. "You can't be in here."

"I think you'll find I can," he said. "You ignored a subpoena. That doesn't exactly make you look like a desirable resident here, does it?"

Did it? She had no idea. She needed to talk to Hannah. A lawyer. Nigel Elliott.

"I'm allowed a lawyer," she said. "I still have rights."

"Sure, honey. I'll let you make a phone call when we get there."

She didn't even ask, "Get where?" She just shook her head. She wasn't going anywhere with this man. He seemed to sense the impasse because he shifted his stance enough that she could see the bulge of a pistol.

Good grief. I'm stuck inside one of my own crime scripts.

"Why me?" she demanded. "I've gotta be the smallest of small potatoes. Why come over here and make such a big deal of tracking me?"

"Glynn always gets the goods," he told her. "You didn't think I was the type to let any of my targets get away, did you? And anyway, don't sell yourself too short. Apparently your episodes for that cruddy little crime show you were working for were the most popular, didn't you know that?"

She didn't, but was hardly going to admit that. "Sure," she said casually. "I was the best writer in the bunch."

"And yet you got paid fifty bucks less a

script than the men."

"What?" Phoebe couldn't contain her outrage. How had she not known? And here she always thought Hank was her friend, her mentor, her scrupulously fair boss. Then again, this man could be lying. She decided to hope that was the case.

"Crummy business, television," Glynn said. "Movies too. No place for decent people to work, that's for sure."

"No," Phoebe agreed. "Good entertainment needs some indecency."

"Cute. Now, pack a bag, sweetheart," he ordered. "I'm taking you home."

"No," she said. "I'm entitled to a lawyer. And if this warrant was real, you'd be with British police," she improvised.

"Oh, honey, really!" Glynn laughed. "Do you think the cops here have any love for Commies? Ever heard of a fellow called Philby?"

"No, but the Communist Party is perfectly legal here," she said.

"Sure, sure, and if I tell a cop you ducked a subpoena and were suspected of treason, how much love do you think they'll have for you? Think about it."

She thought. Maybe this was the FBI's greatest success. As innocent as Phoebe, as all of them, might be of the crimes for which they were accused, there was something about the way they were treated that almost made them feel as though they deserved it.

"I'll give you five minutes," he said. "Start packing."

"No. I'm allowed to talk to a lawyer. I have rights."

"You resisting arrest, sweetheart? Do I have to start searching this dump for more evidence?"

"Evidence of what? What are you — ?"

He took the photo of Mona in the Groucho costume, and ripped it in half.

"Some Reds can hide stuff in photos. Lucky you, you're not one of them."

He might as well have ripped Phoebe in half. She launched herself on him with a howl of rage, punching and kicking. He made a swift move and suddenly she was pinned to the ground, pain shooting up her arms. He pressed a knee into her chest to keep her down, tore the watch from her wrist, and smashed it on the floorboards. Tiny shards flew everywhere. Some pierced Phoebe's cheek. He made a show of examining the watch's interior.

"Nothing hidden in there either. So far, so good. You're looking mostly clean, sweetheart. If you can play ball, you might get treated like a friendly witness."

She wanted to say, "I'd rather be treated like a Salem witch." But she knew if she opened her mouth she'd spit at him, and that would only bring more pain.

"Miss! What the devil, miss?" Freddie, a guardian angel in short pants and a school cap, was at the door, holding an envelope.

"Hey there, sonny," Glynn greeted him. "Miss Adler's had some trouble but she's all right now. Aren't you, sweetheart?" he asked Phoebe.

"You're hurt, miss!" Freddie cried, hurrying to her. "Can I help?"

"There's a good boy, you help Miss Adler wash her face," Glynn instructed.

Phoebe swelled with hope. Glynn must not know the power of Freddie if he was granting them a few minutes alone. She pretended to be more hurt than she was, leaning on the boy and limping into the bedroom for the washstand. As soon as she was sure they were out of sight, she held a finger to her lips, then seized a pen and paper and scribbled furiously. Freddie refused to take any payment. He knew very well he was being charged with the most important mission of his life.

Hannah hung up and promptly dialed Nigel Elliott's number. She'd said nothing to

Sidney, but he'd heard enough on her end to look appalled.

Nigel was in, luckily, and she liked him all the more for being just as appalled as Sidney.

"If the man gets her to the American embassy, we're sunk," Nigel fretted. "She's on US soil then, and in their custody, no matter if it's a ruse and done illegally. I'll make a call. Instruct her to stall as long as possible."

"I can't, she doesn't have a phone!" Hannah cried.

"Oh dear. Then I advise you to have someone go round to her flat and attempt to intervene."

Hannah slammed down the phone and grabbed her hat.

"You can't!" Sidney cried. "We've got a meeting with ITV in half an hour!"

"I've got to," Hannah insisted. "She's my friend and she's in trouble." She hurried down the steps, struggling into her coat, Sidney hot behind her.

"Keep the heid!" he shouted. "You're a single mum now, you're flat-hunting, you're under watch yourself and a hair away from who knows what. And you're ready to drop yourself into Loch Ness with the monster's mouth wide open?"

They were outside. Cabs zoomed by, but Hannah didn't raise her hand. Sidney was right. Horribly, miserably right. It was a risk she couldn't take.

"Shirley," she said, bounding back to the office two steps at a time.

"That's more like," Sidney said approvingly, between pants. "If your fella's like some, the mere fact of a black woman in his presence will tip him off balance. Americans are odd ones."

Beryl was reading, not bothering to look up either when Hannah and Sidney ran out, or now as they came back in. Hannah made the call and, breathless though she was, relayed enough so that Shirley assured her she was out the door. Hannah slumped in her chair with her head in her hands. Sidney slid over a tin of Walkers.

"It could be a bit of luck for the program, anyway," he said sorrowfully. "We say we had no idea Phoebe submitted that script. We kick off a wee bit of fuss about her deception, declare all the other writers clean and cleared, and then they're all safe. And the show is safe too."

"But Phoebe isn't," Hannah said irritably, knowing and hating that Sidney was right. They could say Phoebe had used a front. Her friendship with Joan would lend credence to the story, implying that Phoebe was whom Charlie had meant but been reluctant to name directly out of respect for his wife. CBS would pounce on this easy solution, make a lot of noise about how swiftly the problem was handled and that the episode in question was being removed, when in fact all anyone would do was change the title and Phoebe's nom de plume. It would be over before it began.

"You've sent Shirley, she's more than capable, and if that Elliott fellow is anything like I think, he's the best hope for Phoebe now," Sidney said. "You've done all what a friend could possibly do. We'd best be leaving for the meeting."

"Yes, of course," Hannah answered mechanically. She glanced at her in-tray, which included a note from her solicitor saying the settlement was being processed. She smiled grimly. Money didn't solve everything, but it solved some things, and she knew one more thing she could do for now to help Phoebe.

Phoebe dressed carefully, so as to look the picture of ladylike charm. Her good suit and best shoes, her hair neatly combed. Then she packed a bag. The whole time, her mind was racing, trying to make sense of it all.

They'd always said the FBI couldn't touch them here. Scare them, sure, they could do that if they wanted. Touch them, no. That warrant must be fake. Glynn must be acting outside the law. But she needed a lawyer, or Nigel Elliott, to confirm that. Her heart soared suddenly. If Glynn had broken the law, a deal might be struck! She would agree to say nothing about his actions; the FBI and HUAC would agree to wipe her name clean. She would be Phoebe Adler again.

She just needed someone to come and help her.

Freddie didn't return upstairs, which was wise, but she wished he could tell her if he'd gotten through to Hannah. She packed as slowly as she could, straining her ears for the sound of a savior coming up the steps.

"I hope you're nearly done in there, honey," Glynn called. Phoebe was sorely tempted to answer, "Yes, dear."

When she couldn't postpone it anymore, she returned to the living room. Agent Glynn had made coffee and was reading one of her library books.

"Well, don't you look the picture of domesticity," Phoebe said.

He grinned. "You're a funny one, aren't you? Guess that explains the writing. You're pretty good, I gotta say."

"That's nice to hear, thanks," she said, thinking what a peculiar conversation this was and wishing she could tell Reg about it. Reg. Had Freddie tried to find him? Not that he could do much, but he would be such a comfort right now. Or between them, they could at least take Glynn down, even with the gun.

"Ready, honey?" he asked.

"That depends," she said. "Where are we going?"

He gave her a baleful look and glanced meaningfully at the broken watch on the floor and two halves of the photo. "We're not really going to have this conversation again, are we?" he asked. "Now come on, it's time to pay the piper."

"I don't remember hearing any music," she muttered. But she snatched the two halves of the photo, stuffed them in her jacket pocket, and tagged after him.

It was only when they got out to Meard Street and she saw the car that her full brain kicked in. Nothing good ever happened when a woman got in a car with an armed man.

"No," she said in a shaky voice. "No, you have to tell me where we're going."

"You're the criminal here, honey, I don't have to tell you a damn thing."

"I'm not a criminal," she said, feeling close to tears. "I'm not."

"Someone else'll have to be the judge of that," he told her, pressing a hand into the small of her back and shoving her toward the car. She inched along, wondering how far she'd get if she dropped her bag and ran. Would he really shoot her, here, in the fading daylight, in London? He wouldn't, would he?

They were at the door. A driver stared straight ahead. This had to be a dream, it had to. She hoped she was sleeping next to Reg. Any second, her shakes and whimpers would wake him and he'd whisper, "Phoebe, wake up."

"Phoebe!" she heard. There. She was about to wake up.

"Get in," Glynn snarled, his hand pressing into her spine. That was right. A nightmare was at its worst before it ended.

"Phoebe! Don't get in!"

It must still be a dream, because that mellow, honeyed voice had never sounded shrill. Never sounded terrified. Phoebe turned and saw Shirley running up Meard Street.

"Bitch!" Glynn snapped. He slammed his hand on the back of Phoebe's neck and pushed her into the car. She kicked hard,

518

but he was more than ready for her — a few well-trained moves had her subdued in seconds, stilled by pain and shock. All she could do was turn and look out the window at Shirley, who was memorizing the registration number. For whatever good that would do. Tears rolled down Phoebe's cheeks. Still, Hannah had tried. And she would do more. Phoebe had true friends here. They weren't going to let her go without a fight.

London unspooled out the window. Phoebe thought of Reg and all the places they'd been together. And all the places they planned to go. She thought of Robin Hood and the sort of England he'd fought for. She thought of Hannah, Shirley, Freddie. The other exiles. Even the Other Girls. And Mona. Who was here and then gone only yesterday. How perversely lucky Mona didn't need to know about any of this. She clung hard to her own powerful innocence and laid a hand on the window, as if she could reach through it and brush her fingers against the city as it rolled by.

She mechanically noticed the car had stopped. Glynn was dragging her out.

"All right, all right, I can walk," she muttered. "So where the hell am I?"

"Congratulations, sweetheart," he said. "You're as good as home."

Then she saw the sign. They were in the American embassy. Which was technically American soil. She was officially their legal prisoner.

Glynn escorted her down what felt like several corridors. Phoebe wasn't paying attention. She was thinking frantically, wondering how to get out of this mess. Could she claim she was engaged to a British national? Reg would back that up, if she was allowed to send him a telegram. Perhaps Hannah, with Nigel's help, could secure the sort of British lawyer to make such a stink about the illegal wiretappings and harassment that it would end up easier to make them all just go away. Perhaps she could start screaming and not stop till they threw her in a loony bin. That didn't seem like such a bad option. Certainly it wasn't far off from her current predicament.

There was a lot of chatter, but it was all just background noise as Phoebe attempted to form a plan. There had to be a way out. There just had to.

"Miss Adler?" A pleasant female voice snapped her back to attention. A sleek woman in a pinstriped suit smiled warmly. "I'm Miss Gould. Care for some coffee?" she asked. Phoebe swore she heard a hint of the Lower East Side, recognizing a woman who'd worked her way up and out, probably to Barnard and now the State Department. But not too lacquered to still be friendly to a fellow New York girl.

"No, thanks," Phoebe said. "But I'd like to make a phone call, if I can?"

"Sure, I can get you set up for that," Miss Gould agreed. "They just need to check your passport. Do you have it?"

"What do they need to check it for?" Phoebe asked.

"Oh, just your residency here, make sure it's all on the up-and-up." Miss Gould gestured lightly, giving Phoebe to understand she found some of the protocol silly. She was still a Lower East Sider at heart, even for all her polish. Mildly comforted, Phoebe handed the woman her passport. "Thanks," Miss Gould said. "I'll get this all taken care of. And your phone call. You sure you don't want coffee?"

Phoebe nodded. Glynn was busy with something or other and directed her to a chair. She sat to keep from pacing. Better not to let anyone know she was agitated. It felt like hours must have passed. She looked at her naked wrist. Horatio Adler had said the watch would last forever if she took good care of it. *I'm sorry, Daddy. I tried.*

When neither Miss Gould nor Glynn returned, Phoebe started to feel a new sort of anxiety. There seemed to be no one around. No one at all. The screaming plan was starting to look promising again, when at last she heard raised voices. She clenched and unclenched her fists, readying herself for the unknown.

"Well, well, well, if it isn't the charming Miss Phoebe Adler," Nigel Elliott said, appearing like a ministering angel. Phoebe almost threw herself in his arms as he kissed each of her cheeks and squeezed her hand.

"I can't tell you how much I was hoping for you," she said. "I'm so sorry, I think I'm in a heck of a jam."

He sat her down again, keeping her hands in his. "You are," he said in a low voice. "It was rather off, the way they got you here, but you're here and that makes things thorny. Britain has no love for the blacklist, but a few of our own from MI5 seem to have been engaged in actual espionage on behalf of the Soviets. It's quite a blow. I'm not in a good position to argue for the protection of an American Communist."

"But I'm not!" Phoebe was outraged. Nigel gave her a stern look.

"Did you tell Agent Glynn you'd submitted a script to *Robin Hood* under a false name?"

Phoebe bit her lip. "I . . . okay, I did. But that was because I'm on the blacklist. Being on the blacklist doesn't mean I'm a Communist." She paused, thinking of Anne and Shirley and Will and even Charlie. "And anyway, being a Communist doesn't mean I'm a criminal."

"Being a Communist *shouldn't* mean you're a criminal, no, but too many people have carved out some fine careers believing otherwise. And there's the matter of that subpoena. I'm afraid right now you're guilty till proven innocent." He handed her a cigarette. "It looks as though they're going to fly you back to DC, today most likely."

Phoebe reeled. "But they can't! Why? What if Reg comes down, says we're engaged?"

"If you were *married,* perhaps, but you're not. And the British government won't make an official complaint about your treatment whilst you're potentially indeed a matter of some concern." He looked around and lowered his voice further. "I'm arranging to go with you. Officially, of course, I'm traveling for my own business. Once we're on the plane, we can discuss strategy. I'm quite sure after I've been able to chat to a few chums, I can sort something out for you. I just need time."

Phoebe's eyes welled up. "You'd do all that for me?"

He patted her hand again. "I've always liked you, even without owing you my life. And London is all the better for people like you in it."

Glynn returned, accompanied by Miss Gould. "We're clear to go," he said to Phoebe, though he was glowering at Nigel. "You'll be allowed to sit with your 'representative' there, so long as there's no funny business."

"I was supposed to make a phone call," Phoebe protested. "And where's my passport?"

"It's been sequestered," Miss Gould said smilingly. "But I've let them know you were cooperative."

Betrayed. Betrayed by a neighborhood girl. Not that Phoebe had had a choice. And maybe Miss Gould didn't, either, but Phoebe hated every last bit of her anyway.

"I need to send a telegram," she said, more to Nigel than Glynn. "It's urgent."

"You don't get any more rights now, honey," Glynn informed her. "Let's go."

Nigel took her arm protectively, and Phoebe clung to him. She couldn't believe she was actually having to leave, without even being able to say goodbye.

Since the day she'd started building planes, she wanted to ride in one. Faced with the chance at last, Phoebe would give anything to be huddled over her typewriter in her damp little flat instead. But the huge silver beast was stunning, she had to admit. The acme of postwar freshness, brimming with speed and power and possibility. For a moment, as the engines roared and the plane sped down the runway and then tipped upward and went up, up, up, leaving the earth behind, Phoebe almost forgot her horror at why she was getting to fly at last.

"You can really get on one of these whenever you want?" she asked Nigel as they broke through the clouds into blue sky.

"A diplomatic passport is most useful that way," Nigel said. "Though I do prefer sailing. One meets such fascinating people."

She wanted to ask him if this whole business of being a diplomat was really code for his MI5 affiliation, but now was not the time. Whatever it was, Nigel clearly had enough sway to be able to bear Phoebe off to the first class lounge for a drink. Glynn shrugged.

"Do whatever you want. It ain't like you

can run away."

"Charming fellow," Nigel said when they were out of earshot. "A Hound indeed."

The lounge was small but very elegant, all dark paneling and leather chairs. Nigel ordered them gin and tonics.

"Your Miss Wolfson is a very fine woman. I do admire her. You did very well, you know. The program is quite in the clear, thanks to your admittance of guilt."

"There's nothing I wouldn't do for Hannah, or the show," Phoebe said. "I mean that. I just wish . . ." She took a shuddery breath. "What's going to happen to me?"

"You're going to have a hearing. Beyond that, it rather depends."

A hearing. The thing Mona had insisted she run from was going to happen. And if she didn't name names, or admit Communism herself, she could be convicted of contempt and go to prison. There wasn't even anyone left to visit her.

"I can't go to prison," she said. "I look lousy in stripes. Look, Glynn busted into my place, faked a warrant, broke my stuff —"

"Forget all that. He can say you resisted arrest, that he was working with the CIA and MI5, and it can all be arranged. None of that matters until you're cleared."

"You think I can be cleared?" She had to be. She couldn't accept anything else.

"It does happen. There's the easy route, of course. Give them names they already have, you surely know some. Then you're seen to be cooperative. Play a bit innocent and dim — no jokes or cleverness — and they'll likely decide you're not worth any further trouble."

"I can't name names," she said. "Play dumb, sure, but name names, no."

"People under —"

"No." She wasn't arguing. Just stating a fact. "It's not who I am. I won't play their game. I'd rather go to prison."

"Now you do sound like a fool," Nigel said scornfully. "You're not a martyr, Phoebe, and there's little money in it."

She knew what he meant. It wasn't hard now to understand why Charlie had taken that path. She'd get her name back. But the name would be tainted, if not from being on the blacklist, then by having named others.

"I don't care if I stay on the blacklist forever," she said with vehemence. "All I want is to go home. To London."

She hadn't known till just then how true that was. London had Hannah, Reg, Shirley, Freddie, and opportunities. She'd become a better writer there. Possibly even a better person. New York still held a part of her heart, but she knew that one walk through a London park with Reg would make New York melt away. She couldn't imagine living anywhere else.

"Good girl," Nigel congratulated her. "Well, as I say, you have to mind your tongue. They want to catch you out, and they're clever. Everything you say becomes something else. And you're at a disadvantage. You're not pretty, you're not famous, you're not brilliant —"

"This is delightful."

He gave her a reproachful look. Phoebe sighed. She knew what Nigel meant. She wasn't the sort to sway the public to her side.

"And that subpoena is quite the sticky wicket," he continued. "You'll have to play the fool there. Beyond that, well, I suppose you've heard of Lillian Hellman?"

"She's only the most famous female playwright in America," Phoebe said. "Maybe the world. Good luck finding a girl who sits down to a typewriter and writes 'Act One' without hoping to be the next Lillian Hellman."

"So you know of her," Nigel said. "Good. Then you likely know she was blacklisted as well and brought in to testify. They took every penny she had. But she avoided prison."

"I'm not Lillian Hellman," Phoebe pointed out. And what worked for one was unlikely to work for another. But she listened, just the same. And began to see a possibility.

However unlikely.

CHAPTER TWENTY-ONE

Glynn assumed control of Phoebe just before they landed. Nigel melted away, promising to arrange her a lawyer and telling her not to worry. A hard directive to follow, but she had to try. Mona would expect nothing less.

Like most New Yorkers, Phoebe thought of Washington, DC, as nothing but a self-important small town. The drive past all the huge white buildings did nothing to change her perception. Once, she would at least have felt a swell of pride in this, her nation's capital. Now she just felt revulsion for all it was doing to her and so many others — this persecution in the name of patriotism. *It's not right,* she thought, over and over. *It's just not right.*

They gave her a room in a small hotel. She was surprised, expecting to be kept more of a prisoner, but Glynn explained that she was being watched. Besides, without her passport, where could she go now?

The room wasn't much, but it had a bathtub, so she filled it full of sudsy water and soaked a long time. It was tempting to make a phone call, just to talk to someone. Hannah would be so comforting right now. And Reg, who must be so worried about her. But the phone must be bugged — the whole room was likely bugged. She had to keep Hannah safe. As for Reg, she wasn't letting anyone listen to what they had to say to each other. Reg was for her alone.

She wondered when she'd hear from Nigel, and how. He needed to be careful himself, of course. He was a powerful man, but he had a secret that could hurt him. If someone didn't like his helping her, they would only have to string together enough of an accusation — the word "proclivities" would likely be used — and then not his wife, his wealth, his name, or his position could be trusted to protect him.

Some kind of nutty world we live in.

She propped up the two halves of the photo of Mona. She wished she could be her sister walking into the hearing. Mona wouldn't need jokes to make the committee look like fools. And if she were sent to prison, she'd be friends with all the inmates within a week.

"Give me strength, Mona," Phoebe whispered. "You always said I was the luckiest Adler. If that's true, let me have it in droves. If I get out of this, I'm going to keep living for you. I promise."

A knock came much earlier than she expected. Phoebe opened the door to a tall man with a briefcase. He had a chiseled chin and cheekbones to rival Hepburn's.

"Miss Adler?" he greeted her in a deep voice. "I'm Mr. Briggs, your attorney."

She had to hand it to Nigel. The man looked straight out of central casting.

Briggs was looking her up and down like she was cattle on the market.

"Very good, very good. Nigel said you cleaned up nicely." He studied her hair. "Let's adjust this." To Phoebe's astonishment, he produced several pins from his pocket and twisted her hair into an elegant bun.

"You do this for all your clients?" she asked. "Or just the most hopeless?"

He pulled her into the corridor, closed the door behind them, and lowered his voice. "I do it for the ones I believe in."

"You must not know a lot about my case," Phoebe said. But she couldn't help feeling hopeful. Briggs took her to a coffee shop around the corner, bought her coffee and doughnuts, and whispered instructions.

"We'll do the best we can," he said as they readied to leave. "And, Miss Adler, don't make jokes."

"Don't worry," she assured him. "The last thing I think any of this is, is funny."

Glynn was waiting outside the small room where the committee was convening. His green hat sported a new feather. "It took longer than it should have, Miss Adler, but I knew you'd get here. I always complete my assignments."

Phoebe wasn't even tempted to retort. She felt herself draw closer to Briggs as the one ray of sanity in this strange place. Because standing just behind Glynn, looking almost as pleased as Glynn himself, was Jimmy.

Mrs. Cotley looked at Hannah with little pleasure. Hannah knew what Phoebe's landlady saw. Another American, when two had already been so unreliable. The women were about the same age, but Hannah looked a decade younger — the effects of wealth, comfort, a good tailor, and, until recently, a happier life. She would have liked to tell Mrs. Cotley that the woman had an edge on her. A husband killed in the war was at least noble, and there was a tidy finality about death. A husband who fell out of love with you and went to find love — or anyway, another woman — elsewhere was a messier blow, and one that made even friends look askance at you. It was only having money and *Robin Hood* that would keep people from treating her with open contempt, unless she married again.

"Taken off by a copper, she was," Mrs. Cotley complained about Phoebe. "I can't have that back, not for nothing. This is a respectable house."

"It was a serious misunderstanding, I assure you," Hannah said. "Miss Adler is as upstanding a young woman as you could hope for in a tenant. If you'll just allow me to guarantee her rent until she returns, plus some extra for your trouble, of course, I promise you'll never be bothered by such nonsense again."

"I don't know," Mrs. Cotley said more doubtfully, eyeing Hannah's expensive handbag. "She was sent to me by those Morrisons, and they as good as scarpered off in the night, leaving me two weeks out, them being behind already."

"Shameful," Hannah said. "I'd be glad to compensate you for that as well."

Mrs. Cotley still hesitated, and Hannah wondered if she was being shaken down or if the woman was legitimately unsure about Phoebe.

"Had a man up there, she did," Mrs. Cotley said. "I've got a son to protect."

"Protect from what?" Freddie burst in then, unable to contain himself. "Miss Adler is the best woman I've ever met besides you, Mum, and I want her back here."

"Now listen, Freddie —"

"No, Mum, I won't. You're to listen to me!" Freddie blazed at her, looking both older and younger than his twelve years. "I know her well, and she's excellent, so if this lady is going to pay the rent till Miss Adler returns, you'll take it."

Whether it was the passion of her son, or the sight of the folded notes Hannah handed her, Mrs. Cotley finally relented. Freddie walked Hannah out.

"Miss Adler will be back, won't she?" he asked worriedly.

"Of course she will," Hannah said. Though she wasn't confident. Nigel had said he would move heaven and earth, but those things were very different from the House Un-American Activities Committee.

Hannah dropped a sovereign into the boy's hand. He gazed at her adoringly.

"You know Miss Adler's boyfriend, I think? He's likely in a great panic. When you have a minute, go and tell him I said she'll be fine. He can call me if he likes."

She's got to be fine. She's just got to. She can't go down this way.

"Hiya, Adler," Jimmy greeted her. "How'd you like Limey Land?"

"What the bloody hell are you doing here?" she breathed.

"Picked up some lingo, huh? And wrote some shows. You sure did have all the luck. Anyway, since you ask, I'm here 'cause, you know, 'services rendered.' The Village is crawling with Reds. I'm doing all right, got a lot of work fronting."

Phoebe saw his mouth move, heard every word, and still couldn't believe it. Jimmy! Well, she'd known, hadn't she? Back before she knew, she used him as a model for murderers. And it turned out instead he was a spy, murdering people's careers. She looked at him. Wearing a very good suit, fine shoes, a gold watch. That's what helping the FBI and working as a front for the writers you ruined bought you.

"You sure do look well, Jimmy," she said. He didn't even blush.

The room seemed like something built for television. Five congressmen from HUAC sat at a semicircular table on a raised platform, looming over the witness table. They were interchangeable in dark suits and dull ties. Their severe, brilliantined hair made it tricky to tell if they were graying or balding, which was surely the point. They glared down at Phoebe, and it was hard not to feel small and guilty. She looked around for Nigel, but didn't see him.

A gavel. It began.

"Phoebe Berneice Adler. Are you now, or have you ever been, a member of the Communist Party?"

She clenched her hands together to keep from wiping them on her skirt. She took a deep breath, and leaned toward the microphone.

"No," she said, simply.

She heard rustling behind her. Briggs had told her about the regulars — housewives, mostly — who liked to attend hearings. Phoebe's ladylike look and voice unsettled them. She hoped they were wondering if there must be some mistake.

"Can you account for having been blacklisted?" came another question.

"I wasn't given a reason," Phoebe said.

"We understand you were an instigator during the war," someone clarified.

More rustling. Curiosity. Could Phoebe be a spy?

"Not at all," Phoebe said. "I perhaps annoyed my superiors at the airfield where I worked, but I had to ask for fair wages. Not so much for myself, but lots of the other women were supporting their kids with their men at war. It didn't seem right that they not be paid properly, not when they were doing such fine work."

Now there were murmurs, sounds of displeasure. Some of these women had been on their own during the war as well, and had worked. Plenty of women had said, at least when interviewed, that it made sense to pay them less than men, being weaker and whatnot. But many others felt differently. And if that was all Phoebe had done, well, that wasn't the stuff of treason, was it?

"Nonetheless, you were blacklisted from your work as a television writer and refused to sign a loyalty oath, is that correct?"

There. That looked suspicious all right.

"I was given to understand that signing the oath wouldn't help me," she said.

"So you wanted help? You didn't want to profess loyalty to your country?"

"I have always been loyal to America. That's why I went to work defending her before I was of age. Anyone can sign a paper. That doesn't prove anything."

"But you didn't sign. You weren't even

willing to go that far." The congressman had a bulgy forehead that turned pink when he talked.

"Oh, I would, of course, now that I understand it better. Though my parents and sister — God rest their souls — they always were skittish about signing things. My sister, especially, she wondered if maybe making people sign loyalty oaths seemed a bit Soviet? Or something Hitler made his top men do? Of course, she was awfully ill, confined to a sanitarium, and didn't understand too much about the outside world. Honestly, if President Eisenhower thinks it's right, then I'll be glad to sign."

A gamble, but she knew she had to give at least partway. Briggs's finger brushed hers. Was it congratulations? She knew she sounded like the brassy best friend in countless comedies. She could feel the crowd liking her for it. Convincing the crowd might help convince the committee, Briggs had said. He leaned into the microphone and spoke commandingly.

"My client is prepared to sign a loyalty oath now, should one be at hand."

It wasn't, and the bulgy-headed congressman pushed on.

"You say you are not a Communist, but you have been known to associate with

Communists, have you not?" A question poised to negate her growing popularity.

"I don't know," Phoebe said earnestly. "I don't discuss politics with my friends. Heck, I don't even like to talk politics with my enemies."

Laughter. Briggs exhaled hard through his nose. But she answered a barrage of questions honestly — she had read no subversive literature ("The *Times* and *Herald Tribune*'s crime pages"), signed no petitions ("If people want to complain about something, that's their business"), attended no meetings ("When I wasn't working, I was reading or talking to my sister").

A white-haired man scowled at her.

"Your friend and neighbor in New York was a woman who was not only a registered Communist, she deceived landlords and employers as to her race."

Anne. Intelligent, warm, beautiful Anne. It was indecent, bringing her up here. Phoebe marshaled her rage. Briggs had warned her about this.

"Anne was my friend from our days at the airfield," Phoebe said. "I knew she was a staunch supporter of Roosevelt, and that she paid attention to the news. But she knew I hated politics so we never discussed it. As to her race, well if you saw her, you wouldn't guess she was part Negro." Phoebe took a breath, feeling Briggs tense beside her. He knew what she wanted to say. She wanted to say it didn't matter, it shouldn't matter, it was crazy that anyone thought it mattered. But Washington, DC, was not just the seat of government, it was also the South. Phoebe forced breeziness into her voice. "Though I suppose it explains why she never took up any man's offer of a date." It was sickening, playing into the committee's and audience's prejudices this way, but Briggs's grunt of approval comforted her.

The bulgy man waved this aside and glared down at her.

"Charles Morrison said there were numerous blacklisted writers working on *The Adventures of Robin Hood.* Can you name any?"

"Just myself," Phoebe said.

"His charge was very serious. This show is targeted at children. You ought to understand, Miss Adler, that if you can confirm the allegation and provide us with names, all charges against you will be dropped. Your record will be expunged and your passport returned."

"I understand, sir. All I can say is that Mr. Morrison and I were neighbors, and he discovered I had been able to sell a script. I

541

believe he tried to do the same, and was turned away. In his disappointment, he might well have assumed that I was one of many."

"Those writers could be using fronts!" Jimmy shouted from the audience.

The chair gaveled for silence. Phoebe panicked that this would be the next question — how could she be sure no one else was doing what she said she'd done? Instead, the bulgy man glared at her again.

"Why did you embark upon such a deception? It was very wrong."

Naughty girl. No cookies for you. But this was a game she could play.

"I was desperate," she said plaintively. "I wasn't able to get married, and I had to support myself and my sister. I needed work after I was blacklisted, and no factory would hire me again. I went to London — I didn't know what else to do — and, well, I thought I might as well try. No one was more surprised than I when I succeeded."

"*Robin Hood* is a show aimed at young people. Were you attempting to sway them to a radical point of view?"

"Not at all. I wrote an adventure story. I was only thinking of my sister."

She told the story of the woman who spent her whole short life ill, most of it in the hospital, but yearned for life. The woman now dead, though still so very, very much in Phoebe's heart. Little sighs erupted from around the audience.

"Miss Adler, this is all very well, but you left New York after receiving a subpoena, which you never answered. This is contempt of Congress."

"I'm sorry," Phoebe whispered. "I was frightened. It was all so quick. I knew it meant I'd have a hearing and was maybe supposed to say if I knew Reds, and I didn't — or didn't know I did — and all those men who were so much more important than me didn't give names and went to prison. If I went to prison, Mona would suffer, and I couldn't have that."

"Those men went to prison because they refused to answer questions."

She pressed her tongue to the roof of her mouth. She could feel just how ready they were to cite her for contempt of Congress, turn her over for trial. Why had she ever thought it would be any different for her? No one here got out alive.

Though Lillian Hellman had. It was time to try her tactic. Phoebe steeled herself as the bulgy-headed congressman locked eyes with her — a cobra gazing unblinkingly at its petrified prey.

"You led us to believe you were happy to answer any questions, Miss Adler. So we ask again. Can you name any other known subversives, either in America or abroad, of whom the committee should be aware?"

"I'm so sorry, I should have clarified," Phoebe said. "I'm happy to answer any question about myself that someone has the right to ask."

Pandemonium. The photographers snapped pictures, the audience shouted that a sweet girl like this shouldn't have to suffer more, reporters shouted questions. The chair slammed the gavel again and again until order was restored.

"Miss Adler, Agent Glynn claims to have seen you in company with a great many subversives, both in New York and in London. Do you really expect us to believe you knew nothing of their activities?"

"I was friends with other Americans, that's true, but to me, they were just Americans. I was homesick. As to the rest, I try to mind my own business. That's more than enough to manage. I swear, once my sister died and I didn't have to worry about her anymore, I was going to come home and do right. Mr. Glynn never gave me the chance, what with breaking into my apartment and beating me —"

A fresh cry of outrage arose. The FBI was understood to do what it needed to do in pursuit of dangerous Communists, but beating a defenseless young woman?

The chair gaveled again.

"We understand the agent had clearance to capture people of interest abroad."

Briggs spoke in his silky boom. "It does appear, sir, that he may have overstepped his bounds in both destroying Miss Adler's property, and visiting damage upon her person."

The crowd shouted, but Glynn was louder. "She was trying to resist arrest! Of course she'll say anything. How can you believe anything a named Red says?"

"I agree," Phoebe said. "All of it's my word against his. But I swore to tell the truth, and that's what I've done here."

The chair gaveled again.

"If the agent's methods were unorthodox, he will be properly reprimanded. He was correct, however, in apprehending Miss Adler, who has admitted her deception. I'm given to understand we also have a statement from CBS, saying they've taken further steps to make sure nothing like this happens again."

Phoebe held her breath. *Please. Please let this be over. Please be all right.*

"However," the chair went on. "The flouting of a subpoena will not be allowed to stand. I move your case to trial. You should be aware the usual sentence is up to twelve months in federal prison, plus a fine."

Phoebe gripped the table. Prison! So she was going to prison. She'd never been so grateful that her family was dead and didn't have to see this.

Briggs put a hand on her shoulder, then stepped away, consulting with a congressman. She could see Glynn, shaking hands with Jimmy. They were so pleased with themselves for accomplishing . . . what, exactly?

"When's the trial?" she choked out when Briggs returned and gathered his papers. He held out a hand to help her up.

"There won't be one," he said. He smiled at her. "You're not worth the trouble. You're too small, and you've been publicly punished. The rest is private. They'll keep your passport and you're blocked from working as a writer. They agreed on a fine of two thousand dollars, and then you will be free to go back to New York."

Phoebe gaped at Briggs. Surely he knew she didn't even have two hundred dollars, let alone two thousand. But he seemed pleased with himself and the deal he must have struck. So that was it. It was over. But so was her career. And Reg, Hannah — everyone and everything she now loved were farther away than ever. They might as well be leading her off to prison after all.

Nigel met them back in her room. As soon as they were all inside, he held up his hands and began snapping his fingers rhythmically. Briggs joined him, and they both indicated for her to do the same. Baffled, she started snapping.

"Snapping interferes with any bugging," Nigel whispered. "They'll hear this and some buzzing. The odd words, but not enough to hurt us."

"But . . . it's over, isn't it?" Phoebe asked.

"Come now, Phoebe. Do you think it's ever really over?"

She couldn't speak, just snapped harder and angrier.

"You did very well," Nigel complimented her. "Your Miss Wolfson directed me to pay any fine that might be incurred, that she would guarantee it, so that's settled. In fact, it's a small enough sum that I see no reason not to pay it myself."

"Nigel!" Phoebe cried. "That's too much. You can't, you've already done more than I could ever repay."

"There's no point in being married to an absurdly wealthy woman who despises me if I can't occasionally spend some of her money in a manner she'd find appalling, though she'll never discover," Nigel said happily. "And anyway, you can repay me very well by continuing to do good work and living a happy life."

He sounded like Mona. Phoebe's eyes stung, both because he was so kind and generous and because that work and that life seemed so unattainable. She had no idea how to even begin again. Floyd and Leo might let her sleep on their sofa for a while, and there must be some sort of job she could get somewhere, but she knew she'd have to start writing again. She couldn't not write, it was too much a part of her. And it would mean still living in shadows, sneaking about. For no good reason, except people were afraid. She was sitting in this room, snapping her fingers like a rhythmless Carmen Miranda, because everyone was so very afraid. Phoebe didn't want to live in a world run by Soviets, but she didn't want to live in fear either.

"Nigel. Your diplomatic passport. It allows someone to travel with you?"

Nigel raised an eyebrow in wary assent.

"Phoebe," Briggs said, his voice serious

but his eyes twinkling. "You understand that if you leave the country now, in such a manner, you'll never be able to return?"

"Unless the blacklist ends someday," Phoebe said.

"Maybe," Nigel said, his voice thoughtful. He snapped on, looking hard at Phoebe. "I don't know that I'd be within my privilege, getting you out like that," he said. Phoebe's heart sank. "But let me make a few calls. I might have another idea."

Nigel instructed her to be ready whenever he might return. Briggs took over, changing her hairstyle and watching as she put on more and more makeup. She didn't look different, perhaps, but she didn't immediately look like the woman from the hearing, which Briggs, through snaps, said would help.

Then there was nothing to do but wait. Phoebe paced nervously, trying to make sense of everything.

"I can't write, not officially," she said. "So I'm still on the blacklist? Even though I testified and all?"

"You were polite, but you weren't a friendly witness," Briggs explained. "They won't reward that."

"What a thing," Phoebe said. "What a

thing." She pointed to the phone. "It's bugged, isn't it?"

"That's a fair assumption."

"Let's wait downstairs," Phoebe said. Briggs smiled, interested, and carried her bag down to the lobby. He gave her some quarters and she went to the enclosed phone booth in the corner.

"Floyd? It's Phoebe Adler here. Yeah, yeah, it's a doozy of a story all right. Listen, remember my neighbor, a slimy, stinky, would-be writer?" She spoke carefully. The pay phone was safe, but Floyd and Leo's phone stood a good chance of being bugged. Luckily, Floyd was too savvy to mention any names, and he knew Jimmy by description. "Turns out he's playing a heck of a game with big dogs, and even making extra dough off anyone he sends to hanging."

There was probably better lingo that she didn't know, but the bile in Floyd's voice told her he understood that "big dogs" meant the FBI Hounds, and that Jimmy was playing quite the double game. Word would get around the Village by the drinking hour, and Jimmy would be friendless. Writers would switch to a more deserving front. She hung up, satisfied.

Nigel arrived half an hour later. She wanted to hug Briggs, but kept up appearances and shook his hand formally.

"It's been a pleasure, Miss Adler," he told her. "I'll have our friend keep me up to date on your progress. I have no doubt it will be impressive."

"That's my plan," she said.

Nigel guided her to a big black car with British flags flapping proudly above the headlights. She would feel so elegant and important, getting in such a car, if she wasn't so worried, hoping whatever they were doing was going to work.

"Hey, Adler!" a voice called. It was all Phoebe could do not to vomit. Jimmy. Again. He strutted forward, not noticing Nigel or anything other than her, the woman whose wings he'd clipped.

"No hard feelings, huh?" he said, grinning. "We all have to eat, after all, and come on, you weren't exactly on the up-and-up, were you?"

"Gee, Jimmy, I guess I wasn't, but you sure showed me."

Nigel cut in. "I'm afraid we really must be going."

Jimmy noticed the accent, then took a good look at the car. "Where are you going? What's happening here?"

"For Pete's sake," Phoebe snapped. "What did I ever do to deserve this from you? You did a heck of a job ruining my life already, can't you just leave me be?"

But it seemed he couldn't, because though Nigel practically threw her into the car and they sped off, they both turned and saw Jimmy running for a phone booth.

"Rather a spiteful little squit, isn't he?" Nigel observed.

"I guess he really hated my being better than him." Phoebe shook her head.

"You'd be surprised how many do," Nigel said. "Let's pick up the pace, please."

The driver was even more impressive than the cabdriver who'd gotten Phoebe to the docks, all those months ago. As they reached the airport, Nigel advised her to put her glasses in her bag. Anything to look even less like herself.

Phoebe obeyed with a pounding heart. Taking her glasses off made the world blurry. She clung to Nigel, hop-skipping beside him as he strode through the expansive space. She registered nearly nothing other than the gleam and smell of newness. The way the air shifted as an expensive suit zipped by her, a leather briefcase swinging along. The overwhelming smell of aftershave and brilliantine and power. Nigel ducked and weaved through it all, a man who knew where he was going and expected others to move aside for him.

"Good afternoon, sir, the evening plane?" a man greeted Nigel respectfully.

"Indeed, that's correct, thank you so much, and I expect you can accommodate my guest as well," Nigel said. Phoebe saw the flash of something green. Her first thought was he was bribing the agent, but then she recognized the shape. A passport. Her passport! Somehow cleared, restored, and allowing her free passage again. She couldn't believe it. She was so happy, she felt as though she were floating as they moved along, heading for a plane that someone like Nigel could always get on when he needed to. What an extraordinary life it must be, to command such privilege. She wished she could see people's faces, see the wonder and envy in their expressions. It would be a great story for Reg. Then, even in the blur, she saw the looming figure of a man in a green hat.

"Nigel!" she hissed, trying not to shriek. "Nigel!"

"Ease up a bit, darling, my arm is losing sensation," he warned. "We're quite all right, nothing to worry about."

But there was most definitely something to worry about. Glynn was going to catch them, and the most she could hope for now was that Nigel would wriggle free.

"Nigel, behind us. Glynn!"

"I say, do let us through, will you, important business," Nigel called, parting a small crowd.

"FBI, let me through," Glynn's voice snapped behind them. Much too close.

Phoebe flashed hot and cold. Sharp white spots rose before her blurry vision. "Leave me alone," she heard herself whisper. "Just leave me alone."

"Important business for the British government," Nigel's voice rang. They were on the tarmac, and she could see the plane.

"That woman is not cleared to leave the country!" Glynn shouted. "There's been a mistake!"

Phoebe saw a hand reaching out to stop Nigel.

"I'm sorry, sir, we should probably investigate this."

Nigel spoke with the entitled authority that had built an empire.

"The lady is a legal British resident for the next ten days. After that, she will be returned to American soil should her presence be required. In the meantime, I am escorting her back to Britain. Thank you very much, good day."

And they were climbing the steps into the plane.

"You limey bastard, you can't take her!"

"Sir, that language is not appropriate," someone scolded Glynn. Phoebe didn't dare smile. "I'm afraid I'll have to ask you to return to the terminal."

"I'm FBI!"

Phoebe heard hesitation. Nigel propelled her into the plane, but she knew the debate outside was still going strong. She put on her glasses to watch.

"He can get me, can't he?" Phoebe squeaked. "The FBI has more sway here than you."

"Oh, under other circumstances, that's perhaps correct," Nigel said airily, calling for a drink. "But he doesn't have the friends I have, and didn't make the right calls. He'll have his little tantrum, but he's lost."

Nigel was right. The plane was soon taxiing away, and she was safe.

"And anyway," she said, brightening, "I must have had clearance. You have my passport."

"Ah. Well, that took a touch of bother with a few other friends. I'm afraid when you go to renew your residency, you should expect your passport to be confiscated again. It was only released on a technicality that will be discovered to be a grievous error." Nigel looked smug, and Phoebe raised her brows. He leaned in confidentially. "It will transpire that the person who made the error — not that they *actually* did so, you understand — is someone who's been very active in assisting Mr. Cohn in rooting out homosexuals from the State Department. The rancor he'll incur will quite overwhelm any further concern about your doings abroad, so long as you behave."

Phoebe sat, thinking it all over. The plane took off and she watched the Washington Monument disappear.

"What about Glynn?" she asked. "He could come back and start all over."

"Not at all," Nigel said. "A few well-placed individuals have issued some complaints about his methods. Whether he'll be reprimanded, I don't know, but he won't be traveling to Britain anytime soon, that's certain."

"So. I'm safe?" It seemed impossible to believe.

"You still need to renew your residency, and that's an area a bit outside my sphere."

"What happens if they don't let me stay?" Phoebe's heart was exploding all over again. Why? Why wouldn't anyone just let her live her life?

"Well, your young man could marry you," Nigel advised as casually as if he were suggesting she order eggs Benedict. "Or you can finagle some sort of passage to France and hope they're more accommodating, that can happen. But I shouldn't worry. You've been granted residency before. Honestly, much depends on the mood of the agent at the desk. Be your most charming self and I'm sure they won't resist you."

"Is that the charming self that spurred Glynn to go to such lengths to get me?"

"Ah, well, some of these Hounds get bees in their bonnets about you 'Runaway Reds.'" Nigel was comfortable now, and almost sleepy. "Though I daresay whoever named you must have said something far more extraordinary than that you kicked up a fuss with a union."

"Maybe," she said. "Maybe I'm the next Mata Hari and I don't even know it."

"That's the spirit."

"Nigel. Are you really a diplomat and involved in MI5?"

"I have no idea what you mean," he said. "Where the devil is our supper?"

She would never know. Not that it mattered. It wasn't her business anyway.

She leaned back and closed her eyes. Whoever named her. Whatever they said.

She would never know the answer to any of that either.

To hell with them. I'll spend my life cleaning up my name and then making it big. I'll rub it in their rotten faces, and have a swell time doing it.

For the first time in days, she breathed properly. She was going home.

Chapter Twenty-Two

"Here's to success," Sidney said, handing Hannah a glass of champagne. *The Adventures of Sir Lancelot,* happily approved, was starting production. Episodes for the next season of *Robin Hood* were taking shape. They were more popular than ever. CBS had even sent them an enormous gift basket from Fortnum & Mason — "to make up for that nuttiness." No one asked her to check writers more closely, and she didn't volunteer.

It didn't feel like success, though. Shirley said, "A miss is as good as a mile," but Phoebe had only just managed to stay out of prison, and the show was secured mostly by luck. There could very easily be a next time. A next time, with no Shirley to help. She and Will had made up their minds. They were going to Ghana after all, to help grow its television industry.

"You'll hear more from me than you do

now," Shirley comforted her. "I'll write every day asking your opinion and advice. You'll rue the day we met."

But they both knew that wasn't true. Hannah hardly knew who she'd be without Shirley to see every few days.

"This is the peril, you see, of being the sort of people who want to make a mark in the world," Shirley said. "You've got a legacy. I want one too."

"Sounds more like the peril of being a good influence," Hannah said. "Strife."

Hannah's solicitor didn't even have to raise the hammer on Paul. Paul realized that money would buy him quick freedom, and settled twenty thousand dollars on Hannah in exchange for leaving the country and not looking back. *Is this how love dies, then, with a sum and a forwarding address?*

"You won't be alone for long," Shirley said. "Not unless you choose to be."

"Thanks," Hannah said, squeezing her hand. "I'm not alone, anyway. Not at all."

She bought them a smaller flat in Chelsea. Gemma lit a candle inside it and pronounced it a good home. Rhoda inspected each bare room, looking worried.

"I do like it, but there's not enough space for Daddy."

Hannah sat on the floor and pulled Rhoda

and Julie into her lap. "Remember, I said Daddy wouldn't be living with us anymore."

"But he'll still come to visit, won't he?" Rhoda asked.

Hannah had to believe he must. He couldn't not see his children. But she wasn't sure what to believe anymore. She hugged the girls more tightly, looking hard into each serious little face.

"I'm your mama and your daddy now. I'll work long hours, but I'll always come home. I promise."

Rhoda looked at her thoughtfully for a long time.

"Can I help you read scripts?" she asked at last.

Hannah laughed. "Yes, my darling, of course you can."

"Me too, me read too!" Julie cried.

"You can't read, stupid!" Rhoda shouted.

"None of that now," Hannah scolded. "You'll both help me. The three of us will be unstoppable."

She missed Paul. Missed being in love. Missed feeling like someone was in love with her. But he'd left her the best parts of the both of them. Whatever life he was chasing could never be as good as what he'd left behind.

He was a fool all along, wasn't he?

It probably wasn't true, but it wasn't the worst way to begin to move forward.

"Miss Adler! Miss Adler!"

Freddie barreled into her, his arms hard around her waist.

"I knew you'd be back, I knew you'd beat 'em. I told Mr. Bassill so and he was in a right panic, but I knew it, and I was right!"

Mrs. Cotley, attracted by the sight of Nigel's car driving away, greeted Phoebe with a new respect.

"A strange bit of business, that was, but it's all sorted now?" She studied Phoebe hard for confirmation.

"Yes, Mrs. Cotley. It's all sorted now. I'd like to stay as long as you'll have me."

It wasn't entirely true. She harbored dreams of a home with a private bath and a proper kitchen. But as she walked inside the flat Hannah had preserved for her, Freddie chattering away at her side, she looked around with satisfaction. It wasn't much, but it was hers. For now, that was everything.

Freddie knew where she'd find Reg. And there he was, at their table in the London Library canteen, devouring a pile of books on British and American law.

"Contemplating a change of career?" she asked.

He leapt up and threw his arms around her.

"Oi, do you mind? Some of us are trying to relax," a man complained.

Reg ignored him, smothering Phoebe with kisses.

"I thought I lost you, I thought they'd find a way to keep you there. Your Hannah said that toff was helping, that she felt confident, but I knew she wasn't sure. I've been looking for whatever I could — I knew there must be a way to help you, though of course I knew you'd find a way yourself. You wouldn't be you otherwise."

Phoebe folded her hand in his.

"There's still one problem. I have to renew my residency and they're going to take my passport."

"What if you were married to a British national?" he said slyly. "Wouldn't that smooth the waters?"

Phoebe tousled his hair. "It's the wrong reason to get married."

"What about us being in love? Is that the right reason?" He kissed her forehead. "What about that I don't want any sort of life without you?"

"Let's wait," she said. "Let's assume we'll

have time to really be sure of each other first."

"I'm sure of you," he said. "But I didn't think it would be any other way. I'm just glad you're home."

"Me too."

She called Hannah, who gave her a new address and told her to come for dinner.

"Go take care of the residency now," Hannah advised. "We'll have either a real celebration or a strategy session."

That wasn't as comforting as she would have liked. And she'd heard nothing further from Nigel.

Cassie was on the desk again. Phoebe wondered if there was ever anyone else who worked there.

"Good afternoon." Cassie's greeting was impersonal. Phoebe supposed there was no real reason for the woman to remember her.

"I'm here to renew my residency, please," Phoebe said. "I'm a writer." She slid over her passport with a shaky hand. Cassie took the passport and went to consult the files.

Phoebe glanced at the door, half expecting the officer who took away the Jamaican woman to come in and beckon to her. She couldn't imagine where she'd end up.

Cassie came back with a green file and a

frown. She studied Phoebe. "I'm supposed to keep this," she said, holding up Phoebe's passport. "It's to be returned to your State Department indefinitely. The Americans seem to have accused you of some pretty funny business."

"Me and a lot of others," Phoebe admitted. "Though there's nothing much funny about it."

"You seem to be clear with the British government, though," Cassie went on, reading the file.

"That's nice to know," Phoebe said. "Britain's been good to me."

Cassie looked over the file, then back at Phoebe. "They give me discretion to make some choices," she said. "I don't go a bundle on what seems to have happened here, not when you look perfectly all right." She produced a little booklet, stamped it, and handed it to Phoebe. It was a residency permit. For ten years.

"This lets you work," Cassie explained. "I hope you write something very fine."

Phoebe was speechless. She stared at the little gift, unable to believe it was real. Then she looked up at Cassie.

"Thank —"

Cassie smacked a little bell on the counter, interrupting her.

"Next, please!" she called.

Hannah's new flat was still full of boxes and the smell of fresh paint. But already Phoebe could see it would be a warm and charming family home. Hannah couldn't make a place any other way.

They propped the residency permit up on the sideboard and drank a toast to it.

"I can't ever thank you enough," Phoebe began, but Hannah stopped her.

"We share and share alike, remember? And we help each other out. Anyway, I expect you to get cracking on a cracking new script for me. You'll need a new name, obviously. How about Mona Bassill?"

Phoebe smiled. "Mona would love that."

"I thought as much."

The girls joined them, and Rhoda asked if they could play a game of Robin Hood before supper. As Rhoda put them into position and instructed Julie, Phoebe turned to Hannah.

"The four of us should do something fun this weekend. Go to the Tower of London and tell Rhoda all about beheadings or something?"

Hannah grinned. "She'd be in heaven. What about your Reg, won't he want to come?"

"Maybe another time," Phoebe suggested. "Maybe this time it's just all us ladies."

She was pretty sure she saw Hannah's eyes well up, but she blinked and it was gone.

"An excellent idea," Hannah agreed. "And don't forget, I'm still your employer. I expect a new *Robin Hood* script in two weeks. That won't be a problem, right?"

It certainly wouldn't.

Phoebe decided to walk a little while before getting on the Underground. Tomorrow she would start her new *Robin Hood* script. Then she would write a play, or perhaps a book — about a wheelchair-bound woman who travels the world. That would be in her own name, a name she was going to keep, even if she got married. She hoped someday it would be returned to her in full by her own country. Stranger things could happen.

It started to rain, and she'd forgotten an umbrella. But she kept on walking.

"Getting a bit wet, love," a passerby observed. "Shall I call you a cab?"

"I've been called worse," she said. The man startled, and then a slow smile spread over his face. Phoebe grinned back. "Thanks very much. But that's all right. I think I'll just walk. I don't mind the weather."

And she didn't.

AUTHOR'S NOTE

There is an inherent difficulty in writing about the Communist "witch hunts" in general and the Hollywood blacklist that began in 1947 and remained in force until 1960 in particular, because although they can be understood in context, they are at heart absurd. It is staggering to think that the United States, emerging victorious and a superpower at the end of World War II, should have been so afraid of the spread of Communism that it would start persecuting its own citizens. It is even more incomprehensible that the hugely powerful and influential film industry would have joined in the efforts of the House Un-American Activities Committee (HUAC) and commit itself to purging the industry of anyone suspected of Communist loyalty or sympathy. This was, however, exactly what happened. The path to the blacklist was very much as Hannah and Phoebe describe —

569

the studio heads were terrified of being considered un-American, and a longtime hatred of unions, particularly the Screen Writers Guild, made the persecution of outspoken liberals in Hollywood desirable. Many people have heard of the Hollywood Ten, and some of the other famous men who either were felled by the blacklist or named names. But there were women whose careers were also destroyed by the blacklist, and I wanted to explore their stories.

I came across the story of Hannah Weinstein early in my research, and her daring inspired the plot arc. That she was willing to endanger her career to help others maintain theirs was rare in this period, and she deserves lionization. Though some of the writers who either lived abroad in exile or worked for her from America criticized her for paying only scale wages, it is generally agreed that she provided opportunities when almost no one else was willing to take that risk. For the purposes of my narrative, it worked best to fictionalize much of her life, thus did she become Hannah Wolfson (named for a terrific writing teacher). The real Hannah was already separated from her husband Pete when she came to Europe in 1950, and had three children rather than two. She had a remarkable career long before she ever came to create *The Adventures of Robin Hood.* She was a successful journalist, worked as a speechwriter for New York mayor Fiorello La Guardia, and worked for the presidential campaign of Henry Wallace. Some sources say she used money from a divorce settlement to help start Sapphire; others say she was in fact sponsored by either left-leaning organizations or the American Communist Party to set up a company that would help struggling writers. I prefer the idea that it was Hannah's own brainchild and brilliance.

Likewise, the real Sidney Cole (who was not Scottish, but my version of Sidney felt Scottish from the start) said that *Robin Hood* came about because Hannah wanted to create a British-themed costume series and had a number of ideas, of which *Robin Hood* was one. He claims to have encouraged her to pursue *Robin Hood,* arguing that it would provide a huge amount of scope for stories. Which was true, as the show ran for five years, yielding 143 episodes. Many of the names mentioned (Peter Proud, Terry Bishop, Richard Greene, Bernadette O'Farrell) are real people connected with the show, which was as groundbreaking for its production and cinematography as it was for its stories and secret writers. I did, however, fictionalize quite a lot, starting with the timeline, as the time from conception to sale to shooting would of course take longer than I've allowed here, but for the sake of pacing, I shortened the window. Additionally, the show did film at Nettlefold Studios in Surrey, and Hannah did buy woodland to use for better filming, but I've fictionalized the layout of the interiors and exteriors.

As inspiring as Hannah was, I knew that my main character was going to be a writer experiencing the shock of being blacklisted and having to suddenly navigate treacherous new terrain. In creating Phoebe, I called to mind the classic "career gals" of old movies, and thought of real pioneers such as Madelyn Pugh Davis, the cowriter of *I Love Lucy,* who is obliquely mentioned in the narrative. I thought Phoebe was the sort of person one of my heroes, Nora Ephron, would have been if she were a TV writer at the dawn of the industry. It's also possibly the sort of career woman her screenwriter mother, Phoebe Ephron, was, and so it was only natural to name the character Phoebe.

Many of the harassments Phoebe is subjected to come from real experiences. As outlandish as some of the stories seem, they are true. People knew their phones were being tapped when there was no one at the end of a ringing phone, or if each phone in the house rang at a different time. Most disturbingly, a call might prove to be a recording of a conversation you'd had several weeks ago.

The harassment was extraordinary. Former "Hounds" talk about going into people's homes to search for anything that could be labeled incriminating. Even minor items like grocery bills might be intercepted for scrutiny. All of which was legal. If it seems bizarre that so much effort would be expended on someone like Phoebe, consider that in the case of some suspected Communists, an entire family would be followed every day — including children. There might be two Hounds in two different cars to follow each family member in case they changed direction. Then other Hounds would be assigned to enter the house and search — and all of this paid for by the taxpayers. The stress of life under the blacklist is clear in all the writings about it. Friendships and marriages dissolved, in addition to careers being ruined. Some people's health suffered and never recovered. Others, unable to cope with no work or support system, and ongoing persecution, committed suicide.

Many people fled to Europe and Britain in the hopes of escaping harassment or worse, and being able to continue working.

Though people did indeed have some relief abroad, nearly every situation described or mentioned in the book is based on a real experience. The American embassy tried to insist that UK officials deny residency to American exiles, and letters were often sent to try to get people to bring their passports to the embassy, where they would then be confiscated. Some agencies and producers were pressured not to hire artists. And the real Hannah did report being followed in London. While the level of overseas harassment I create is mostly fictional, many exiles still felt themselves unsafe.

The midpoint near catastrophe, when Hedda Hopper descends on the set of *Robin Hood* and the blacklisted director is forced to hide, is also based on a real incident. The scandal-obsessed Hedda Hopper was a notorious Red-baiter, and was very happy to name names. She came to England precisely to try to catch blacklisted directors on sets. On a film Joseph Losey was directing, he was lucky enough to hide in a building overlooking the set before she saw him. There was a telephone there, and he was able to call the assistant director and carry on working until she left.

That *The Adventures of Robin Hood* was written entirely by blacklisted writers was considered one of the industry's biggest open secrets. Sapphire partnered with American producers, a company called Official Films, who never knew about the enterprise. Hannah did indeed instruct her staff not to open registered letters in fear of a subpoena. It was the president of Official Films, not an executive at CBS, who insisted on meeting at least one writer, and an American script editor in New York acted as a front for this meeting — I wanted to keep this action where we could see it, and Beryl was the obvious person to pretend to be a writer on this occasion.

Hannah herself was classified as a "concealed Communist," and an FBI investigation determined Sapphire was "influenced by Communists." For reasons yet unknown, nothing further was done. It is possible that, because the British press and public were generally sympathetic to the victims of the witch hunts, attacking what was by then one of the most popular programs on both British and American television might have been viewed as unwise.

Though Phoebe is said to be on the blacklist, there was actually a separate "list" for people who worked exclusively in television — a booklet published in 1950 called *Red Channels*. I chose to use only the blacklist for reasons of expediency.

For a few years in the 1950s, people living in exile abroad were offered "golden tickets" to return to the US if they agreed to name names. Many who could not cope with the strain of living abroad and not finding work chose this option. People's passports were indeed seized, or not renewed. This went on until 1958, when the Supreme Court ruled that a citizen's passport could not be revoked under such circumstances.

Two people whose passports were held until 1958 were writers and activists W. E. B. and Shirley Du Bois, on whom the LeGrands are based. Some of the real exiles remembered interacting with the Du Boises in London and Europe, and as they were such extraordinary people, and examples of those outside Hollywood who were targeted by HUAC, I was inspired to create characters based on them and place them in London during these years. In 1961, they did indeed move to Ghana, where Shirley (an incredible woman who deserves her own book) helped develop the nation's first television network.

One of the stranger moments that occurs

toward the novel's end is also based on real reports. During the initial hearings in Washington, members of the Hollywood Ten would snap their fingers as they talked in their hotel rooms, as this was understood to disrupt the listening devices.

The hearings themselves were essentially show trials, as the committee knew if someone was still in the party or not. The investigations stretched far beyond the arts — into science, labor, the armed forces, and the government. It is perhaps no coincidence that many of the people targeted were not just political progressives, but also members or organizers of labor unions, Jews, LGBT, African Americans, and intellectuals. It was very fitting that Lillian Hellman titled her memoir of the period *Scoundrel Time.*

Although HUAC lasted far longer and was more devastating, the Communist-hunting of Senator Joseph McCarthy is better remembered, thanks in large part to the phrase McCarthyism being used to describe such witch-hunting. I chose to effectively leave him out of the narrative because by 1955, he had been denounced and left the Senate. But the damage he did was great, and long lasting. His chief counsel was Roy Cohn, who is also briefly mentioned. Cohn was a closeted gay man who was keen on purging the government of gay men as well as supposed Communists. He is famously a character in Tony Kushner's multi-award-winning play *Angels in America.*

On a much lighter note, bonus points to any reader who picked up that Nigel's club, the Egotists', is a favorite of the famous fictional detective Lord Peter Wimsey.

Hollywood has only recently begun to come to terms with its complicity during the scoundrel years. There was no great reckoning that ended it. Rather, the beginning of the end came thanks to the actor Kirk Douglas, who wanted Dalton Trumbo to write the script for *Spartacus* and insisted that Trumbo be allowed to use his name. Douglas's star power was such that this was allowed, and from there the blacklist crumbled. One can't help but wonder what might have happened if a major star a decade earlier had made the same insistence.

I wrote *Red Letter Days* to tell a story people would enjoy reading. That said, one of the reasons I've always loved history is because it not only tells us who we used to be, it also has the power to show us who we are. It was the blacklist and HUAC that were truly un-American, but they were allowed to happen then. It's my hope that knowing that now should guard against it ever happening again.

ACKNOWLEDGMENTS

Working on this book was a journey into a history both sinister and surreal. I was lucky to have an enormous amount of help and support throughout.

I could never have found as much, and so readily, without the existence of excellent libraries. From the New York Public Library, to the libraries at the University of California, Los Angeles, to the British Library and the Barbican Library in London, I found both books and original source material that were invaluable in bringing life on the blacklist from those pages to these pages.

My professional support team continues to be amazing — my agent, Margaret O'Connor of Innisfree Literary, and two brilliant editors. Kate Seaver, who helped shape the initial story, and then, while Kate was on maternity leave, Ellen Edwards, who with great patience and insight got me through to a (mostly) finished manuscript.

Kate helped with the final hurdle, and I could not have managed without either of them.

Somewhere in the middle of the initial draft, I moved from the States to London (under much happier circumstances than the Americans in the book), and I definitely could not have achieved that and carried on with the book without a lot of wonderful people, starting with Amanda and Alisa in New York, my very lovely mother in Los Angeles, and then my awesome friends in London — Melinda and Michael, and their daughter Anya (whose flight of fancy one summer day inspired a similar flight for Rhoda). Thanks as well to Sheila, Ariane, and Rebecca, and all the people who helped make London home. Melinda and Ariane also turned me into a coffee drinker (one appreciates the irony), and there were days when that cup (or three) of joe was a capable and generous cowriter.

Speaking of joe, the best chapter in the writing was when I met Joe, the love of my life, who helped me in ways I didn't even know I needed, and whose inspiration I look forward to ~~exploiting~~ enjoying for as long as I carry on with this writing lark.

And, finally, gratitude always for readers everywhere.

■ ■ ■ ■

READERS GUIDE:
RED LETTER DAYS

SARAH-JANE STRATFORD

■ ■ ■ ■

QUESTIONS FOR DISCUSSION

1. Hedda Hopper was a real person, who really did wield great power as a gossip columnist, destroying the careers of suspected Communists, homosexuals, and anyone she believed was involved in some scandal. How do you think her newspaper and radio programs were allowed to have such influence? What might have stopped her at the time? How might a similar person be stopped from doing such damage today?

2. Many former Communists were frightened enough by the prospect of being blacklisted or imprisoned that they agreed to "name names." What other alternatives might there have been? Do you think their choices were reasonable?

3. The fears of the spread of Communism, or rather, the fears of the growing power

of the Soviets, were used to justify the actions of HUAC and the FBI. What sort of response in the face of concern might have been more reasonable?

4. Hannah Weinstein really did report being followed while living in London. Do you think the FBI's tactics were just attempts to frighten people, or did they think there was something to learn from their tailing?

5. Wiretapping was just as chaotic as described in Phoebe's experience — either there was silence at the other end or, occasionally, a recording of a previous conversation. How does this invasion of privacy compare with tactics used today, by either law enforcement or sites attempting to tailor marketing?

6. Hannah tells a story about her first foray into television when there were no designated women's lavatories and so she used the men's and hung her handbag on the door handle. This comes from a real anecdote a female pioneer in television recalled. What other hurdles do you think women had to leap if they wanted to be part of the growing industry? How does that compare to today?

7. Though a number of people who lost their work and good name in this era knew either who named them or why they were destroyed, many did not. Discuss whether you think Phoebe is correct and it was her action at the airfield that got her on the blacklist, or another cause. Who might have named her?

8. *The Adventures of Robin Hood* was a hugely popular television series, and many of its episodes were lightly veiled critiques of authoritarianism and the Communist witch hunts. In what ways could the show have shaped the views of its young audience? How can art change the way people think about things?

9. Though Britain dealt with actual spies for the Soviet Union, and was by no means pro-Communist, the British government never emulated anything like HUAC, and the general attitude was that the witch-hunting in America was unacceptable. Why do you think that was? Was it just their experience of the war, or do you think there was something more inherent in British culture that prevented such persecution?

10. Phoebe claims to not want to get involved with a man because she is worried such involvement might mean she won't be able to keep working. Hannah is considered an exception in that she's married with children and yet holds a position of power. Do you think Phoebe would have been able to keep working and build herself up to a staff position if she were married and had children? How do you think it compares to working mothers today in the television — or any — industry?

ABOUT THE AUTHOR

Sarah-Jane Stratford is the acclaimed author of *Radio Girls*. Her work has also appeared in the *Guardian,* the *Boston Globe, Los Angeles Review of Books, Marie Claire,* Bustle, Guernica, and many others. A former resident of both American coasts, she's now living the expat life in London, where when she isn't working, she's exploring and seriously considering learning how to garden.

Connect online: SarahJaneStratford.com; Facebook: Sarah JaneStratfordAuthor; Twitter: StratfordSJ; Instagram: SarahJaneStratford